A Hundred Veils

Rea Keech

ISBN 978-0-9836990-4-0

Library of Congress Control Number:
2015936809

Published by

Real
Nice Books

11 Dutton Court
Baltimore, Maryland 21228

Publisher's note: This is a work of fiction. Names, characters, places, institutions, and incidents are entirely the product of the author's imagination or are used fictitiously, and any resemblance to actual persons, living or dead, or to events, incidents, institutions, or places is entirely coincidental.

Sketches by Barbara Munjal

The cover photograph of "Mount Damavand"and the title page image from it are by Hamed Saber. Licensed under CC BY 2.0.
(https://www.flickr.com/photos/hamed/164348283/in/photolist-5GnTcY-fwk26-hfK9V-TpZ3G-aRoQmt-65D6xA-xEmAu-onuZFd-haSYks-nGz1Qr-8jsgD4-ntSsKe-nxKyYQ-4WtjZs-nPQfBn-6nzmo-q6Ta8C-6kqzZ-isi2Db-4Mv8Zs)

The tile pattern on the cover was created from the photograph "Iranian Tiles 1" of the Sheikh Lotfollah mosque in Esfahan by مانفی. Licensed under CC BY-SA 3.0 via Wikimedia Commons.
(http://commons.wikimedia.org/wiki/File:Iranian_Tiles_1.JPG#mediaviewer/File:Iranian_Tiles_1.JPG)

Printed in the U.S.A.

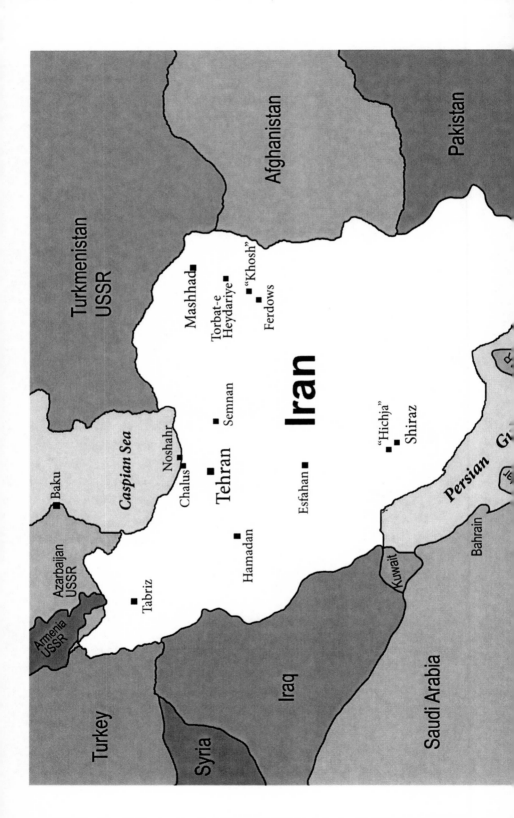

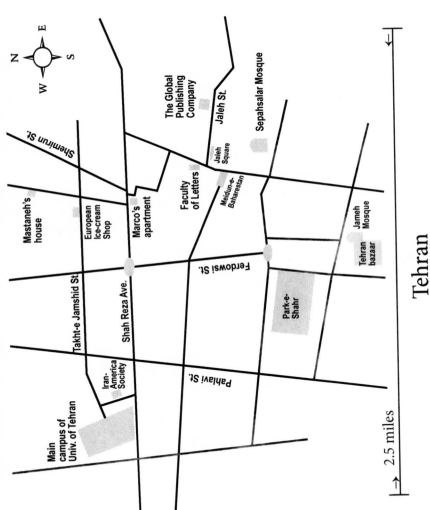

Tehran

2.5 miles

List of Chapters

I

Roses and nightingales

With an abrupt drop, the plane banked sharply. Through his window, Marco could see men, women, and children in pajamas getting up from mats on the flat rooftops below. They were stretching, yawning, turning towards the red sunrise. None looked up. He was flying unnoticed through the bedrooms of hundreds of families.

Don't look directly at the women—cultural-religious thing. The sight of so many women in their pajamas caused this warning to keep replaying in Marco's head as the plane landed in the Shiraz airport.

At the gate, a rag-tag soldier in khaki shirt and mismatched olive green trousers held a machine gun across his chest, not standing at attention but simply loitering, ogling each disembarking passenger like a star-struck girl.

The airport smelled of sweat. Marco stepped around a carpetful of flowers spread in front of a frail man sitting cross-legged on the floor.

"Salaam aleikum."

Marco turned, pleased he had understood the man's greeting, and returned it.

Being spoken to by a foreigner seemed to be a first for the flower man. He jumped up and asked Marco where he was coming from—and got an answer.

Where he was going—and got an answer.

Men in shiny suits and collarless shirts began edging in close enough to take in the action. They stood with shoulders and arms touching Marco, their faces uncomfortably close to his, encouraging him to talk more.

Some pushed through to get a closer look—all men at first. But then some women in paisley chadors, holding the cloth across their faces, edged towards the fringes of the circle that was developing. "Listen to him speak," they said to each other. Marco had pretty much already used up all the Farsi he knew.

A scuffle broke out on the outer edge of the crowd as more and more bystanders tried to shove in to see what was going on. A turbaned mullah had been watching at a little distance but then, as two soldiers carrying machine guns approached the crowd, he shouldered a brown sack and walked away. The soldiers hadn't come to break up the scuffling crowd, however. They simply wanted to see, too.

Marco was twenty-three years old and had never been the center of so much public attention. Now a few more men elbowed in to try out their English—or any foreign language they knew.

"Hello Mister!" This was the country's universal English translation of *Salaam aleikum.*

A portly man with amber *tasbih* prayer beads in his hand said something in Arabic to Marco.

"Idiot. Does he look like an Arab to you?" The women on the fringes giggled.

Marco tried to hear what was being said on the airport loudspeakers. "Today, the King of Kings, Light of the Aryans . . . ." All he understood was that the Light of the Aryans was going to Washington. Marco looked over the heads of the crowd for the baggage area.

The flower peddler put a red rose into Marco's hand, took him by the other hand, and pushed through the crowd. "Pardon the *sholugh,*" he said. Marco recognized the word for ruckus or public disturbance.

Huff and Dooley were standing beside their bags at the unloading area. "Hurry up," Huff said. "There's a jeep waiting for us outside."

Marco looked through the remaining bags and realized his were missing.

A burned-out English expatriate named Boggs picked them up

in the shimmering, furnace-like heat. He was apparently in charge now. Nobody seemed to know Boggs's first name. He had something wrong with one arm. It worked, but it didn't hang straight from his shoulder.

Without any baggage other than the thin vinyl briefcase he had carried with him, Marco climbed into the front seat of the dusty Land Rover while the others loaded their bags into the back. They bounced across a bare valley surrounded by jagged, barren mountains. On the highest peaks, huts perched atop wooden towers. Boggs said they were army observation posts. Below each tower stood a thin little soldier in a bleached-out uniform holding a machine gun.

"What are they on the lookout for?" Marco asked.

"Ghoshghai," Boggs told them. "Tribes. They sacked the city of Shiraz twenty years ago. There's some of them over there."

"The guys in the Archie hats?" Huff said. "They don't look that scary."

Boggs grunted. "The Shah likes to be extra careful."

The open Land Rover left a mile-long wake of dust behind it. When Marco blinked, his eyelashes were crusty. He licked his teeth and felt grit on his tongue. He now realized why Boggs's hair stood up like that.

As they entered the city, Boggs said, "You'll notice you have to use the horn a lot more than in England, or the States." He leaned on the horn, and the Land Rover jerked one way, then the other to avoid a white Mercedes coming head-on. It didn't seem to be quite set in stone which side of the street you drove on.

"What are all those strings of lights everywhere?" Marco asked Boggs. "They look like Christmas decorations."

"Getting ready for the Shah's coronation."

As Boggs came to a stop at a traffic light, all vehicles going in his direction lined up side-by-side across the whole road like horses in a starting gate. The sidewalks on both sides of the road were also used. Vehicles coming the other way did the same on their side of the intersection. Now there were two rows of vehicles facing each other as they waited for the light to change. On either side of the intersection, only one vehicle was in what Marco would have called the proper lane.

"Keep your arms inside," Boggs said. The two phalanxes of vehicles rushed at each other. Bluff—showing no regard for the vehicles coming head-on—was the predominant tactic. Speed and size had the advantage. The Land Rover, on the wrong side of the road but biggish in the current lineup, shot out with horn blaring and claimed a space between two on-coming three-wheelers, which were forced to turn aside, bringing traffic to a stop on either side of them.

"Traffic's not as bad as I thought," Boggs said. He swerved to avoid a donkey backing into the street. "You're going to love Shiraz, the City of Roses and Nightingales. I've lived here for fifteen years, and I never want to live anywhere else. The home of the poet Hafez. I hate it when I have to be in Tehran."

He stopped at a three-story building attached to a cinema broadcasting out into the street the Farsi soundtrack from *The Ten Commandments* at a piercing volume. "Here you are. In there somewhere."

The City of Roses and Nightingales smelled like urine and garbage. Straw and scraps of greenish vegetables floated slowly along in the dark water of the open *jub* or water-supply sluices that lined each side of the street. Vegetable peddlers were washing their produce in the *jubs*. Donkeys were urinating on the sidewalk.

Huff stood beside Marco on the low balcony of the Pahlavi University dormitory, where he, Dooley, and Marco would stay until Boggs decided where the International Teachers Association would send them. Huff's face was engraved with a permanent tight-lipped grin, the kind sometimes described as "shit eating." On the plane to Shiraz he had asked the hostess for Johnny Walker. "It is not," she had told him.

Below in the street, a Ghoshghai squatted on the sidewalk in a felt hat with the brim turned up on all four sides and canvas clog shoes with upturned tips. He was weighing tomatoes on a hand-held scale for a hunched-over figure covered completely by a black chador.

Two young soldiers walked past side by side, pinkie fingers linked together, swinging their arms.

Huff rolled his eyes. "Goddam."

Dooley was still down on the sidewalk buying something. When he came out onto the balcony, he had a copy of the *Kayhan* English language newspaper and a huge paper sack of dried pumpkin seeds.

Marco silently stared down into the street. Despite the blazing heat, every man wore at least a threadbare remnant of a suit coat, usually over pajama bottoms. Two nurses in white uniforms walked together arm-in-arm towards a bus stop at the corner. Except for them, the women were completely hidden beneath black or paisley chadors.

Marco thought about the letter in his pocket. He had written it on the plane but was ashamed of the pleading tone he'd used and didn't know if he would actually mail it.

"Look at this," Dooley said. "It's the year 1346. We're going back in time." Dooley had an omnivorous, indiscriminate appetite for facts and food. He took off his gold wire-framed glasses and wiped them on the huge thigh area of his khaki pants. "*Khaki* is a Persian word," he told them. "So is *pajama*." He said *pajama* only referred to the bottoms. "They're baggy, unisex, one size fits all."

It might be fun to wake up on a rooftop in pajamas, Marco thought. Of course, Elaine wouldn't have thought so. A picture of his ex-fiancée in her overpriced pink designer pajamas flashed into his mind. She had met somebody "more attuned to her lifestyle," she had told him. And now here he was in Iran, moving on.

"Not still brooding about that bitch dumping you, are you?" Huff said.

"No. Well, maybe a little," Marco admitted.

"Get over it, I say." Huff rolled his eyes towards several formless female figures squatting on the sidewalk holding dirty black chadors in their mouths to hide their faces as they picked through a pile of pomegranates. An ironic grin spread over Huff's face. "You're sure to find somebody new here. Oh, yes, I'd say you came to just the right country."

"Not actually," contradicted Dooley, who never understood sarcasm. "Even getting a look at a woman here is difficult. The customs here—"

"We know, we know." Huff cut off what was about to become one of Dooley's rambling expositions.

Marco had a more immediate problem. Boggs had told them to wear coats and ties to a welcome ceremony that evening by the education ministry. "I'll just go down and buy a coat," he said, since all of his clothes were missing.

He walked fast trying not to step in donkey droppings or on the piles of fruit, seeds, and vegetables spread out for sale on the sidewalk. He passed a row of shops that sold nothing but square-toed shoes, shops that sold only Ghoshghai hats, pajama shops—he paused, but then went on—and turned into the first tailor shop. The word for coat was coat.

"Hello Mister."

Marco looked around and immediately saw his mistake. Ready-to-wear was an American concept. The reason everybody in the country looked like he was wearing a tailor-made suit was because he was.

The proprietor tried out his English: "You are welcome. Please. You drink the tea."

He poured a little *estekān* glass of tea and put it in front of Marco on a small white saucer along with a bowl of sugar lumps. "You are welcome. Please. You drink the tea." Marco now realized he had already heard all the tailor's English.

The welcome ceremony was held in the Cedar Gardens on the outskirts of the city near the tomb of the poet Hafez. The garden, bordered on every side by long rows of thin, towering cedars, was a peaceful and beautiful oasis walled off from the cacophony, odors,

16

and heat of the city. Above the deep green of the trees, light brown ranges of mountains loomed in the distance against a cloudless blue sky. In the early twilight, cool air radiated from the trimmed hedges, the vast beds of roses, and the water in the central fountain.

A violin quartet played Mozart's *Eine Kleine Nachtmusik* while waiters in starched white coats stood everywhere with silver trays of hors d'oeuvres. All the guests—men and women—wore elegant clothes that could have come from New York, London, or Paris. There must be two Irans, Marco thought.

"Now this isn't bad," Huff said.

A loud *caw* came from the top of a cedar tree.

Huff smirked. "But that definitely sounds more like a crow than a nightingale."

Beyond the fountain, where most of the dignitaries and guests were gathered, there was a long table covered by a white cloth. Lined up from one end of the table to the other were bottles of Pepsi Cola.

"I see that Johnny Walker is not," Huff said.

Dooley took a Pepsi.

Huff was talking to a gray-haired man from the provincial Ministry of Education. "We have just the person to answer your question about American literature," he said, turning towards Marco. Marco stepped forward wearing a coat with huge padded shoulders, wide stripes, and sleeves that didn't come very far down his arms—a loaner from the tailor.

The minister took in a sharp breath.

"I see he's impressed with your zoot suit." Huff grinned. To the gray-haired man, he said, "I'd like to introduce you to Mr.— No, I guess I'll let him tell you his name himself." Huff's smirk deepened.

"Mark O. Something-or-other," Marco said. The family name was muttered. "I'm pleased to meet you."

"Pleased to meet you Mister Marco," the gray-haired man said.

It seemed to work every time. Since his first Farsi lesson, "Marco" had worked out this way to avoid using his last name, which in Farsi meant *penis*.

Pajama party

ساقیا جام می‌ام ده که نـگارنده غیب

نیست معلوم که در پرده اسرار چه کرد

—Hafez

Sāghiā, jām-e-meyam deh ke negārandeye qeib
Nist ma'lum ke dar pardeye asrār che kard.

Huff was sent to teach at the University of Esfahan and Dooley to teach at a boys' high school in a northern province. Marco didn't know if he would see either of them again. While Boggs was waiting to confirm Marco's assignment, he sent him on an overnight trip to the nearby village of Hichja in the desert foothills of the Zagros Mountains. The idea was to practice his Farsi. It was there that Marco met Farhad.

The bus was festooned with plastic beads and silk tassels. Above the windshield hung a large picture of the Shah in a white military uniform decorated with about a square foot of military medals and ribbons. On the dashboard was a smaller picture of Mohammad's grandson Hossein Ali in a white robe. The picture of Ali was surrounded by red tassels and decorative script from the Koran. Like a Catholic holy card, Marco thought.

As the bus leaned into curves at the edge of cliffs, several passengers began throwing up in the aisles. Marco noticed others holding flowers to their noses. He tried to open a window, but it was stuck. Never mind. This trip was just a kind of initiation devised by Boggs that Marco had to get through. In a day or two he would get his permanent assignment, probably in Tehran.

Out of the window, as far as he could see were endless plains of tan dirt and endless ranges of tan mountains. Now and then there were sheep or goats. Some had their heads down as if grazing, but no matter how hard he tried, Marco couldn't make out what they could possibly be eating.

The bus stopped in the village, and the driver's assistant opened the door. Marco stepped down and immediately drew a crowd.

"Do you know where you are?"

"Did you come here alone?"

"Where is your mother?"

As instructed by Boggs, he told the villagers he had come for sightseeing. Apparently, it hadn't occurred to Boggs that they might take this for sarcasm.

"There is nothing here," they said.

"For sightseeing you want to go to Esfahan."

"We don't even have a cinema. The nearest cinema is in Shiraz."

As the crowd waited for an explanation, a little bald man in a shiny suit sidled up and stood right next to him without saying anything.

Marco had no friends or relatives in Hichja. He had no business to undertake. There was no sightseeing. Finally he had an inspiration. "I want to see your mosque."

It was as if he had declared a town holiday. The mosque! Well, all right, then! Someone shouted, "Clear the way. He wants to see the mosque." In a great state of excitement, the whole town accompanied Marco to see the mosque, as if they expected through his eyes to see something they had never noticed before, that had lain hidden all their lives.

A mullah, followed by a gangly teenage boy with his hair cut close to his head, came out of the madreseh, the school attached to the mosque. The boy began speaking, not to Marco directly but to the whole crowd, in a formal, public voice, quoting heavily from the Koran, Marco presumed. His eyes glared, and spittle dripped down one side of his mouth. "Shut him up," somebody yelled from the crowd.

"What an embarrassment. Go home, Mohammad."

"Move aside. We're showing our guest the mosque."

At the side of the mosque, Marco caught sight of a tall, curly-haired young man wearing a sleeveless undershirt and vivid blue and white pajamas. He was laughing with a woman in a chador and a little girl holding her hand. As the crowd approached, the couple turned, froze, then rushed off somewhere behind the mosque.

"Was that Farhad?" Mohammad said. "Who is he with?"

"Mind your own business," somebody shouted at him.

Inside the mosque, the smell of dirty feet hit Marco as he walked in his socks onto an expansive floor covered from edge to edge with Persian carpets in deep red, yellow, blue, and white floral patterns. Yellow tiles with elaborate light blue designs covered the walls. The mosque was a concentrated cache of color secreted in the monotone dust of the village, a shady and quiet haven open to anyone who wanted to pray or think in peace. Marco felt like standing there longer, but the crowd was watching him, waiting for some reaction. He nodded and left.

Next, they took him to see the bazaar. On the way, the serious little bald man who seemed to be sticking by Marco's side brushed against the mullah. The mullah addressed him as "Bikhod." The crowd laughed, and Marco heard others address the bald man as "Bikhod" while they approached the arched, enclosed marketplace.

"It's late. Maybe he wants to eat," someone said.

The crowd seemed to agree that Marco was hungry. They led him to what passed for a restaurant in Hichja—two small tables set up at opposite sides of a dirt walkway through the bazaar. The proprietor stood beside a brazier of sizzling shish-kabobs. He dispersed the crowd and greeted Marco with a hand over his heart.

Only one of the tables was empty. The little bald man quickly sat there and called for tea.

"Now where is Mister going to sit?" the kabob man scolded him.

"*Befarmāid,*" called the customer at the other table. Please. He had a thick black mustache and a gold tooth that gleamed when

20

he smiled. He put his hand over his heart and gestured for Marco to sit with him and share his food. He stood, shook hands, and introduced himself—Mr. Sufizadeh. He wouldn't sit back down until Marco sat first. Then he moved his plate of minced lamb kabob closer to Marco.

"*Somagh*," the kabob man said putting a shaker of reddish-brown sumac down on the table. Mr. Sufizadeh sprinkled some on one skewer of the marinated meat, again saying "*Befarmāid.*" Seeing no utensils, Marco picked up a piece with his fingers. Mr. Sufizadeh and the kabob man watched intently as he chewed.

"Good." Marco bobbed his head.

The two men relaxed and smiled.

Mr. Sufizadeh said he was an oil tanker driver, originally from Hichja. He had moved his family to Tehran. "Because I'm in Tehran as much as any other city," he explained. "So when I drive to Shiraz, I always stop here in Hichja to visit my parents." He ordered more kabob and some tea. "But it seems my parents went to Shiraz this morning to visit relatives and see a movie."

Marco told him he was a teacher, and the truck driver started to talk about sufi poetry. Marco tried to follow, but his Farsi wasn't up to it.

"We need my nephew Farhad," Mr. Sufizadeh said. "He speaks English like an American."

"I'll get him," the kabob man's assistant said. It seemed like everybody in Iran had an assistant.

When Farhad arrived, Marco realized he was the young man he had seen beside the mosque talking to a woman and her child, then rushing away when the crowd approached. He had thick eyebrows that almost met in the middle, a thin nose, and a rather mischievous smile.

Farhad and his uncle shook hands. The uncle brushed his mustache against both of Farhad's cheeks. Farhad put his hand on his chest. The uncle put his hand on his chest. Farhad put his hand on his chest again. They shook hands again. Uncle asked nephew to sit down. Nephew couldn't sit down until uncle sat down. It took a while to sort itself out.

In very good English, Farhad said to Marco, "We have to do that."

"Oh. Well. Sure," Marco said.

"So, what are you doing here?" Farhad asked him. "Not that everybody doesn't want to see our village. Yes, they *come from far and wide.*" He squinted at Marco as if to see if he'd used the phrase correctly.

"I'm just here for a day. I think I'm going to be sent to teach at the University of Tehran soon."

"Tehran! Oouee!"

"So you've been to Tehran?"

"Naw. But I'm going next week."

Farhad said *naw* and *yul* as he'd heard cowboys say *yes* and *no* in movies. He said he was about to start at Tehran University's Faculty of Translation.

Farhad's uncle invited Marco to visit him if he came to Tehran. He took out a piece of paper and started writing down his Tehran address. The bald man, who was sipping tea across the aisle from them, suddenly stood up and started to come over to the table to see what Farhad's uncle was writing, but the kabob man stopped him. "Please. Leave these customers alone. Go home, now, Bikhod. What a nuisance."

"I'm going to take the visitor to the town guest room," Bikhod insisted. "I need to write down his information."

Marco feared another *sholugh* would break out. But Farhad rebuffed Bikhod and continued talking to Marco, who was now surprised to hear that Farhad knew the word *asshole* in English.

"We'll *all* go," Farhad's uncle said. Mister wants to hear some poetry." There wasn't much the little bald man could do about it. Mr. Sufizadeh brought along his traveling bag. Farhad came along, too.

The guest room was on the second floor of a mud-brick house next to the bus stop. The landlady led them past the *hoz*, the traditional pool in the garden, and up an outdoor stairway.

"We'll need the form," the little bald man told her.

Ignoring him, she showed the guests into the room and began laying out three clean sleeping mats on the floor. Apparently it was out of the question that Marco would stay there alone for the night.

"We'll need the form," the little man repeated. He asked Marco to show him his passport.

"What's the hurry?" Mr. Sufizadeh interrupted. "Let him unpack." As he said this, everyone turned to look at Marco's small black airline briefcase. It couldn't hold much more than a toothbrush and a clean pair of socks.

"I mean, let him relax," Mr. Sufizadeh said.

"That's all right," Marco said. "I'll be glad to fill out the form Mr. Bikhod needs."

At once, the whole room erupted. The landlady squealed and pulled her chador across her face. The little man stared malignantly at Marco. Somehow he had been insulted.

In English, Farhad managed to say, "What did you call him? Don't answer that." He bent over, holding his breath and shaking. "That's not his name."

"But that's what people call him—the mullah, the restaurant owner—"

"It just means *worthless*," Farhad said. There were tears in his eyes from trying to hold back laughter as he rushed out onto the stair landing, closing the door behind him. Marco heard something that sounded like "Oouee." The landlady got up and followed him, a single sparkling eye visible behind her chador. From the landing, Marco heard Farhad say something else, then another squeal from the woman.

If the little bald man, whatever his name, had left at this point, Marco would have counted himself lucky. He was beginning to fear there would be more fun in store, this time at his own expense, if he had to fill out the guest log in this atmosphere charged with such emphasis on one's *name*.

"I'm sorry, sir," Marco told the bald man. "My Farsi. I misunderstood."

The form was finally brought in and duly filled out by Marco, who registered himself as Mark O. without incident. The landlady looked doubtfully at Marco's thin briefcase and asked the uncle and nephew if Mr. Marco had pajamas. Mr. Sufizadeh had already changed into his.

"Of course, he does," Farhad said—before Marco could say *no*. "Americans are civilized, too."

The landlady left the men to themselves. Farhad's uncle took a bottle of araq out of his bag and poured four tea glasses full of the clear homemade vodka. He said in Farsi:

> *O Sāghi, bring my cup of wine, since no one knows*
> *What fate our unseen Author has hidden behind the veil.*

"Beg your pardon?" Marco said. It looked as if Mr. Sufizadeh was talking to him, but he didn't understand.

"He's quoting Hafez," Farhad told him. "Might as well drink because we don't know what lies ahead. *Sāghi*—that's the wine pourer in the tavern." When Marco took out his notebook, Farhad said, "Not much use writing that down. There haven't been any *sāghi* for six hundred years."

"*Bezan bālā*," Mr. Sufizadeh said. Down the hatch. He, Farhad, and Bikhod drank theirs in one gulp.

Farhad went out to get some pistachios.

As Mr. Sufizadeh continued to recite Hafez, Bikhod kept drinking. Saying "With your permission" each time, he poured himself glass after glass. "Where are those pistachios?" he muttered. He was drunk now. The top of his bald head was flushed red.

Farhad came back up the stairs—followed by Mohammad, the mullah's student who had delivered the harangue at the mosque.

"Akh!" his uncle and Bikhod said almost in unison.

"So, good night, Mohammad," Farhad said at the doorway. But Mohammad slipped past him into the room.

Farhad dropped a sack of pistachios on the table and handed something to Marco. "A present from my mother." It was a pair of blue and white striped pajamas exactly like the ones Farhad was wearing.

Mohammad sat down cross-legged at the table with the others.

"What the hell?" Bikhod said. "Who invited you?"

"May the peace of Islam be upon you, and Allah's graces," Mohammad said.

"What's this *pedar sag* doing here?" Bikhod's speech was slurred, but Marco recognized the phrase *father-dog*.

"God is great," Mohammad said. His eyes began to glaze over as they had outside the mosque earlier that day. "Woe to the unclean, the idolater, the unbeliever. Hell lies waiting for those who do not follow the way of Islam."

Farhad egged him on, translating a few key words for Marco. He turned to Marco and with a deadpan expression said, "I haven't been counting, but I think this is his seventh *first point*."

Mohammad frowned deeply and lifted up his chin when he spoke. Marco caught the word for alcohol, a substance forbidden in Islam, and glanced at the table in front of him. Farhad had cleared away all the glasses except the one in front of Bikhod, next to which sat the nearly empty bottle of araq.

Nodding seriously as if translating, Farhad said to Marco in English, "He's just repeating phrases he heard in the mosque. He wasn't good at any subject in high school, so he went to study with the mullah." Marco nodded gravely, and Mohammad—encouraged—raised his voice. He started pausing now and then for Farhad to translate. Rather than translate, Farhad gave a running commentary: "He just mispronounced the word for materialism; that's why my uncle smiled. He thinks America is in the middle east. He's big on avoiding lust; you get the idea he's been on the receiving end of this part of the lecture a few times. This is good: you should put ice on your balls to drive Satan out. He's getting off the track now. Repeating himself. He might have already used up everything he's got."

Farhad and his uncle kept saying "God is great" and "Praise God" from time to time whenever Mohammad started to slow down. This was a show they were putting on, largely for Marco. Farhad glanced at Marco now and then to see if he was enjoying it.

When Mohammad flagged, Farhad turned to Bikhod and tried to get him going, too. "Sir, but what about the Shah's six-point program of modernization? What about the White Revolution?"

"You see what's standing in the way," Bikhod said, his speech slurred. "We're going to keep throwing more and more of these ignorant fanatics into prison until His Majesty is free to carry out his enlightened reforms." Marco was pleased to understand some stock phrases that he had memorized from newspaper and radio reports—the part about reforms, that is. He had to look up the word for prison.

Bikhod held his face close to Mohammad's and kept hurling insults. Mohammad raised his voice and put his hands to his ears as if calling the faithful to prayer. Neither could have understood what the other was saying.

"Is this what you call a *Mexican standoff*?" Farhad asked Marco.

As Marco was wondering how it would end, Bikhod's body slowly began to tip backwards until he fell flat on his back with his legs still crossed and knees sticking up into the air.

"*Kesāfat!*" Farhad said. Unclean. "Let's get him out of here before he throws up."

Farhad and his uncle dragged Bikhod out of the room by his arms. Marco and Mohammad followed them down the stairs and into the garden, where Bikhod regurgitated a green mixture of pistachios and araq.

"Pig!" Farhad's uncle said. "Let's wash him off." They dragged him to the *hoz* and dunked his head into the water. Bikhod regained consciousness briefly, but passed out again as they dragged him out to the street and left him there.

"The light of day will reveal his corruption," Mohammad said.

To prevent Mohammad from following them back to the guest room, Farhad said, "Good night, Mohammad." When Mohammad looked disappointed, Farhad told him, "Mr. Marco and I are going to Tehran soon. Maybe you can come to visit us there and give us more of your guidance." To Marco he added, "Although he might have to ice his balls down more often in Tehran."

Farhad's uncle nudged Bikhod a little with his foot. "He's a dangerous man to anger," he said. "But he never remembers anything that happened when he wakes up."

Back in the room, Marco asked Farhad, "Why did your uncle call that little man dangerous?"

"He's our local SAVAK agent," Farhad told him. The Shah's equivalent of the CIA. Not his full time job. They're everywhere. They send reports of suspicious activity, things like that."

"Now we can enjoy the evening," Farhad's uncle said. "Let's listen to some poetry." He produced a short-wave radio from his pack and tuned it to a station broadcasting *Golhaye Rangarang*, a program of Persian poetry sung to santur, violin, and flute. Farhad and his uncle knew every line. Marco was entranced by the sounds alone.

"With your permission," Farhad said to his uncle, "I'll just smoke one cigarette before I go to sleep." He took one from the table and, not seeing a match, picked up the form that Marco had filled out for Bikhod, rolled it up, and held it in the charcoal fire below the samovar. He used it to light his cigarette, then let the whole thing burn and dropped the ashes into a tea glass.

Wayfarers

به کوی میکده هر سالکی که ره دانست
دری دگر زدن اندیشه تبه دانست

—Hafez

Be kuye Meikadeh har sāleki ke rah dānest
Dari degar zadan andisheye tabah dānest.

Marco sat alone in his Tehran apartment. He had been sent to teach at the University of Tehran, but classes wouldn't start for a few weeks. He raised the reed *hasir* blind and opened the large glass door to his bedroom balcony on the third floor, then stood looking down at the walled, gated garden below. Beyond the wall, mostly blocked from his view, was the narrow alleyway or *kucheh* that led to Shah Reza Avenue. Now and then he heard people talking to each other, but here in Tehran, he felt isolated from their lives. Turning away from the window, he picked up the letter he had written asking Elaine to take him back. He read it once again and put it away in his briefcase. Take him back? Even if she did, she'd never come to a place like this. Elaine didn't like foreigners very much.

Every day he walked to the post office to see if he had a letter from his mother or even perhaps from Elaine. He didn't. Every day the post office clerk encouraged him: "Maybe tomorrow."

One day, the door buzzer rang.

"Farhad!"

"I got your address from the University office. The gate was unlocked. Are you sick or something?" Farhad said in his perfect English. "You don't look too good."

"It's just . . . do you know *diarrhea*?"

"We invented it. Don't worry. My aunt has some pills that will

28

seal you right up." He looked around Marco's apartment. "You have a shower and hot water. This is nice."

"How about moving in here?"

"Really?"

Farhad came back later that afternoon bringing with him a bundle of clothes and a Shiraz carpet. They put the carpet down in an empty room, Farhad dropped his bundle on it, and he was installed. Marco's room had a bed but no carpet. Farhad's room had a carpet but no bed. Each thought the other was missing the more important item.

From his pocket, Farhad pulled out two tiny white pills. "From my aunt," he said. "For your condition."

"Thanks. What is it?"

"Opium."

Marco found that indeed just one pill sealed him right up.

The next day, Farhad came back from his aunt's with a low canvas cot and a red curtain to put across the entrance to his room, which had no door. "My aunt insisted I needed these," he explained. "And some guys are going to bring over a bookcase she doesn't need. And a dresser for you."

In the early evening, they went out for a stroll, a *gardesh*, as it was called. They walked down the wide, tree lined Shah Reza Avenue taking in the sights. It was the last month of summer, and the fragile, light green leaves of the tall, skinny poplars quivered as the cool night air of the sky met the heat still rising from the sidewalks. The night coolness sank lower as the sun disappeared behind the jagged geometrical horizon formed by the rooftops in the distance. The avenue was filled with people, but in the busy city of Tehran it wasn't as clear as in Shiraz who was out for a *gardesh* and who was actually going somewhere. In Hichja no one had been going anywhere.

They turned onto a side street.

"Look at that." Farhad laughed. "That little restaurant. See what it's called? The Kaleh-pacheye-Victor Hugo."

Marco didn't get it.

"You know, we sometimes eat a stew of sheep's head and feet. *Kaleh-pācheh*. That's the Victor Hugo Sheep Head and Footery, I guess you would call it. Oouee! We're going to love Tehran."

Farhad stopped to buy a single cigarette at a little table on the sidewalk lit by a gasoline lantern. He lifted the globe of the lantern and leaned down to light it. "Remember that form you filled out in Hichja?"

"The one you burned?"

"Yul. There was trouble."

"You're kidding."

Farhad blew a smoke ring into the evening air. "Everybody in town knows you stayed there. They also know that the next day our part-time SAVAK agent couldn't seem to find the form. They love telling him he let some kind of spy slip through his fingers."

"Get serious."

"I mean, you know. No form, no papers. You just drifted in and out of town, *leaving no record*."

"Come on. I would think I looked more like a vagabond than any kind of agent."

"Yul. That's what I told them." Farhad raised his head, blew another perfect smoke ring, and eyed Marco. "That you weren't an agent, I mean."

They headed back towards their *kucheh*, and Farhad stopped in front of a tavern on the corner. "Look. The Meikadeh Hafez. The Hafez Tavern. Great name. Wonder if it's owned by a Zoroastrian like in the old poetry? We've got to go in here."

They sat down at the counter on little stools, and Farhad ordered two glasses of araq. He held up his glass to Marco. "*Nushi jun!*" To your health. He looked around. The customers—all men and all older than Farhad and Marco—seemed like regulars. The proprietor was a tall, powerful-looking man with long sideburns. The customers called him by his name, Adarvan. Farhad turned to Marco and nodded. Yes.

Farhad held his glass up again. "To you, Mr. Adarvan, and the Meikadeh Hafez." He gulped down the araq and recited lines from Hafez about a *Meikadeh* or tavern:

A wayfarer finding his way to this tavern's lane
Would be a fool to knock at any other door.

"*Bārak' allāh*," a few of the customers said. Nice.

"For the wayfarers," Mr. Adarvan said. He filled up Farhad's and Marco's glasses again. "*Befarmāid*," he said. On the house.

Farhad put his hand over his chest, and Marco copied him.

Marco was still thinking about *Mr. Worthless*. "Could he really cause any trouble?"

"Naw. His only job is to get information on any stranger who comes into town and send a report to SAVAK—and he screwed that up. Now he just wants everybody to forget the whole thing."

As they ate *kālbās* sausage sandwiches, Farhad looked Marco over. "Sorry to say this. But you look a little . . . *scruffy*. Is that the right word?"

"Yeah. I lost all my clothes except the ones I was wearing."

"We can take care of that. We'll go to my uncle and aunt's house."

"The uncle I met in Hichja?"

"Right. His daughter can sew anything. My cousin. She'll fix you up."

As they left, Adarvan said, "Please come back again." A few customers turned and put their hands over their chests.

The next morning, Farhad took Marco to a tailor his uncle knew to get measured for a suit, and he helped Marco bargain for it.

"Next what?" he asked.

"Underwear? Shirts?" Marco suggested.

"Naw. My cousin can make those for you."

Not Kansas

چو من فانی شدم از جان کهنه

مرا افتاد با جانان ملاقات

—Attar

Cho man fāni shodam az jān-e-kohneh
Marā oftād bā jānān molāghāt.

It was only a short bus ride to Farhad's aunt's house. Marco took the letter to Elaine with him, wondering if he really should mail it.

From behind the wall, they heard the sound of girls laughing, then saw a volleyball fly up into the air and drop down behind the wall again. Farhad rang the bell at a high wrought-iron gate. "*Yā'allāh*," he said, the standard warning that somebody was coming in—and a notice to any women present that they might want to retreat.

"Welcome," the girls practically sang together. They rushed to take down laundry that had been hung out to dry, then disappeared into the house behind armfuls of clean white clothes. There was a *hoz* in the center of the garden, and the ball was floating at the edge. Marco picked it up and Farhad took it inside.

His uncle was away driving his oil tanker. His aunt was a cheerful-looking woman with slight traces of gray in her hair and a broad smile.

"The Honorable Mister Professor Marco," Farhad announced. He spoke Farsi so everybody could understand.

"We are your servants," his aunt replied. "We're humbled by the honor of your visit."

"You don't have to use a lot of *ta'ārof* with him," Farhad told his aunt. He said foreigners didn't use elaborate expressions of formal courtesy.

His aunt seemed doubtful. "I know you're not saying they're uncivilized." She showed them into a room with no furniture except a low table in the center. A red floral Shiraz carpet covered the whole floor, and cushions were placed on the carpet for them to sit on around the low table. Elaine would have hated this, Marco thought. As they sat down, the three daughters stood in the doorway looking in.

His aunt served her guests some tea.

When Marco took a sip, she gasped. "No sugar?"

"No thanks."

"Your heart will contract," she told him. "Please, drink it with sugar."

Marco put a lump of sugar in his mouth and sucked the tea through it, Iranian style. Mrs. Sufizadeh smiled and nodded. She turned towards the door. "Girls, come in to meet Mr. Marco, Farhad's friend. Bring some fruit, please."

The three daughters filed quietly into the room. It was a modern Tehran family, and none of the women wore chadors, inside or outside.

His back to the doorway, Farhad pretended not to notice the girls coming in. "They say I'm going to marry one of my cousins," he told Marco, still speaking in Farsi. "It's a scary thought."

"Hah! Farhad, you're destined to die single," the middle and by far most beautiful daughter said. Her long black hair floated and glistened as she turned her head. "It would be too cruel a fate for anyone to marry you."

"Ah," Farhad said. "This young lady with such poor judgment about men is my cousin Mastaneh."

Marco stood up, and she held out her hand. He tried to keep his composure as she smiled at him with her deep brown eyes. "A pleasure to meet you," she said. "I'm sorry I don't speak English."

"The pleasure is mine." He stood looking at her, still feeling the softness of her hand after she had let go.

Farhad coughed. "Uh, and this is her older sister Maryam, and this is little Mina."

They both shook hands with Marco, even Mina, who was just starting elementary school.

When they sat together at the table, their mother said, "Girls, give Mr. Marco some fruit." She poured him another glass of tea and watched to verify that he took a lump of sugar with it.

The girls peeled apples delicately, listening while their mother asked Farhad about his course at the university. They were absent-mindedly putting each slice of peeled apple onto the fruit plate in front of Marco. Soon his plate was piled quite high.

"You can talk to Mr. Marco," Farhad encouraged his cousins. "He speaks Farsi."

"Why is your hair that color?" little Mina immediately asked him.

"Impolite!" her mother said. "Not that kind of question."

Pointing her delicate fingers at the ridiculous heap of slices on Marco's plate, Mastaneh smiled. "Mr. Marco, I hope you like apples."

Little Mina giggled.

"With your permission," Marco said. He took the last apple slice that Mastaneh herself had put on the plate. Her eyes met his.

It was then that Farhad announced, "Mr. Marco doesn't have any clothes."

Everyone stared at Marco as if he might be naked.

"Some *father-dog* stole his baggage at the airport."

"Watch your language, Farhad," his aunt scolded.

Mastaneh quickly volunteered, "I could make Mr. Marco some shirts."

"And some underwear," Farhad said.

Marco felt he was blushing.

Mastaneh said, "Mr. Marco, if I have one of your shirts, I'm sure I can make more the same size."

Farhad looked at Marco. "Any problem with that?"

"Except . . . I just have this one."

Farhad's aunt said, "We will discuss this matter later."

34

In English, Farhad told Marco, "That means never. It's how we end awkward discussions in Iran."

"Speak Farsi," his aunt said. She sipped some tea. The conversation seemed to have died. Then she said, "How is your *problem*, Mr. Marco?"

"Problem?" Mina said.

"Problem?" Maryam said.

"Prob—?" Mastaneh began.

"Diarrhea," Farhad said.

The conversation stopped.

"Oh, I'm fine now." Marco thanked Farhad's aunt for the pills.

Maryam, some years older than Marco, cleared her throat. "Mastaneh, maybe he knows that novel you're reading."

"Are you kidding?" Farhad interrupted. "He knows everything about literature. He's a professor at the university."

Mastaneh broke off a sprig of grapes with her long fingers, looked at Marco from behind hair that had partly fallen across her face, and said nothing.

Maryam explained that Mastaneh was reading a Farsi translation of *Huckleberry Finn*.

"Yes," Mastaneh said. "There's part of it I don't understand."

Farhad said, "Why don't you get the book? Tell Mr. Marco what part you don't understand."

"I left it at the office."

"Then bring it to our apartment after work some day," Farhad said.

"I don't want to take up Mr. Marco's time."

"Please. It would be my pleasure." Marco was happy to be able to use a stock phrase of formal *ta'ārof*, which, in this case, he really meant.

"He can read Farsi, too," Farhad declared. "A little. Try him."

"Can he read poetry?" Mina said. "It's hard."

"Let him try," Farhad said. "Get one of your father's books."

Mina brought a ragged book of Attar's poetry and opened it to a random page. "Can you read this, Mr. Marco?"

"I'm sure I can't."

"Try."

He took the book and puzzled out a verse, which he figured meant this:

> *As I left behind my bygone life,*
> *I chanced to meet the Beloved.*

"*Āfarin!*" Mrs. Sufizadeh exclaimed in her high-pitched voice. Excellent! Marco glanced at Mastaneh. She was holding her hand over her mouth.

When the conversation turned back to family relations and friends in Hichja, Mrs. Sufizadeh seemed concerned. "Mr. Marco, this must be boring for you. Mastaneh, maybe Mr. Marco would like to see some of the sketches you've made." Mastaneh demurred, but Marco insisted.

She took him into the adjoining room. In one corner was a loom and a sewing machine. In another was an ancient-looking roll top desk. She opened the desk.

Marco had expected sketches of flowers and bowls of fruit and bunny rabbits, but she showed him something quite different. There were glimpses of Hichja farmers bent over carrying sacks of straw, scratching irrigation ditches in the dry earth of walled gardens, and cutting rows of wheat with heavy scythes. There were high school sketches, mostly of girls—studying, trying on clothes, cooking, drinking tea together. The sketches of boys were drawn as glimpsed from windows of a house or through a bus window—kicking soccer balls in the streets, walking with their open books under the street lights at night. Mastaneh had done a sketch of Farhad, too. She caught perfectly his curly hair, thick eyebrows that almost met in the middle, and thin nose.

Marco looked up. Mastaneh was watching him.

"They're wonderful," he told her. "Let me see the rest."

There were sketches of men and women haggling over the price of everything from carpets to carrots in the bazaar. Marco's favorite was a drawing of the mosque in Hichja, not an architectural sketch but a close-up view inside the entrance, where a line of human posteriors rose up in the foreground—her townsmen at prayer. Marco could feel her love and understanding of her country and people.

"I love these," he told her.

"Akh," she exclaimed. *"Ta'ārof nakon!"* No need to be polite.

"Seriously!" he insisted.

Now everybody at the table was looking over at them.

"Talk to him in English," Mina called.

"I'll believe that when I hear it," Farhad commented.

Mastaneh bowed, cleared her throat, and in a slight British accent said, *"How good of you to come, sir."*

"Dorothy! Talk like Dorothy, Mastaneh!" Mina was getting excited. "Please. Please."

In an American accent this time, Mastaneh said, *"Mr. Marco, we're not in Kansas any more."*

Mina clapped.

Farhad said, "Too bad we just heard the only two things she knows how to say in English. Her pronunciation is great, though, isn't it, Marco?"

"Like a nightingale," Marco said.

Farhad looked pleased. "I've never seen her blush before."

On the way back to the apartment, they passed a yellow mailbox, but Marco didn't mail the letter he'd brought with him. When he got back to his room, he tore it up and threw it away.

Dating

یا رب این شمع دل افروز ز کاشانه کیست

جان ما سوخت بپرسید که جانانه کیست

—Hafez

Yā rab ihn sham'-e-del afruz ze kāshāneye kist?
Jān-e-mā sukht beporsid ke jānāneye kist?

The next day, Farhad went to his first class at the university's Faculty of Translation but decided he already knew more English than the teacher and went out looking for a job. It wasn't easy because Tehran was beginning to fill up with people from the provinces coming to town to look for work. Farhad said there were very few salaried jobs available, most of which were in government agencies or government-connected businesses. These positions were doled out to relatives, friends, and supporters of government officials and rich entrepreneurs in a system of favoritism and influence called *pārti bāzi*.

The streets of Tehran were filled with people without jobs—somehow surviving through their own desperation and wit. A man came down the *kucheh* in front of Marco's apartment every morning with a dented metal pan announcing himself as an *āb hozi*, a cleaner of the *hoz* found in most courtyards. He was followed later by a man shouting *kot shalvari*, the coat and pants man, a buyer of used clothes to re-sell to a dealer. Turkoman and Bakhtiari tribesmen with leathery, sun-wrinkled faces slowly walked the streets in silent dignity, each with a tribal carpet over his shoulder—for sale. A man stood at a crowded corner with a parrot on his shoulder. The parrot, imported illegally, was for sale.

The university's Faculty of Letters, where Marco would teach, hadn't opened for the school year yet. Thinking about Mastaneh, he picked up a notebook Farhad had left on the dining room table. There were some passages from Hafez Farhad had translated into English. On one page, he found these lines:

> O Lord, from whose house is she
> who lights a candle in my heart?
> Ask whose beloved she is who set my soul on fire.

He went to the small hallway window that faced north and gazed out at the perfectly symmetrical snow-covered peak of Mount Damavand. The fall sky was topaz blue in the early evening, with orange streaks that deepened into crimson at the horizon drenching the mountain peak in a deep pomegranate red. Something he had heard at Farhad's aunt's house was bothering him.

Farhad came in. "From my aunt." He handed Marco a cloth-tied bundle containing three white shirts along with some undershirts and baggy green shorts with elastic bands. "Actually, Mastaneh made them."

"That fast?"

"Yul. She said she started as soon as we left. She saw we were the same size and made them by measuring some things I had left in my aunt's house."

Marco laid out each item carefully on the table. "I need to thank her."

"Sure." Farhad lit a cigarette and blew a smoke ring up towards the ceiling. "You seem *moody*? Did I use that right?"

"I was just wondering. When we went to your aunt's house, you said something about one of your cousins being your fiancée. I took it you meant Mastaneh."

"Yul. They've always said that."

"I mean, is she?"

"You think we really marry our first cousins? We're not back in Qajar times."

"So it's just a joke."

"Yul. I'm not saying people don't marry their cousins sometimes.

You know, in villages."

"Like Hichja?"

Only a few days after he started looking, Farhad burst into the apartment. "I got a job." Beaming, he handed Marco a green bottle of Star beer he brought from the Meikadeh Hafez.

"Great. Where?"

"At the Iran-America Society. Teaching English."

"That's great. What's the Iran-America Society?"

"Like the British Council, or the Alliance Française. Some kind of propaganda agency. It's part of the USIS. They call it the USELESS."

"Anyway great."

"Yul. I already taught two classes. Actually, my title is switchboard operator. But an American teacher quit, and they needed somebody right away. They watched me teach the two classes and hired me *on the spot*." He looked at Marco. "Is that right?"

"It sure is."

"Come on, let's celebrate. We'll go to the House of Heaven."

"No. I don't feel like it."

"OK. We don't have to go to the House of Heaven. We'll go down to the south of the city where we can find some women to sympathize with us—if you know what I mean."

"Hmm."

"There are plenty of them. Beautiful, too. We just pick them up and bring them back here."

Marco said he wasn't in the mood. "In the States, we usually just go on dates with girls. I know you can't do that here. It's just, that's what I'm used to."

Farhad knew the word, he knew what it meant, but he couldn't imagine why a man would want to do such a thing. "You're sitting there, just next to the girl, right? So, I don't get it. Doesn't it make you want to 'do' her?" He used a literal translation of the Farsi slang expression, which worked well in English, too. "So. You've stirred yourself up all for nothing. How is that enjoyable?"

"You get to know each other."

"But if you can't do them, wouldn't it be better not to know them? The whole thing seems pointless."

"See, if you like them, and they like you, sometimes you end up 'doing' them, as you say."

"Aha. This is starting to make sense. But I still couldn't do it. What if you like them and they reject you? I couldn't stand that."

"You try another person."

"I don't know. I'd rather go for the *sure thing*." He lit a cigarette. "But I'll tell you what. Let's do it. Let's give it a try. Some students in my class at the USELESS are kind of *emruzi*, modern. Give me another day. I'll arrange everything. We'll go on a date. A *double date*, right?"

The next day, Marco reluctantly went with Farhad to meet two girls in their late teens in front of the Cinema Golden City. "Which one do you want?" Farhad whispered. Marco didn't care.

The two couples sat in the back of the theater, where Farhad put his arm around his "date" and started kissing her. Marco just sat there watching the movie until his date lifted his arm up and put it around her shoulder. "Let's go," Farhad said, only a few minutes into the main feature, and the four of them returned to the apartment. Before they sat down, Farhad said to his date, "I want to show you something in my room." He turned and to Marco he said in English, "I put some condoms on your dresser. You know, just in case."

Farhad and his date came out of his room again in ten minutes. "Still sitting here?" he said. Marco hadn't wanted to show his date anything in his room. In fact, he was finding it hard even to carry on a conversation with her. "Not my type," he muttered to Farhad, who immediately said to Marco's date: "Come on. I'll show you, too."

In fifteen to twenty minutes, Farhad had "done" both of them, and they were on their way.

"This dating's not bad," Farhad said. "But I still think the girls who do it are sluts."

The Emperor of Ice-cream

The doorbell buzzed. It was Mastaneh. "Sorry. The courtyard gate was open. So I just came up to your door." She looked at Marco timidly, her deep brown eyes highlighted by long, black eyelashes—eyes more beautiful than any Marco had ever seen.

"The gate's always open. Come in. Farhad's not back from work yet."

"Then I'd rather not come in, if you don't mind. I hope you understand." Some of Mastaneh's long hair fanned across her delicate shoulders and made a brilliant contrast with the white of her blouse.

"Yes, I understand." Marco knew that in Iran a woman couldn't enter the house of a man who wasn't a relative.

"I don't know if you really have time to answer some questions about this book. I'm sorry to bother you. I can't read it in English."

"*Ghorbān-e-shomā*," he said. I am your sacrifice. Marco had often heard people use this polite *ta'ārof* phrase to mean "I'd be glad to."

Mastaneh gasped. Her face reddened.

He stood there confused. "Did I say something wrong?"

This made her smile. "It's just, there are some things men don't say to women. Like *I'm your sacrifice.*"

"Oh."

"It's kind of strong."

"I'm sorry. Only to other men?"

"Yes. Unless you—never mind. Yes, only to men." She looked radiant with her blushing cheeks.

Marco was afraid to say anything more.

She touched his arm. "Don't worry, Mr. Marco. You'll catch on. I'm glad you can talk to me in Farsi."

"Mastaneh, the European Ice-cream Shop is on the way to your house. Maybe we could go there?"

"I don't understand. Go together to an ice-cream shop?"

"I guess I shouldn't have suggested it. I'm sorry."

Mastaneh looked down at her book and, still looking down, she took a breath and said, "I'll do it."

They sat in leather and chrome chairs while a waiter in a white jacket and black tie brought them peach melbas on a silver tray, placing the tall glass dishes on a small, shiny black table. French *chansons* played in the background, and elegant young men and women dressed in the latest fashions from Paris or Berlin were socializing not over cocktails but over elaborate dishes of ice-cream or fruit desserts.

"What an absurd place!" Mastaneh whispered. "An Iranian ice-cream shop with a menu in French!"

Marco nodded.

"But ice-cream is my favorite thing in the world!" She turned her eyes one way, then another, and spoke in a lowered voice. "We have a word for these customers. I wonder if you know it: *farang-rafteh.*"

"People who've been to Europe and come back?"

"Or act like they have." She glanced around. "But, look, nobody's staring at us. I didn't know it was possible to sit and talk to a man in public like this."

She tasted her peach melba. "Okh, Mr. Marco, this is the most delicious thing I've ever eaten in my life."

Relaxed, now, and happy in her disguise as a *farang-rafteh,* Mastaneh became talkative.

"In fact," she said, "I'm reminded of the famous lines of the poet Hafez of Shiraz." She had a playful smile.

"What lines?"

"Just a minute. Let me try to recall." She breathed in and then recited a spontaneous pastiche of a Hafez lyric, substituting *waiter* for *sāghi,* the beautiful wine-pourer celebrated in ancient Persian lyrics, and *peach melba* for *wine.* Marco didn't get it all, but it ended something like this:

Youth and beauty turn to dust,
And farang garments tatter.
Lo, Hafez, leave this useless life,
And, waiter, fill the goblet up
With heaven-sent peach melba.

Some customers laughed, and a few applauded, including the waiter, who Mastaneh hadn't realized was standing behind her. She had begun in a normal tone, but Persian lyrics need to be declaimed in stylized, sonorous tones, and she had forgotten herself.

"Excellent!" a man wearing tinted glasses at a nearby table called out. Mastaneh held her napkin over her mouth with both hands and looked around only with her eyes, her face flushed. Others said, "Well done!" —despite the implication that the vibrant pleasures of the past had degenerated into these effete pleasures of the European Ice-cream Shop. They seemed to find Mastaneh's poem all the funnier because the joke was on them.

"I'm sorry," Mastaneh said. "I guess I ruined the *ambiance*." She put her napkin back over her mouth to stifle a laugh. Her cheeks looked hot. Marco wished he could touch them.

He said, "I like the way Iranians can laugh at themselves."

She sipped some water. "Not all of them can, of course."

"A notable exception being the top *farang-rafteh* himself?" He meant the Shah.

Mastaneh now spoke in a low voice. "Please be careful, Mr. Marco. Especially in a place like this."

"Sorry. I can't get used to watching what I say."

Marco didn't want the afternoon to be over. "And about *Huckleberry Finn*?"

"Can I wait and ask you about it the next time Farhad brings you to my house?"

When Marco called for the bill, the waiter said, "*Pas de prix, monsieur.*" Mastaneh didn't understand.

"There's no charge, Miss. It would be like charging Hafez."

44

Marco walked her home but stopped as they turned into the narrow *kucheh* that led to her house. He looked around. No one was there. He took her hand. She looked into his eyes for a second, then quickly turned and ran away towards her house.

Walking back to his apartment, he realized he hadn't asked her whether he could mention their ice-cream "date" to Farhad. Mastaneh hadn't told him to keep it a secret, but he knew a woman's reputation could be damaged by being seen with a man in public.

Maybe Tehran was different, he hoped. It was the home of the Westernized Shah and had been made into a comfortable city for his Westernized supporters to live in. Through money, determination, and imperial edict, Tehran had been forged into a place where the Shah's foreign supporters—industrial moguls, arms salesmen, government officials—could feel somewhat at home when they came to pay their tribute. Farhad had taken him to the Marmar Bar, which could have been a London pub. He told Marco about places he had heard about at the Iran-America Society—the tea dancing at the Café Lyons, set up exactly as it was in France, the Pension-e-Swiss modeled after an Alpine hostel, and a German restaurant that served Bavarian food. Russians could drink Stolichnaya vodka in any of the Armenian- or Zoroastrian-owned cafes. And for the Americans there were Hollywood action movies.

Any of these foreign visitors or Westernized Iranians who wanted to prepare European meals could buy what they needed at Iran Super on Takht-e-Jamshid Street, where even the butchers spoke English, French, German, and Russian. Marco once considered buying a jar of peanut butter there but was unwilling to part with a week's salary for it.

It was his turn to buy food for the dinner. He bought carrots and potatoes at one sidewalk shop, onions and green beans at another, and seventy-five grams, one *sir*, of ground beef at a third. He turned at Pich-e-Shemirun and headed down Kucheh-e-Hamin'oddoleh towards their apartment, walking slowly, trying to think of what to say to Farhad. He girded himself and opened the apartment door.

"Where have you been? You're usually home before now."

Marco felt his face flush. "Mastaneh came by. She didn't come in. I walked her part of the way home, then bought this stuff for dinner." He wanted to tell Farhad the truth, but he thought it would be better not to use the word *date*. He started cutting up the onions, trying to think of a way to explain how he happened to have ice-cream with Mastaneh.

"You're looking *nārāhat*," Farhad said. Uneasy. "What's wrong? Want to try dating again—with different girls? Maybe we can find one you'll like."

"One I like? But, you know, if I liked a girl, I might just want to sit and talk to her."

"You're losing me, Professor Penis."

Obviously the conversation wasn't going in the right direction. Now it seemed impossible to mention the European Ice-cream Shop. He said, "I'm just thinking. Isn't it a double standard to say that women who sleep with men, or even date them, are whores, but the men who do it are only acting natural?"

"Double standard," Farhad repeated, fascinated by the term. He said it again, letting it sink in. "This is a good term."

"You get the idea of what it means?"

"Double standard. A double standard. Sure. It is."

"So it's not logical. It's not fair to women."

"Definitely. It's not logical." He dipped a lump of sugar into his tea. "But I still can't help it. That's the way I feel."

Alkinoös's palace

As Marco was looking over the textbooks he was to use at the university, Farhad burst into the apartment with another of his announcements.

"My uncle's back in town. He wants to see you again. We're

invited for dinner. Let's go."

Marco put on a shirt that Mastaneh had made. Some foreigners in the country complained that Iranians were dishonest in their dealings with tourists and visitors. Marco himself was surprised that even people like bus token sellers tried to shortchange him occasionally. And, of course, as soon as he arrived in the country, someone had stolen all of his baggage and clothing, either in the Tehran or Shiraz airport. But almost as if in recompense for this loss, Marco's clothes were gradually being replaced, piece by piece. Marco now had pajamas from Farhad's mother in Hichja, shirts Mastaneh made for him, and a "loaner" suit coat which the tailor in Shiraz had insisted that Marco keep. He had a new suit made by a friend of Farhad's uncle for which he was charged almost nothing and a pair of square-toed Iranian shoes that some other relative or friend of somebody had made for him.

"What you need is a pair of light-tinted sunglasses," Farhad told Marco. "I'll get them for you."

Marco pictured the kind of glasses he'd seen customers in the European Ice-cream Shop wearing. "Black frames? Square-ish lenses?"

"Exactly."

"I don't know."

But on the way to Mastaneh's house, Farhad stopped and said, "Wait. Let's go in here." It was one of a row of several almost identical shops, none bigger than Marco's kitchen. The wizened proprietor sat motionless on a stool opposite a framed picture of the Shah wearing square-ish, tinted sunglasses. "Welcome," the old man said.

"We're looking for sunglasses," Farhad told him.

"I might be able to help you," the shopkeeper said with a deadpan expression. Farhad and Marco looked around, noticing for the first time that nothing else was for sale in the shop.

They rang the bell, and Maryam, the oldest, swung open the heavy gate, her sisters in line behind her. "Welcome," they all said together.

"It's Farhad and Mr. Marco, disguised as Tehranis," Mastaneh said. "Farhad, those glasses had to be your idea."

"How do you like them? Made in France. We got them cheap."

"Ah."

"What do you mean 'Ah?' They're expensive glasses. We bargained him down."

"I didn't mean anything," she said. They look fine, I suppose." Mastaneh glanced briefly at Marco but didn't speak to him directly.

"Mastaneh likes Mr. Marco's eyes," little Mina put in. "Now she can't see his blue eyes."

"Ah," Farhad said.

Mastaneh pinched her little sister's arm.

If Mastaneh had told her sisters she liked his eyes, Marco wondered, had she also told them they went to the European Ice-cream Shop together? He needed to know.

Maryam said, "Now you're embarrassing Mr. Marco, everybody. Mastaneh and Farhad, can't you stop your bickering? And, Mina, there are some things you're not supposed to repeat, you know."

"Sorry, Mr. Marco," Mina said.

Farhad picked her up and swung her around so her legs flew out.

"Papa's in town," Mina said. She ran back into the house ahead of them.

As he went inside, Marco took off his sunglasses.

Mr. Sufizadeh gave Marco a bear hug and a mustache-kiss on each cheek. He told his wife, "We're old friends. I met Mr. Marco in Hichja, you remember I told you?"

Mr. Sufizadeh, Farhad, and Marco sat at the table while Mrs. Sufizadeh came into the room and started up a samovar on the floor near the doorway, then left. Her daughters alternately brought seeds, nuts, and fruit for their father and the guests, then left.

"Mr. Marco, you're famous in Hichja," Mr. Sufizadeh laughed. "The mysterious stranger." His gold tooth shone beneath his mustache.

Farhad translated the word *mysterious* for Marco. He went on in English. "Remember Mohammad? My uncle says the mullah kicked him out of the madreseh, so he put on a turban and declared he'd learned all he needed."

"Speak Farsi," his aunt said. "I'm sure Mr. Marco can understand. Just don't use words like *mysterious*."

Farhad nodded. He said, "Mohammad might come here to visit us. You don't mind, do you, Marco?"

"Heaven forbid!" Mrs. Sufizadeh's voice rang out. "You don't have to open your home to crazy people, Farhad. Even if they're from your hometown."

"He's harmless," Farhad said.

"I hope he's harmless." Mrs. Sufizadeh glanced at her husband.

In English, under his breath, Farhad said to Marco, "My uncle got into some trouble a long time ago. For being in the Nationalist movement. He quit, gave up politics, but my aunt still worries."

"Farsi, please." Mrs. Sufizadeh tapped the table in front of Farhad.

Her husband changed the subject. "Farhad tells me you're studying Persian poetry, Mr. Marco."

Mastaneh knelt silently behind Farhad and Marco, reaching between them to put three little tea glasses and a bowl of sugar lumps on the table, then put the teapot next to her father. Marco saw only her hand and long-sleeved white blouse, but he knew it was Mastaneh. Then she disappeared.

"Right? Marco? You know some Persian poetry now, right?" Farhad repeated.

"Oh. Just a few poems. I can't understand the ones that have Arabic in them." Marco showed Mr. Sufizadeh the notebook he kept of Farsi words and some translations of poems he'd made.

"This is your handwriting?" Mr. Sufizadeh asked. "Ah. I see. Yes." He tilted his head, eyes glimmering, trying not to smile.

"What are you girls looking at?" Farhad raised his voice to the girls peeping into the room. "Impolite!"

"We want to see Mr. Marco's handwriting, too," Mina said.

"Come in if you're that curious," their father said. "Mr. Marco, I hope you don't mind." The three girls sat on cushions just out of reach of the table.

"I'll show you *my* handwriting," Mina said. She took Marco's notebook, wrote something, and handed it back to him. "There, can you read it?"

Marco read: "I have an American friend named Marco."

"Mastaneh's being strangely quiet today," Farhad observed.

Marco was trying not to look at Mastaneh directly. Had she mentioned the ice-cream shop to anybody? He needed her to give him some kind of sign, but she sat back from the table, almost behind him. Then she said, "May I see your notebook, Mr. Marco?"

Watching her turn through the pages slowly on her lap, everybody stopped talking, as if expecting a witty remark. Farhad, at least, was obviously hoping for one. "May I show you a better way to write this word?" Mastaneh asked.

Marco turned and watched while she wrote: ***I work at the Global Publishing Company.*** Her fingers left moist blurs over one or two words. It was readable, though. Marco swallowed hard.

"Do you see?" she asked.

"Yes."

"That's not my best writing, though. I'm going to erase it." She did so and closed the notebook.

Marco was losing track of the conversation but forced himself to listen.

"Maryam is my inventor daughter," her father said. "She invented a new kind of machine for ironing clothes. I'm going to try to have one made."

"Mr. Marco wouldn't have much need for that," Farhad said. "He arrived here without any clothes, as you know."

"Like Odysseus," Mastaneh said.

"Mastaneh is my literary and artistic daughter," Mr. Sufizadeh explained. "She's always quoting people I haven't heard of."

"Thank you for making me the shirts, and things." Marco

addressed this to the whole family.

"We'll make you more clothes," Mrs. Sufizadeh told him. "Mastaneh has *talent flowing from every finger.*"

"Let me measure him," Mina said.

"And this is my bold-faced daughter," Mr. Sufizadeh concluded.

The women began setting the table and serving the men without putting any plates on the table for themselves. The three men ate radishes, radish greens, leeks, spring onions, tarragon, mint, flat bread, purple onions, salted vegetables, yogurt, cucumbers, chicken soup cooked with lemons, saffron rice, and *gormeh sabzi*, a thick vegetable stew with hunks of lamb. Marco had barely started on his huge plateful when Farhad and his uncle were finished. "We eat fast," Farhad said. After he refused more food about three times, he ate another complete plateful.

"I eat slow," Marco said. He was trying to eat fast enough to show how much he liked the food but slow enough not to be given another plateful.

Mr. Sufizadeh called to his wife, "You and the girls should sit down, too. We can all fit at the table."

Mastaneh sat next to Marco, saying "With your permission."

"I guess you don't sit on the floor in America when you eat," Maryam said. "Do you keep your shoes on even when you eat? I hear Americans watch television while they're eating."

Marco said his family didn't watch television when they ate but did wear shoes.

"Do you eat pig?" Maryam wanted to know. "Papa says Americans eat pig. And lobsters."

They waited while Marco looked this one up. Even Farhad didn't know the English word for lobster and was as curious as the girls to know if Marco had ever eaten one.

"Yes, I've eaten lobster," Marco said. "They're good." He knew shellfish were forbidden to Muslims.

Mastaneh caught some food in her throat and took a huge sip of water. Everybody except Marco laughed at her.

"I'm going to try it, then," Farhad said. "I'm sure Mastaneh would like to try it too. We'll serve it at our apartment to anybody who wants to come."

"If you eat it, then I will too," Mastaneh said.

Her mother gasped.

"What is a lobster?" Mina asked.

"Where would you get a lobster?" Maryam said.

"If you get one, I'll eat it," Mastaneh declared. She was more herself since she had written, then erased the message in Marco's notebook.

Farhad asked Marco if he had ever ridden in a *Fordmustáng*.

"I know what that is," Mina said. "A fast sports car. I saw it in a magazine."

"My mother has one," Marco said

"Akh, God the Merciful!" Mrs. Sufizadeh shrieked. Even Marco couldn't help laughing.

"Who drives her?" Mina wanted to know. When Marco said his mother drove the car herself, Mrs. Sufizadeh called on God the Merciful again.

"How about a Phantom jet?" Farhad asked. "Have you—"

"No, my mother doesn't have a Phantom jet," Marco teased.

"God the Benefactor be praised," Mrs. Sufizadeh exclaimed. "What is a Phantom jet, anyway? This is what our Shah wants to buy from America."

"I really don't know what they are," Marco said. "I don't know what the Shah wants to use them for."

"He's a boy," Mr. Sufizadeh said. "They're toys for him to play with."

Maryam said, "I have a question, Mr. Marco. Is it true the Americans are going to land on the moon?"

Mrs. Sufizadeh shook her head.

"What's the matter, Maman?" Mastaneh asked her. "Wouldn't you like to live in America and drive a fast car and eat lobster and pig with your shoes on and have yourself shot up to the moon?"

Mastaneh's mother put her hands on both cheeks. "No, dear, I wouldn't." She looked at Marco. "No offense, Mr. Marco."

While the women finished eating, Mr. Sufizadeh poured more tea for the men and recited a poem which ended with a phrase about the moon. Farhad followed by reciting a poem that began with a reference to the moon and ended with a phrase about wine. They looked at Marco, giving him a chance to cap Farhad's verse. When it was obvious he couldn't do it, Mastaneh came to his rescue with a stanza that began with wine and ended in the phrase "hold your tongue."

"By the way," Farhad said to Mastaneh. "I hear you came to visit us when I wasn't home."

Marco held his breath.

"You didn't tell me about that," Mina said.

"She told *me*," Maryam said, looking over the top of her glasses.

"Why didn't you tell me?" Mina said. "Can I go too?"

"I didn't go in," Mastaneh said. "Farhad wasn't there, and I didn't want to inconvenience Mr. Marco."

Certainly some kind of *ta'ārof* phrase must be required of Marco here, but the danger of getting it wrong, or implying that he would like Mastaneh to visit him when he was alone kept him mute—or not exactly mute: he uttered something like *uhh*.

"Never mind," Farhad said. "Mina and everybody's coming the next time—for the lobster dinner."

The requested information

Marco tried to go to sleep. When he closed his eyes, he pictured Mastaneh's hand putting plates on the table. He felt her blouse brush against his hand. He thought up things he would like to say to her, seeing if he knew the Farsi words he would need. Nobody knew he was thinking about her like this. He was welcomed into her family and trusted like a cousin and nephew, like Farhad. Iranians didn't really marry their first cousins, Farhad had told him. "We're not living in Qajar times," he had said when Marco asked him about that. But although the Qajar dynasty went back to the eighteenth century, it had hung on until about forty years ago.

Marco couldn't ask Farhad where the Global Publishing Company was because it would be obvious he got the name from Mastaneh. He asked at the Meikadeh Hafez when he went to get a beer and a sandwich. The proprietor, Adarvan, didn't know. He lifted his head and asked in a deep voice if any of the customers knew. All conversation stopped. Then an animated discussion broke out. Some said it might be here, some there. Everybody seemed to have an opinion, but nobody actually knew. Outside, he stopped a taxi, but the driver didn't know where it was. "There are some bookshops near Se Rah-e-Jaleh," he said. "Must be a small place. Maybe ask at the post office."

Before he could ask at the post office, class began at the University's Faculty of Letters, which was near Se Rah-e-Jaleh.

Seventy students jumped to attention in unison when Marco walked through the classroom door for the first time. The sudden roar of seventy chairs scraping the floor together hit Marco like a cannon shot, and he stood deafened by the absolute silence that followed. Men, dressed in dark, shiny suits and ties, and women, in skirts and blouses, stood stiffly with their hands at their sides waiting for him to . . . do what?

He said, "Good morning." They remained standing. Were they waiting for permission to sit down?

"Si-sit down, please." He wasn't allowed to use Farsi in the class. But most of them didn't understand him, and he had to motion with his hands.

The men sat on one side of the room, and the women sat on the other. This was the first class of their first year at the university, the first time they had ever been in a class of males and females together, and, for many of the girls in class, the first time since they

54

were young children that they had been in the presence of strange men without being covered by a chador. No chadors were allowed on university grounds, by edict of the Shah.

Marco called the roll:

Ghalamkar, Azadeh
Gharari-e-Mazandarani, Sassan
Ghobtoddin, Ebrahim
Ghods, Davud
Ghorbaghi, Abbas . . . .

The university divided all the students into classes alphabetically, and Marco had a class of 70 students whose last name began with *gh*, a sound Marco previously made only when he was gagging.

At the first break in his first three-hour class, Marco took his seat at the table in the teachers' room. A miniature-sized man put a small glass of dark brown tea front of him on the green felt tablecloth.

The other English teacher, Dr. Zaban, said to Marco in English, "I am just telling your colleagues. It is our custom, for the man which he bring to us the tea, we give to him every month one toman or two. For to buy the tea."

Even a couple sips of the stale, strong tea gave Marco stomach cramps. He would gladly pay the man not to serve it to him. But, grateful for any information that would help him fit in with the Iranian faculty, he went into the booth where little Hassan made the tea and washed the glasses. He gave him three tomans. "May your hand not hurt," Hassan said. "I am your sacrifice." The little tea man cupped the coins in both hands and bowed his head.

There were only a few minutes left before the next class session, and Marco wanted to see if the Iranian faculty knew the place where Mastaneh worked. "Have you heard of a place called the Global Publishing Company?" he asked Dr. Zaban.

"I am surprised you know this place," he told Marco. "This is publisher of books in the Farsi, translations from your English and

European books. How you are knowing about this place, if I may ask?"

"A friend mentioned it."

"You are studying the Farsi, I know. Perhaps you see how the books has been rendered into the Farsi."

"Yes."

Dr. Zaban translated their conversation for the philosophy and Persian literature professors. They immediately asked who the friend was who had mentioned the Global Publishing Company. But at that point the tea man stepped out of his booth into the corridor and rang a brass bell with a black wood handle, the signal to return to class.

Marco didn't make it back to the teachers' room for the second break. The students surrounded him asking him questions. How could he live away from his mother and family? How old was his sister? Was she married? Did he vote for President Johnson? When the class was over, Marco walked down the corridor towards the teachers' room with barely any voice left. The other teachers were already gone.

Hassan, the tea man, came up to him. "Sir, I have the information you requested."

"Beg your pardon?"

"I'll take you to that place you are looking for, if you will do me the honor, sir. It's walking distance."

The Global Publishing Company

Hassan took Marco by the hand and led him down Jaleh Street past shops with iron curtains, some half drawn down. In the shop windows on the first block, there were pieces of used machinery. In the next block, newspapers and magazines. Then books.

"Here it is, sir. The Global Publishing Company. Shall I go in with you, sir?"

"No thanks," he told Hassan. Marco tried to give him another toman, but the tea man wouldn't take it.

He walked into the little dimly lit shop. There were books on shelves along the walls, but nobody was there.

"Yā'allāh," the tea man suddenly shouted behind Marco, almost scaring him to death. Hassan seemed to feel responsible for seeing this through.

Marco heard an old man's voice, then a girl's behind an inner door that he noticed in the back of the shop. "Thanks," he said to Hassan. "I'm all right now." But Hassan left only after bowing to Mastaneh as she peeped out from the partly-opened inner door.

"Welcome," Mastaneh said, business-like. "Please come in. I'll introduce you to the owner."

Marco had to bend down to get through the doorway to the rear of the shop. The front room smelled like dust, but this bigger room that Mastaneh took him into smelled like the kerosene burning in the samovar. A bald man wearing thick, round, frameless glasses stood stacking thin books on a table.

"Mr. Ketabi, this is the gentleman I told you about," Mastaneh said. "The professor at the university and expert in Western literature."

"You draw forth my shame," Marco said holding his hand over his chest. "Nothing is farther from the truth." He hoped he was getting better at ta'ārof. Mastaneh smiled, almost laughed, watching him jump through the hoops.

"Would you mind getting some tea?" Mr. Ketabi asked Mastaneh.

"Please, no, no tea," Marco said.

Mr. Ketabi led him to an area where there were cushions on a red and white Turkoman rug. When they sat down, he said, "I am Mastaneh's uncle's cousin. We're related, though our families are from different cities, and we didn't know each other until we came to Tehran. And how about you, Mr. Marco? How do you happen to know Mastaneh?" He asked Marco if he was married and how old he was. "Ah, you're the same age as Mastaneh."

Mastaneh listened attentively to Marco's answers without interrupting and only afterwards said, "Akh. Mr. Ketabi, please don't embarrass Mr. Marco with these personal questions."

"Yes, yes, yes." Mr. Ketabi started nodding, first at Mastaneh, then at Marco. "Business. Yes. Of course. I understand you've read a lot of books, Mr. Marco. Mastaneh tells me you can explain some of the scenes she's trying to draw. She's the most talented artist in Tehran."

How would the unflappable Mastaneh shake off this *ta'ārof*? Now it was Marco's turn to smile at her.

"Correct," she said in a lilting voice.

"And the humblest," Mr. Ketabi added.

Mr. Ketabi turned an easel to show Marco a pencil sketch Mastaneh had just completed for the Farsi translation of *Huckleberry Finn*.

Marco was shocked. "What's this?" he asked. The emaciated face of a man tortured by a vision of the depths of human evil stared out in anguish, his flaming eyes crying out in despair.

"Can you read Farsi?" Mr. Ketabi asked. "There's a caption."

Below the sketch was written a translation of Huckleberry Finn's words: "All right, then, I'll go to hell."

"This isn't Huck Finn," Marco said.

"I was afraid of that," Mastaneh said. "I don't think I understand that part of the book."

"No."

"It's here. Let me see. Huck decides not to turn Jim in. Then he says, 'All right, then, I'll go to hell.' I don't understand."

"He's been taught the wrong thing. Helping a slave to escape was considered theft."

"But he does it anyway?"

"He follows his heart, not the law or religion."

"He's not going to hell?"

"No. He thinks he is, but we know he's not."

Mastaneh looked at Mr. Ketabi. "Ah-hah," she said.

"I see, I see." Mr. Ketabi nodded repeatedly. "Mr. Marco, Mastaneh and I in fact had a little argument over this, and it seems that Mastaneh was right." He took the sketch pad off the easel and held it on his lap. "But look at this sketch. Mr. Marco, if I could put this illustration on the cover, it would sell the book. The illustrations are very important. You are sure this could not *perhaps* be Mr. Huckleberry Finn?" Mr. Ketabi the businessman narrowed his eyes and looked steadily at Marco.

"No. Sorry. Maybe you could use it for Kurtz in *Heart of Darkness*," Marco joked.

Mr. Ketabi's spirits improved immediately. "I don't know this book. Mastaneh, dear, what about you? We must get it. You see, Mr. Marco, you've helped us a lot in only a few minutes." He started nodding again, first to himself, then in Mastaneh's direction, then at Marco.

"Mr. Professor Marco, I hope you can come to lunch next Thursday." He turned to Mastaneh. "What food does Mr. Marco like?"

"Lobster, I believe."

"Unholy girl! Mr. Professor Marco comes here out of the goodness of his heart to help us and you make jokes at his expense. –Mr. Marco, you must have some tea."

The work at Global Publishing obviously proceeded at a rather slow pace. No one came to the front of the shop to buy anything, and the decision not to use Mastaneh's sketch for Huck Finn seemed to be regarded as the bulk of the afternoon's work. Marco wasn't interrupting anything. He drank several glasses of tea, slowly, while Mr. Ketabi slowly nodded off to sleep. They weren't exactly alone, but this was close to it. In a soft voice, Mastaneh said, "Mr. Marco, I'm very glad to have met you."

"Would you just call me Marco, without the Mister?"

"I couldn't let my family hear me call you that." Mastaneh hesitated. "Actually, Farhad told me 'Marco' isn't your real name. He told me to ask you what it is some time. What is he talking about?"

"He said that?"

Mastaneh put her finger over her mouth and Marco lowered his voice. "Mastaneh, it's very embarrassing. You know how words mean one thing in one language and another thing in another language? I don't like to use my last name in Iran, that's all."

"How bad could it be? Tell me what it is."

"It's bad."

"Just say it. Out with it."

"It's ... it's ...." Marco said the word. Her mouth dropped open. "Sorry. That's my family name. Now you know."

Mastaneh gave Marco a disappointed look, as if he had made a joke in very poor taste. At the same time the body of Mr. Ketabi began to quiver. "Khakh-khakh-khakh khakh-khakh." At first Marco thought he might be choking. No. He was laughing.

"You were supposed to be asleep! Impolite old man!" Mastaneh held her hand over her mouth.

"Khakh-khakh-khakh khakh-khakh." Mr. Ketabi was out of breath and panting. He sat up straighter and wiped the tears from his eyes.

"Mr. Ketabi, this is no way to treat a guest," Mastaneh said.

"Haaaaaaa." Mr. Ketabi exhaled and put on a serious face, except for his eyes. "Mr. Marco, please forgive me. There's no excuse for—"

"Let's face it. I have a funny name," Marco said. "Nobody can hear it without laughing."

"I'm not laughing," Mastaneh said. "People can't help what their name is." Her voice was quavering.

Mr. Ketabi looked at her.

"Heee...!" Mastaneh held both hands over her mouth and ran out into the front room of the shop.

Travelers on the Golden Road

"So, you must have the class roll down by now?" Farhad had drilled Marco until he could pronounce all their full names without stumbling.

"They seem impressed. But somebody told them Americans call each other by their first names, so that's what most of them want me to do."

"Men and women still sitting apart?"

"No, it's mixed up now. Like in an American classroom."

"How's *The Golden Road to English Literature* going? I was looking at it: *Robinson Crusoe*. I don't hear you talking like this."

"That's 18th-century English."

"Qajar period."

"Some of the selections are even earlier. I have a hard time answering the students' questions sometimes. Like how far is it from Lambeth Stairs to the Horse Ferry on the Thames River? You see, John Evelyn wrote his 1683 diary that he walked that far on the ice."

"Yul, it would be nice to know how far that was."

"Davud usually helps me out. He's older, and he's lived in England."

"Any beautiful girls in the class?"

"Definitely."

"*You need to get on that.* That's from an American at the USELESS."

Abbas Ghorbaghi, a uniformed officer of the Shah's gendarmerie who attended classes, caused a minor *sholugh* at the beginning of the semester. Since there was such a disparity in English ability, and since Marco wasn't allowed to use Farsi, self-designated translator-assistants tended to appear in the classes. They interrupted briefly to explain things to the rest of the students in Farsi. Most were deferential and helpful. But Ghorbaghi stood up and practically took over one early class, insulting a student who had made a mistake.

"Sit down, please," Marco said.

Ghorbaghi turned to Marco and began shouting at him in Farsi. He deserved an older and more experienced instructor. He said, *The Golden Road to English Literature* is a ridiculous textbook."

"Sit down, please," Marco interrupted again. Now Marco was getting angry.

The officer kept on talking.

"Sit down."

When Ghorbaghi didn't move, Marco packed his books into his briefcase and walked towards the door himself. There was nothing that could make him put up with this. He would rather quit the job, return home, and be drafted into the Vietnam war. It was as simple as that.

Before Marco got to the door, Ghorbaghi threw his *Golden Road to English Literature* on the floor and stormed out. Marco then walked back to the desk, unzipped his briefcase with hands trembling in anger, and continued the lesson without comment. Ghorbaghi never returned to the class.

This was the only unpleasant incident that Marco ever experienced in his classes, and he easily ignored it. The other students were polite, friendly, and good-humored. They gathered in the hallway asking him questions during every break, and Marco seldom had a chance to make it to the teachers' room for tea before the next class began.

Davud Ghods was the first to invite Marco to his house for lunch after class. He was a stout, well-dressed older student whose English was the best in the class—the only student who had a car, a new Russian Volga that reminded Marco of a 1955 Studebaker but of which Davud was quite proud.

His apartment was in the fashionable Shemirun section in the north part of the city, furnished like the rooms of elegant Parisian hotels Marco had seen in movies. Davud's wife served *fesenjun*, an eggplant and ground walnut dish, because she had heard it was Marco's favorite. They sat at a long, polished rosewood table with Davud's sisters, cousins, and a sister-in-law who had just returned from Israel. Marco felt like he was in Europe.

"They're very interesting stories in *The Golden Road to English Literature*, are they not? Too difficult for some of the students, of course." Marco thought Davud might have been referring to the Colonel Ghorbaghi incident and didn't respond.

Davud changed to a different type of question. "Why do Americans keep their left hand on their lap when they eat? I've heard a reason, but I don't know if it is true."

"What's that?"

"They say it is because in the old days Americans needed to have their hand near their gun."

Marco dismissed the idea with a laugh—but brought his left hand up on the table.

Sassan Gharari-e-Mazandarani usually rode the bus with Marco part of the way home. Both of them liked to ride on the top deck and enjoyed the stiff, spring-less ride and the view of the city from the window. Sassan was a shy student who wore the same threadbare but impeccably cleaned and pressed suit to class every day. He was from a small village near the Caspian Sea, and his family were rice farmers.

One day he said, "Mister Marco, I do not know. Is possible you come my room eat the lunch? It is poor. It is not house. One room only."

"I'd be glad to come."

"Do you come the next week?"

It required three transfers to get to the poorer section of town where Sassan lived. They entered a dry cleaning shop and then climbed up a back stairway to Sassan's room, leaving their shoes in the hallway.

"Please, you wait. I go to the downstair."

When Sassan returned, he said, "Please, sir, take off your pants," holding out to Marco the pajamas customarily offered to visitors. But these were starched, pressed, and very neatly folded. Sassan smiled. "Is poor here. I have nothing. But dry clean is free."

They hung their suit coats on wooden pegs in the wall. Then, since there were no more pegs, Sassan laid their trousers over the bedding folded in a corner of the room. They sat on the simple cotton rug with a tablecloth (starched and pressed) spread out between them. Sassan put two plastic plates and two soup-sized spoons on the tablecloth. Marco wondered how he was going to be able to cook a meal. The small sink out in the hallway with a single cold water spigot must have served as the kitchen sink as well as a lavatory. It was probably used as a washtub as well. Then he noticed an electric rice cooker on the floor at the side of the room, already steaming.

Sassan lifted the top off the rice cooker. "Is Japanee. It has the clock and ready when you come back. Cook very good."

"It's nice."

"Please, you take when you leave."

"Thank you, but my roommate's getting one tomorrow," Marco lied. He had to stop admiring things in Iran.

Sassan excused himself again and from somewhere downstairs brought up more food to go with the rice. Invisible assistants behind the scenes—members of the dry cleaner's family, perhaps—were helping Sassan entertain his teacher. Marco ate some of everything he was offered. As soon as they had finished, there was a light knock on the door. When Sassan opened the door, a tray with two glasses of tea and a bowl of sugar lumps had been set on the floor in the doorway.

On the rug near the wall was a stack of books, on top of which Marco recognized *The Golden Road to English Literature.* "How do you like those stories?" Marco asked.

"Mr. Marco, I tell to you truth. I study to be ingénieur. Why I have to read about 'Day of Triffids'? I think you say us in class the Triffid is not."

"Right. Triffids are just imaginary. I don't know why we have to use that book. I know the classes could be better—"

"I like American teacher," Sassan interrupted.

"You do? Why?"

"Because American teacher tell the colonel to sit down."

Cold-hearted foreigner

It was the day he was invited to lunch at the Global Publishing Company. As Marco entered the campus gate, little Hassan was waiting for him in the Faculty of Letters courtyard.

"Sir, a message."

"Beg your pardon?"

"From Global Publishing."

Hassan handed Marco a small piece of paper folded and pasted shut with an X written across the flap. Marco gave Hassan a toman.

"May your shadow never decrease."

He slid the note between the pages of *The Golden Road to English Literature*, not wanting to read it in the faculty room in front of the others as he sat at the long table and braced himself for the obligatory morning round of bitter tea and broken English.

Hassan set a glass of very dark tea in front of Marco. It was chilly enough in the mornings now to want to drink something warm, but not that. He drank it anyway.

When the class began, Marco opened *The Golden Road to English Literature* to the selection from "The Day of the Triffids." The note from Global Publishing fluttered out and down onto the classroom floor, settling with the X facing up. In a rare moment of absolute silence, approximately 140 eyes focused on the note, then on Marco's face. Sassan, who always sat in the front, instinctively got up to pick it up for Marco but seeing the seal and the large X over it, stopped and backed up towards his chair, still hunched over. There were a few titters. Marco picked the note up. A few of the women put their hands over their mouths.

"Maybe a letter from his mother."

"What? What did Mr. Davud say?"

"His mother? Ah. A letter from his mother."

"How do you know? How does he know?"

"It must be. Let's ask."

"But maybe it's not. Who's going to ask him?"

Marco raised his voice: "A letter from my mother."

"But—"

"I forgot to open it," he added. "I'll open it after class."

Marco opened the envelope in the toilet attached to the teachers' room. He didn't have his dictionary with him and was glad to see that the note was written as if to a child:

I have to take Mina to the dentist's. So I have to cancel lunch this afternoon. Maybe you can come tomorrow? Mastaneh.

Out in the courtyard, a group of young women from his class were still waiting around. The only way they could talk to him was in a group like this. Azadeh, a pretty student who could speak English more confidently than the others, asked him questions while the rest listened admiringly. "Your mother is well? It must be."

This encouraged the others to join in.

"She asking you come to the home? If my mother, this is what she write."

"Mr. Marco, did you write about us in your letter to your mother?"

They seemed overjoyed to have finally made some kind of personal connection with him. Like all Iranians, they stood closer when talking to somebody than Americans were comfortable with, and Marco, occasionally taking a step or two away, eventually found himself backed up against the tiled gateway to the school. He told them about his mother, mentioning things from letters he had actually received. They listened more intently than they ever had in class. He told them about his sister, that she was getting married soon. He described his brothers. They wanted to get back to the sister.

"If my sister marry, anywhere I am in the world, I go to the wedding. This is sure," Azadeh told Marco. "Why you did wait until after the class, you open the letter? We are thinking all the class what is in the letter. You are not thinking this? How you could teach the class and not open this letter?"

The others nodded in agreement. How could this foreigner be so cold? As he walked away, he heard one of the women use an unfamiliar word, *bi-bokhār*. He looked it up that evening: *steamless*.

Visit of the Two-bit Angel

Marco ate a bowl of lemon-flavored chicken soup in the Meikadeh Hafez. Then he went home and lay on his bed. He took out Mastaneh's note and read it again. He smelled it. Nothing.

The door buzzer rang. It was a thin woman in a paisley chador. "I'm so sorry, sir. My name is Fereshteh. I met Mr. Farhad on Ferdowsi Street, and he asked me to come to see you."

"I don't understand. Come in."

"He said you needed cheering up, sir. You were *nārāhat*." Uncomfortable. Farhad had previously translated it as "uneasy."

"He told you that?"

Her lips closed into a thin line.

"What did he say, exactly?"

"He said you were lonely."

"No. I don't know what he means by that." Marco looked away.

"You don't know what lonely means?" Fereshteh put her little hand on Marco's arm and looked him in the eyes. "I mean, Mr. Farhad gave me money, sir. To cure your loneliness."

"*Father-dog!*" Marco used one of Farhad's favorite expressions. "Sorry. I'm not lonely. What did you say your name was?"

"Fereshteh, sir. The police call me *Fereshteye-Do-Hezari*. But I don't mind. I have to feed my baby somehow."

Fereshteh, the Two-bit Angel, Marco translated for himself. He wasn't going to let Farhad get away with this.

"Never mind. I understand," she said.

"Sorry."

She started to go. "Excuse me. I hope you don't mind if I ask. Are you in love, sir?"

"What? Did Farhad tell you to ask me that?"

"Oh, no, sir. I just got that idea myself, standing here with you. I don't mean to get personal, sir."

"You can tell if somebody's in love by looking at him?"

"I was in love, sir. Once."

"You mean when you had your baby?"

"Yes."

"What happened?"

"You can imagine, sir. He took advantage of me. Then left." Fereshteh looked steadily into Marco's eyes, and thinking about Mastaneh he felt a pang of guilt. The coils of Fereshteh's dull brown hair hung across her forehead and down beside her cheeks enhancing her childlike appearance. "Something's on your mind, sir. I can tell that."

"No," he said. "But I'm confused. Maybe you can tell me something. Why aren't men in Iran allowed to be friends with women. Girls." Marco changed to the word for unmarried women.

"You see, it's dangerous. For the girls."

"Their reputation, you mean."

"Reputation is everything, sir. I can tell you that." Fereshteh pursed her thin lips.

"But just being seen with men shouldn't be cause for a bad reputation."

"No doubt you're right, sir. Is this how they think in your country? I wish I lived there."

Neither said anything for a moment.

Then Fereshteh said, "Who is the girl, sir? Are you in a difficult situation?"

The buzzer for the door rang.

"Farhad must have forgotten his key again." But when Marco opened the door, Mastaneh was standing there.

"*Salaam*," she said. But then she saw Fereshteh and gasped.

Fereshteh said, "*Salaam*, Miss" and walked directly into Marco's bedroom. Mastaneh turned to leave without saying anything.

"I got your note," Marco said.

Mastaneh stopped and looked back. Her eyes were watery with tears.

Fereshteh now whisked out of Marco's bedroom. She was holding an armful of Marco's dirty underwear. "Is this all the laundry you need washed, sir?"

"Uh, yes, that's all today," Marco told her.

"The dishes are washed, sir. So I'll just wash these clothes before I go." She walked towards the shower room with the clothes.

Mastaneh stood in the doorway. Her face was flushed. "Marco, forgive me. You can't imagine what I thought. I'm so embarrassed. Don't ask me."

Still, she didn't walk in. From the shower room came the sound of rushing water.

"Just let me close the door, if you don't mind," Marco said.

Mastaneh took a breath, then stepped inside. "I finished taking Mina to the dentist's earlier than I thought. So I stopped by. I wanted to show you this." She took a wad of tissue from her jacket pocket and opened it. "Look. Mina's tooth. The dentist pulled it out."

Fereshteh came out of the shower. It was actually a full-sized room with a shower in it, large enough for washing clothes and hanging them up. "I'll leave now, sir."

Mastaneh stood back and let Fereshteh pick her chador up off the chair.

"Shall I serve you some tea before I go, sir? Miss?"

Mastaneh said, "My cousin's not here, it seems. I won't be staying."

Fereshteh shot a glance at Marco.

Marco ignored her. "Do you know what children do with their teeth in America when they fall out?" He explained about the Tooth Fairy.

"I'm going to do that tonight," Mastaneh said. "I'm going to tell Mina about the Tooth Fairy. I'll put a toman under her pillow while she's sleeping."

Marco noticed Fereshteh standing with two glasses of tea in her hands.

"Oh, sorry, sir," she said. "I didn't mean to be listening to what you said. It's very interesting. In your country they believe in fairies, too?"

"And some people believe in angels," Marco said.

"I wouldn't let a fairy come near my baby at night," Fereshteh said.

"This is a good fairy."

"Still."

Marco looked at his watch. It was getting near the time Farhad usually came home.

"I'll be going now, sir," Fereshteh said.

"Wait, please," Mastaneh said to Fereshteh. "I'll go, too. It's late. Good-bye, Mr. Marco. Maybe I'll see you at the office."

Marco stood at the open door watching the two of them walk down the stairs. When they turned out of sight on the landing, he went into his room and out onto the balcony and watched them walk out together through the garden.

Level seven

در چشم من نیاید خوبان جمله عالم

بنگر خیال خوبش مژگان من گرفته

—Rumi

Dar chashm-e-man naiāyad khobān-e-jomleh ʿālam
Bengar khiāl-e-khubash mozhgān-e-man gerefteh.

"How was it?" Farhad said as soon as he came home. "*Safā?*" He used the Farsi word for pleasure.

"Oh, I . . . ."

"The Two-bit Angel! Don't say Farhad doesn't take care of his friends."

"I didn't really . . . I mean—"

"You didn't do her?"

"No."

Farhad looked disappointed. But then he said, "I know. It's not the real thing. Not like the love they sing about in the poetry, huh?" He recited some lines from Rumi:

No worldly beauty can reach my eyes
For the wondrous vision of her
Has blinded me to all else.

Then he blew a smoke ring—at the world, as it were. "The Arabs say there are seven levels of love. I think it's seven. Oouee. Back in Hichja. My first time."

"Level seven?"

"Maybe. I don't know. I'm just saying it was good."

"So you managed to have a girlfriend in Hichja?"

71

"Not a girl. A married woman. Somebody's second wife. Only a few years older than me. Her husband is almost always out of town. I miss her since coming to Tehran."

Her name was Fatimeh. She was married to a well-to-do older merchant who traveled and wanted a second wife who would live in Hichja. She lived in a house with her mother, visited only from time to time by an absentee husband she disliked. She fell in love with Farhad when he was eighteen—saw him walking along the street in front of her house in the evenings studying his books by the street lights. She had a daughter.

Marco said, "I think I saw her. I'm sure that was you and Fatimeh and her little girl, standing by the mosque when I went to Hichja."

"Oouee! Right. And all of a sudden this crowd of people comes rushing towards the mosque, following you, and there we were standing right there. Know where we went? We hid in the madreseh. All three of us. Nobody was there."

"It's a small town. How did you ever get to be with her alone?"

"Easy. One winter night when I was walking by, she cracked open the door and smiled at me. And that was it. Believe me, I didn't care about anything. I just walked right up, she opened the door, and I walked in. She smiled at me. What else could I do?"

"I see what you mean."

"Her husband was away, her mother was visiting a friend. I don't think anybody saw me go in, but I don't know. I didn't care. All she had on was a chador, and she dropped it on the floor. I didn't know what to do. Then she showed me."

Farhad's eyes glazed over as he sipped some tea.

"Too bad she's married," Marco said.

"Yul. She's beautiful. She says her daughter looks like me. She says look at those eyebrows, look at that nose. Her mother says the same. Her mother likes me. She hates Fatimeh's husband."

"So do you think she's your daughter?"

"*I will neither affirm nor deny it*—I got that at the USELESS."

"*Pedar sag!*" Marco said. Father-dog. "Did I use that right?"

Flan

Marco found it hard to get away from students who wanted to talk to him after class or eat lunch with him. Azadeh was particularly persistent. "Come to eat with me and Parvin in the Planning Organization cafeteria. And you can meet my uncle. He works in the organization."

"I'll eat with you ladies some time," Marco promised. I can't today. I have an appointment."

"Appointment? We wonder what is this appointment."

"Yā'allāh," Marco said as he entered the Global Publishing Company. Mastaneh and Mr. Ketabi were standing side by side waiting for him. They both shook hands with him—the expected and obligatory greeting instituted by the Shah's father, Reza Shah, as a sign of Westernization. Women always shook hands, too, but women never kept hold of his hand the way some men did. Marco stretched the handshake with Mastaneh as long as he dared—long enough to make her take a breath and open her hand.

"Come back to the production room," Mr. Ketabi said. "Lunch is ready."

They left their shoes in the outer room of the shop, the "sales room." In the inner "production room," the little table on the Turkoman rug had been covered with a white cloth, and there was a huge plate of saffron rice covered with pieces of chicken, along with flat bread, raw onions, radish greens, mint, yogurt, and tea.

Mastaneh was pouring tea for him. "Remember what my mother told you. You have to drink tea with sugar or your heart will shrink."

"This is true," Mr. Ketabi said earnestly.

Marco and Mastaneh sat across from each other. As Marco shifted a little from a cross-legged position and stretched one leg slightly out, his foot touched what must have been Mastaneh's knee under the table. She looked him in the eyes across the table with a totally expressionless face, daring him to leave his foot there. He did. Never moving her knee, Mastaneh began to chatter in her most formal voice, asking if "Mr. Marco" would like some more rice, if "Mr. Marco" liked radish greens, if "Mr. Marco" was comfortable sitting cross-legged on the floor Iranian style.

"I'm very comfortable," Marco said. "I don't think I could be sitting in a more comfortable position." In fact, his legs were getting stiff, but nothing could have made him budge in the slightest.

"You know," Mastaneh said, "I think this is the best way to sit. Don't you think so, Mr. Ketabi."

"It's more intimate than sitting in chairs," Mr. Ketabi said.

"Exactly the word I would have used!" Mastaneh said. "Mr. Ketabi has a wonderful way of putting things, I've always said."

"This is not true, Mr. Marco. Mastaneh, dear, you know you're always suggesting a different word when we're writing notices for our new books."

"But we must be boring Mr. Marco," Mastaneh said. "Let's talk about something of interest to him. Mr. Marco, are you still studying sufi poetry? My father asked us in his last letter."

"I've read some translations and tried to translate a few poems myself. Farhad says he'll help me, but he's usually too busy."

"Ah, yes, he is a busy boy. I'm sure my cousin never misses a class at the university. But what about your students? Maybe some of them could help you?"

"Actually," Mr. Ketabi interrupted, "Mastaneh knows more about Persian poetry than any young person I've ever met."

"Mr. Ketabi forgets I don't know English, and the university students do," Mastaneh said. "What are your students like, Mr. Marco? I know there are both men and women in your classes. Farhad says the women are beautiful."

"He does?"

"And they must be very intelligent."

"Oh, I don't know."

"They're lucky."

"Mastaneh, dear, do me a favor, please," Mr. Ketabi interrupted. "Would you get down that book of Hafez's poems with the English translations? I want to give that book to Mr. Marco."

"Excuse me, Mr. Marco," she said. "I'll have to get up. To get that book."

Marco watched Mastaneh stand up and walk in her black skirt over to a shelf on the wall. He looked down at her bare feet, strangely excited. In Iran, even if a woman wore a chador, you could see her bare feet when she walked inside the room. In a culture so preoccupied with preventing exposure of the female body, feet didn't count.

"What is it, Mr. Marco?" Mr. Ketabi asked.

"Oh, sorry. I was just thinking how much I like some Iranian customs. Thank you for the book."

"Mastaneh, dear," Mr. Ketabi said. "Would you do me one more favor? Would you go down to the French bakery and get some flan. It seems we forgot dessert. Take the money from the jar."

"Don't bother, please," Marco said.

"Mr. Marco, I insist," Mr. Ketabi said. Mastaneh left quickly.

"I wanted to have some time to talk to you," he said to Marco. "You mention our customs. I wonder how much you understand how we try to protect our women, guard their purity—do you know this word?"

"Yes. Yes, I do."

"May I speak more plainly? I wonder if you realize women are not supposed to be together with men before they marry. We don't have this custom of men and women associating with each other before marriage."

"Yes. I do know that. I hope I—"

"Please, Mr. Marco, I only want to speak in general now. I know you're a good person. That's why I'm talking to you. As you know, Mastaneh's father is often away driving a truck and can't be here to look after her as he would like to."

"Yes. I've seen how much he loves Mastaneh and all his family.

What should I do, Mr. Ketabi?"

"I can't answer that, Mr. Marco, but may I mention one more thing? We always fear that foreigners with different customs might hurt our daughters' reputations—and then suddenly leave the country, perhaps without ever realizing they have caused any harm. I'm sorry to speak so directly."

"I understand everything you've told me. To hurt Mastaneh is the last thing I would ever want to do."

Mr. Ketabi smiled. "Then perhaps we should change the subject a bit. I didn't mean to say that all foreigners were alike, Mr. Marco. And of course in every country people fall in love and . . . . Sorry. What I mean is, I noticed right away that you and Mastaneh are interested in the same things, in art, in books, for example. I was surprised that a foreigner could understand Mastaneh's humor as you do. This surprised me very much."

"I probably miss the point of a lot of things she says. But she makes me laugh with her eyes. If you know what I mean?"

"Oh, yes, I do, Mr. Marco. Khakh-khakh khakh. We laugh in this shop all day." He wiped his bald head with a handkerchief. "Sometimes we laugh about you, Mr. Marco. Mastaneh imitates the way you speak Farsi, for example. Khakh-khakh khakh. I'm sure you wouldn't be offended if you were here. She remembers every word she's heard you say. That's the truth." He stared at Marco through round glasses that made his eyes look bigger. "I can easily picture you two as a married couple, Mr. Marco, except . . . ."

When Marco didn't say anything, Mr. Ketabi changed tacks again. "I know you live with Mastaneh's cousin. I've never met him, but I know he speaks English very well. He knows about America and American customs. A person like this, I could imagine living in America. Do you agree?"

"I think Farhad could live anywhere."

"Yes. This is my point. But I find it hard to imagine Mastaneh living anywhere but in Iran. Mr. Marco, this is an Iranian girl. In America, I believe, Mastaneh would be out of place. I don't know if you understand what I mean."

"I do."

"But how about you, Mr. Marco? Could you ever feel at home in Iran?"

"I don't know."

Mastaneh called out an ironic "*Yā'allāh*" and whisked back into the shop carrying an unbelievable amount of flan.

"Khakh-khakh-khakh." Mr. Ketabi's whole body shook with amusement. "Could you find any flan, Mastaneh?"

"I found a little," she said. "We have to treat our guest right. It's a duty."

"And I don't suppose there's much change from the money you took?"

"None, actually," Mastaneh said.

"Khakh-khakh khakh. You know, Mr. Marco, Mastaneh herself is quite fond of flan. I thought she might be enthusiastic about going out to get some."

"I tried to find lobster on the way but couldn't. I hope you like flan as well, Mr. Marco?" She slid her knees beneath the table across from Marco. "There. I'm sitting right here and not moving again until we see about this flan. If you don't like it, Mr. Marco, I'll eat yours."

"Impolite!" Mr. Ketabi scolded.

Marco noticed, though, that both Mastaneh and Mr. Ketabi were politely waiting for him to start eating first. He enjoyed being in this country.

Faces

Farhad was reading his favorite magazine, the satirical *Tofigh*. "Look at this cartoon. It might not seem like it, but it's criticizing the Shah. You can tell by his face."

"His face?"

"Yul. You always see pictures of him looking powerful, self-confident, assured. Right? But here he looks—I don't know—a little childish, like a spoiled child. People here really care about what a person looks like. His *ghiāfeh*. His appearance."

Marco was starting to wonder how widespread the opposition to the Shah was. "Some students have warned me about anti-Shah groups. They say there are a couple of guys in the class I shouldn't associate with. I don't get it, though. One is poor, working hard to be an engineer. Another knows Arabic well but no English—and tells everybody he's not interested in learning it."

"Probably an Islamic fundamentalist of some kind. You stand for everything he's against."

"But he's nice to me, really funny."

"Maybe he's not like most of the West-haters."

"You mean there are a lot of them?"

"Remember that broadcast we heard from Najaf on the short-wave radio one night? By the man I told you the government doesn't allow us to listen to? His name's Khomeini. A lot of people listen to his broadcasts. He says there's a higher authority than civil law."

"Yeah, in the States, the Bible people are like that."

"But here's the real reason they listen to him. His face. You can see pictures of him pasted onto walls now and then. Until they get torn down. What the people like is his *ghiāfeh*—the proud frown, the powerful glare. And there are people out there who'd like to crowd behind him and use that face to scare the world into respecting them."

The next day after class, Marco headed towards the Global Publishing Company again. This time Davud caught up with him just beyond the university gate.

"May I drive you home, Mr. Marco?"

"Oh. Thanks, but I have an appointment."

"I am wondering where you walk. It is not in the direction of your home."

"It's just, I feel like taking a walk before going home."

"Walking is good. But also we see you sometimes talking to Mr. Sassan, and we wonder about that. This is after you make Colonel Ghorbaghi leave the class. We don't want you to get involved with a radical."

"Radical? Oh, don't worry. Mr. Sassan doesn't seem like a radical."

"And also Mr. Ebrahim. Is different groups, but they want to cause trouble for government."

Marco dismissed the warning. "They never talk about politics."

"This is good. But people are saying there could be trouble. Government is always watching us."

Here it was—what Farhad called "the Iranian paranoia."

"Believe me," Davud said.

Sassan and Ebrahim passed by. They put their hands on their chests and bowed to Marco and Davud. Davud put his own hand on his chest. "Good-bye, sirs. I am your sacrifice," he said with utmost courtesy.

"Okh, Marco, I thought you weren't coming." She pushed her glimmering black hair aside with her long fingers.

"Mastaneh thought you might be eating lunch with your students," Mr. Ketabi said.

"Mr. Ketabi, that's not true. I never said such a thing."

"Ah-hah," Mr. Ketabi said. "Anyway, we hope you will have lunch with us again today. We will have *āb-gusht*."

It was one Iranian meal that Marco didn't care for. "I can't eat a whole serving, though."

"I can't either," Mastaneh said. "Mr. Marco and I could share one bowl, perhaps." The next moment Marco had his toes against Mastaneh's knee and was dipping his unleavened bread into the same bowl of fatty stew that she was eating from.

After lunch Mr. Ketabi said, "Mastaneh, why don't you show Mr. Marco the picture you drew this morning for *René*? —For some reason, Mr. Marco, she said it would amuse you. As for me, I think it's excellent."

With a sparkle in her eye, Mastaneh showed Marco a sketch of the old American Indian chief Chactas in Chateaubriand's *René*. Headband, feathers, loincloth, walking stick—he looked convincing enough to be a Natchez Indian to Marco. The face, however, made him burst out laughing.

"Has my assistant got it wrong again, Mr. Marco?"

"No. Not at all. This could definitely be Chactas. It's great."

"But you laugh."

"The only thing is, he has her cousin Farhad's face!"

"Do you really think so?" Mastaneh teased. "This is my idea of an American Indian."

"I have never met her cousin," Mr. Ketabi said. "It does look like an Indian to me. Although truly I wouldn't know."

"It's perfect," Marco said. Farhad's high cheek bones, slightly almond shaped eyes, straight, prominent nose—in this outfit he could easily be an American Indian.

"Ah, I'm glad the face looks realistic," Mr. Ketabi said. "I certainly want to use this sketch in the book."

Mastaneh smiled, nodding her head.

Mr. Ketabi asked Marco to look at some more sketches Mastaneh had done for Global Publishing's Farsi versions of European and American literature. "She's having problems with the sketch of Odysseus," Mr. Ketabi said.

"I won't show him that one," Mastaneh said.

"But he can see it right there against the wall."

Marco turned and saw a very young, thin Odysseus, light hair, perhaps in his early twenties, with a rather featureless naked body, holding a branch to hide himself in front of Nausicaa, who stood surprised and speechless before him, the ball she had been chasing lying at his feet. This figure of Odysseus, however, had no face at all, only a faint gray outline for where it would go. As for Nausicaa, her face looked just slightly like Mastaneh's.

"Nice," Marco said. "I know the scene."

Mastaneh turned the sketch around towards the wall. "It's not finished," she said. "I'm still working on this one."

"Maybe you need to do some more research," Mr. Ketabi suggested. "Do you hear me, Mastaneh? I said maybe you need to—"

"Yes, I heard you," she said. "We will discuss this matter later."

The Coronation of the King of Kings, Light of the Aryans

پادشاهی کو روا دارد ستم بر زیر دست
دوستدارش روز سختی دشمن زورآور است

—Sa'di, Golestan

Pādeshāhi ku ravā dārad setam bar zir-e-dast
Dustdāresh ruz-e-sakhti doshman-e-zurāvar ast.

Marco walked towards home along with the *gardeshers* who were taking in the cool evening air on Shah Reza Avenue, then rested on a bench near a lighted water fountain at Meidun-e-Ferdowsi. The sidewalks were crowded with visitors in town for the Shah's coronation—which he had delayed for years until he felt totally assured of his absolute power. Strings of colored lights were hung on buildings, lamp posts, walls, and trees. Huge new pictures of the Shah and Farah, the Shahbanu, appeared everywhere. Workers were carrying crates of food and drink into restaurants and taverns in the expectation of good business in the coming days. But a lot of other shops that didn't expect to do much business during the holiday were already closed.

"**I** can't believe the USELESS is going to be open all through the coronation holiday." Farhad frowned and reached into his coat pocket to pull out half of a cigarette he had saved. "The Alliance Française is closed, the Goethe Institute is closed, but we're open. There aren't any classes, but I'm supposed to help with "receptions and presentations." *Father-dogs*! Sucking up to the Shah." He blew a smoke ring up towards the ceiling. "Oh, well. At least they're paying me extra."

"The university's closed tomorrow for the coronation. Then there's no class Friday, Saturday, or Sunday. Four days in a row off. I was hoping we could go to your aunt's house, or something."

"Sorry. That's what I thought, but I have to work all those days. I guess you could walk along Shah Reza in the morning, and maybe you'll see the motorcade going up to the palace. Give the empress a kiss for me."

Marco left early the next morning and took a taxi straight to the Global Publishing Company. He was less interested in the coronation than in seeing Mastaneh. Mr. Ketabi had said, "Come whenever you can," and he was going to take him up on the invitation. The shop might be closed like a lot of shops, but if it was open, Mastaneh would probably be there.

The door was shut, but there was a light on inside. He knocked.

"Oh!" Mastaneh kept her hand on the door handle.

"Sorry. I guess you're not actually open today."

"Mr. Ketabi's taking a few days off. It's just me."

"I see."

She stood there.

"Could I come in?"

"Oh. Yes. I was just surprised."

Leaving the shop door open, she led him to the low table back in the production room where she'd been sitting. She put down a cushion for him on the carpet. When he sat down, she said, "Mr. Ketabi's not here."

"You said. Is it all right if I stay a while?"

"I mean, I guess."

"I won't stay long." He looked at the book she had open on the table. "What were you reading? Oh, Sa'di. *On Kings.*"

"In honor of the coronation." She chuckled.

He read:

> *A shah who tolerates oppression in his reign*
> *In hard times finds his friends oppressing enemies.*

"One of my father's favorite passages," she told him.

He looked into her eyes, but she didn't say anything more.

"Sometimes I try copying out poetry," he said. "I'm still having a hard time with handwriting."

She smiled. "Yes, I saw your notebook at my house. Remember?"

He knew he was blushing.

"But, you know, I taught Mina to write. I wonder if I could help you." She gave him a pencil and pad of paper. "May I watch you write something?"

He started writing, and she seemed to be trying not to smile. "Do you mind? Here's how I showed Mina." He took a breath when she put her hand on his to help guide the pencil. "This part stays above the line, this part comes below. *Pa-de-shah-i   pa-de-shah-i pa-de-shah-i.*"

Marco had a hard time concentrating on the handwriting, but he wanted to keep the lesson going. "Show me how to make that final *i* after *king*. Mine are really ugly."

"Loosen your hand. Relax. Give me your fingers. Hold them like this." She moved behind him to line up her writing arm with his, resting her other arm against his back as if she were teaching her younger sister. "Over, back, and around. Good. Over, back, and around."

She leaned gently against his back.

"There," she said. "They're starting to look better. Not so

big." Her hand was still resting softly on his, no longer guiding. Wondering how long she would keep it there, he kept writing, slowly.

Suddenly, horns blared in the street. People were shouting. They rushed to the doorway. Men and women were throwing flowers in the path of a motorcade led by black Mercedes sedans.

Mastaneh pulled Marco's coat sleeve. "Look! The long car with the Red Lion and Sun flags and the motorcycles all around it—that must be the Shah and the empress Farah."

Women were giving out high-pitched trills and everyone was yelling *Zendebād Shāhanshāh*, long live the King of Kings. "It's nice, pretty," Mastaneh said.

"They all seem to love him."

"Yes. I guess they do."

"Farhad says some don't."

"I know. You can't help seeing Sa'di's warning hanging like a cloud over his head."

They were standing in the doorway, the street packed with a seemingly endless line of cars, the sidewalks filled with bystanders cheering and shouting. Mastaneh was still holding the pad of paper Marco had been practicing on and drew a quick sketch of the procession.

"I can't believe how fast you can draw. It's as if you can freeze the scene on paper as it's happening."

"I wish I could freeze time, too. Here we are, standing together, and, for this one instant, no one's paying any attention to us. It feels good."

He put his arm around her waist, and she took a sharp breath. "Nobody's looking."

Tentatively she slipped her arm around him, too.

"I love being with you, Mastaneh."

"Um-hm."

The motorcade had passed, but cars and taxis were still following behind, blowing their horns. Feeling Mastaneh's body against his, Marco gathered up his nerve. "Doesn't look like you're going to have much business today."

"That's what Mr. Ketabi figured."

"You could probably close the shop."

"We'd never get anywhere in this traffic. The city is pretty much shut down."

"I mean we could have some tea right here."

"Oh." She stood hesitating. Then she took a deep breath and said, "All right."

A sea without a shore

افسوس که بی گاه شد و ما تنها
در دریائی کرانه اش نا پیدا
کشتی و شب و غمام و ما میرانیم
در بحر خدا به فضل و توفیق خدا

—Rumi

Afsus ke bigāh shod o mā tanhā
Dar daryā'i kerāneyesh nā peydā.
Keshtiyo shab o ghamām o mā mirānim
Dar bahr-e-khodā be fazl o tofigh-e-khodā.

She closed the shop door behind them as they went back to the inner room, where she picked up a box of matches to light the samovar. He took them from her hand. "I don't really want any tea."

"We're just out of vodka."

He stood in front of the easel. "Still no face on Odysseus, I see."

"No." She bit her lip. "Should I finish it now?" She picked up a pencil. "Do you mind holding still for a second?" She licked her pencil. Gradually a face started to appear on Odysseus. It looked more and more like Marco's. "There."

"Nice."

"You like it?"

He pointed to the figure. "But my body doesn't look like that at all."

"Impolite!" She pulled his hand away.

He held on to hers. "I see Armenian men kiss ladies' hands. Like this."

She gave a little start. "Yes, that's their custom. I didn't think Americans did that."

"They don't."

"*Pedar sokhteh*!" Rascal.

"You didn't like it?"

"I didn't say that. And now that I think of it, I'll have Odysseus kissing Nausicaa's hand."

"I don't know. He's supposed to be hesitant to approach her."

She was focusing all her attention on the sketch. "But he might slowly build up his nerve and kiss her hand. I see him as a gentleman. That's what I like about him." She started altering the drawing. "My father, too. He liked him the first time he met him, he told me. He looked lost."

"Your father met Odysseus?"

"What?" She blushed and seemed confused as she turned back from the sketch. "My father was talking about you, I mean. A nice gentleman, lost."

"Oh."

"I thought the same thing."

"You did?"

"I liked you from the first day you came to our house. That's all I'm trying to say."

"You know I liked you the minute I saw you, too, don't you?"

She looked down, still blushing. "And now? Now that you've met about seventy beautiful university students? Who speak English?"

"None as beautiful as you."

"Okh, now you're lying."

"It's true. And you're more interesting than any of them."

"I wanted to go to the university, but I couldn't. I passed the *concours* entrance exam, but we didn't have the money."

"I can't see you as a university student. All they do is memorize what's in their books. You try to figure things out for yourself."

"That's what my father taught us."

Marco thought about his trip to Hichja. "I guess I *was* kind of lost when I met your father. But when I came to your house, I started to feel like I had a family in Iran."

"You do have one." She put down the pencil and pulled her hair away from her face. Her voice became weaker. "Farhad says you have a girlfriend in America."

"Had. Not any more."

"Oh." She looked into his eyes, then looked down. "I guess you didn't kiss her on the hand."

"What do you mean?"

She kept her eyes averted. "You probably kissed her like they do in the movies."

"The movies?"

"I can't imagine kissing like that."

He smiled. "But you can imagine kissing?"

There was no answer.

"Like you kiss Mina?" he suggested

"Maybe. I don't know."

"Would you kiss me like that?"

She let him pull her towards him. "You want me to?"

"*Khāhesh mikonam.*" Please. The Farsi word literally meant *I beg you.*

She gave him a quick kiss, her lips incredibly soft against his cheek. He put his arms around her and could feel her shaking.

She whispered in his ear, "Marco, we shouldn't be doing this." She put her hands on his chest and pushed away. "My mother says if a woman is with a man, then marries somebody else, she might always remember the first love, all through her marriage."

Marco took her hands again.

She said, "And I guess that goes for men, too. I mean, you had a girlfriend."

"I haven't thought about anybody but you since we met."

"Is it possible?"

"And now your kiss is the only one I can remember."

"I want that to be true." She held their hands to her heart. "Marco, I'm afraid." She was trembling.

"I'm sorry. I should go."

But she held on to his hands. Her eyes were closed. He stepped closer—and kissed her. The touch of her lips on his was more tender than he had imagined. Her breath mingled with his. He pulled her close, and she rested her warm cheek against his, her arms around his neck.

She whispered in his ear. "Marco, I dreamed of this."

"I love you, Mastaneh."

"I don't know what to do." She collapsed kneeling onto a cushion, breathing heavily, her cheeks and neck flushed.

He knelt beside her.

"I feel lost, Marco. I wish you knew Rumi." She recited some lines:

Alas, we've passed beyond time and are alone
On a sea with no shore in sight.
Boat and night and clouds and we sail
On the sea of God into the grace and fortune of God.

Lost on a shoreless sea. It was exactly how Marco was feeling. Were they really in God's hands now? That's what Mastaneh seemed to be saying.

"Marco, we can't stay here. I'm afraid of what I'll do. I'm sorry. Can you understand? I want to go home."

He took her hand and kissed it again. "I'll go with you. We'll have to walk."

The hand of God

از سر جان چون تو برخیزی تمام
من کنم ان ساعتت در جان نشست

—Attar

Az sar-e-jān chun to barkhizi tamām
Man konam ān sā'atat dar jān neshast.

"So," Farhad said. "Did you see the Benz parade?"

"*Zendebād Shāhanshāh!*"

"Right. At the USELESS, we all went out to watch when the Shah turned up Vesal-e-Shirazi Street."

"We went out as he passed by, too."

"Who?"

"The Shah."

"I mean who went out. You said *we*."

"Oh, right. I wanted to get a book from the Global Publishing Company. Mastaneh was there."

"What is it?"

"What?"

"The book."

"Oh. Just a book of Rumi's poems. I forgot and left it there."

"She gave it to you? It's basically love poems—the ghazals are. Or maybe her boss gave it to you?"

"No, she did. She's nice. I like her."

"Yul, she has a lot of spirit. It's fun joking around with her."

"She seems very, sort of, traditional. I mean, she's not at all interested in learning English."

"Naw, she's all poetry and art and shit." He cocked his head to gauge whether he'd used *and shit* correctly.

"I guess tomorrow I'll go back and pick up the book."

"Her boss is always there, right?"

"Um, I don't know."

"It's just, it's better not to go there when she's alone. I know Americans would do that, but we don't. Anyway, it probably doesn't matter. God help any guy who thinks he can get anywhere with that girl."

Marco went straight back to the Global Publishing Company the next morning. Mastaneh had already put cushions at opposite sides of the table and set out tea and a plate of grapes. He sat down across from her. This was a lot more formal than he'd expected.

"I've been talking to my sister Maryam." She nodded towards the bowl of sugar lumps as he picked up his tea. "Because I've been thinking. About yesterday."

"Oh."

"I told her we kissed."

Marco put a lump of sugar in his mouth and sipped some tea through it.

"She said she was afraid of this. I said, why? She said she could tell we liked each other. I said, what should I do? She warned me."

"Oh."

"About what could happen. She said Marco's going back to America eventually. Then what?"

Marco sipped more tea and felt the sugar dissolving on his tongue.

"She said she believes you're a gentleman, but—"

He reached across the table and took her hand. She pulled it back. "Maryam says my reputation will be ruined if we—you know. She's right."

"I'm sorry. I realize I shouldn't be here. This is putting you at risk."

"But I wanted you to come."

He looked towards the door, then knelt up, getting ready to stand.

She said, "I mean, could you stay here? In Iran? Maryam says you probably couldn't."

"I don't know. You make me want to stay here. I'd be leaving everything behind. It would be hard. What else did Maryam say?"

Mastaneh smiled. "She quoted some lines of poetry, of course. You know what our family is like."

"What lines?"

"Never mind. I shouldn't have mentioned it." She moved and knelt next to him, pulling on his arm for him to sit back down. "Let's just finish our tea."

"All right. But what lines?"

"It's really all about union with God, you know. Attar's poetry."

He looked into the depths of her eyes, captivated. He had never known anyone like this. He struggled not to touch her, holding onto the edge of the table. She kept her eyes on his as if she read his mind. After what seemed a long silence, she quoted the lines of Attar:

> When you have left your life completely behind,
> At that moment, I will have entered your soul.

He didn't know if he understood.

"It's just Sufi ideas," she said. "Union with God, it means, but . . . ."

"It applies to human love, too?"

"Yes."

"Believe me, I've been thinking I'll have to give up my life in America."

"I can tell."

"Should we stop being alone together until I'm sure I can do it?"

"That's what Maryam thinks." She dropped her gaze. "Because Maryam thinks I could never leave Iran."

Marco's voice was shaking. "What should we do? Maybe we should just see each other at your house. Whenever Farhad takes me there."

She nodded. Tears were running down her cheeks. As he started

to get up, she threw her arms around him, sobbing. "Wait. No."
She held her warm cheek against his.

He pushed her hair from her face. She looked up, and he kissed
her. She was breathing hard, holding him. Marco wanted to stop,
but he couldn't. He moved his hands down her silky white blouse,
then onto the soft navy blue skirt—and then the smooth skin of
her thigh.

"*. . . enter your soul*," she whispered. "Okh, Marco."

There was a knock at the shop door, a customer. Marco stayed
in the back room while Mastaneh rushed out. The customer wanted
a copy of *Little Women*, which Mastaneh had illustrated. "That will
be twenty-six tomans," he heard her say.

"Oh, sorry. I only have twenty-five."

"Good enough. Let me wrap it."

She came back. "Mr. Ketabi will be happy. —What's the matter?"
She followed Marco's eyes and saw that her blouse was half pulled
out of her skirt. "Akh, what did that man think?" She tucked in
her blouse and lifted her hands to her cheeks.

He put his arms around her.

"Marco, was that the hand of God stopping us from making a
big mistake? I mean, the feeling was so powerful. I would have—"
Softly in his ear she said, "Please, I need to go for a walk."

Baharestan square was lit up with gaudy coronation lights. They
sat side by side on a bench eating *shishlik* kabob, feeling safely lost
in the crowd of people enjoying the holiday. Looking at the crowd,
she said, "I want to be with you. But what should we do? Word
spreads. I don't want people to look down on me."

"No."

"They say terrible things about women who are with men before
they get married."

"*Father-dogs!*"

Mastaneh laughed. "You've been around Farhad too long. He
might be one of those *father-dogs* himself."

"Maybe. I feel guilty. He doesn't know anything about us."

"I hope not!"

"Sometimes he calls you his fiancée."

"I'm not. And never was."

Marco stared ahead at a small lighted fountain shooting silvery water up into the air. He said, "I can try to be a gentleman, Mastaneh-*jun*." It meant Mastaneh, dear, and it was the first time he'd used it.

"A gentleman. All right. And I'll be a lady."

The evening air was getting cool, and she slid closer to him on the bench. "But . . . ."

"What is it?"

She turned towards him, and under the *shishlik* wrapper on their laps he felt her leg touch his. The deep brown of her eyes reflected the light of the fountain. "Marco, maybe I was wrong. I don't know. It's possible. Do you think it's the force I feel *drawing me to you* that's the hand of God?"

A gentleman caller

"**Y**ou look all excited these days," Farhad told Marco.

"Oh, it's the whole coronation thing, you know."

"*Pedar sag!*" Farhad tended to curse in Farsi.

"Or maybe I've been drinking too much tea."

"So. Let's go to the Meikadeh Hafez and see if Adarvan has some cognac to calm you down."

The tavern owner kept their glasses full. Marco tried to keep up with Farhad's *bezan bālā* down-the-hatch shots and was getting tipsy. "So how are the 'presentations and receptions' going at the USELESS?" he asked.

"They had me serving drinks to these American guys, probably spies. Why do they cut their hair like that?"

"The USELESS guys?"

"And embassy guys."

"Real short? Flat on the top?"

"Yul. Grown men. They look ridiculous." He downed another glassful. I heard one of them tell another, 'We're not worried about the fucking rag-head mullahs. It's the Commies we have to look out for.'"

Marco just shook his head.

"Nasty *mother-whore.* As if this country belonged to him. I got him, though."

"What do you mean?"

"Before I brought him another drink, I spit in it."

"All right!"

"Anyway, I couldn't see being a waiter. So, the next day, three girls show up not knowing classes were still canceled. Oouee!"

"What?"

"I took them upstairs for a private lesson."

"Like with those 'dates' we brought back to the apartment?"

"Yul. One at a time. In the director's office. He was downstairs."

Marco let this sink in. "Aren't you ruining those girls' chances of getting married?"

"Naw. Believe me, they want it. And they have money. They'll get married. Besides, there's this thing we do in Iran. I can't tell you now. I'd have to use a Farsi word, and these guys here would understand." He held up his glass. "Down the hatch."

Marco asked Farhad again when they got home about that "thing we do in Iran."

"It's called *lāye pā.*" Between the legs.

"That's what you do with the USELESS girls?"

"Yul, that's what they want. I think women invented it. It feels good for *all involved.* Is that used right? Plus, they can still call themselves virgins."

"Would you call them virgins?"

"You know what I call them."

94

It was the last day Mr. Ketabi would be on vacation. Marco bought a box of flan on the way to the shop.

The door was open, and Marco walked in. *"Yā'allāh."* There was a vase of flowers on the table.

"I thought it was a bit dingy in here," Mastaneh said. "It's all right for a bookshop, but—"

"Not for a *shoreless sea*?"

"Uh-huh. What's in the box? Is it flan?"

He put the flan on the table, and they sat down next to each other.

"Looks like you're reading some kind of manuscript."

"I told Mr. Ketabi I want to do more work in color. He said he had some translations of foreign poems in that drawer over there. I picked this one."

At the top of the manuscript, Marco saw *The Eve of St. Agnes, A Poem by John Keats.*

"What a beautiful story! Madeline prays, goes to bed without dinner, dreams of her lover Porphyro, and he appears. Their families don't want them to marry, so they run off together. We don't have stories like this."

"No?"

"No. We have *Layla and Majnun*. Majnun can't have Layla and goes insane. Layla is forced to marry someone else. Then she dies. Then Majnun dies. Both of their lives are miserable. That's the kind of story I grew up hearing."

"I see what you mean."

"Marco, I don't want our story to be like *Layla and Majnun*."

"No."

She put her arm through his and leaned her head on his shoulder. "I dreamed about you last night. In my dream we were together."

"Tell me about it."

"You know, we were just lying down holding each other."

"In bed?"

"I don't know. Dreams are kind of mixed up."

"We weren't doing anything?"

"Impo . . . No!" She pursed her lips. "We were naked, though, if you want to know."

"Look at me." He touched her cheek.

"I don't know why I said that. I just meant it was like Madeline's dream in the Keats poem." Her face was flushed. "Now I don't know why I even said *that*."

"I knew what you meant." He pulled her close and kissed her. She put her arms around his neck, and he was awash in the shoreless sea.

They sank down on the carpet, her head on a cushion, and he touched her face, then breast. It was covered only by her silky white blouse, and he felt her nipples beneath his hand. He kissed her cheeks, her neck. His hand was on her leg under her skirt, and he moved it higher.

"Okh!"

He knelt up, starting to take off his jacket.

She closed her eyes. "Marco, but . . . ." She pulled the cushion over her face, then sat up, holding it on her lap.

"What's wrong?"

Stroking the cushion, she swallowed hard. "Nothing. I guess. It's silly."

He saw her hand was trembling, then thought he understood. "That's Mr. Ketabi's cushion."

"You see what I mean?" she said. "And his table. And carpet. And shop!"

"I know." Yet Marco was excited even more by the sight of her sitting there, hair in disarray, blouse untucked and partly open, skirt raised almost to her waist, legs apart in a sort of child-like disregard. She seemed unaware of her effect on him.

"I'm sorry," she said.

Marco looked around the room, the vision of Mr. Ketabi's welcoming, trusting smile forcing itself into his mind. Slowly his passion began to cool, replaced by a wave of guilt. He knew the mood was broken. "Not here?"

"I can't."

"I guess not." He tried not to look at her.

"I love you. It's just . . . ."

Marco put his coat back on. He sighed. "Well, I brought you some flan."

She smiled. "And the tea is ready."

Big sister

When classes started again at the university, Azadeh cornered Marco in the hallway and gleefully announced that her family had been invited to the Niavaran Palace to view the coronation ceremony. "It was a wonderful holiday, are you agree?"

"It was momentous for me."

"Espell, please." She looked the word up in her well-worn dictionary and smiled. "Yes."

As soon as class was over, he went to Global Publishing. Mr. Ketabi came to the inner doorway. "I understand you were here while I was gone."

Marco stiffened.

"Helping Mastaneh with her work," Mr. Ketabi added.

"Oh. I didn't do much, really." He saw Mastaneh make a comical face standing behind Mr. Ketabi.

They sat down for tea and *shishlik*. "Mastaneh tells me you like *shishlik* perhaps even better than *āb gusht*."

Before they finished eating, Maryam came into the shop unexpectedly. As she shook hands with Mr. Ketabi and Marco, she took a brown wool bag from her shoulder.

"Please," Mr. Ketabi said, "join us for lunch."

Maryam knelt at the edge of the table. She wore a long gray jacket that looked like a factory uniform but didn't take it off. "I don't have time to eat," she said. She folded her hands on her lap.

"Mr. Ketabi, did you enjoy the coronation holiday?"

"Yes, I went to see my brother in Semnan."

"And you, Mr. Marco?"

"I, uh, maybe you heard, we saw the motorcade drive by."

Maryam smiled. She flipped her glasses down from over her head and looked around the production room. "I was curious to see what kind of place Mastaneh worked in. It's not at all like where I work—rows of women sitting at tables cutting out designs for curtains and tablecloths. It's cozy here. I understand why Mastaneh enjoys it."

Mr. Ketabi said he was lucky to have her.

Maryam opened her bag. "Mastaneh forgot this poem. It's short. I read it. Very interesting. I thought I'd bring it to you on my lunch break."

Mr. Ketabi said her kindness was great.

"It's a handwritten manuscript. Is it an original translation?"

"Yes, it is."

"Beautiful language. It doesn't say who translated it."

Mr. Ketabi's face reddened. "Actually I translated it myself. A long time ago. From a French version. So it's not exactly—" He broke off, a worried look coming over his face. "You see, Mastaneh thinks she can use it to practice illustrations in color."

"I see." Maryam turned through the pages. "When I read it, I was trying to imagine what kind of pictures they would be."

Mr. Ketabi coughed. "There are castles, stained-glass windows, tapestries, knights and ladies."

"Yes. And there are some scenes I guess you would call more *exotic*?"

There was a silence. Marco looked up the word in his dictionary.

"Maybe Mr. Marco doesn't understand," Maryam nodded to him, "but, in our culture, for example, these lines here, describing the girl, uh, undressing for bed—I mean, I hope my sister wouldn't make a drawing of that."

Mr. Ketabi emitted a kind of moan. "This is all my fault. Miss

Maryam, I hope you aren't getting doubts about what kind of books we publish here. Certainly, there was never any intention of publishing this poem."

"And yet you gave it to Mastaneh to illustrate?"

"He didn't give it to me." Mastaneh raised her voice. "I picked it out of Mr. Ketabi's archive drawer myself."

"Mastaneh, is that supposed to make me feel any better?"

Marco was still trying to think of a response to Maryam. He wanted to say Keats's description, even in his "culture," was exotic but not salacious. What was the word for *salacious*? He decided to keep quiet.

"In any case," Mr. Ketabi said, "I'm going to put it back in my archive for good."

Marco couldn't help feeling relieved, but Mastaneh said, "Please don't, Mr. Ketabi. It's a beautiful poem."

Maryam interrupted, "As for me, I would feel better, Mr. Ketabi, if you did put it away. I'm sorry to say that." She refused tea and said she had to get back to work.

When she left, Mr. Ketabi took off his glasses and held his head in his hands, moaning again.

Mastaneh put her hand on his shoulder. "It's all right, Mr. Ketabi."

"But now what does your sister think about our business? This is terrible."

"The fact is, I think Maryam was worrying about me and Marco, not about what kind of books you publish."

Mr. Ketabi bobbed his head in confusion. "Worrying about you and Mr. Marco? But we were talking about the poem."

"And the poem is about a girl who dreams of a man she loves, and then she runs away with him."

Mr. Ketabi tilted his head.

"And Maryam knows I like Mr. Marco."

"Yes. How dense I am. It never occurred to me she might be worried about you and Mr. Marco." His head bobbing, Mr. Ketabi seemed lost in thought. "I worry a little, too, but then the worry fades away. Seeing the two of you brings back memories of my own past, and that makes me happy." He stared down at the manuscript.

Mastaneh said, "Maryam just worries too much."

He cleared his throat, shifting on his cushion. "I did talk to you once, Mr. Marco, about differences in customs. Do you remember?"

"Of course. It was something I'll never forget."

"You did?" Mastaneh said. "What did you tell him? Mr. Marco, you never mentioned this to me."

Mr. Ketabi said, "I told him I don't want you to be hurt."

"I won't be," Mastaneh said. "I'm not afraid." She turned to Marco and repeated, "I'm not afraid."

Mr. Ketabi nodded. "Then I'm not, either." He picked up the manuscript carefully in both hands. "Some day, perhaps, I'll tell you how I came to translate this poem. For now, I'm putting it away." As he took the poem to the cabinet, he said, "But, we all know, the truth is there's always a risk in choosing to be happy."

Marco rode home with Mastaneh on the bus, aware as always that the other passengers were probably interested in what an American and a beautiful Iranian girl without a chador were talking about, and so they spoke under their breath.

"Was Maryam angry?"

"No. I've just upset her. With all my questions."

"Maybe you could tell her there's nothing to worry about. You're not really going to do anything."

Mastaneh raised her eyebrows to say *no*. "I've said enough to Maryam already."

Asynchronous communication

Now that the university was back in session, Marco found it harder to get away after class to visit Mastaneh at the shop. The students, the boldest ones, all wanted him to eat lunch with them. The first day back, Azadeh reminded Marco of his promise to go with her and her friend Parvin to the cafeteria of the Planning Organization.

"Today?" Marco said. "But there's somewhere I was planning to go."

"You promise."

Marco gave in. The Planning Organization cafeteria looked exactly like the cafeterias in Washington, D.C., government office buildings. He slid his tray along the chrome rails and looked through the glass.

"I think you find the food you are liking," Azadeh said. "Like America."

"And also food we like," Parvin added. Marco noticed now additional items that couldn't be found in a D.C. cafeteria, including boiled sheep's stomach and tongue, grilled sheep testicles, and yellow lemon-soaked chicken.

"What do you eat? Azadeh asked him. "I and Parvin usually eating the *escrambled-egg* mix with the sheep brain."

"I'll have that too," Marco said without thinking. Trying to make conversation with the two women in English wore on him, and he let his attention drift. He heard them talking, but he wasn't taking in what they were saying. He wished he could be eating at the Global Publishing Company. With Mastaneh he could talk in Farsi about things that were interesting to him. Was his Farsi as comical to her as Azadeh's broken English was to him? He wondered if Hassan had received a message from her that he hadn't been able to deliver.

"Next time, you must come up to my uncle's office in the Planning Organization," Azadeh said. "He want meet you."

As winter approached, Marco saw Mastaneh as often as he could at Global Publishing. Mr. Ketabi was always there. When Marco touched Mastaneh's knee under the table now, she seemed less mischievous, more moved, but Mr. Ketabi didn't seem to notice the change. Whenever Mr. Ketabi went to get tea or went to the other room to get a book, Marco and Mastaneh looked silently into each other's eyes.

Farhad did seem to notice a change in Marco. He was more curious than suspicious. One weekend, he said, "Come on. Let's go to my aunt and uncle's house."

Mastaneh's father was in town. He brushed his mustache against both of Marco's cheeks. "Welcome, Mr. Marco. Still talking about you and *Mr. Worthless* in Hichja, you know."

Mastaneh's mother said, "Your name is heard a lot in this house, too. Welcome."

After the men sat down, the women joined them, Maryam at first taking the place next to Marco, but then slipping aside for Mastaneh to sit there.

"Why does Mastaneh get to sit next to Mr. Marco?" Mina asked.

"You wanted to sit next to Papa," her mother answered.

"I do."

"Hmm. I guess she was just wondering," Farhad commented.

Maryam changed the subject. "How are your classes at the university, Farhad?"

"Excellent."

"Uh-huh," she said dryly.

Mastaneh's father said, "They miss you in Hichja, Farhad. Your mother and father send their love." Then he added, "Lots of people in Hichja miss you."

Farhad just nodded. Marco didn't know how secret Farhad's affair with the level-seven woman in Hichja was.

Now it was Mastaneh's mother who changed the subject. "They say it's going to be a cold winter."

"I hope it snows!" Mina wiggled back and forth on her cushion.

"What's wrong with Mastaneh?" Farhad said. "She hasn't said a word. How is it going at the Global Publishing Company, Mastaneh?"

"Excellent."

"Good. Good. Marco said he saw you there. I've never been. I should stop by some time."

"I am unworthy of your interest."

Her mother said, "All right, children. I think it's time to eat."

Marco and Farhad shook hands with everybody as they left. When Mastaneh shook Marco's hand, she managed to slip him a tiny folded-up note.

He read it in his room:

I love you.

He put the note in his briefcase but kept taking it out to read again.

Through the cold winter, he kept going to Global Publishing when he could, but now he never stopped wondering if Farhad would "stop by." The idea of Farhad dropping in and seeing him there with Mastaneh frightened him. He started to cut his visits short and went there less often. Now Hassan frequently handed him notes from her:

My dreams are crazy. You wouldn't believe.

Yesterday Mina asked me, "Do you kiss Mr. Marco?"

Maryam says she wants us to be happy. ???

This is my last note. I can't trouble Hassan any more. Just come to me whenever you can.

Merry Christmas

مست مستم ساقیا دستم بگیر

تا نیفتادم ز پا دستم بگیر

—from a popular song of the time

Mast-e-mastam, sāghiā, dastam begir.
Tā nayoftādam ze pā dastam begir.

The university was closed for winter break. While the students went back to their hometowns to visit their families, the faculty stayed to grade the *concours*, the university entrance examination for new applicants.

Farhad and Mastaneh were leaving, too. Her whole family had wanted to go back to Hichja to visit grandparents, family, and friends, but Mina had school and Maryam had to work. So only Mastaneh could go.

"Mr. Marco, it's going to snow!" Mina told him. "They said so on the radio."

Marco knelt down to Mina's level. "I love snow," he told her. He could barely keep himself from hugging her. Instead, Mastaneh came up and hugged her. She glanced at Marco, then gave Mina a little kiss. "It's all Mina can think about. She's still talking about the last time it really snowed here, a couple of years ago."

Cloth-wrapped bundles were piled on the dining room table in her house—gifts and supplies to take back to Hichja.

"Couldn't you take Mr. Marco with you?" Mastaneh's mother said. "He could squeeze in the truck."

"The teachers have to stay and grade the *concours*," Farhad said. "It's too bad. But I'll say hello for him to *Mr. Worthless* and Mohammad."

104

Mr. Sufizadeh was in the terminal on the outskirts of town getting the truck filled and waiting for them to bring the bundles in a taxi. As they started to carry them out of the house, Mina cried that she wanted to go, too.

"Marco's going to stay here so he can play with you when it snows," Mastaneh told her.

When the baggage was piled up on the sidewalk, it was obvious it wouldn't fit into a single taxi. Mastaneh said she would take as much as she could in one taxi, and Farhad could take another. That way, Marco could come to the terminal with Farhad, too, if he wanted. He did.

"Or we could all take a *taxi-bar* together," Farhad suggested.

"No," she said. "See you at the terminal."

When she left, Farhad shook his head. "Did you see that? My fiancée, and she didn't want to ride with me."

"She's not really your fiancée, of course?"

"That's what they say."

"But it's a joke, right? That's what you told me."

"See. If I married for love, I'd marry Fatimeh."

"The level-seven girl in Hichja?"

"Right, but I can't. She's not a virgin. Can you imagine?"

"Not to mention, she's married."

"So I'll probably just end up marrying Mastaneh. That's what people expect anyway."

"What? You can't."

"She's not that bad. I thought you liked her."

"But she's your cousin. You said people don't marry their cousins any more."

"They mostly don't." He took a cigarette from his coat pocket and held it. He seldom had any matches. "There are worse things. Of course, you're right. I'll find somebody else. These people." It wasn't clear whether he meant Mastaneh's family, or his, or Iranians in general, or all the people in the world. "They think they can take control of your life."

A man smoking a cigarette walked by, and Farhad stopped him to ask for a light. "Anyway," he said blowing out a huge puff of smoke, "right now Fatimeh knows I'm coming and she's waiting for me because word spreads fast in Hichja—as you know. Wish you could come too. You should meet her."

He waved his hand. A three-wheeled *taxi-bar*, really a motor scooter with a covering, a flat seat for the driver, and an open deck for parcels in back, struggled jerkily but determinedly across three lanes of heavy traffic and stopped at their feet.

"Where do we get in—front or back?" Farhad asked the driver.

"In the front. One on each side."

They perched on the narrow bit of seat available on each side of the driver. He clanked the gearshift lever on the handlebars, and with a low-geared jerk and a two-cycle popping sound they were off, blue smoke rising behind them.

"I'm surprised Mastaneh didn't want to ride in one of these," Marco commented.

"Hmm."

The tiny vehicle had a great advantage in heavy traffic because it could drive up on sidewalks, squeeze between lanes of cars, and weave through jammed intersections. The driver buzzed the horn authoritatively as if escorting dignitaries. "I can speak seven languages," he declared in Farsi. He watched Marco's face for a reaction.

Marco kept looking straight ahead and said, "Really?"

"Yes," the driver said in English, swerving around a pedestrian.

"How are you?" Farhad asked in English, testing him.

The driver said, "Yes."

Farhad said, "Do you know French?"

"Yes!" he beamed.

"Do you know German, too?"

"Yes!"

"How about Russian?"

"Yes!"

"May I fuck your sister?"

"Yes!"

The machine finally jerked to a stop at the terminal. "It's that truck over there," Farhad told him. "How much is the fare?"

"Whatever your heart wishes."

As they got off, Farhad told Marco, "If you get lonely, you could look up the Two-bit Angel. You can find her on Ferdowsi Street in south Tehran."

Mastaneh arrived and asked her taxi to wait and take Marco back. After her father loaded everything into a compartment under the truck, he brushed each of Marco's cheeks with his mustache. "Sure you can't come along?" Mastaneh looked as if she was hoping he would change his mind.

"I wish I could."

"*Felān khodā hāfez*," Mastaneh said, shaking his hand, holding it a bit long. Good-bye for now.

With Farhad and Mastaneh gone, Marco turned to the job of grading university entrance exam essays. The teachers sat inside a long paneled room at the main campus with a proctor standing at each door. None of the teachers were allowed to leave the room until all the papers in that day's batch had been read and rated by three people. Dr. Khodpour, the head of the English Department, came into the room and gave them a speech about the seriousness of their task.

The work for the day was finished by late afternoon, and Marco walked home under an unusually deep gray sky. This was the time for taking a *gardesh* with friends. He walked in the general direction of Mastaneh's house without intending to go there. He reached the street that connected her house and his, then turned towards home. The European Ice-cream Shop was about midway between their two houses. He looked in the window. Well dressed customers sat nibbling fancy dishes of ice-cream or fruit. Most of them seemed to be couples. Crowds of people brushed by Marco as he stood looking into the shop. He seemed to be the only person in the city walking alone.

Outside the ice-cream shop doorway, a man in a shiny suit with padded shoulders stood idling, fingering his amber *tasbih*. He wore black-framed, tinted glasses like many of the *farang-rafteh* customers in the ice-cream shop and seemed familiar.

"Hello, *mein Freund*," the man said in a mix of English and German. "It is long time, *nicht wahr*? Are you find good apartment for living?"

Marco realized it was the man who had shown him an apartment for rent when he had first arrived in Tehran. It was owned by a woman he said was a friend of his who lived on the ground floor and whose daughter lived on the third floor. The middle-floor apartment was for rent. "Is good, yes?" the man had said. "You like old, you go down. You like young, you go up." Then he had added, "But not go down too often. I also go down."

Now the man suggested, "Maybe you come with me, we visit landlady and daughter? I think now is good time. Your face is not happy, looking in ice-cream shop. Is your Christmas season, *nicht wahr*?"

"Oh, I was just thinking about something. Thanks, anyway."

The man shook his hand. "*Fröhliche Weihnachten*, Mister!"

Marco turned up the collar of his overcoat and walked on, shivering. The sky was a heavy dark gray.

He worked a few more days grading *concours* essays. Once he took a walk to Jaleh Square and passed by the Global Publishing Company but didn't go in. The next day, he went to check his mail at the post office. "Maybe tomorrow."

As he left the post office, he almost bumped into a woman in a chador. It was Fereshteh, the Two-bit Angel.

"Ah, sir. What a surprise!"

He stopped.

Fereshteh said, "I was just mailing a letter. To my mother in

Hamadan."

Marco asked about her baby.

"He's getting bigger and bigger, sir. Thank you."

There were glances from passersby at this woman standing on the street talking to a man. The presumption that she was a prostitute, in this case, was well founded.

"Then, unless you need me further, sir, I should go. I'm happy we met." She adjusted her chador exposing less of her face.

"Yes."

She didn't seem willing to be the first one to walk away. "I feel you're still troubled, sir, like before."

"A little."

"I can't forget that beautiful girl who came to your apartment."

"Yes."

"Do you know? When we left your apartment, she gave me a *cheshmazan*. She had brought it to show you, but since I had a baby, she gave it to me." This was a talisman made of incense, myrrh, and silvery and gold paper from a cigarette pack to hang over a baby's crib to ward off the evil eye. "I'm sure she'll get another one that she can show you, sir."

Marco noticed it was mostly women who looked at them as they passed. Some peered sideways around the edges of their chadors. Those without chadors rolled their eyes more subtly.

"My mother tells me when you're troubled, sometimes it helps to talk. I don't mean to presume."

"Talk?"

"We could, if you would like, sir."

He took her by taxi to a traditional *chelo kebāb* restaurant on Takht-e-Jamshid Street. Since he was accompanied by a woman, the waiter showed them to the *haram* section shielded from the rest of the restaurant by a curtain. They were alone.

"I don't eat much, sir." She had soup, and he shared part of his huge plate of rice and kabob with her. She said, "I saw that young lady's eyes when she looked at you. She was afraid, but I could also tell she loved you. You should marry her, sir."

"She would have to come to America, or I would have to stay here."

"Ah, I never imagined you might not stay here. I was thinking you came here to live. You seem to fit in here."

"But it's hard to leave your own country."

"I suppose. If you have a good life there."

"What about you, Fereshteh? Could you leave Iran?"

"I don't know. To make a fresh start? Maybe."

"Anyway, when I'm with her, it's hard to think of the future." He lowered his voice. "I want to make love now, and I think she does, too."

"This is not something that surprises me, sir. The first thing I would say is make sure she doesn't have a baby before things are decided." She sipped some water and coughed before she could swallow it. "Haaa, I sound like my mother."

"Yes, but I also worry about ruining her reputation. I mean, she's my friend's cousin. There's this talk that they're engaged."

"Okh."

"I mean, they both say they're not. But I still worry. Could their families end up insisting?"

"I don't know, sir. You're in more trouble than I thought."

"And if that happened, if their families forced them to marry —I've heard women are rejected for not being virgins. I've heard they're even given physical examinations sometimes."

The waiter came in and stood by the table. Marco asked for more yogurt to get rid of him.

"Examinations?" Fereshteh said. "That's not something to worry about. Believe me, I know about these things. It's impossible to tell." When Marco didn't seem convinced, she said, "I'll tell you something. One doctor told me I could pass this kind of examination!"

Marco couldn't help smiling.

"He told me why, but I don't want to get into it."

"No."

"Sorry. I've gone too far, sir. Anyway, there's no doubt about it. The best way is to get married first. —There! I sound like my mother again."

While they were still alone at the table, Marco gave some money to Fereshteh.

"Please. The meal was enough."

"It's for your baby."

"Thank you, and good luck, sir. Do the right thing. Oh, and I should wish you a happy *Eid-e-Noel*." Merry Christmas.

On the day after the grading was finished, the air felt sharp and icy. Thick clouds covered the city. Marco went out early to the Meikadeh Hafez and bought two bottles of beer. The tavern radio was playing a popular song by Golpa in which the enamored addresses his beloved as a tavern cup bearer, or *sāghi*, saying that he is drunk with love:

> *I'm drunk, o sāghi, take my hand.*
> *Lest I stumble and fall, take my hand.*

When Marco got back to the landing of his apartment, there was a thin box wrapped in shiny red paper leaning against his door.

His name was written on the outside. Inside was a necktie and a note: *"Merry Christmas. I came back early. Mastaneh."*

He sat down on his bed and held up the necktie—maroon and gray silk, very smooth. He pulled off his tie and put on Mastaneh's. If Mastaneh had gone to work today, she would still be there.

"**Y**ā'allāh," he said as he went inside.

Mr. Ketabi came out of the back room. "Mr. Marco. I must wish you a happy *Eid-e-Noel*. Please, come in. Mastaneh, it's Mr. Marco."

The low table in the back room had been turned into a *korsi* for the winter, a brazier of charcoal under it and a thick cover over it going down to the floor. They put their legs and arms under the cover to keep warm. Mastaneh said, "Merry Christmas, Mr. Marco. You look particularly well-dressed today."

"Oh, yes, I have a new necktie."

"Very nice."

Mr. Ketabi chuckled. "Yes, yes. Very nice, indeed. Well, well." He took his hands out from under the *korsi* and looked at his watch. "Oh, my. It's almost time for closing. A little early, perhaps. Three or four hours early. Since it's supposed to snow, though. God light our paths. Mastaneh, dear, you and Mr. Marco go on. I'll take care of the coals and close up the shop."

Huge soft snowflakes were falling as Marco and Mastaneh stepped out into the street. When they looked up, the sky was white. Neither said anything about where they were going. The street was unusually empty and quiet. The snow kept falling heavier and heavier until it was impossible to see very far ahead. Mastaneh took Marco's hand and held it tight.

Snow

میان ما و تو امشب کسی نمی گنجد

که خلوتیست مرا با تو در نهان امشب

—Attar

Miyān-e-mā o to emshab kesi nemigonjad
Ke khalvatist marā bā to dar nahān emshab.

The blanket of snow had suddenly hushed the city and obscured the view from Marco's balcony. Even with the balcony door wide open, his room was sealed in by a dense, milky glimmer radiating upward from the snow into the whitened sky, dulling the image of the other buildings in the distance. The opaque light made it impossible to guess the time of day. Below, in the courtyard, the rounded tops of tulip trees now and then shed sparkling streams of excess snow into the still air, and an angular ridge of snow raised the top edge of the wall enough to remove the *kucheh* from view. Mastaneh stood next to Marco. The strange hush and sense that they were hovering over the city in an impenetrable sanctuary was overpowering.

She covered his trembling hands with her gloved hands to warm them, and they stood together without talking. The snow bathed her face with a dreamlike light. "Are those tears?" Marco asked. Her deep, beautiful eyes were sparkling.

"No. It's the cold. Can we go inside and close the door?"

His room was lit only by the glow reflected through the glass balcony door. The only sound was the flutter of the flame in the kerosene space heater outside of his room.

"They look like tears." Marco wiped one away.

The room was getting warmer. She pulled off her black leather gloves and unbuttoned her coat. He helped her take it off. "Your face is cold, but you're warm underneath."

She touched her forehead. "What does it feel like to be drunk?" She seemed a little unsteady, and he took her hand. "It's my name, you know."

"I know *Mastaneh* means *intoxicated*. It always seemed a strange name."

"My father chose it. The feeling you get from mystic unity with the One." She looked around his room. "Nice. No carpet, though."

"I know."

"That's why you don't take off your shoes when you come in? Akh, my boots are dripping on your floor."

"You can put them over there."

She put her hand on his shoulder to take her boots off.

"You can stand on that little tribal rug. By the bed."

"Oh!"

"What?"

"It's a Ghashghai *gelim*. From Shiraz, right? I have a rug just like this by my own bed."

"It must be a sign."

"Yes. —Akh, Devil! Don't tease me. I'm nervous." She looked down at her white socks. "They're wet. Look. My footprints on your rug. Sorry. I should take off my socks."

"Sit down here."

"Your bed! Your quilt. Your pillow. Your dresser. Your little briefcase." She sat on the edge of the bed and took off her socks. Her hand touched a book lying on the bed. What's this? You're reading Attar?"

"It's Farhad's. He lent it to me."

She started leafing through it, then stopped. "Okh!"

"What?"

"Here." She read:

> *No one can come between us tonight*
> *For the night hides our secret seclusion.*

He sat next to her, and she turned away towards the balcony window. He pressed his face against her long, soft hair. She turned towards him, and they kissed. Her cheeks and lips were still cold. The tips of their tongues touched.

"Marco," she gasped. "Do you feel like this snow is our blessing?"

"Yes. Like it's guarding us from harm."

"I'm not afraid."

"But you're shaking."

"It's just, my feet are cold."

He knelt and put his hands on her feet. "This will warm them."

"Yes." Soon she said, "That's all right. You can stop." She was breathing heavily.

"You can put your feet under the quilt."

"Okh, I want to. On the same bed you sleep in."

"Go ahead."

"It's crazy. In real life, I'm afraid to do what I freely do in my dreams."

He pulled back the quilt.

She stood up with her back to him. "Get under with my street clothes on?"

"You could."

"My mother would have a fit." She was shivering.

"Just get in."

Her back still to him, she unsnapped her skirt, letting it drop onto the rug. She took a deep breath and unbuttoned her blouse, but then left it on. She quickly jumped into the bed and pulled the quilt up almost over her head. She was lying face down with her hair spread out on his pillow.

Stirred by the sight, he said, "I'm coming in, too."

"Oh, God."

She stayed on her stomach, not moving, while he slid down under the quilt and covered her cold feet with his legs. "Better?"

She didn't answer, but soon they felt warm against him.

"Aren't you too hot now? Let me pull the quilt down." She didn't move as he uncovered her. He slid his hands up the back of her legs, then over the short mini-bloomers, touching the frill around the waist and each leg. She lay still except for a slight trembling, and he heard her muffled breath against the pillow. He touched her under her blouse and kissed the back of her neck. She let him take one of her hands from under the pillow, hold the cuff, and pull her arm out of the blouse. Then the other. He kissed her back and rested his cheek against it, reaching under her silky little bloomers to feel her there, too. "Okh!" she said, but still didn't move. He pulled her bloomers down, and she shifted her weight slightly to let him get them off, still pressing her face against the pillow. He swept the hair from her cheek, and she turned over. Her eyes were moist, radiant. "Are we going to make love?" she said.

"Yes."

They lay beside each other. Both were breathing heavily, and neither spoke. He heard his heart throbbing in his ears. She reached for his hand and held it against her breast. "Feel!"

"I can see your heart pounding."

She stared at the ceiling. Gradually, a serious look came over her face. She turned to him and said, "Do you look down on me now?"

He squeezed her in his arms. "How can you ask that?"

They walked out into the snow together hoping to catch a taxi, but the only transportation still running was the bus. She said her mother would assume she had worked all day at the Global Publishing Company.

"Will you come back tomorrow?"

"Yes. No, wait. Tomorrow is Friday. No work. Come to our house. We can play with Mina in the snow."

The bus was less crowded than usual, and the driver's assistant had a portable radio tuned to the *Golhaye Rangarang* program. A love song. A woman in a chador was staring out the window tapping her finger lightly on her handbag along with the music. A middle-aged man looked up from the newspaper he was reading to listen, his head back against the seat rail and his eyes closed. Another man glanced now and again at Mastaneh and Marco.

He walked her down her *kucheh* in the whirling snow, and when they stopped in front of her gate, she touched her cheeks and said, "Will they know? Will they be able to tell?"

He pulled her close and gave her one last kiss. "Just tell them it's the snow."

Courtship rituals

When he went back to Mastaneh's house the next day, all three sisters were outside with their mother, ankle-deep in snow. "It's Mr. Marco," Mina shouted. "Open it! Open it!" She was too short to reach the latch.

As he looked through the wrought-iron grate, Mastaneh lobbed a huge ball of snow two-handed over the gate and onto his head. Mina opened her mouth, but no sound came out.

"Just wait!" he said, wiping the snow from his face. Mastaneh opened the gate and ran.

Mina pulled him by the hand into the courtyard. "Come on. Snow fight." It seemed to be mother against daughters.

Mrs. Sufizadeh looked years younger out here in the snow, her cheeks red, her movements quickened in the chilly air. Her dark eyes flashed a brilliance he hadn't noticed until now. Mastaneh's eyes. Her smile was girlish, uninhibited, as her daughters tossed handfuls of snow up into the air over her head. She chased them with snow she scraped off the edge of the *hoz*—and caught them.

"Time out. Time out," the older girls called. Mina stood defiant, ready for another chase.

"Mr. Marco, go the other way around," her mother shouted. He grabbed some snow and they trapped Mina between them.

"No fair," Mina laughed as she was pelted from both sides.

"Come on, everybody," Maryam said. "Enough fighting. Let's make snow fairies." She stood at the side of the *hoz* forming figures from snow and sliding them across the thin layer of bluish ice to the others.

Mastaneh made one of her own, but Mina put her hands on her hips and tilted her head.

"It's an American fairy," Mastaneh said. "A tooth fairy. They look a little different."

"Aiee." Her mother held her hand over her mouth. "It looks

like it bites."

Mastaneh smashed it in her gloves. "Maybe Mr. Marco can show us what they look like."

"I can't, but I can make something else." He lay on his back moving his arms and legs back and forth. He didn't know what Muslim angels looked like, but he hoped they had wings.

"An angel!" Mrs. Sufizadeh said. Mina flopped down to make one herself. Mastaneh and Maryam glanced at each other, then both lay down and did the same. Their mother gave a high-pitched laugh, sprinkling snow onto all the girls' faces. "I wish Papa was here."

When Marco and the girls got up, their backs were white with snow. Mrs. Sufizadeh brushed Mina off. "It's cold. I'm going inside to fix us some lunch."

Mastaneh and Maryam brushed each other off, and Mina brushed off the back of Marco's legs. She jumped up a few times trying to get the snow off his back. "Uh. Uh. Help me."

Maryam pointed with her chin. "Go ahead, Mastaneh."

"Hold still." Mastaneh took off her glove, and he felt her finger moving across his neck to remove the snow inside his collar. He shuddered as the cold finger moved down inside his shirt but he didn't want to move.

"Got it yet?" Maryam said dryly.

At lunch, Mrs. Sufizadeh was still exuberant. The others were hungry and dove into their rice and stew, but she just poked at hers with her spoon. "You know, I first saw your father in the snow."

"Yes, Maman. You told us," Maryam said.

"I want to hear it again," Mina insisted.

"Don't worry. You're going to," Mastaneh told her.

"It was on a trip in the Zagros mountains," their mother continued. "Lots of people were already there when our bus stopped. We were sitting in the tea house watching the boys sliding down the snow trail in their boots, no skis." She put some rice on her spoon but didn't eat it.

"And the best-looking one was Papa," Mastaneh said.

118

"Not only the best-looking. He was the one who kept helping the others when they fell down. That's what I noticed, too."

"And you found out he was from Hichja," Maryam said. "And then you watched him playing soccer there. And he wasn't that good at soccer, but the other players all liked him."

Mina was stuck on the snow trail scene. "Papa still picks me up when I fall down."

"That's just my point," Mrs. Sufizadeh said. "I was able to see how he acts when he didn't even know I exist."

Maryam was interested in the topic. "In the West, they go out together to see if they like each other."

Her mother said, "That's good, I guess. But then they're trying to impress each other, wouldn't you think? So can you be sure?"

"The same with *khāstegāri*," Maryam said. Matchmaking. "You can't know what they're really like."

"I'm going to marry Farhad," Mina put in. "Or maybe Mr. Marco."

Her mother laughed. "I think we need to get Maryam married first. She's the oldest."

"Mother!" Maryam held her napkin across her face, but Mrs. Sufizadeh continued, "Mr. Marco, do you know any single teachers at the university who might want to get married?"

"Please, Mother." Maryam pushed the rice around her plate with a piece of thick *barbari* bread. "Anyway, I don't know about teachers."

"What's wrong with teachers?" Mastaneh wanted to know. "How impolite!"

"Sorry. No, it's just like Maman says. I don't like arrangements, that's all." She sipped some tea through a sugar lump and cleared her throat. When she didn't say anything more, her mother said, "What?"

Maryam put down her *estekān*. "There is a man at work I like."

"Okh!" Mastaneh put her hand on Maryam's.

"I don't really know him. He fixes the machinery when it breaks down. So I only see him every week or so. It's like Maman says, he doesn't even know I exist."

"Does he have a mustache, like Papa?" Mina needed to know.

"Yes, actually." Maryam was blushing now.

"And?" Mastaneh tapped her hand.

"I watch him fix the looms. He's really clever. They say he's single."

Another tap.

"He just walks by us women at the table and goes straight to the electric looms where the men are working. He makes them laugh. I hear them talking. They call him 'Mr. Engineer.' They all like him."

"That's what I'm talking about," Mrs. Sufizadeh said. "See how he is when he's not trying to impress you." She frowned. "You'd think he'd be married already."

"He's kind of short. So I don't know. Maybe that's why."

Mrs. Sufizadeh put down her spoon with a clank. "Short? You say he's a clever man. Nice. Everybody likes him. With a mustache like Papa. —Maryam, what does it matter if he's short?"

"It doesn't matter," Maryam said. "I wish I could find a way to talk to him."

"Do what Maman did!" Mina urged, making all the women laugh. When Marco sat there an outsider to the joke, Mrs. Sufizadeh was easily persuaded to tell once again how she had walked by the soccer players in Hichja day after day until finally the ball rolled out of bounds right at her feet. "I picked it up and threw it back. Not to the nearest guy but all the way in to Mr. Sufizadeh. I still get embarrassed when I think about it." She picked up the spoonful of rice again. "But it worked."

"I don't think he plays soccer," Maryam said. "So I'll have to think of something else." She turned towards Mastaneh. "Maybe I could just lob a ball of snow onto his head."

Wind in my ears

بـه کام تا نرساند مرا لبش چون نای
نصیحت همه عالم بـه گوش من بادست

—Hafez

Be kām tā naresānad marā labash chun nāi
Nasihat-e-hameh 'ālam be gush-e-man bādast.

Marco straightened up his room, put water in the kettle, set the kettle on the heater, washed some dishes, put tea in the pot, put a bowl of sugar lumps on the table, combed his hair, brushed his teeth, opened the *hasir* blind and looked out the balcony window, paged through the *Divan* of Hafez, got up and checked the water in the kettle, sat down at the table, looked out the dining room window.

He heard somebody running up the stairs. Mastaneh. She was out of breath, her hair blown wildly across her face by the wind.

"I was hoping you would come."

"Maman thinks I'm at work! I told Mr. Ketabi I'm going back to Hichja again."

She set a drawing pad down inside the door. "I started a sketch of the snow from your balcony. I need to fill in a few things."

She started unbuttoning her coat, then stopped. "I mean, is it all right?"

He unbuttoned it the rest of the way for her.

"Marco, do you know what I can't get out of my mind? You'll think it's ridiculous." She giggled. "Reaching my finger under your collar to get the snow out!"

They stood on the balcony. The snow was disappearing from the streets, but not from the rooftops or courtyards.

"I don't want it to melt." She took a handful from the edge of the balcony and watched it turn to water and drip through her fingers. He warmed her hand between his.

The kettle whistled. Marco said, "Tea?"

"No thanks. Can I finish this sketch?"

He stood behind her watching. She captured the precise feeling of standing on the balcony in the snow two days before—the large flakes of snow, the sense of a magical, grace-like light flowing into his room, even, somehow, the uncanny silence. After a few more strokes, she said, "There."

"Amazing. It brings back everything. And we're not even in the picture."

"Like what we did was just a dream? That's the idea I meant to give." She breathed in deeply. "It was wonderful."

"Yes."

"I think it's enough to last me for the rest of my life."

He moved the hair away from her face. "Is that what you want, Mastaneh-*jun*? Just to remember that one time?"

The wind made a rustling noise in the heater vent. She gazed down at the courtyard. "I don't know. It scares me. I'm thinking maybe we should stop."

He tried to keep from looking like a man sinking in quicksand. "Look at me."

"I can't. You know why." She pressed her face against his chest. She was trembling.

The flame in the heater fluttered wildly as the wind blew across the chimney pipe outside. Mastaneh pulled tight against him. "Listen to the wind. It's almost scary."

"It's just wind."

"*. . . wind in my ears*. Marco, do you know what Hafez says?"

> *For until I taste his lips on mine,*
> *All the advice of the world is wind in my ears.*

She threw her arms around his neck. "Oh, God. Forget what I

said. I take it back. It *wasn't* enough to last the rest of my life." He felt her tongue touch his lips.

They lay in bed talking. They hadn't eaten anything that day, but neither was hungry. He streamed his fingers through her hair, pulling it up to his lips.

She said, "It's strange. I don't feel afraid right now."

"No."

Her sketch of the snow scene was leaning against the wall. He said, "Did you always want to be an artist?"

"I've always drawn pictures. I don't know. I wish I could do something more."

"Like what?"

"I wish I could be a nurse. But it's not fated to be."

"Not fated? That's doesn't make sense. You can go to nursing school."

"You sound just like an American. I heard that on the radio: *Americans say you can be whatever you want to be.*"

"Heh."

"I applied to the Pahlavi University nursing program in Shiraz. I didn't get in. They only take people right after high school. They said I'm too old."

He took her hand.

"I had to save some money before I applied, and then I was too old. But anyway for the past two summers I've volunteered in the hospital there. Nurse's aide."

"*Bārak'allāh,*" he told her. Good for you.

"Hah. Now you sound like an Iranian."

"Which do you like better?"

"I like both."

"Should I grow a mustache?"

"Akh!"

"Do you love me. Just me?"

She sat up in the bed. "Can you really ask me that?"

They sat at the dining room table. He poured some tea. Waiting for the tea to cool, she seemed nervous. "What days does your maid come in?"

"Who?"

"She was here when I dropped by with Mina's tooth. She mentioned she had a baby."

"Oh. Actually, she doesn't come here any more. We wash our own clothes now."

"She was nice. She said she wouldn't let a tooth fairy come near her baby. I had the feeling she didn't have a husband, and that's why she had to work as a maid."

He nodded.

"Too bad." The wind swept across the vent outside making the flame in the heater flutter. She ran her fingers around the rim of her glass and looked across the table at the doorway covered by a red curtain.

"Farhad's room," he explained. "No door."

"Oh."

"He has no idea about us. He'll hate me if he finds out."

Partly under her breath she muttered, "Hypocrite."

"You're right. I feel bad about it."

"I meant Farhad. He'd be furious at me, too, if he found out."

Maybe we should stop, she had said.

"But if he says *āgh* to me, I'll say *ogh* to him. Hichja's a small place. Everybody knows what goes on." A cloud slowly passed over her face. She pursed her lips.

The old fear welled up again in Marco that she had a stronger attachment to Farhad than she admitted, or that she even realized herself. He said, "But *āgh* or *ogh* wouldn't hurt him as much as it would you."

"I don't want to think about that."

He sipped his tea, without sugar, looking at Farhad's red curtain. She touched his cheek. "Marco, where are you?" She kissed him.

They were lying in bed as the sun was starting to set. He said, "Come out into the hallway. I want to show you something." They wrapped themselves in one sheet. "Look." The small window framed a breathtaking view of the pink, snowcapped peak of Mt. Damavand, far north of the city. "The glow of the sunset brings it close. You feel like you could reach out and touch it."

"Yes. Go on, Marco."

"I like to watch it until the pink totally fades away."

"Then what?"

"Then the peak moves farther and farther away as the sunset fades. Then you can just see the tip, and it's way in the distance until finally it's dark, and you can't see it any more at all."

"Then what?"

"Then? Then I go down to the corner and buy a bottle of beer."

"Akh, Marco. *Aghlet bereh bālā*! Lift up your mind! You were doing so well until you said that. You don't compose poems to capture the experience? Or write memoires or something?"

"No, I just come back and correct the students' compositions."

"All right. Then what? When you're finished reading their papers?"

"Before the snow?"

"All right, before the snow."

"I thought about you. About how I could never have you."

American Ramazan

With the university closed and Farhad away in Hichja, they fell into a routine. Mastaneh left her house in the mornings as usual as if she were going to the Global Publishing Company but went to Marco's instead. Mr. Ketabi assumed she was in Hichja.

They ate nothing during the daytime, only drinking tea which he kept warm on the kerosene heater. Sometimes just after sunset, before he took her home, Marco ran down to the Meikadeh Hafez to get a chicken sandwich and brought it back to the apartment. "Our Ramazan," she called it. "How long do these American Ramazans last?"

Each night, they emerged from the apartment just as it started to get dark. Although Tehran was much like a European city in many ways, it was presumed that a woman walking alone on the street after dark was a prostitute, and she could be arrested. He walked with her to her courtyard gate, giving her a quick kiss and retreating as soon as she rang the bell.

One morning, she arrived later than usual and carrying a small package.

"What's that?"

"Oh, something. I'll tell you afterwards." She put the package out on the balcony.

"Ah, afterwards."

Her face reddened.

"After what?" he persisted.

She put her palms on her cheeks. "After nothing."

Afterwards, she lay on top of him and looked down into his eyes, her hair bathing his face. "I love you, Marco," she said. "You asked me if I loved only you, and I'm going to prove it." Covered only by his undershirt, she slid open the balcony door to retrieve the package she had set out in the snow. "Are you ready?" Her face was ashen, and her expression more deadly serious than Marco had ever seen it.

"I don't know," Marco said. "Mastaneh, sweetheart, you don't have to prove it."

"Just watch me." She held the package almost at arm's length, put it down on the bed, and slowly opened it, biting her lower lip. "Lobster!" she gasped, keeping her eyes on what was actually a very large shrimp as if she were afraid it might bite her. "I'm going to eat it." She gulped and then put her hands over her mouth, still staring at the shrimp. "You just eat some first," she said through her hands.

Marco sat on the bed and pulled the package towards him. Mastaneh jumped. She stood motionless keeping an eye on the shrimp. He stopped smiling. The thought of letting her go through with this gave him a strange thrill.

He picked up the shrimp and peeled off the shell. She turned away in horror sucking in air through her teeth as the shell crackled in Marco's hands.

"Look. It's good," he said. He ate some.

She ran her tongue over her upper lip and hunched up her shoulders, breathing hard. Suddenly she dropped down onto her knees by the bed. "I love you, Marco," she said. She closed her eyes, picked up the shrimp, and put it into her mouth, for a moment letting it sit on her tongue without chewing. He could see goose bumps on her arms. With her eyes still closed, she slowly began to chew.

Marco was transfixed.

She chewed and swallowed every bit, then gasped. She threw her arms tightly around his knees, her head against his legs.

"Mastaneh!" he breathed. "O my God!"

Basse-couture

One morning Marco was still in bed when Mastaneh rang at the door. When he opened it, she stopped in the doorway staring at him.

"Marco! Where did you get those?"

He was in his bright blue and white striped pajamas. "From Farhad's mother."

"Akh."

"What?"

"*First* of all, you look ridiculous in those baggy things. *Second*: Maman and my grandmother in Hichja share material when they make new pajamas for their families each year. So *third*: I and both of my sisters have those exact same pajamas."

"Yeah? Draw a picture of me wearing these."

"I don't know if I can draw a picture of you."

"Try."

He sat on his bed cross-legged while she sketched. Now and then she looked up from her sketch, held her hair to the side with one hand, and stared penetratingly at Marco. Her eyes moved up and down over his body. She licked her fingers and smeared the penciled lines in places. He was embarrassed, then began to be aroused by being looked at so closely, with such intensity.

"Good. I'm finished. There, Mister Marco, is your sketch. But you have to tear it up as soon as you look at it."

The sketch was from a perspective that emphasized and exaggerated the pajamas. It was mostly pajamas. And—could it be true?—there was just the slightest suggestion that Marco had an erection. Mastaneh never put titles on her sketches, but this one had a title at the bottom in Farsi: *Mr. Penis, Wearing Pajamas.*

"*Pedar sokhteh!* Rascal! This.... Ha! What a fool I was to tell you my real name."

She pulled it out of his hands and turned towards the heater. Marco couldn't bear to see it destroyed. He grabbed her from behind and pulled her onto the bed. She twisted, trying to get free, and the sketch slid to the floor. He kissed the back of her neck. She sighed, then relaxed. He kissed her cheek.

"I can't touch you," she said showing him her fingers.

He spat on his own fingers and cleaned the graphite off of hers. They fell into each other's arms.

When he was getting dressed to take her home, he said, "Mastaneh, I don't want to be just a penis wearing pajamas."

"Marco, no. It was just a joke. You're a different organ. You're a heart."

"That's better."

"Yes." As Marco tucked in his shirt, she added, "A heart with a penis. Wearing pajamas."

Lovers' migration

ای عاشقان ای عاشقان هنگام کوچ است از جهان

در گوش جانم می رسد طبل رحیل از آسمان

—Rumi

Ei āsheghān, ei āsheghān, hengām-e-kuch ast az jahān.
Dar gush-e-jānam miresad tabl-e-rehil az āsemān.

Marco wished more than anything he could sleep with Mastaneh all night long, and he told her so. She only smiled. Instead, every evening he took her home, walked back to his apartment, and dropped into bed alone.

Now it was the last day of the holiday. He heard her running up the stairs.

"I had to bring the snow sketch back." She came in out of breath as usual. "Mina saw it. She asked me where that balcony is."

"What did you say?"

"I just imagined it." She took it from the pad. "Can you keep it for me?"

"At least until Farhad comes back." He put it over his dresser. "Then I'll have to hide it. With the pajama sketch."

"You didn't burn that?"

"Never."

They sat down at the table, and he made tea. Some of Marco's books were scattered there. "Do you mind if I look at these?" She picked up his ragged copy of *The Golden Road to English Literature*, holding it delicately as if anything of his was a valuable item. "Your students can read this?"

"Some of them can."

She turned the dog-eared, tea-stained pages gently with her

glossy fingernails. "Ro-bin-son. *Robinson Crusoe.* I've read this in Farsi."

"The whole thing?"

"Yes. Hmm. Ah. *Jane Eyre.* This one, too." She closed the little book softly and sighed. "I wish I knew English. We studied it in school, but I hated it."

He poured some tea.

"I wish I could be a student in your class."

"You'd be the best one."

"Liar. But I know I would work hard. I would do all the home-work."

"Come here." He hugged her. "You're *my* beautiful teacher."

"Farsi, you mean?"

"Not just that."

"Wisdom comes not from reason but from love. That's what Andre Gide says."

It wasn't by any plan that they stayed in his room day after day without going out. Having a place to be alone together was such a rare, fleeting gift they didn't want to waste it on meals, walks, or, in her case, work. They talked about everything except their future. She told him Maryam had managed to get introduced to the man who fixed the looms at work by going to her boss with an idea for eliminating a defect in the tablecloths. "Maryam told her boss she needed to speak to the 'engineer' himself. We'll see how it works out."

Marco told her about his classes. "There's one student, Ebrahim. He knows almost no English but tries to talk to me anyway. He says, 'I like Mr. Marco. I no like English, I like Arabi. I no like West, I like East.'"

"Hah. At least he's honest. Tell me about the women."

"The women? They're all dull and ugly as sin."

She turned away with a little pout on her face.

"It's true. On my life. On my father's grave. May I die unburied."

She put her hands over his mouth. "Stop. You sound like Farhad. Talk like Marco. That's what I like."

A little before the time she would normally go home, she said, "Let's cook dinner ourselves. What food do you have?"

"Eggs."

They went out shopping for groceries. Picking out carrots, potatoes, and onions together, they didn't arouse the public curiosity they were sometimes bothered by. The shopkeepers treated them like a married couple.

"Oh, these eggplants look good," Mastaneh said. "How much are they?"

"They have no worth. Take them, please."

"I insist," she said. "I'll give five rials."

"I couldn't take money for them."

The Iranian way of buying vegetables, Marco saw. Finally, the shopkeeper agreed to take six rials—just for her, he said. When Mastaneh next looked at the acorn squash, Marco warned her, "You know, there's only one frying pan and one pot."

There was almost no light left in the sky when they got back. On the landing outside his door, Mastaneh pointed to a smaller door off to the side. "Where does that go?"

"I don't know."

"Now, if it was me, living here, I would know."

"It's out here in the hallway, so—"

"Open it."

"You think?"

"*Achi machi tarachi lā tarachi.*"

Marco was dumbfounded.

"It's from a story. Words to open a cave."

"Ah. Open sesame."

"Just open it. It doesn't have a lock."

It was a narrow stairway to the roof. They set the groceries down in the hallway. She held onto his coat from behind as they went up. As they emerged on the roof, the vibrant red peak of Mt. Damavand loomed up on the horizon, still lit by the last dying rays of the sun.

"Even bigger than it looks through my window," he said.

She squeezed his hand. "Did you ever see anything more beautiful?"

He saw her brown eyes turn to gold as she gazed breathlessly at the mountain. Yes, he thought. I've seen something more beautiful.

Their footsteps made no noise in the snow that lay in patches on the rooftop. Mastaneh spread out her arms. "It seems like we could walk right into the sky." She stepped up onto the low wall at the edge of the roof.

He stepped up next to her. Neither looked down.

"Sufis believe you have to die to this world to be truly alive."

"Maybe that's what happened. We've entered a different world."

"You feel that too, Marco? Rumi calls it migrating from the world." She quoted a couplet:

Lovers, oh lovers, the time to migrate from the world has come.
The drum of heaven is sounding the departure in your soul.

They stood on the wall holding hands until the mountain peak had disappeared and the sky was completely dark.

Sleepover

شب قدری چنین عزیز وشریف
با تو تا روز خفتنم هوس است

—Hafez

Shab ghadri chenin aziz o sharif
Bā to tā ruz khoftanam havas ast.

"It's late. We're not going to have time to cook this," he said.

She turned to him with an impish look on her face. "I don't have to go home tonight."

"What! You didn't say anything all day."

"Surprise."

"Devil!"

"Remember my mother said the family was going to meet my father in Esfahan? Maryam got off work, but I told them I couldn't. Too busy!"

In the narrow kitchen, they stood side by side cooking. It all had to be fried together in one pan because rice was cooking in the pot.

They ate slowly, savoring the sense that they were a couple and this was their household. They washed the dishes together in the little sink.

"We have a shower," he told her.

"I remember."

"It'll take a little while for the water to warm up."

They left their clothes in his room. Wrapped in towels, they went into the large shower room together.

She let one end of the towel drop but held the other end in front of her. "I've never taken a shower with anybody else before. Not since I was practically a baby. Don't look at me."

133

"Want me to leave?"

She took a breath. "No."

The shower took much longer than either of them expected.

When they were back in his room, he said, "Did you bring a toothbrush?"

"I want to use yours."

"Want to wear my pajamas, too? They ought to feel familiar."

"No, thank you."

They lay naked under the warm quilt. He was excited. "I hope I can go to sleep."

"We can listen to *Golha* on the radio. That's how I usually go to sleep."

They lay in each other's arms listening as the plaintive minor chords of the violin rang out in the cool dark night, and a female voice recited a poem of Hafez:

> *On a night so grand and precious as this*
> *To sleep with you till morning is my only wish.*

"That's meant for us, Marco." She pulled him closer. "I wish this night would never end."

Suddenly, the bed shook back and forth, first sharply, then with a gentler rocking.

"What's that?" Marco sat up, looking around.

She held his arm. "An earthquake tremor. Wait. It's probably nothing."

"Should we run outside?"

"Maybe. Wait. There, it stopped."

"That was scary."

"It was just a tremor."

"The building was shaking."

"Don't worry, Marco. It's over. Lie back down with me." She put her arms around him. "You get used to it."

"I don't know."

"You're wide awake again, aren't you?" She lay over him and kissed him. "Do you realize what we're doing, Marco? We're sleeping in the same bed together. All night."

They made love until they both settled into a deep, peaceful sleep.

The door buzzer rang. Marco tensed in the cold daylight. The buzzer rang again, louder and longer. Mastaneh woke up. "Oh, no," she whispered holding the quilt up to her neck.

A female voice rang out: "Mister Marco! Anybody there?"

"Who's that?" Mastaneh whispered. "It sounds familiar."

They sat perfectly still. The buzzer rang a few more times. Marco could feel his heart throbbing. Mastaneh was squeezing his arm.

"Mister Marco!" the voice called outside of the apartment door.

"Do you know her?" Mastaneh frowned.

"No. Wait. Listen." They could hear her walking back down the stairs.

Mastaneh crept naked to the blind at the balcony and spread apart two narrow slits just enough to look out. Marco peeped out beside her. A young woman was just pulling her chador back over her head and opening the gate to leave. She had a large bundle tied up in a greenish cloth that she carried with her as she walked away.

Mastaneh was dressed in a few seconds. "I'm confused. She called your name. I have to go. Good-bye." She gathered up what she had brought with her and ran out the door.

Marco stood naked in the doorway unable to run after her.

By the time he had gotten dressed and slipped Mastaneh's two drawings behind the dresser, Farhad walked in. "*Salaam*. Back a little early. I brought you something." He gave Marco a small package tied up in what seemed to be the same cloth that the woman's bundle was tied in. "Pistachios, dried apricots, sunflower seeds—stuff from my mother." He looked around. "Fatimeh didn't get here yet? That's funny."

"Fatimeh? Somebody did ring the bell. I didn't open the door."

"Didn't open the door? What the hell? Why not? We came back

from Hichja together. I sent her ahead of me so nobody would see us together. You didn't open the door? She was supposed to call out your name. *Father-dog!*" He threw his own bundle onto the cot. "Come on. Let's go."

"Where?"

"We have to find her. She probably thinks she had the wrong address." Then he stopped. "But we can't let anybody in my aunt's family know she's here. That's important. They know who she is."

"I can't go with you. I have to go—"

"Where? The university's still closed until tomorrow."

"I just need to see somebody."

"See somebody? You're acting weird."

Just then the doorbell buzzed again. It was Fatimeh. "*Salaam.* She dropped her bundle and threw her arms around Farhad, then noticed Marco and looked embarrassed.

"Professor Marco. Fatimeh." Farhad introduced them, and Marco shook her hand. She smiled but didn't say anything.

"You can talk to him. He speaks Farsi."

Fatimeh looked back and forth between Farhad and Marco as if this were one of Farhad's jokes.

Marco said, "I am very pleased to make your acquaintance."

Fatimeh uttered a little gasp and blushed. She shook his hand again, as if for a real greeting this time, and apologized for being "impolite."

Farhad picked up her bundle and carried it to his cot. "That was a long bus ride, Fatimeh-*jun*. I need some rest. How about you?"

"Your room?" she smiled. "No door."

"I have this curtain. That's all we need."

Farhad said Fatimeh was going to stay with them for a while. "Her husband told her he was going to divorce her as soon as he got back from Mashhad. So she's here to look for a job in Tehran."

Marco saw his chance to leave. "Need anything from outside?" They didn't.

136

II

شرکت جهانی نشر

The green bundle

چه دانستم که سودأ مرا این سان کند مجنون

دلم را دوزخی سازد دو چشمم را کند جیحون

—Rumi

*Che dānestam ke sodā'ye marā in sān konad majnun
Delam rā duzakhi sāzad, do chashmam rā konad jeihun?*

Marco took a taxi to the Global Publishing Company on the chance that Mastaneh had gone there. As he passed Jaleh Square, he noticed army trucks parked along the street.

Mr. Ketabi came out of the inner room. "It's Mr. Marco!" he said. "Mastaneh, it's Mr. Marco. Did you hear me?"

Mastaneh stood in the doorway to the inner room wringing her hands. Marco wondered what she had told Mr. Ketabi.

"And now, I hope you can excuse me." Mr. Ketabi said. "This is terribly impolite, but I have an important appointment. If I'm not back by six, please lock up the shop for me, will you, Mastaneh, dear?" He obviously wanted to leave them alone to talk.

Mastaneh came into the room and knelt down across the *korsi* from Marco. She was waiting for him to say something.

"That was a shock," he said finally. "We almost got caught."

"Who was that woman, Marco? She called your name."

"It's not important. I can't tell you."

"Please don't keep secrets from me."

"I can't help it."

"When you don't tell me who it was, that makes it worse." She was clutching the *korsi* cover in both hands.

"Mastaneh, it's nothing to do with you and me, I swear."

"You don't need to swear."

"Can we just forget it?"

"I mean, she was carrying a bundle. It's clear she was planning to stay at your apartment." Tears were forming in her eyes. Marco moved to her side of the table, but she slid away. Finally, she said, "Don't you realize. The neighbors will start talking. You're going to get in trouble." She put her hands on her face. "*I'm* going to get in trouble. People have probably seen me going into your apartment. And now this woman. They'll think we're both—you know what they'll think. *Khodāyā*." Oh, God.

"She's not a prostitute. I hope that's not what you think."

"No. But she might be somebody that I don't want to be like."

"You don't even know who she is."

"Maybe I do."

"How could that be?"

"Do you realize villages in Iran get bulk supplies of cloth, meters and meters of the same kind of cloth all in one shipment? So you can imagine what happens. We make our own clothes, and so lots of different families end up with clothes made out of the same material."

He thought of the pajamas Farhad's mother had given him.

"And nowadays a lot of people in Hichja have things made of the same green cloth that woman had her things tied up in."

He remembered the green bundle Farhad had just brought back to him from his mother.

"I have to tell you. There's a woman in Hichja. She's the second wife of a man who's never there. Everybody knows she loves Farhad. Everybody knows they find ways to be together. Maybe the people in town feel sorry for her and don't blame her, but they still see her as a loose woman." She sniffled. "Just tell me. Is that who it is?"

Marco couldn't keep it from her any longer. "Yes. It is."

"I knew it! I can't believe he would bring her here, to his apartment—to *your* apartment."

"She doesn't seem like a bad person to me."

"She's very nice. But I couldn't stand it if people tsk-tsked about me the way they do about her. If they find out about us, they will."

Marco didn't have an answer for that.

Mastaneh said, "I was always ashamed of Farhad for carrying on with Fatimeh. This makes me realize I'm doing the same thing."

He felt a lump in his throat as he saw a latent feeling of regret starting to overcome Mastaneh.

She said, "And now people are going to find out."

"Just because Fatimeh is staying with us?"

"Her husband might come looking for her. He probably knows about Farhad already, the way people talk. He'll ask questions. If he finds out she's staying at your apartment, he might even suspect you—of something. He'll find out about us. My family will find out." She was crying. "Won't you tell her she can't stay with you?"

"That wouldn't be easy. I'm sorry."

She sniffled. "I want to go home."

"All right, I'll get you a taxi. There are soldiers and trucks on the street out there."

As Marco and Mastaneh passed a canvas-covered personnel carrier, several uniformed men with shaved heads whistled and called Mastaneh a foreigner's whore. Marco hailed a taxi. When it stopped at her *kucheh*, Mastaneh said, "I need to go home alone."

"Park-e-Shahr," he told the driver. He wanted to sit somewhere and think. The last patches of snow were still covering the grass. He sat on a bench by himself turning up his collar and staring at the pieces of ice floating in the little pond. He thought of the first time he had sat in this park with Farhad. A little village boy who had just arrived in the city had sat on the bench next to them and offered them drags of his one cigarette. He showed them his money—five tomans—but said he couldn't offer them any of it at the time because he didn't have any work yet and might need it. He had asked Farhad where they were going to stay for the night. Marco thought the question strange, but Farhad had said in English, "You see? He thinks we're here in the park because we don't have any place to go. Like him. He'll have to sleep here tonight."

Marco walked home from the park taking his time, wishing he had a place to sleep other than his apartment. It was getting dark, but he didn't want to go home yet. When he came to the Meikadeh Hafez, he went in. The purplish fluorescent light and baby blue walls made him squint at first.

"Hello Mister." Adarvan gave him a toothy smile. "*Kālbās* sandwich and a Star beer to go?"

Marco sat down on a stool at a tiny round table. "Yes, please, but I'll eat here."

One of the customers recognized Marco. "Alone tonight?"

Marco nodded, and the man raised his glass. "*Nushi jun.*" To your health.

There wasn't much talk. Most of the men drank cold vodka straight, in one gulp, from thick water glasses. They nibbled on a few pistachios, wolfed down sandwiches, and left. The few who stayed longer were listening to a radio broadcast of a poem by Rumi:

> *How did I know love would drive me so mad,*
> *Make my heart a hell, make my two eyes a river?*

One of the customers, probably an Armenian, turned to Marco and wished him a "Happy Your New Year." "Get him a cognac," he said, and they clinked glasses. "*Nushi jun.*" The other men nearby raised their glasses, too.

"He looks like he needs another," one of the men said. "*Befarmāid.*" On me.

Behind the red curtain

By the time Marco got home, the apartment lights were out. Behind the red curtain to Farhad's room, he could hear Farhad and Fatimeh talking. He went quietly into his own room and closed the door, trying to go to sleep, but he could still hear them.

"Not now," he heard Farhad say. "I'm too tired. I need to think."

"Think? What's wrong?"

"I'm wasting my time at the university, not learning anything. Even if I wait it out and get my degree, I'll still probably have the same job I have now."

"Teacher?"

"I call myself teacher. I teach a few classes. Really, I'm a telephone receptionist. That's all."

"I'll make you feel better."

"I just want to talk. I'm not going to waste my time any more. I'm going to do something, but I don't know what yet. I'm thinking."

Fatimeh said a few more things in a lower voice.

Farhad said, "No. Just sit here next to me."

"Sure."

"Did you ever answer the telephone a hundred times in one day and say the same thing a hundred times to a hundred people?"

"It might be fun to do that one day. Then I'd quit."

"But I might have to be working there the rest of my life."

"It's a good enough job, isn't it?"

"I'm going to end up a fifty-year-old switchboard operator. Knows a little English. Peculiar. Hums to himself and drums on the desk with his fingers. Said to have had a lot of girlfriends in his day. Some say he still does—at his age! Imagine!"

"Hm-huh." Fatimeh had a laugh or giggle that sounded to Marco like a bell.

"It's not really funny, though. I feel like I'm in prison."

"How about me? I'm an old man's second wife. He drops in

now and then when he's passing through town. I'm shut up in the house. It really is a prison. You get used to it, though."

"You do? You shouldn't."

"I mean, I'm worse off than you. Here I am looking for a job. The best I can hope for is cleaning people's houses and washing their dirty underwear—something you'll never have to do in your life, no matter what happens to you."

"I guess you're right."

"My uncle told my mother we can live with him in London."

"Yeah, I know. That was a year ago. Anyway, how could you do that? You're married."

"Yeah."

"Your husband's really going to divorce you?"

"He says so. He told my mother he's going to hurry before the law is changed. Until then, all he has to do is say he divorces me in front of two witnesses, and that's it."

"He's crazy. You're beautiful."

"Hm-huh."

"Hey! Watch it."

"Don't be so jumpy," she said. "I'm just lying down beside you."

"Then what about your daughter? I mean if he actually divorces you."

"My mother's making plans to take her to a friend's house or somewhere. He'll have a hard time finding her."

"Good idea, I guess." There was a pause. "Want to share a cigarette?"

Farhad and Fatimeh talked more quietly then. Marco was finally getting sleepy and couldn't follow their conversation. He heard them talking about the streets and houses and people of Hichja. They recalled sneaking cigarettes together in garden huts and being scared by the moaning of jackals at night. Marco heard them laughing softly together as he finally drifted off to sleep.

The next morning Farhad came out of his room as Fatimeh

was going into the shower. "Oouee. I did her five times last night."

"Oh, man."

"She wanted to do it more. I couldn't."

"Oh, man."

"She's supposed to be staying at her cousin's house looking for a job."

"Supposed to be? She's not really going to stay there?"

"Naw. I want her here."

When Fatimeh was dressed, she made a breakfast for the three of them. She turned her chair sideways facing Farhad and put her bare feet on the rungs of his chair with her knees touching his leg. "I didn't know if Americans eat eggs," she said.

"They do," Farhad told her. "But with the shells on."

She didn't mind Farhad teasing her. Her way of getting back at him was just to touch him or lean on him since she noticed this seemed to embarrass Farhad in front of Marco.

"Watch out! Let me drink my tea," he said, twisting on his chair.

One shelf of Farhad's bookcase held all of his clothes. To get ready for work, he only had to pull on his shirt, trousers, and coat. Two minutes. His socks were there by his shoes where he took them off. His tie was always ready since he never untied his "sign of western civilization" but kept it as a loop and merely pulled it over his head, slipped it under his collar, and tightened. It was five minutes before he was due to start at work, but he couldn't leave before smoking the one cigarette he had saved on top of his bookcase the night before. "I'm turning my life around," he said, blowing out a perfect ring of smoke. "Thinking about the future."

"Doesn't sound like you," Fatimeh said.

"Believe me. See this cigarette? I knew I would want it this morning, so I saved it last night." After a few more drags, he knocked the fire off the end and put the remaining half into his shirt pocket, nodding meaningfully to Fatimeh. He walked out the door saying, "*Be good, y'all.* –Got that from a guy at the USELESS."

Where nobody cares

"Farhad's funny, isn't he?" Fatimeh poured Marco a glass of tea. "You start work late?"

"Yeah, not until ten." He sipped his tea.

"Oh!"

"I know. It's kind of an easy job."

"No. It's how you're drinking that tea." She pushed over the bowl of sugar lumps, and he picked up the smallest one he could find, put it on his tongue, and took another sip of the tea through the sugar. She smiled.

"Are you really a university professor?"

"Yeah."

"Hm-huh! Those pajamas! They look familiar. I made pajamas for my daughter with the same material."

"Oh."

"They're still talking about you in Hichja, you know."

"What do you mean?"

"*Mr. Worthless.*"

"Oh, right."

"Mr. Sufizadeh keeps telling that story to everybody."

"He does? So, you're friends with him?"

Fatimeh drew back a little. "What do you mean?"

Marco saw that even the suggestion that a woman is friends with a man is an insult to the woman in this country. "No, I mean, I guess you know the Sufizadeh family. That's all."

Immediately embarrassed that she'd taken offense, Fatimeh put her hand on Marco's. "Sure. Sure, I do. Everybody knows them. He's Farhad's uncle, you know. We mainly know the grandparents now that the rest of the family's moved to Tehran. What's the matter? You look a little nervous."

"No. It must have been that sip of unsweetened tea."

"Got to watch that."

"I've met the Sufizadeh family here in Tehran."

"Yes. You're lucky. Living here."

"What do you mean?"

"Here in Tehran you can do what you want. Nobody cares who comes to see you, who you're living with."

"Well . . . ."

"In Hichja they expect me to stay in the house and cook and take care of my mother and daughter and just wait, doing nothing. Farhad knows my daughter better than my husband does."

"Too bad. At least you have Farhad."

She dipped a lump of sugar into her tea and put it into her mouth before taking another sip, then looked at the apartment door. "Do I?"

Marco saw an opportunity and couldn't help asking, "Fatimeh, it's not true, is it, that Farhad and Mastaneh are engaged?"

She blushed, tears forming in her eyes. "Farhad says it's not true." Then, with a sigh she added, "But he can't marry me. And they like each other. So, I don't know."

"I didn't mean to upset you. I'm sorry."

She wiped her eyes and smiled. "You seem more upset than I am, Mr. Marco. Please, it's nothing to do with you. Let's cheer up."

She said the plan was to find a job in Tehran so she could support herself after her husband divorced her. "But I know it's almost hopeless. They say there's only one job for a divorced woman. Do you know what it is?"

Marco didn't answer.

"Never mind. I'm off." She stood up. She had on a dark gray jacket, matching skirt, and white blouse. "How do I look?"

He wanted to say "beautiful" but said, "Very nice. I'm sure you'll get a job." She shook hands with him as she left.

Mastaneh can't hate this person, he thought. I won't let her.

Blockade

There were army trucks in Jaleh Square when Marco walked through the Faculty of Letters gate. He hadn't been prepared for the hatred of the Shah that he was running into everywhere. The International Teachers Association officials and his Iranian Farsi instructors in the States had given the impression that the Shah was the one enlightened shining star in the Middle East. The Shah was called a reformer, a modernizer, an educated, visionary leader. It was the Shah, under pressure from the United States, perhaps, who had instituted a sweeping land reform in the country, dividing up the holdings of powerful landowners and making it possible for farmers to own the land they worked on. The Shah modernized education and extended it to women. He instituted religious freedoms, ending blatant discrimination against non-Muslims. He brought the Ghoshghai, the Turkoman, and other tribes under control and maintained a unified country. And he was fiercely anti-Communist, accommodating towards Israel, and prone to spend huge sums of money in America.

Marco had expected to find the people of Iran grateful and contented. He did find many people who were, Iranians like his student Mr. Davud, who had managed to become wealthy under the Shah's regime. But Marco was gradually seeing what American policy makers somehow didn't seem to realize—that the people's silence and lack of open criticism didn't mean approval. And now Marco was becoming aware that there were organized, clandestine movements that were not only anti-Shah but anti-America as well. His official mission in the country was to serve as an "ambassador of good will." What the hell? Marco thought.

He saw Hassan and stopped. "Any news from Global Publishing?"

"No, sir. There was no message today. There's a blockade in the street, you know."

Dr. Zaban was the only teacher besides Marco who appeared in the teachers' room that morning. "The others are afraid to involve if there is demonstration," he told Marco. "The Colonel Ghorbaghi, perhaps you remember him. He come back asking questions this morning, asking which students they planning demonstration. Perhaps is better you also go home."

"What about you?"

"Is my job, teaching. I stay."

"I'll stay too. I heard a student say nothing was going to happen today."

After class Marco started off to see Mastaneh. Hassan stopped him. "Excuse me, Mr. Marco. They say it's dangerous. You see the trucks, the gendarmes. It's especially dangerous for a foreigner if there is a protest. Perhaps you should go straight home today, sir. Use the other gate."

"I'll be all right."

"These protesters are anti-Shah and anti-American, sir."

"I'll just slip down to Global Publishing anyway before—" Marco now saw that the whole street was blockaded in the direction of the Global Publishing Company. Wooden rails were set up across the street, and gendarmes were stopping traffic and pedestrians and forcing them to turn around and head north. Two armed soldiers came to the gate Marco was about to go through and locked it with a chain from the outside.

"I'll show you the other gate, sir. You'll have to take a different bus home."

"What bus would I take to get to Global Publishing from the south?"

"In the south there's another barricade. The only way to get into that quarter of the city is early in the morning before they put up the barricades, then late in the afternoon when they take them down again. Global Publishing might be closed today anyway, sir, because of the disturbance."

"But—"

"I have a way to deliver a message to your associates there, if you wish," Hassan said. "It will get there tomorrow."

Marco quickly wrote *When are you available to discuss our business?* He gave his note to Hassan and went home.

Makes no difference

Fatimeh followed Farhad out of his room. His shirt was unbuttoned, and her blouse was pulled out of her skirt.

"Oh, you brought some food, Mr. Marco," she said. "We were going to get some, but we lost track of time."

Her cousin's wife had objected to her moving in with them. "She's young," Fatimeh said, as if that explained it. It looked to Marco like she was settling down where she was.

Marco helped them in the narrow kitchen where he and Mastaneh had cooked together only a few days before. The room held all three of them only if they stood side by side. Marco cooked the meat, and Fatimeh and Farhad, standing shoulder to shoulder, peeled the vegetables.

"Stop eating the carrots before we cook them," she told Farhad.

"All right," Farhad said, and he ate a piece of raw potato.

"Akgh," she said. "You can't eat potatoes raw."

"It's the American way. Ask Marco."

"I will not. I don't believe anything you tell me."

"I swear to God," Farhad said.

"Probably everything you tell me is a lie."

"I told you you're beautiful."

"Rascal! I'm getting out of here." But she couldn't move. Farhad was in the way. She pushed against him.

Farhad said, "See if you can squeeze by."

"Hm-huh!"

During dinner, Farhad entertained her with imitations of characters at the Iran-America Society. "It's filled with Armenians, like the American embassy is," he said. "One old man, Yusef—the Americans call him Joe—must be eighty years old. He walks like this." Farhad slid his legs forward without lifting up his feet. "Here's the way he uses the telephone—picks it up, holds it with the mouthpiece sticking above his head, and shouts: 'Halooo. Haloooooooo. Right, right.' After he hangs the phone up, he looks down at it and shouts: 'I'll be right there. Good-bye.'"

Farhad could imitate anybody. He gave Fatimeh his impression of Marco looking the Hichja SAVAK agent in the face and politely addressing him in an American accent as *Mr. Worthless*. He did a Prime Minister Hoveyda speech, puffing on an imaginary pipe and spinning out a stream of words with no meaning whatsoever. He imitated the pompous pontifications of the Shah. Farhad's solution to living with the pains of a repressive regime was humor.

After dinner, Farhad lit a cigarette, blew a smoke ring up towards the ceiling, and said, "I think I'm going to go to bed early tonight."

"Hm-huh!" Fatimeh said. "Maybe I will, too."

Early the next morning, after Fatimeh left to apply for a job her cousin had recommended, Marco told Farhad, "You and Fatimeh are a perfect couple."

"Yes, we get along well," he said. "Too bad."

"What do you mean?"

"Too bad she's not the kind of girl I can love."

"But I would almost say you do love her."

"Naw. What do you mean? How could I? I'm not the only one who's done her."

"But that's in the past. It seems like she's left her husband."

"What difference does it make? The past follows you. It's part of you."

"But the two of you look like you belong together."

"Too bad."

"She's the reason you were so excited about going back to Hichja for the break, I'm sure."

"Maybe. I've known her for a long time. What does it matter?"

"But she's in love with you. Anybody can see."

"Maybe. It doesn't make any difference."

"Because any girl who lets you 'do' her is a whore?"

"Basically. At least that's what people think."

No luck

Now Marco had to enter the university by the back gate.

"A message, sir."

In the toilet, Marco opened the envelope and read: *Please don't send me any more messages—as long as that woman is there. I'm sorry.*

Hassan rang the bell to announce the start of the first class. When Marco walked in, he was thinking of Mastaneh's message and couldn't remember what the lesson was for the day.

Edging up to the front row, he glanced at Azadeh's desk to see what book she had opened. *Conversation Exercises.* The idea was to help the students talk to each other in English. This never worked. They only chattered in Farsi until he declared the lesson over. But Marco always gave it a try.

"All right, so, today's lesson, as you see, is arranging for a language tutor," Marco said. In his mind, he heard *Please don't send me any more messages*, and he paused before turning his attention back to the lesson. The class was strangely quiet, watching him.

"The words to be used in the conversation are *tutor, fee, instruction, private, William,* and *Margaret.*" Marco cleared his throat. "All right, so you see the situation. William wants to arrange for Mastaneh to tutor him—"

The students, who had resumed murmuring steadily, suddenly hushed again and stared at Marco when he mistakenly said an Iranian girl's name instead of the name in the book.

"I think she's name is Margaret," Azadeh said.

"Right. Of course."

"What is 'private'?" Azadeh wanted to know. "Do William and the Margaret meeting alone for the tutor? If I am Margaret, I am not consent to this."

Several of the students murmured their agreement and looked at Marco in confusion.

"You know, why don't we just turn to *The Golden Road to English Literature* instead?" Marco said. "H. G. Wells, *Invasion from Mars.*"

He gazed out from his balcony. Mastaneh would probably never want to come here again. He left his room and saw Fatimeh's bundle of clothes on the floor outside of Farhad's room. He picked it up and put it behind the red curtain.

Fatimeh came back, dressed in her job-hunting outfit.

"No luck again," she said.

"Sorry."

"At least I can help around here." She took some dishes into the kitchen. Then she came back with tea and opened a package she had brought. "Try this. My daughter loves it."

It was baklava. She turned her chair towards Marco's while they ate it, but she didn't put her feet on the rung. "What's America like?" she asked him.

"I don't know. It's more . . . impersonal than it is here."

"That's what my uncle says about London. He lives there."

"Does he like it?"

"He says he can make money there. He told my mother he could get us a visa to stay with his family. If I get a divorce. He thinks I could find a job there." She took a well-worn envelope out of her handbag. "Look at this."

There was a London return address written in an Iranian hand. The letter was addressed to Fatimeh's mother.

"My uncle's invitation. He's been waiting for us to answer him."

"Maybe that's what you should do."

"It's scary, though."

The door opened. "*Yā'allāh*," Farhad said. "What's that? Baklava?" He picked up a piece and ate it.

"The job didn't work out," Fatimeh told him. "I don't have any luck."

"Come here." Farhad led her towards his room. "Come in here with me. Maybe your luck will change."

Haji gives a warning

Fatimeh was out looking for work again. Marco picked up one of the student themes on the dining room table. Two pages were joined by a pin through the upper right-hand corner. This seemed to be the back of the paper—holes on the right-hand side—but it was hard to tell. There weren't any capital letters or indentations in the writing, which went past the margins from one edge of the paper to the other—no waste. He flipped the whole thing over so the pin and holes were on the left. This couldn't be the beginning; the writing ended half way down. He un-pinned the pages and examined them like pieces of a puzzle. The content should give a clue where to begin reading, but one page began with "then," another with "so," another with "not," and the half-page with "and."

Farhad burst through the door. "Hurry up. We have to clean this place up."

"What's the matter? Stop pacing around."

"Haji's coming."

"Who's that?"

"The landlord. Shit."

"I never met any landlord. His name's Haji?"

"It's just what they call him. Since he's been to Mecca."

"So how do you know him?"

"He called me at the USELESS. There've been complaints about women going in and out of the house."

"Oh."

"He's coming here to talk to us. I told him the only woman who ever came in here was your Farsi tutor. Let's get your beer bottles put out of sight somewhere."

"Is it a big deal?"

"He's a Haji. An important person. Rich enough to go to Mecca. And religious."

"I'll take the bottles back for the deposit."

"He's coming any minute."

"It's not like it's against the law to drink beer."

Farhad ignored this and put the empty beer bottles into a pillow case. They cleaned up the best they could. "Put the radio under your bed or somewhere," Farhad said.

"The radio? Are you serious?"

"Yul. These religious people think listening to music is sinful."

"Goddam," Marco said, using his friend Huff's favorite expression.

Farhad looked him over.

"What?"

"And you better put on your coat."

Haji himself, a short well-fed looking man with a permanent five-o'clock shadow—no razor ever cut his beard—wore a tight-fitting suit but no tie. His collarless shirt expressed his contempt for Western civilization. Farhad went through the most elaborate display of *ta'ārof* Marco had ever seen. It threw the man off guard, and when Marco chimed in with some flattering expressions of his own, Haji struggled not to smile. They begged his eminence to deign to sit on the humble mat set up for him on Farhad's rug. The tea was ready. Marco listened to Farhad's explanation while he went to get it.

"Yes, Haji, sir, we are still shocked by what you told me. We discussed it, and we can not imagine how a mistake like this could have been made. Mister Doctor Marco is a distinguished professor at the University of Tehran, and I myself am a humble student at the same university. The only thing we can think of is that, yes, once a week or so, perhaps, Professor Marco's tutor, who happens to be female—another distinguished member of the Faculty of Letters at the university—might be seen arriving to give him his lesson."

Marco carried the tray into the room and placed it on the rug in front of Haji. As he did so, he noticed Fatimeh's brassiere hanging from the top of Farhad's bookcase directly behind the landlord's head. There must have been a look of panic on Marco's face.

"There's no need to be alarmed, Mr. Marco," the landlord said. "Your friend has basically explained the situation to me."

Marco tried to catch Farhad's eye.

Haji went on: "I told your friend, having a tutor come in to give you a lesson is one thing. I can't disapprove of this. What I don't want is for various women to be going into and out of the apartment at all times of day and night."

"Of course," Marco said. "I understand."

"You can be sure this will never happen," Farhad asserted.

"Certainly not. We understand," Marco repeated.

"It's the last thing we ourselves would want," Farhad added.

"Definitely," agreed Marco.

Haji seemed satisfied. "Very well, then, I'll be going. I'm sure there will be no more complaints."

When Farhad began the farewell *ta'ārof*, begging his excellency to honor them longer with his presence, Marco tried again to catch his eye again to indicate the brassiere.

"Oh, yes, Haji, sir, I believe Mr. Marco is reminding me of something I promised him I would mention to you. I hate to bother you with these details, but the thermostat on the hot water heater is broken. It won't shut off automatically after the water is hot."

"Can't you just turn it off when you're finished taking a shower?" Haji said. The businessman in him was breaking through the Islamic fundamentalist.

"Certainly," Farhad said. "That seems to be the solution. It's just, how can I put this? Americans apparently expect the water to be kept constantly hot, but not overly hot."

"Why would they want that?"

"I see what you mean."

"You can just put in some kerosene and light it up whenever you need hot water, and turn it off when you're finished using it."

"Yes, of course. But it seems to be a matter of safety, Mr. Marco believes. It has a thermostat, but the thermostat is broken. It is supposed to shut off by itself in case somebody forgets to turn it off."

"Be vigilant," Haji said. He stood up to go.

"I could just show you the part I'm talking about," Farhad said. He would have to lead Haji past the bookcase to get to the shower room. Luckily, Haji wasn't willing to look at it.

"As I said, be vigilant. I'll take my leave now."

When the door closed behind Haji, Marco pointed to the brassiere. Farhad grabbed his stomach and doubled up on the floor in laughter.

Steam

Farhad was behind his red curtain with Fatimeh. Now and then Marco heard Fatimeh's stifled giggle. He fell asleep thinking about Mastaneh.

He was startled awake by Farhad's shouting. He got out of bed but couldn't see anything. He seemed to be in a warm cloud.

"What the hell?" Farhad shouted. "Come here and look at this."

Steam was shooting out from the hot water faucet in the kitchen. "It's shut, but steam's still coming out," Farhad said, standing in front of the sink in nothing but his shorts. The steam was hissing and coming out heavier and heavier. "What's that noise?" Fatimeh called. She came out of Farhad's room wearing only a towel.

The whole apartment was now filled with steam, most of it coming from the shower room. When they rushed in, steam was shooting in thick, staccato spurts from the showerhead, and the hot water heater was rumbling.

"It's the damn thermostat," Marco said.

"*Termo-estát?*" Fatimeh repeated.

It was getting hard to see in the steam. Fatimeh reached up and opened the shower room window to try to clear the air. Marco bent down to turn off the water heater. At the same time, Farhad turned open the shower faucet to ease the pressure of the steam in the pipes, but this let out a new blast stronger than anybody expected. He jumped aside just in time to avoid being hit in the face, but the steam hit Marco on the arm. He yelled out in pain.

"What are you doing?" Farhad yelled to Fatimeh. She had thrown her towel over Marco to block the steam and stood naked, out of reach of the steam, holding her hands up to her face. Then Farhad noticed Marco on the floor. "Marco, don't get up. The steam will hit you again."

They dragged Marco onto Farhad's carpet, just outside of the shower room. Fatimeh put on one of Farhad's undershirts.

"I don't know what to do," Farhad said.

"Run outside," Marco said. "I got the water heater turned off. But just to be safe." He was still speaking in English. "I'll follow you out."

"What? What?" Fatimeh said.

"Get some cold water maybe," Farhad told her. "We'll pour cold water over his arm."

Farhad and Fatimeh ran back and forth from the kitchen with a pot and a tea kettle full of cold water, taking turns pouring it over his arm. The water was drenching Farhad's carpet. As soon as one of them stopped pouring, Marco felt the pain return.

"We'll just keep pouring it on all night if we have to," Fatimeh said.

"Shouldn't we get out of here?" Marco asked.

Farhad looked around. "Don't worry. Look. The steam isn't coming out as fast now."

They wrapped the towel around Marco's arm and kept it wet. Marco sat up, supported by Farhad from behind and Fatimeh on one side. "I think I'm all right," he said. The steam slowly began to clear. He lifted the wet towel. His arm was red and a little blistered, but it didn't hurt as much as before.

"We'll take you to the hospital," they said.

"I'll just keep this over my arm," Marco told them. "I'm all right. The skin isn't broken." Fatimeh was holding his hand.

"Fatimeh, you didn't get burned, did you? Put on some more clothes," Farhad said. The undershirt was drenched and sticking to her body from the steam.

Marco was recovering quickly. "Don't go to any trouble," he told her. "Your humble servant is content to sit here in your shadow and enjoy the bounty of—"

"Impolite!" Fatimeh said, dropping his hand and running into Farhad's room.

"Owww," said Marco.

She came back wearing her blouse and Farhad's pajamas and sat down beside Marco.

"Fatimeh-*jun*, would you still call this foreigner *steamless*?" Farhad asked. *Bi bokhar*, or "without steam," Marco had learned, was a term Iranians sometimes used to describe foreigners. Less emotional and spirited than Iranians, perhaps even dull and uninteresting—that was how they sometimes viewed Western people.

"Maybe he used to be steamless," Fatimeh said, "but I think we broke his *termo-estát*."

Farhad had his arm around Marco. Fatimeh put her hand around him, too, and the steamless Marco now sat on a soggy carpet clutched on either side by two decidedly steamy friends.

Green medicine

The next day Marco's arm hurt when he tried to use the blackboard. After class, Azadeh and her friend Parvin rushed up to him in the hallway.

Azadeh looked worried. "You not move your arm, Mr. Marco. Why?"

"Just a little burn. It's getting better."

More students gathered around. Marco noticed the tea man Hassan listening from a distance in the hallway. He hadn't had a chance to talk to Hassan before class.

In Farsi, Azadeh announced, "Mr. Marco is hurt!" A chorus of Okhs and Akhs and the Iranian tsk-tsk sound broke out. Marco saw little Hassan immediately turn around and disappear.

"It's nothing," Marco told them. "I'm fine."

When Marco returned home from class, Mastaneh was on the landing outside his door waiting for him. "Okh, Marco!" she said. She started to grab his arm but held back. "Which arm is it?" She couldn't have stood any closer without touching him. "Let me see, may I? Mr. Hassan from the university told me what happened."

"Oh."

"Farhad didn't get hurt, did he?"

"No."

"I mean, nobody else got hurt?"

"Just me."

"Does it hurt a lot?"

"It hurts a little." Marco didn't feel like downplaying his injury at the moment.

It was cold standing in the doorway. She and Marco were both shivering. He opened the door, but Mastaneh just stood in the doorway.

"Why don't you come in?"

"I can't, Marco."

He hung his coat on the doorknob and rolled up his sleeve. The burn had left a little streak of red on his arm.

"Okh. Here." She took a bottle of green liquid from her coat pocket. "May I put some of this on you?"

"I beg you."

Her hands shaking, she took the cap from the bottle. She bit her lip and wiped the green liquid over his burn.

"It feels better already."

"It doesn't work that fast," she laughed. "Please, Marco, whenever anything happens like this, will you just come to our house right away?"

"You said not to send you any more notes. So I—"

"I mean, not as long as . . . ." She glanced inside the apartment. Farhad's red curtain was drawn aside, and there was Fatimeh's green bundle sitting on top of his cot. There was a quaver in her voice. "Put the medicine on twice a day. I can't stay. Good-bye."

"Wait. I want to talk to you."

"I can't." There were tears in her eyes. "One of the neighbors gave me a funny look when I came in just now. That never happened before."

Marco didn't mention the landlord's warning.

"There's going to be trouble. I can tell. My father heard that Fatimeh's husband is coming back to Hichja from Mashhad. They say he's going to divorce her. If she's not there, he could come here looking for her."

"I hope not."

"It would be safer—for you and me—if you ask her to leave."

"Mastaneh, I can't do that."

She put both hands to her head. "Marco, I'm afraid. I'm sorry. We have to stop seeing each other." She turned and ran down the stairs.

"How's your arm?" Farhad asked when he got back. "I brought some medicine for it." He gave Marco a bottle of green liquid exactly like the one Mastaneh had brought. "Put this on twice a day." Then he noticed Mastaneh's bottle on the table. He laughed. "Oh. Who brought you that?"

"Um, one of the students gave it to me at school."

"Girl or guy?"

"Uh, a girl."

"Ah-hah! Beautiful?"

He thought of Azadeh. "Not bad. But not my type."

"Yeah?"

"She has an uncle in the Planning Organization."

"Now there's an organization that ought to be called the USELESS. I agree. Stay away from girls who have uncles in the Planning Organization."

Fatimeh rushed in with a package wrapped in newspaper. "Dinner," she said, dropping vegetables on the table. Marco had already put the two bottles of medicine in his dresser. "Here, Mr. Marco. This is for you." She took out a bottle of green medicine. "Put this on twice a day. Look. I'll do it for you." When Marco hesitated, she said, "Don't worry. It doesn't hurt."

Farhad just smiled and went into the kitchen to start cooking the dinner.

Fatimeh held Marco's arm and started spreading the medicine on. "What's the matter? It doesn't hurt, does it?"

"Oh. No. I was thinking of something else."

She sighed. "I know. You're uncomfortable with me here," she said in a low voice.

Marco lifted his head *no*, Iranian style. Farhad came out of the kitchen and put some rice and vegetables on the table. "Any luck looking for a job?"

"No."

"That's all right," he told her. "It took me a while, too. You can stay here as long as you want. Right, Marco?"

Fatimeh looked at Marco.

"That's right," he said. "As long as you want."

Missing

The street in front of the Faculty of Letters was still blockaded. Guards stood watch by the entrance gate to the campus. Marco realized he wouldn't make it to the Global Publishing Company today either. And now he wondered if he should even try. Mastaneh had seemed determined when she said they should stop seeing each other.

When he called the roll in his class, he noticed that Sassan, the student who had served him lunch in his room above a dry cleaner's shop, was absent.

After class, Azadeh told him, "We worry about Mr. Sassan. He absent three days now."

"Yes, that's strange."

"We hope is not true what they say. They say he is arrest."

"Arrested? How can that be? What for?"

"They say he is member of Fedayan-e-Khalq."

Farhad had told him this was an anti-Shah leftist movement, but he knew little more than that.

Azadeh said, "We worry because we know you talking to him."

"Oh, but he never mentioned anything like that."

Azadeh shrugged.

Since he wouldn't be able to get to Global Publishing, he made a decision. "I think I'll go to Sassan's place and see if he's sick."

"Please don't do that. You don't want get mixed up with these people."

A little bell rang as the shop door opened. A sweat-covered man was pulling down a huge, hissing press onto some white cloth. He turned and pursed his lips when he saw Marco. He didn't respond to Marco's *ta'ārof* greeting.

Marco said, "I came to see Mr. Sassan."

"He's not here."

"I don't know if you remember me. I'm his teacher. I visited him here once for lunch."

"I remember."

"He's been absent three days. I was wondering if he's sick."

"He's not sick."

"I don't mean to be nosy. I just wonder where he is."

"Maybe you could tell *me*."

The dry cleaner's wife appeared in a doorway at the back of the shop. She stood silent, watching from a distance.

The dry cleaner said, "You came to visit. Then a Colonel Ghorbaghi comes here asking questions."

"What!"

"Sassan's just a poor farm worker's son. He studies his books all day long. He wants to be an engineer."

"I know."

"What do you people have against him? He hasn't done anything wrong."

"You don't understand. I'm trying to find out what happened to him."

"One day he didn't come back. That's all we know."

His wife came up and stood beside her husband. She said nothing but gave Marco a pleading look.

"I'll let you know if I hear anything," Marco said.

The dry cleaner looked skeptical. But his wife let go of her chador and grasped Marco's hand. "Please," she said. "He's a good boy."

Marco sat on the upper deck of the bus remembering his ride with Sassan through the crowded streets of the south of Tehran. How could anybody imagine he had anything to do with Sassan's disappearance, with his arrest, if that's what happened? Was it just because he was an American?

"Yes," Farhad told him when he got home. "They say America controls the Shah."

"But I'm not America."

164

"Yul, but they don't get the difference. They figure you're here *giving the Shah a hand*." He raised his eyebrows to see if the expression was correct.

"All I'm doing is teaching English."

"Like I say. Giving him a hand." Farhad turned and blew a smoke ring across the room. "The Shah's men made sure the language I studied was English."

"What do you mean?"

"You know I love languages. Back in high school I was taking a course in Russian broadcast over short-wave radio." He gave Marco a little demonstration of his Russian. "Remember *Mr. Worthless*? I'm sure he's the one who called the SAVAK thugs on me. They took me to the police station in Shiraz and questioned me for a whole day. I was only fifteen. They broke my radio, told me to concentrate on the language being taught in school, English."

Marco squirmed. "That's criminal!"

"Yul, I guess. That's the way they do things here."

"I see why your uncle and . . . his daughters . . . never want to talk about politics."

"Yul. Now you see what can happen. Maybe that student Sassan was seen with the wrong people. Maybe somebody *had it in for him*."

"Actually, that might be possible." Marco told him about Colonel Ghorbaghi.

"So. Maybe it's personal. Maybe Sassan told some students he liked the way you got Ghorbaghi out of your class. Maybe Ghorbaghi heard about it. Found out where Sassan lived. It doesn't take much to get arrested in this country."

The Planning Organization

Sassan wasn't in class the next day either. After class Azadeh reminded Marco of his promise to visit her uncle in the Planning Organization.

"Today?" Marco said. "But I have something important to do today." He hadn't had time to see if Hassan had a message from Global Publishing. Not that he expected any.

"Yes. You promise," Parvin pouted.

"All right."

The Planning Organization was in a modern high-rise building near the Faculty of Letters. Azadeh was proud to have an uncle who worked there. She obviously considered the organization a monument to the Shah's Western efficiency. It was filled with European- and American-educated economists, business analysts, city planners, political scientists, engineers, and agricultural experts. Farhad had a different slant on the organization. He described it as a bureaucracy that produced reports the Shah could show to American ambassadors and presidents to prove he was a force for modernization in the Middle East. The organization had produced a five-year plan that pleased President Johnson and *got him off the Shah's back*, as Farhad put it. The newspapers and radio announced the start of endless studies, which Farhad said were the groundwork for the Shah's taking control of all aspects of the economy and eradicating all political opposition.

They went up to the seventh floor to visit Azadeh's uncle, who worked in the economics division.

"Elevator like in America?" Azadeh asked.

"Fancier," Marco said.

They waited in an expansive outer office with Scandinavian teak furniture arranged on a huge Esfahan carpet more tightly woven than any Marco had ever seen. Even Parvin, who was also about to meet Azadeh's uncle for the first time, looked at the carpet amazed.

166

A woman in a beige business suit sat at a wide desk, empty except for a telephone, and asked them if they would like tea or coffee while they were waiting.

"Shall we have Turkish coffee?" Azadeh suggested and nodded to the secretary.

When they had finished it, she and Parvin turned the little empty cups upside down over the saucers. "We do this for seeing the future," Azadeh told him. "Do you turn yours too?" Azadeh looked at the configuration of the grinds on the sides of the cups. Marco, Parvin—and the secretary—waited for her interpretation.

"Mine show to travel," Azadeh said. "I am happy for this." She took Parvin's cup. "For Parvin. This is difficult. Let me look it more." She lifted the cup and let the dregs drip around the inner edges. "I think is no travel. Staying here with many other people. But for them is big change coming. The life will change, everything different, nothing same. Is perhaps difficult change." Azadeh put the cup back on the saucer.

"And now, Mr. Marco, do I read yours?" She held his cup by the handle between her thumb and forefinger, tilted it, and said, "Okh!"

Parvin audibly sucked in her breath—as did the secretary. Marco looked over at the secretary. Embarrassed, she opened a drawer of her desk and started rearranging some things inside it.

"It is problem in the love," Azadeh said. "That is what I see, Mr. Marco."

The telephone on the secretary's desk rang. Azadeh's uncle could see them now. The secretary showed the guests into a sitting room connected to the uncle's office that was lit by a wall of gleaming copper-tinted windows giving a view of the eastern part of the city. Marco, Azadeh, and Parvin instinctively walked across the thick Western-style carpeting and looked out. From the centrally heated, climate-controlled building they looked through the tinted glass down onto Jaleh Square and the streets and winding *kuchehs* beyond. Marco was able to pick out the Global Publishing Company. The blockade was still in the street.

New, modern buildings rose up everywhere they looked. There was furious construction going on. But the projects didn't have any obvious benefit for the peasants pouring in daily from desert villages, the people who passed their lives sitting motionless on stools in front of doorways, sleeping on the sidewalks, or washing their vegetables in *jub*s that others washed their feet in. These people could not be seen—or smelled—from the windows of the Planning Organization.

Behind them, they heard someone say in English, "Beautiful, isn't it?"

They turned around to greet Mr. Ghalamkar, Azadeh's uncle, and the *ta'ārof* began—in English. Ghalamkar spoke in perfect American English without any trace of accent. He was a model of elegance, refinement, good manners, and understated self-assurance.

"My niece has told me a lot about you," he told Marco. "She says you're an excellent teacher."

Marco knew the expected Farsi deferential reply but couldn't immediately come up with the appropriate equivalent in English. "Uh, that's . . . ," he said. Then he settled on, "Your English is perfect, Mr. Ghalamkar."

"I went to college in the States," Ghalamkar told him. "UCLA. Do you know it?"

"Yes, of course."

"I went to Berkley for my Ph.D. Economics. I just got back a few months ago from doing some post-grad work at Princeton. So I've lived in the States quite a bit." When Marco didn't say anything, Parvin said, "Mr. Marco is *deraf-dogér*." She was clearly unaware of the negative connotation.

"Ah." The uncle smiled.

Marco felt himself blushing. "I'm in the International Teachers Association," he told Azadeh's uncle. "Maybe you know what it is. Most people here don't seem to know about it."

"Yes," Ghalamkar said. "I know it. Going off to help poor countries. Is that the general idea? Maybe you can understand why we're a little touchy about that."

Marco only nodded.

"So we're both idealists, it seems," Ghalamkar said to Marco.

Marco squirmed, trying to think of a reply.

"Mr. Marco hurt his arm," Azadeh said.

"Oh?" Ghalamkar said. "Are you all right, Mr. Marco? I hope it wasn't serious. Can I help you see a doctor or go to have it checked at a hospital?"

Marco said he was all right.

"How did it happen?" Ghalamkar asked.

"The thermostat on the water heater doesn't work. Steam built up in the pipes and shot out when we opened the faucet."

"But the landlord should be notified of this. It seems dangerous. He should fix it."

"Actually, my roommate and I had asked him to fix it."

"Middle Eastern inefficiency?" Ghalamkar said.

"No, that's not what I meant."

"I could never get my landlord to fix anything in the States either." Ghalamkar smiled.

Azadeh said Marco had previously gone to lunch with some other students.

"So you're making friends," Ghalamkar said. "I hope your friends are good influences on you."

Azadeh said, "Mr. Davud is good for Mr. Marco."

"It's a sign of the forward-looking determination of our government, isn't it, Mr. Marco, that Jewish people like Mr. Davud have such freedom and can be so successful in our country? Getting to know Mr. Davud will probably show you a good deal about the difference between Iran and other Middle Eastern countries."

Marco said, "One of my students is missing."

"I've heard that from my niece. A Mr. Sassan Gharari, I'm told."

"Do you know where I could ask about him, find out what happened to him?"

"That's not a good idea. My niece and I are worried you might be influenced by the wrong people and maybe even get into trouble.

She told me about your argument with Colonel Ghorbaghi."

"It was just about how he behaved in the classroom," Marco said.

Ghalamkar laughed. "Right. Mr. Marco, I've got to admire you Americans for the way you stick to your principles. Here it's sometimes considered a little dangerous. Good for you, though."

Azadeh said, "And I told him about Mr. Ebrahim, too."

"You see," Ghalamkar said, "it's just possible my niece might be right about these students. There are two kinds of—what shall I call them?—renegade groups that emerge from time to time. I don't know if you've heard of them. There are Marxist-Communists— Azadeh thinks Mr. Sassan might be associated with these. And there are radical religious fundamentalists—and Azadeh suspects Mr. Ebrahim is connected with these. None of these opposition groups has the slightest chance of success, but it might be better to be aware of them."

Marco nodded.

"Just a word to the wise," Ghalamkar said. "My niece respects you a great deal, Mr. Marco."

The clamor of traffic hit them as they walked out the door of the Planning Organization. They were back in the real world. The two girls spoke to each other in Farsi. Azadeh said, "I don't want school to end."

"I know why," Parvin teased her.

"What do you mean?"

"Because you're going to miss seeing Mr. Marco."

"Of course, we'll all miss him." She assumed Marco couldn't understand Farsi.

Parvin suggested they share a taxi home. The girls lived in the north of the city, and Marco's stop was first. He sat in the front and the two girls sat in the back. Azadeh took something out of her purse. "For you," she said. "A pass to the Planning Organization cafeteria. My uncle gave it to me. Now you can eat lunch with us for free every day."

"Oh, I can't accept this," Marco said.

"Please." She reached over the seat and dropped it in his lap.

"*Lotf-e-shomā ziād*," Marco said. Your kindness is great.

On hearing him speak Farsi, Azadeh grabbed Parvin's arm. The taxi driver grinned. "This is your street, sir. Kucheh-e-Hamin'odd-oleh. Where should I stop?"

"That building there with the gate."

Marco heard an "okh" from the back seat when he spoke Farsi to the taxi driver. Azadeh and Parvin looked at each other. They leaned forward and shook hands with him before he got out of the taxi. Azadeh held his hand longer than he expected.

A marriage proposal

"**So** the *mother-whore* wouldn't give you any help finding your student?" Farhad poured Marco a cup of tea.

"No."

"Worthless *father-dog*! And his niece gives you a pass to the Planning Organization cafeteria! Professor Marco, you're getting mixed up with the wrong crowd." He gulped down his tea. "Your student's probably not at the police station, but we could check anyway. Let's go."

"Maybe you shouldn't go, Farhad. You know, that problem when you were studying Russian in Hichja. Maybe they have a record of that. Where's the police station? I'll go."

"Not without me."

The police station on Takht-e-Jamshid Street reeked of sweat. "This is a professor at the University of Tehran," Farhad said. "He wants to report one of his students missing."

"Over there." The uniformed sergeant behind the desk pointed with his chin to a line of folding metal chairs against the wall. Morose-looking men and women were sitting on all but the last one. Marco and Farhad stood.

"Next."

All but Marco and Farhad rushed at the desk.

"Sit down. Sit down." The sergeant pointed to the woman who had been sitting on the chair first in line. "You. In that room."

It was a long wait. When they were finally called in, Marco had to present his residence permit and work permit for identification and wait for the clerk to copy everything down. The clerk wanted to write down information on Farhad, too, but Farhad said his name was Hossein Ali and he was just Marco's translator. With Farhad's help, Marco was finally able to file a missing person report on Mr. Sassan-e-Gharari-e-Mazandarani.

"I have a feeling I'm never going to see him again," Marco said as they walked home.

When they turned down the *kucheh* to their apartment, there was a taxi waiting in front. A young woman called out, "Mr. Marco." Azadeh got out of the taxi. She saw Farhad and said, "Oh."

"I'm surprised to see you," Marco said. He introduced Farhad.

"A pleasure to meet you," Farhad said. "Mr. Marco has told me wonderful things about you. Please, come in."

"I'm sorry. I just have something to give you, Mr. Marco. Your housekeeper said you weren't home, so I waited in the taxi a while."

"Housekeeper? Oh."

Azadeh said, "Mr. Marco, I just give you this. We can discuss about it later."

The driver leaned out of the taxi window. "That was a long wait, Miss. Do I go now?"

"No. Now you can take me back." She took off in the taxi.

When they went inside, Farhad called to Fatimeh. "Have you gotten the house straightened up for us, Housekeeper?"

"*Father-dog*! Is that what she called me?"

"Yeah. And she probably thought I was the house boy."

Fatimeh said, "No offense, Mr. Marco. I mean, she was very polite and pretty."

Farhad asked Marco, "So what do you have there?"

They sat at the table and looked through the papers Azadeh had given him.

"All English," Fatimeh said, disappointed.

"It's an application for admission to the University of Texas," Marco told them.

"Texas!" she exclaimed. "Why would anybody want to go there?"

"What do you mean?"

"I've seen movies. Cowboys with guns are always shooting each other there."

"Oh. Yeah. And this is an admission essay she wrote. I guess she wants me to check it over."

"She wrote that?" Fatimeh sounded impressed.

"Hmm, no, I think her uncle probably wrote it for her."

"*Sister-whore!*" Farhad said. For Fatimeh's benefit he spoke in Farsi.

Fatimeh pointed to the last paper. "What's that?"

It seemed to be a letter. As Marco read it, he started shaking his head.

"What is it? What is it?" Fatimeh looked back and forth between the letter and Marco's face.

"Impolite!" Farhad said. "It's a personal letter."

Marco put the letter down and didn't say anything. Fatimeh and Farhad sat perfectly still looking at him. Then they turned to each other. Farhad said, "A love letter, of course."

Marco picked up the letter again. "It sort of is."

"Okh!" Fatimeh grasped Farhad's hand.

"But not exactly. She's determined to go to America."

Farhad said, "Oh, I get it."

"What? What?" Fatimeh wanted to know.

Marco slid the letter over to Farhad.

"Just tell us," Fatimeh said.

"All right. She says she wants a visa to America. She'd rather have a permanent one than a student visa if possible."

"And so she wants to marry you," Farhad said.

"Okh!" Fatimeh said.

"She says she has lots of money. Actually, *too much money*."

"How much?" Farhad asked.

Now it was Fatimeh's turn to say, "Impolite!"

"Doesn't say."

"Does she love you?" Fatimeh said. "Does it say that?"

Marco looked at the letter again. "It says she likes my smile."

"Yes," Fatimeh said.

"Says she thinks it's a good plan."

Fatimeh said, "And?"

"That's about it."

Fatimeh looked towards the window. "That's pretty much what my husband said to me when we got married."

The American way

After class the following week, Azadeh approached Marco before he got to the teachers' room.

"Perhaps you read my letter?"

"Yes." He lowered his voice. "Azadeh, I don't really want to get married."

She pouted. "I was thinking you like me."

"I do like you. But I don't want to get married."

"Perhaps I mistake by writing a letter. My uncle warned me this is not the American way."

"I just don't want to get married. I'm sorry."

She turned away.

"I did look over the application and essay. And I can write you a letter of recommendation."

Parvin and some others came up to talk. Word was out that the blockade was in place to prevent a demonstration. "We are sorry it interfere with your walks down Jaleh Street," Azadeh said.

"Mysterious walks," Parvin added in Farsi. Marco knew the

word. He had learned it at Mastaneh's house.

When class was over for the day, Dr. Zaban took him aside in the courtyard. "I have heard from the department chairman something, Mr. Marco. He asked me to tell you *not to drop worms*. This is what we say."

Marco took it to mean not to stir things up.

"Did you make a report about Mr. Sassan Gharari missing?"

"Yes. I just wanted to do something, at least."

"The police, they have reported this to our chairman. He says making reports is his job."

"I'm sorry."

"Never mind, Mr. Marco. I know you have a good heart. I will tell him that's the way they do it in America."

"Is this the way they cook eggs in America?" Fatimeh had asked him the first time she made breakfast. "This is how Farhad likes them." When Farhad wasn't there, she would say, "Farhad's *place is empty*." She never relaxed until he came home from work. And Farhad was the same when she was gone. Although he never said her place was empty, Marco could tell he was *nārāhat*, "uncomfortable," as Farhad sometimes translated it. When he and Fatimeh were together, they talked and talked. They shared jokes that Marco didn't understand. And they spent an astounding amount of time behind the red curtain of Farhad's room.

Each day she went out to look for work. And each day Farhad seemed relieved when she hadn't found a job yet.

Marco walked home. He wanted time to think about things. He bought vegetables on Shah Reza Avenue and some ground lamb at a butcher shop, thinking about the time he and Mastaneh had gone shopping for groceries together. He got home later than usual. Farhad was pacing back and forth in the apartment. "Have you seen . . . . Hi. Have you seen Fatimeh?"

"I just got home."

"Yul, I mean I thought she would be here by now. Did she say where she was going?"

"I left before she did this morning."

"*Father-dog*! Where is she?" He lit a cigarette and took a deep drag, then sat down and gazed over towards the red curtain of his room.

"She could still be out looking for a job."

"Naw. It's dinner time."

"She'll probably show up soon."

"Yul. I guess I'm getting used to having her around."

"I noticed that. Did she ever say how long she was going to stay here?"

"No. Of course, I know she has to go back sometime. She has to deal with that divorce thing—if that's really going to happen." He was shelling peas into a bowl. "She told me her mother took her daughter Ziba away somewhere so the husband couldn't find her." He looked out the tiny kitchen window. "Ziba loves peas. She plays with them before she eats them, lines them up like this, in a circle."

Marco said, "If Fatimeh's really going to get a divorce, then I guess you two could get married."

"I suppose that's done in America. It's not something I ever saw myself doing before."

"But now?"

"Shit, I don't know."

"Are you worried about losing face?"

"Losing face. I haven't heard this."

Marco explained.

"Yul, that's it. I would lose face. How could I face people? I know what they'd say. Why did you pick *her*? Somebody else's castaway. And her kid."

"Fatimeh says she's your kid."

"OK, she might be mine." He puffed out a series of smoke rings up towards the ceiling. "I named her, you know. Ziba. Beautiful." He smiled to himself.

176

"But don't people in town know about you and Fatimeh already? You didn't lose face when you started seeing her?"

"Naw. She did, not me. That's how it works. I could even live with her. But if I married her, then I would lose face." He picked up a lump of sugar and put it on his tongue to sweeten the tea. "I can't believe I even mentioned marrying her."

The dinner was getting cold. "Go ahead and eat," Farhad said. "I'll just wait a little longer." He drank another glass of tea. "*Pedar sokhteh!*" The scoundrel. "She knows better than to be walking alone through the streets at this hour."

"Maybe she went to her cousin's."

"His wife said she couldn't stay there."

"Maybe she went to your aunt's house."

"Naw, I was just there before I came back here."

Marco thought about the letter Fatimeh had showed him from her uncle in London. Farhad had scoffed when he told him about it.

"I guess you checked in your room," Marco said.

"Obviously she's not there." He frowned. "What do you mean 'checked?' Oh." He went into the room and looked around. "*Pedar sokhteh!*"

All of Fatimeh's things were gone.

Demonstration

Marco hadn't seen or heard from Mastaneh since the day she brought him the green medicine. Hassan had said it was possible to get to the Global Publishing Company early in the morning before they manned the barricades. The shop was probably closed because of the blockade, but Marco was determined to give it a try today before going to class. He had something to tell Mastaneh: Fatimeh had left.

The shop door was closed, like most of the shops on the street. He knocked on the door anyway. He knocked again, louder.

Mr. Ketabi's face peeped out through the window. He opened the door without saying anything and closed it immediately behind Marco. "Merciful God!" he exclaimed. "What confusion in the streets!"

"I was afraid you might not be here."

"I've been here every day. Working on galleys in the back with the shop closed."

Marco didn't have much time before he had to leave for school. He said, "I was wondering about Mastaneh."

"She's not here yet. I'm worried about this *sholugh* in the streets. It seems to be getting worse."

He took off his glasses, wiped them, and put them back on again. "I feel that you and Mastaneh have had some kind of misunderstanding. She said she has heard something from her cousin that upset her."

"Heard something from Farhad? What?"

"I'm afraid she didn't say, Mr. Marco."

"Did she say anything else?"

Mr. Ketabi rubbed the top of his head. "She just said she didn't want to talk about you. I'm sorry."

"Oh."

"Mr. Marco, I will say one thing. I believe Mastaneh loves you. I'll tell her you came. And that you want to see her."

"Thank you."

"And anything else?"

Marco didn't want to mention Fatimeh to Mr. Ketabi. "That's all, I guess. Thanks, Mr. Ketabi. *Lotf-e-shomā ziād.*" Your kindness is great.

Jaleh Square was already packed with people. A group of mullahs and shabbily dressed men congregated on the corner opposite the university entrance, and Marco had to weave his way through another crowd loitering directly in front of the entrance. Guards were opening the gates only for students with identity cards and people they knew.

"It's Professor Marco," Hassan said, and a guard let him in.

In the teachers' room, Dr. Zaban said a rumor was going around that an anti-Shah demonstration would start at noon. He was told to dismiss the students at ten o'clock. In the classroom, more than half of the seats were empty, with more women than men attending.

"Can we go to home?" Azadeh asked.

"If you want," Marco said. "We'll all leave after the first class."

Outside, in Jaleh Square, horns were blaring; the engines of heavy trucks groaned, brakes squealed, and people could be heard shouting to each other. It wasn't close to ten o'clock yet, but Hassan came down the hallway ringing the bell to end the class.

"Go straight home," Marco advised the students. "If you stand around, it's going to look like you're part of the demonstration."

Teachers and students pushed their way together through the crowd outside the gate, but Jaleh Street was even more crowded. It didn't seem to be a demonstration so much as a crowd that had showed up to watch one—a gigantic *sholugh*. Trucks full of gendarmes now crept through the traffic with their horns moaning and gears whining. Trying not to look too much like an American, Marco put on his sunglasses, wishing he also had a hat. He started to head south but couldn't force his way through the crowd that was coming towards him. He was pushed back towards the university along with some other students who also had to give up the idea of making their way south on Jaleh Street. A moving wall of agitated people forced Marco in the opposite direction of Global Publishing.

To get out of the crowd, Marco and a group of students shoved their way into a double-decker bus a block up from the square. They climbed up to the top level and looked out the windows.

The street was packed with more people than vehicles now, but the bus driver seemed determined to continue on his route. He lurched the bus forward up to a wall of pedestrians, then screeched to a halt, scattering them. The bus lurched forward again, scattering others, then stopped dead again. The driver leaned on the horn and eased forward, tapping the rear bumper of a taxi and pushing it forward until it hit the van in front of it, then jerked to a halt again. It was impossible to stand up inside the bus.

"Say a prayer for Mohammad and his family!" a passenger yelled out. The whole bus answered the invocation in unison: "*Allāh homā saleh Allāh Mohammad va āleh Mohammad!*" Marco's friend Huff called this the "scare prayer" because Iranians chanted it on buses when they careened around cliff tops or had near misses with trucks coming the other way.

Before the bus could go a block, though, it was stalled completely. Out of the rear window Marco saw a formation of young men and women, some with scarves over their mouths, rushing out from behind a building with arms linked. Another loosely organized group forced their way into the square from across the street at the same time. Marco tried to hear what they were chanting. It sounded like "criminal Shah" and "America's dog." He tried to read the signs and placards they were carrying. Some said "Death to the Shah." Some said "Death to America." He sank down in his seat. A third group emerged from the *kucheh* between two buildings where Marco had seen people gathering earlier that morning. Mullahs in robes and turbans followed behind men carrying placards saying "America the Great Satan" and "Free the prisoners." They chanted in unison, "Down with Western decadence!"

By now the older people and children were standing with their backs against the shops and offices along the street. Young men and women completely occupied the street, weaving around the stalled taxis, trucks, cars, and buses. Most of them were shaking their fists in the air and shouting. Some had rolled up flyers in their hands. A few carried signs or banners held up by sticks on each end. A group of about ten or fifteen stopped behind the bus Marco was on and set fire to a poster of the Shah in his uniform.

Behind all these, still generally moving north, another group was carrying a makeshift facsimile of the American flag upside down. They were trying to burn this, too, but having a hard time setting it on fire.

"Don't worry, Mister," a student sitting next to Marco said. "We are safe on the bus."

Helmeted soldiers poured out of the personnel carriers that had been maneuvering into the street at Jaleh Square. They carried machine guns in one arm, aimed into the air with their fingers on the triggers, walking slowly along the edges of the demonstration—but not directly interfering. Heavy army trucks approached from the opposite direction with rifles sticking out the windows. Students who had made their way up the street were now running back down towards the square, some of them bent over as if to avoid being shot.

The soldiers on foot in the square seemed to be under different instructions from the soldiers coming down the street in trucks. They had been guarding against violence, keeping the demonstration confined to the street. But as soon as they saw the trucks approaching, they started firing their guns into the air. Students dropped their placards and ran. Others were trapped between the trucks and the foot soldiers. Some of these were arrested and dragged into the back of the trucks. Marco slid down even lower in his seat, peering over the window ledge.

Demonstrators and onlookers disappeared as fast as they had appeared. Vehicles caught in the street slowly started to move again, and a white ambulance with the imperial Iranian Lion and Sun insignia stopped near the bus Marco was on. As the bus pulled around the ambulance, Marco saw the medics putting the limp body of a woman on a stretcher.

The bus driver ignored his stops for the next five or six blocks until they were well above the demonstration scene. As soon as the bus stopped, Marco and most of the others got off. Marco looked around to get a sense of where he was. It was a good hour's walk from home. Amazingly the demonstration and blockade seemed to be over. He was still shaken as he started the long walk home.

Sniffing out decadence

Marco climbed the stairs to his apartment and found Moham-mad, the teenager from Hichja who had declared himself a mullah, sitting on the floor outside his door. He was dressed in a brown robe and dirty white turban. The ineptly tied turban was sliding down over one eye. He recognized Marco and stood up. "*Salaam,*" he said. "I've accepted Farhad's invitation to visit here. I'm sorry to be a bother to you in your house." He brought inside his bundle, tied with green cloth, along with some leaflets he had been carrying.

Marco served him some tea. On one of the leaflets, he noticed the slogan "Death to America."

"You're a little late for the coronation," Marco teased.

"I've come for a different reason." Mohammad looked around the table. Marco slid a bowl of sugar lumps towards him, and Mohammad put his hand over his heart. "I'm here to attend a kind of meeting."

"A meeting?"

"A meeting of the righteous. In the street." He picked up one of the leaflets. "Maybe you would be so kind as to help me. I don't know the city. This is the location."

"That's Jaleh Square!"

"You know it? This is good."

"There's no date. Do you mind if I look at the other leaflets? Hmm. No date on any of them."

"God will direct the believer."

"But I'm afraid you might be too late."

"It is never too late to submit to God's will."

"I mean, there was a . . . meeting . . . at Jaleh Square. It was this morning."

The reality was gradually forcing its way into Mohammad's brain. He reached up under his turban and scratched his head. "You know this?"

"Yes. I was there."

"At the meeting? God be praised!"

"No. I work near there. It was an anti-Shah demonstration. There were some mullahs there, following along behind the others. It's all over."

Mohammad slid both hands up under his turban to scratch. It unraveled onto the table. "All over?" he said. He sighed, rolling his turban into a ball.

"You must be hungry. How about an omelet and rice?"

"I couldn't trouble you. Maybe I should go back."

"All the way to Hichja? You have to stay a while. Farhad will be back soon."

"Are you sure it's all right? I mean, Farhad did say I could visit."

"Of course. We have plenty of room."

Mohammad sighed again.

"You must be disappointed. But there's a lot to see in Tehran. Tomorrow I could take you to Sepahsalar Mosque."

"*Ghorbān-e-shomā.*" I am your sacrifice.

"It has eight minarets. And a huge madreseh attached."

"I'd like to see the mosque." He fidgeted with his turban. "The madreseh? I don't know."

Marco knew that Mohammad had been dismissed from his hometown madreseh in Hichja. "The mosque, then. We'll just visit the mosque."

"Do you think I would meet anybody who was at the meeting?"

"We'd just be going to see the mosque. Not to meet anybody."

"What were they saying at the meeting? Were they denouncing the Shah's rule that mullahs have to have a degree in religious studies?"

"I didn't hear anything about that."

"They should. It's a ridiculous rule."

"Hmm."

"We know the word of the Prophet. That's all we need to know."

"Hmm."

"I mean, what *were* they saying?"

"I heard them chanting, 'Down with Western decadence!'"

Farhad walked in. "What? What? Oh, Mr. Mohammad." He hugged him and kissed him on the cheek.

"I'm sorry to be a burden to you," Mohammad said.

"Not at all," Farhad told him. "It sounds like you're here on a mission to wipe out Western decadence?"

"*Enshā'allāh.*"

"How do you like the French omelet I see Mr. Marco made for you?"

"Delicious. Thank you again, Mr. Marco."

"How about some barley water," Farhad suggested. This was the Farsi term for beer. He unwrapped a green bottle from a piece of newspaper and got three glasses.

"It's a bit bitter," Mohammad said. "Good, though," he added politely.

"Drink it down and we'll go for a *gardesh*. See what we can do about that Western decadence."

It was dark, but the streets of Tehran were well lit if a little emptier than usual. Marco recalled a *gardesh* he had taken with Farhad and two friends when he first moved into the city. Reza and Mahmud, high school friends from Hichja, stayed one night with them in the apartment. They were "unofficially on leave" from their Literacy Corps assignment in a remote village. Their eyes popped out at the short skirts and sleeveless blouses of the Tehran women. Reza had a hard time keeping his hands off them.

Marco and Farhad walked on either side of Mohammad, who had insisted on wearing his mullah outfit. They were getting more looks than the women. Mohammad seemed pleased.

Farhad asked him, "Do you find the women more beautiful here than in Hichja?" He stepped aside to let a young woman in a very short black leather skirt slip between him and Mohammad.

Mohammad didn't answer. "Could we get some more of that barley water?" he said.

"Better not," Farhad said. "It's not really good for you."

"Show me some Western decadence."

"It's everywhere you look."

Mohammad looked around. "Exactly what is decadence, anyway?"

"It's something in the air. Can you smell it?" Farhad lifted his chin and sniffed. "There. There it is."

Mohammad did the same. "I . . . I'm not sure." He stopped short and sniffed again, longer.

Some people bumped into them from behind and gave them a puzzled look.

"We're sniffing out decadence," Farhad explained.

Sightseeing

Early the next morning before class, Marco took Mohammad to see the huge 19th-century Sepahsalar mosque in the south of the city. They moved shoulder to shoulder with the crowd entering the enormous *musallā* or prayer hall, which could easily have contained the entire mosque of Hichja. Mohammad's eyes traced the steps of the *menbar* all the way up to the platform at the top where the mullah would stand to lead the prayers and preach under the elaborately carved wooden dome.

"I'll just go up there to do my preaching," Mohammad said.

"No. Shsh! Don't do that."

"I must. I'm called to preach. I smell the decadence even here."

"That's just dirty feet." Marco held him by the arm. A few people glanced sideways at them. It would be mortifying to cause a *sholugh* in a mosque.

An elderly mullah edged up to them. "Is something wrong," he said in a low voice. He looked at Marco. "This is a mosque where people come to pray."

"I'm going to preach," Mohammad declared.

"Your accent," the mullah said. "Are you new in Tehran? No one preaches here except the imam of the mosque."

Mohammad looked a little cowed.

"You're welcome to pray here," the mullah said.

A few men came up to see what was going on. "If there's any argument, it would be better to take it outside."

"Of course. There's no argument. We're just going," Marco said.

"This isn't right," Mohammad muttered. But he followed Marco out.

They turned a corner, and Marco breathed a sigh of relief. "My class starts in twenty minutes." He gave Mohammad some money for a taxi. "I have to leave you now."

"Leave me?"

"You could go to see the bazaar."

"Alone? Where is Farhad?"

"At work." He thought a minute. "Want to go see Farhad? It's all right, I guess." He hailed a taxi and gave the address of the Iran-America Society.

Marco got to the university a little late. "Bah-bah!" Dr. Zaban exclaimed when Marco walked into the teachers' room. "You are safe! Some of your students have been asking. We didn't know."

The hallway was buzzing with talk of the demonstration—what they saw, what they heard, who wasn't there for class. Some of Marco's students ran up to him.

"You are here!"

"We worry!"

"This is terrible thing! Some students they are not here."

"Tsk-tsk!"

"Do we have class today?"

Marco led them into the classroom. They were too excited to sit down at first. But when he said, "I need to call the roll," they shuffled quickly into their seats. Now everybody would find out for sure who was missing.

"*Alhamdulellāh!*" Ebrahim shouted out in joy when his name was called. Hallelujah! The class roared in laughter. Other than Sassan, no one in Marco's class was absent.

After class, in the teachers' room, Hassan caught Marco's eye and discreetly jerked his eyebrows up in the sign for *no*. No message.

As Marco was about to leave for the Global Publishing Company, Dr. Zaban stopped him. "Mr. Marco, this is very strange. We have received a message from the Iran-America Society. There has been . . . I don't know the English word for this. Do you know the word *sholugh*?"

Marco stifled a gasp and nodded.

"They would like for you to go there at once. They want you to—" He looked in his English dictionary. "*Vouch.* To vouch for someone."

Marco's taxi stopped behind an olive green Land Rover with tinted windows. Two armed guards standing by watched Marco go into the building.

"I'm looking for—"

"Everybody's busy." This had to be Jusef, the scatterbrained Armenian receptionist/registrar cum janitor that Farhad had often imitated. "Come back tomorrow."

An English class let out, and the Iranian students filed down the hallway. Farhad was talking to some of the women. "Ah, here he is. I have important business with Mr. Marco." Farhad took Marco into the empty classroom. "Did you send Mohammad here?"

"I didn't know what else to do with him."

"Great. He walked into the first classroom he saw. It was mine. He looked at the women. Blushed beet red. Then started preaching against lechery. The son of a whore was getting pretty worked up. Worse than you saw him in Hichja. One of the girls started crying. I told him to leave. He started lecturing me for promoting lechery. Some of the other teachers heard him and a bunch of us took him up to the main office. *Father-dog!* Then Mr. Richmond, the director, came in. Mohammad was still ranting on. He wouldn't shut up. The director called for help. Now there's a SAVAK guard in there and Mohammad's handcuffed to a chair."

"Oh, shit!"

"He said his American friend sent him here."

"Oh, shit!"

"I couldn't believe he even remembered your name. And he knew where you worked."

"Shit!"

"So anyway, come on. Let's go. We can't let them lock him up."

The director sat behind a huge desk in a rumpled herringbone sport jacket—obviously an American. He hung up the phone when he saw Farhad and Marco come in.

Farhad introduced Marco. " A professor at the University of Tehran."

Marco moved to shake Mr. Richmond's hand, but the director immediately broke out. "We've had a terrible shock. I assume you speak English? This man, this mullah, broke in here and I don't know what. Insulted the students. They say one of them was in tears. He frightened everyone. He says an American sent him here. Do you know him? Did you send him here?"

"Mr. Marco. It's me," Mohammad called out. The guard slapped his head and told him to shut up.

"I know Mohammad," Marco admitted. "He's staying with us for a few days. I guess Farhad told you. They're from the same hometown. He's our guest."

"This person is your guest? I can't understand that. Why would you let such a person in your house?" He glared at Marco a moment, then said, "How do I even know you're an American?"

Marco showed him his residence permit.

"I can't read that! Don't be absurd." He pointed to the guard. "Show it to him."

When the guard verified Marco's citizenship and place of work, Mr. Richmond said, "All right. Here's what we're going to do. This whole incident is a bad reflection on me and the organization. It shouldn't have happened. I want you to get this damned mullah out of here right now and make sure he never comes back. And you, what's your name? Farhad. If he ever shows up here again, you're out of a job, you understand?"

The guard took the handcuffs off Mohammad and said in Farsi, "Get the hell out of here and don't come back or you'll end up in prison for a long time."

Mohammad sulked and didn't say anything all the way back to the apartment. When they were there, he said, "I see now. I see what they mean. The government is our enemy. America is our enemy."

"Whatever," Farhad said. "But just promise me one thing. You'll never go back to the Iran-America Society again, all right? You can never go back there."

Mohammad sipped some tea, then smiled. "But I am welcome to go back whenever I want."

"Ridiculous. How can you say that?"

Mohammad reached under his robe and pulled out a card. "I'm a member. See? Mr. Yusef gave it to me. A very nice man."

Sholugh at the bazaar

Marco managed to slip out through the Faculty of Letters gate without talking to any of the students. He wanted to tell Mastaneh that Fatimeh had left—and find out what Farhad had told her that upset her. He'd been afraid to ask Farhad about it. But Mohammad was waiting for him on the sidewalk outside the gate.

"I'm your sacrifice, Mr. Marco. Farhad said you might take me to the Grand Bazaar."

"Now?"

Mohammad stared at him blankly. Clearly, Marco didn't have a choice. "All right. Let's go."

When they got to the bazaar, Marco said, "This is it. I wonder, could you look around here on your own? I need to take care of some business at a publishing company. I'll give you money to take a taxi back to our apartment when you've seen enough."

Mohammad looked down the endless, winding lanes and up at the huge tiled arches and domes. He reached out for Marco's arm. "You're not leaving me?"

"It's just that I have an important message I need to take to somebody."

"I beg you. Stay with me." He gripped Marco's arm like a vice. It seemed cruel to leave him.

Mohammad held on tightly as they entered the convoluted passageways of the crowded bazaar. Mounds of pomegranates, beets, melons, sunflower seeds—anything you could imagine eating—were followed by clocks, radios, mirrors, and tableware as they turned a corner, then by hanging carcasses of chickens, sheep, and goats in another lane, then by gold bracelets and necklaces, then by silver and brass trays, samovars, Persian miniature paintings, and carpets. They went down a passageway that led to the Jameh Mosque. Mohammad stopped at a display of amber prayer beads, *mohr* prayer stones, and paintings of Hossein Ali. He let go of Marco's arm. "*Allāh akbar!*" he cried out, startling the proprietor and the nearby shoppers. Now that he was suddenly the focus of attention, Mohammad was emboldened. He jumped up on a pile of carpets. "*Allāh akbar!*" he sang out, louder. People pushed forward to see what was going on. "I smell decadence!" Mohammad shouted. "I smell decadence!" The crowd grew.

Marco stepped back and watched from behind a huge pile of apricots. Two ragged laborers stopped beside their cartloads of figs, listening to Mohammad's rambling exortation. Shoppers in the connecting passageways approached, and merchants came out of their stores fingering their *tasbih*. The crowd was growing, pushing forward as Mohammad's harangue reached its pitch. "*Allāh akbar!*" some shouted, encouraging him. "*Alhamdulellāh!*" Someone yelled out, "Follow the path of God!" Another shouted, "Not the path of the West!"

All shopping in this corner of the bazaar had stopped, and some of the merchants began to get uneasy. "All right. All right," one said. "We understand. Good enough." Marco saw a well dressed rug merchant squeeze past the crowd and go out to the street. Another merchant said, "God is great! But now let's not block the corridor. We need to get back to business."

The rug merchant came back pushing his way through the crowd with two policemen in blue uniforms. The police, looking considerably less threatening than the gendarmes who had been called to handle Mohammad the previous day, took his arms and pulled him off the pile of carpets. "Come with us. This is a public disturbance." They took him out of the bazaar and onto the sidewalk.

"*Allāh akbar!*" someone yelled out. "We want to hear him speak."

"No we don't," another person yelled. But he was drowned out by most of the others shouting "*Allāh akbar!*"

Marco wanted to slip away. Instead, he was pushed forward by the crowd, which now surrounded Mohammad and the two policemen.

"They arrested two mullahs in the demonstration yesterday!" someone yelled. "What is this? What's going on? The government is turning against Islam!"

Mohammad shouted, "*Allāh akbar!*" over and over, pleased to have finally attracted some kind of following. Even the policemen looked nervous. One fumbled with a walkie-talkie, not able to get it to work.

Mohammad's eyes were flashing, and his voice grew more menacing. The crowd roared. It looked bad for the policemen—and maybe for Marco, too. He couldn't see any escape route. Luckily, the focus was on Mohammad, not him. He wished he had his hat and sunglasses. Mohammad was working up the crowd with his passionate outbursts. "He's speaking the word of Allah," someone shouted out. "You can see it in his eyes!"

The walkie-talkie squawked.

"Enough!" shouted the policeman holding it. He stood in front of Mohammad. "Stop talking and leave right now, or we'll call in the gendarmes."

"You better get going while you can," someone in the crowd yelled. The voice sounded familiar, but Marco couldn't place it. Just then Mohammad looked out, scanning the crowd. "Mr. Marco," he yelled, cupping his mouth with his hands. "There you are, Mr. Marco!"

The crowd turned towards Marco, and he realized he had no choice but to go forward. "Yes. Yes. Come with me, Mohammad. We'll go home now."

"What's going on?"

"Who's that?"

"How can he . . . ?"

"Is the mullah being taken away by some American?"

Marco stood trembling, not knowing what to do.

Mohammad grabbed one of Marco's hands and held their arms up in the air together. "Allāh akbar!" he yelled.

"What the hell?" somebody in the crowd shouted. There was a general mumbling.

"Stand back!" one of the policemen shouted at the crowd. He seemed about to use the walkie-talkie.

"Mr. Marco is my friend," Mohammad yelled towards the crowd.

"Is this true?" the other policeman asked Marco. "Can you get him out of here?" He shouted for a taxi. "Quick." He put them into the taxi while the other policeman held off the crowd.

Back at the apartment, Mohammad said, "But did you see them? They were opening themselves up to my words."

"Maybe some were. But you're going to get yourself into serious trouble in Tehran, believe me."

"No, I won't. In Hichja they say I cause trouble. Here they listen."

"Because here they don't know you yet. Mohammad, I hate to say this, but you're going to have to leave."

That evening Farhad agreed. "I'm glad you told the fool he has to go. You wouldn't believe all the questions they asked me at the USELESS. But he's a guest from my hometown, you know—I can't tell him to leave myself. It's not our custom." He blew a ring of smoke up towards the ceiling. "I'll take him to the bus station in the morning and buy him a ticket."

West-sickness

After class the next day, Marco tried again to get to Global Publishing, but Ebrahim took him aside. "I sink im-por-tant," he said.

"We can speak Farsi outside of class."

"You speak Farsi! *Jallāh hāleq!*" Wonder of God! "Mr. Marco, I saw you yesterday at the bazaar. Can we go somewhere and talk?"

He took Marco to a tea house in the bazaar district. All of the customers were men, mostly laborers in collarless shirts and threadbare suit coats, in some cases worn over pajamas. Some of them sat with their legs tucked under them on the chair seats.

"Yesterday, I saw you with a mullah at the bazaar," Ebrahim began. "He was stirring up the crowd."

"Oh, you were there?"

"In the crowd. I live near there. I was surprised you have a friend like that."

"I know what you mean. He's from my roommate's hometown. He was visiting."

"Ah, a roommate. Also a mullah?"

"No. He's nothing like Mohammad. And Mohammad's not really a mullah."

"He speaks with fire, but . . . ." Ebrahim screwed up his face. "Can you understand what he says?"

"Me? No. Maybe the parts about miniskirts and Satan and

being unclean. I never get the references to the Koran."

"Heh-heh, neither do I. When he tries to quote Arabic, I hate to tell you, but it's mostly gibberish."

Marco laughed.

"You know, Mr. Marco, my number is zero in English class, but in Arabic and philosophy, my number is very good, best in the class."

Marco nodded.

"Mr. Marco, this is what I wanted to warn you about. A couple of times your friend mentioned "my Society." If this is an Islamic society opposed to the government, it's not wise to mention a thing like that in public."

"Society? Oh. No, I'm sure it's not an anti-government society."

Ebrahim smiled. "And about 'decadence.' He seems to think it's something you can smell."

Marco coughed and took a sip of tea. He knew Ebrahim was opposed to Western influence in Iran. As Ebrahim put it in class when he was called on and couldn't answer the question, "I don't like West. I like East." This was one of the few things he had learned to say in English. Another was "Do you give me the number?" Will I get a passing grade? He said this ironically with a glimmer in his eye, knowing the answer was no—and the class always laughed. A fish out of water in the English class, he managed to keep his sense of humor. Azadeh and others suspected Ebrahim of being subversive, perhaps a member of a society like the ones he referred to, but everybody liked him. Marco was glad to have a chance to get to know him better.

"Mr. Mohammad says decadence comes from America. Although he doesn't seem to know where that is."

Marco laughed.

"Did you smell any decadence in America, Mr. Marco?" Ebrahim grinned, but his eyes looked serious.

"Oh, well, you know, when you're around a bad smell all the time, you stop noticing it."

"And you're here to get some fresh air?"

"More like just to have a look around."

"This is good. I wonder, do you know the word *gharbzādegi?*"

"I've heard it. My roommate listened to a speech on the radio once. By Jalal Al-Ahmad, he told me. I heard that word, but it was all too deep for me. I didn't understand it."

"*Gharbzādegi* means we're held down by assuming that the ways of the West are superior to ours. *West-sickness.* Mr. Al-Ahmad is a brilliant man. We need somebody who can bring his message to the people."

"Mr. Mohammad?"

"Akh!"

Boro bekheir

Farhad still hadn't heard from Fatimeh. "She never told me a thing before she left. *Pedar sokhteh!*"

"I'm sorry."

"Never mind. What do I need her for? I've got a fiancée."

"Why do you say that? Mastaneh isn't really your fiancée."

"I guess not. I don't know. Come on, let's go to my aunt's. Now that that *father-dog* Mohammad is gone."

"OK. What's that you're carrying?"

"Just something from a bakery."

Mastaneh wasn't in the room. "She's been acting funny lately," her mother said.

Farhad said he would cheer her up. "Mina, tell Mastaneh I have something she likes, would you?"

When she came in, eyes lowered, Mastaneh sat at a distance from both Farhad and Marco.

"I brought something," Farhad said. "I don't know if anybody here likes it." He opened his package on the table.

"Flan!" Mina said. "Mastaneh, flan!"

Mastaneh said, "Thank you, Farhad. We haven't seen you for some time. We thought something might be wrong."

"Oh, I've been a little busy. With work. Right, Marco? Busy with work."

"Right," Marco said. "And with that guest from Hichja."

"Guest? What guest?" Mina said. "Who was your guest?"

Mastaneh seemed to be examining her flan.

"It was Mohammad," Farhad told them.

"Mohammad from Hichja?" Maryam flipped her glasses up over her head.

"He's gone back now."

"*Māshā'allāh!*" his aunt said. God's will be done.

"Still," Mastaneh said, poking at her flan. "You must miss having a *guest* around."

Before Farhad could say anything, Maryam interrupted. Mastaneh had probably told her about Fatimeh staying with Farhad. "All right. Let's not talk about guests any more. Here's some good news. Papa's coming back." Maryam looked at her watch. "He should be here any minute."

When he came in, all three girls stood up and hugged him. Mina held on to his hand.

"Bah-bah!" he said. "Everybody's here." He brushed Farhad's cheek with his mustache, then Marco's. Maryam brought him some tea. "From Grandma and Grandpa in Hichja," he said, opening a bundle wrapped in a familiar-looking green cloth. There were dates, pistachios, even eggplants, and Marco noticed a small jar of green medicine.

"How are Grandma and Grandpa?" his wife asked.

"They're fine. And, Farhad, they say you've had a visitor here." His gold tooth gleamed when he smiled.

Farhad spilled some tea on a napkin, and Maryam tried to come to his rescue. She said, "Yes. Mohammad. We've just been talking about him."

"Oh, right. They say his head is in the clouds since he came back from Tehran. He's been to the big mosque, he says. He keeps talking about some secret society he joined."

"You let him join a secret society?" Mrs. Sufizadeh glared at Farhad. "That's what got Papa in trouble years ago!"

Mr. Sufizadeh, too, looked a little worried. "We can't tell if he joined a Marxist society, a nationalist society, some combination of one of these with an Islamic program of revolt, or what. It's not clear he himself knows what kind of society it is."

"It's not a secret society," Farhad told them. "It's the Iran-America Society. Where I work."

Mr. Sufizadeh burst out laughing. "What? Are you serious? Oh, this is good. Mr. Marco, I guess you can imagine, *Mr. Worthless* gave Mohammad some grief over this secret society he's in. Neither one of them could read the membership card he produced."

"*Alhamdulellāh*!" his aunt said.

Mastaneh sat poking at her flan. "Any other news from Hichja?" she asked.

"Big news!" Her father looked at Farhad. "Fatimeh's there alone, waiting for her husband to come and divorce her."

"Alone?" his aunt said. "What do you mean?"

Maryam said, "Divorce her?"

"She might have been expecting it. It seems she came to Tehran a while ago to try to find a job. By the way, Farhad, Fatimeh told Grandma she saw you when she was here."

"Oh, yes, that's right."

"You almost forgot, did you?" his aunt said in her high-pitched voice. "Devil!"

"I don't understand," Farhad said. "Where are Ziba and Fatimeh's mother?"

"Fatimeh won't say. She's afraid her husband will take Ziba away from her when he comes to divorce her."

"Poor dear," Mrs. Sufizadeh said.

"Here's the thing," Mr. Sufizadeh added, looking worried. "The husband's furious. He wants Ziba, and Fatimeh isn't going to tell him where she is. I hope there's not going to be any trouble."

Mina started crying. "No, no. I like little Ziba. He can't take her!"

"Fatimeh's there alone?" Farhad's hands were shaking. "Waiting to face an angry husband when he comes back?"

His uncle said, "Yes. He's driving in from Mashhad."

His aunt said, "So what are you going to do, Farhad?"

Farhad was rocking back and forth looking from his uncle to his aunt.

Maryam spoke up. "Everybody knows you like her."

They stared at Farhad, waiting for him to say something.

"Sorry to mention this, too, but you know they say Ziba looks just like you, Farhad," Maryam added.

Her mother exclaimed, "You can't let that man take Ziba away from her. What are you going to do, Farhad?"

"I don't know. I don't know." Farhad sat twisting his napkin. "I don't know."

Mastaneh's eyes were teary. She said, "It's no secret you love Fatimeh, Farhad. She's free now. Or will be soon. And she needs you."

"I can't believe you're saying this to me."

Farhad reached for a cigarette but didn't take it out of his pocket in his aunt's house. Marco had never seen him speechless before.

His uncle said, "I'll tell you what. I'm driving back to Hichja tomorrow. Farhad, you could come with me. If you want to, I mean."

Farhad looked at Mastaneh. She nodded once.

"Yes. Yes, I do."

In the courtyard, everybody hugged Farhad, but Mastaneh hugged him the longest. "*Boro bekheir, pesar,*" she told him. "*Mard beshi.*" On your way, kid. Become a man.

Bloody handkerchiefs

Farhad spread out a cloth on the floor and started pulling clothes off his bookcase shelf and throwing them on top of it. "You didn't say much."

"No. It seemed like a family thing."

He threw some books and a notebook on top of the clothes and tied up the bundle. He was packed. He lit a cigarette. "So. You think I should go?"

"Yes."

"You realize how hard this is for me?"

"I think so."

"I mean, I can't let that bastard take Ziba, that's for sure."

"No."

"I know Fatimeh must be scared."

"Yes."

"I mean, she needs me to be there."

"You don't have to convince me."

"I know it's simple for you. You just think we ought to get married and that's it. But to me it's not that simple."

"The purity thing?"

"And what people will say. Do you know what a wedding ceremony here is like, a traditional one? Everybody makes it their business to see if the bride is untouched. Sometimes they wait outside the bedroom, and the man passes out a bloody handkerchief. To show it's the bride's first time. I grew up assuming I would do that."

"I don't know. It sounds like some kind of business transaction. Like when you open up a package that was delivered to you and sign a receipt saying you received the goods undamaged."

"It *is* like that." He frowned so hard his black eyebrows met. "And you know what? There are a lot worse ways the goods could be damaged. All they look for is the one little thing any idiot can understand."

"I know."

"Because that's easier than looking at the whole person. They don't know what Fatimeh is like. I do."

"It's too bad you have to worry about all this."

"Yul, I worry about my parents thinking I deserve something 'better.' Worry about how my friends Reza and Mahmud will laugh at me. Worry about how even that idiot Mohammad will mouth off something about the need to shun adulterous women."

"Farhad, Fatimeh is a wonderful person. Your parents will change their minds once they know her better. And if your friends try to make you feel bad, it's going to be out of jealousy. They know how great she is. They're going to be jealous that you got her."

Farhad threw his arms around Marco. "That's exactly what I think. I can't believe you said that. You think that, too? *Screw 'em!* Is that right? Is that what you say?"

"Exactly."

Farhad went to Mastaneh's house the next morning and rode back to Hichja with her father.

Back to normal

Marco looked for Hassan in the courtyard before class.

"A message, sir!"

It said, *I would like to see you at Global Publishing today.*

Although there had been rumors after the demonstration that the university was going to be closed, it never was. The Shah's forces must have decided everything was under control. The only student at the Faculty of Letters who was missing was Sassan, who had disappeared before the demonstration. There was still no news of him.

Marco handed back the students' papers. "Mr. Ebrahim Ghobtoddin." He hadn't written anything at all. Instead, he had drawn two pictures, one of Marco holding a book with *ingilisi*, English, written on the cover, and the other of himself holding a book entitled *arabi*, Arabic. Both faces were quite true to life.

"Sorry," Marco said. "It's good, but—"

"What? What? Good? Mr. Ebrahim's paper is good? We want to see."

Ebrahim held up his drawing, beaming.

"*Alhamdulellāh!*" Davud called out. The class went wild, and Ebrahim took a few bows. Things were back to normal.

Marco rushed towards the gate immediately after class. Ebrahim and some other students were in the courtyard waiting to talk to him, but he put his hand on his chest Iranian style, bowed, and said, "Sorry. Something important to do."

Mastaneh and Mr. Ketabi were standing in the doorway of the shop.

"Welcome, welcome." Mr. Ketabi shook his hand and led him inside. "Come in. I have prepared some lunch."

Mastaneh shook his hand, too, rather demurely. Something was clearly bothering her. She said almost nothing through the lunch. Afterwards, Mr. Ketabi said, "Would the two of you mind watching the shop for a bit? I have to go buy some ink."

Mastaneh said, "But—"

"Some *more* ink." He slipped out the door.

Mastaneh was staring at the tie Marco was wearing, the one she had given him. He took her hand. She pulled it away. "Farhad told me. About the student in your class. He said you might marry her."

"What? That's ridiculous."

"You mean it's not true?"

"No."

"But why would he lie?"

"He wasn't exactly lying—more like imagining. Here's the thing." He used one of her father's favorite expressions.

"Akh! Marco, there's a thing?"

"I did get a letter from a student. Farhad saw it. She wanted a

201

visa to America. She said she had money and . . . she mentioned marriage. It was absurd."

"Absurd? But Farhad said you might do it."

"How could I even think of it?"

"That's what I wonder."

"Please believe me. I couldn't."

She stared down at the table, still with a deep sense of sadness in her face. And loss. Marco remembered her tears when she'd urged Farhad to go to Fatimeh. He said, "Is there something else wrong, Mastaneh? I know you're sad to lose Farhad."

"Yes, but he's still my cousin. I'll always have him."

"I gave him some money. I didn't have much."

"I'm sure my father will give him some."

"It all happened pretty fast."

"It didn't seem fast to me. He's been with her for years."

"I'll teach his afternoon classes while he's gone. He said if he doesn't come back in a week, tell them they need to hire somebody else."

"Mm."

She was wiping her eyes when they heard Mr. Ketabi's "Ahem!" at the door. "I hope you two have been able to settle your little misunderstanding," he said. "Everything back to normal?"

Marco wasn't sure.

The European Ice-cream Shop, revisited

Nobody knew when or if Farhad was coming back. Until he did, Marco had agreed to substitute-teach for him at the Iran-America Society. That meant most days he wouldn't be able to go to the Global Publishing Company. After his own classes, he had just enough time to eat a sandwich and get to Farhad's first class.

The students there were different from the university students. Their English was quite advanced. Some had American or British accents. The men had expensive-looking suits and wore bright, audacious ties and tinted glasses. The women wore heavy makeup and revealing blouses or sweaters. *Gharbzādegi?* West-sickness?

After class, he went to see Jusef, the receptionist who had given Mohammad the membership card. He told him Farhad would be away for a while.

"Don't worry," Jusef said. "I'll handle the phone while he's gone." The phone rang. Jusef looked at it and said, "Hello." He picked up the receiver. "Who? I don't know. Maybe he went home for Noruz."

"All right, then," Marco said. "It looks like everything is in good hands here."

He ate dinner alone for the first time in a while. He had the apartment to himself again now, but he didn't know if Mastaneh would ever come there again. He walked to the hall window. It was almost spring, almost the beginning of the new year in the Iranian calendar, and the snow was beginning to disappear from the peak of Mt. Damavand. He thought maybe he could make out a little bit left of a rosy glow on the top. He wasn't really sure.

He went out for a walk as the sun was setting and people were going home from work. It was a *gardesh*—he wasn't going anywhere in particular. Before long, he turned and started walking along the street that led to Mastaneh's *kucheh*. A bus whined past him and squealed to an abrupt stop at the corner ahead of him. Mastaneh's stop. She wasn't one of the people who got out. He looked down her *kucheh*. He'd never gone there uninvited yet. He turned, walked home, and went to bed.

"A message, sir." Hassan had found a corner in the corridor for delivering messages to Marco without anyone noticing. Marco gave him a toman. The message said: *I thought you might come yesterday. But I understand if you have somebody else now. Anyway, Mina says she has a toothache, so I'm leaving early to take her to the dentist's this afternoon. I won't be at work.*

Ebrahim was the first to approach Marco after class. He spoke in a low voice, in Farsi. "I don't know if you would be interested, Mr. Marco. There is a scholar in town, Mr. Shariati."

"My roommate has mentioned him."

"Perhaps you would like to go with me to hear his lecture."

"Thanks, Ebrahim. I'd go, but I can't understand formal lectures. I can talk to people in Farsi, but lectures are beyond me. How about this? You go and then explain the main idea to me afterwards."

"You mean I will be the teacher?"

"That's right."

Azadeh stopped beside them, and Ebrahim said goodbye.

"What is this, Mr. Marco? I don't think you should let Ebrahim teach you anything." Azadeh was serious.

"You don't? Sorry, Azadeh, I have to go."

"You have time for other student but not for me."

"I just have something to do. That's all." He didn't have to teach Farhad's class that day, and he wanted to try to get to the Global Publishing Company before Mastaneh left.

"I think you will cancel when you hear this." She made sure no one else was listening. "I have information about Sassan."

"What?"

"From my uncle."

"What is it?"

"I cannot tell you here."

"Is it good or bad?"

"I have paper to show you."

"All right. Quick. Come into the teachers' room. Dr. Zaban's probably still there. We'll give it to him."

"I did not bring with me to university."

"Why not? What is it?"

"My uncle said show you, then give back him."

"But you didn't bring it."

"We must meet private."

"Your uncle's office?"

"No. He does not want. Please, you go to home. I pick you up in taxi."

"Just tell me now. What's the information?"

"He is not good friend for you."

Other students were starting to notice Azadeh and Marco talking together. They didn't come up to join in, probably realizing it was a private conversation. "All right," Marco said. "Whatever you want."

A taxi beeped in the *kucheh* almost as soon as he got home. He got in.

"Where are we going?"

"I know a place." She gave a street address to the driver. When they got out, she was holding some papers in a binder.

"Where are we? No, not here." Marco stopped.

"It is European Ice-cream Shop. Very nice place."

"Somewhere else. Not here."

"You look very strange, Mr. Marco. Taxi is gone."

It was *gardesh* time, and the crowd had to swerve to avoid this couple standing in the middle of the sidewalk—Marco, an American, apparently arguing with an attractive Iranian girl in a low-cut blouse and very short skirt. Everybody slowed down to take a look. Marco heard a woman go "Tsk-tsk."

"All right. Let's go inside," he said.

They sat by the window. Azadeh put her binder on the table and studied the menu. "This is what I will have." She pointed to *nougat glacé.*

Marco said he would just have tea. "So. What do you want to show me?"

"Several things." She showed him a newspaper page. "Look here." It was a routine police report. "Can you read this name?" One name was underlined. Sassan Gharari-e-Mazandarani.

"Missing persons," Marco said. "I filed this report myself with the city police. We know he's missing, Azadeh."

The waiter made some room on the little black table to put her *nougat glacé* on a saucer beside the newspaper. Marco's tea was served Western style, in a cup with lemon and a little silver bowl of ground sugar with a spoon. Marco noticed people on the sidewalk glancing in from time to time as they walked by the window. Azadeh offered him a spoonful of *nougat.*

"No thanks. You said you had something else?"

"Can I finish this *nougat* first?"

"Let me look at what you brought while you're eating."

It was a copy of an official-looking report of some kind, hand written in very small script. Marco had a hard time reading it. He read out "National Police Headquarters."

"Shhh! Mr. Marco, not so loud."

"What am I looking for?"

She pointed with her *nougat* spoon to a heading on the document. "Reported to be Members of the Fedayan-e-Khalq." He looked down the long list of names. There was Sassan.

"Mmm. Good," Azadeh said. "You should try some of this, Mr. Marco."

"So probably the national police picked him up. Is that what you're saying?"

"Mmm."

"You could have just told me that. Isn't that what we all suspected? Now I know why, maybe, but does this help us find him?"

"Find him? I don't think we find him."

People continued to look in the window as they passed. The ice-cream shop floor was raised above the sidewalk so that the tables were at about eye level.

"Mr. Marco, I have one more thing I show you."

"What's this?"

She leaned towards him, unfolded a paper on the table, and, in a low voice, said, "From bank. See? My name. And see? Here." She pointed to a number of rials so large Marco couldn't even try to calculate it in dollars. It was obviously a whole lot.

"This is your bank statement?"

"Yes. I hope you will change your mind." When Marco looked up, he noticed two faces looking in the window. It was Mastaneh and Mina. They were probably on their way to his house after going to the dentist's.

Returning things

اگر چشم و دلم غیر تو بیند

در ان دم چشمها را کور خواهم

ببستم چشم خود از نور خورشید

که من ان چهره ی پر نور خواهم

—Rumi

Agar chashm o delam gheir-e-to binad
Dar ān dam chashmhā rā kur khāham.
Bebastam chashm-e-khod az nur-e-khorshid
Ke man ān chehreye por-e-nur khāham.

He rang at her gate—uninvited. Mastaneh's mother let him in. "Mr. Marco. Welcome. I thought it was Farhad. I thought maybe he came back."

"Who is it Maman? Is it Farhad?" He recognized Mastaneh's voice from another room.

"It's Mr. Marco."

"I'm not feeling well, Maman. I can't come in." After a moment, she said, "Does he have any news of Farhad?"

"Why don't you come in here and ask him yourself, dear?"

"I'm sick."

"Impolite! You're not that sick." She asked Marco if he knew what was wrong with her.

"Maybe if I could talk to her."

"I wish you would." She went to Mastaneh's room, and Marco couldn't hear what they were saying. When she came back, she told Marco, "All she will say is to tell you *congratulations*."

"You see, there's some mistake. There's nothing to congratulate me about. Would you please try again to get her to come out?"

Her mother came back again and said, "It's no use. I'm sorry, Mr. Marco. I think we'd better leave her alone."

"I understand."

In case she wouldn't talk to him, he had slipped a note into a book, a few lines from a Rumi ghazal that meant something like this, he figured:

> *If my eyes and heart see someone other than you,*
> *In that instant, let my eyes be blinded.*
> *Let me close my eyes to the light of the sun itself*
> *Since I want to see only your face full of light.*

"Would you just give her this book that she lent me, please?"

"This is not good," her mother said. "Returning things. What does it mean?"

"I'm not sure."

Ashura

He walked down Shah Reza Avenue remembering his first days living alone in Tehran. He passed the shop where Farhad had bought him sunglasses. The street was eerily empty and quiet. Many of the people on the sidewalk were standing still, looking towards the street. As he approached the Meikadeh Hafez, he saw Adarvan, the tavern keeper, standing outside in front of the closed door. He was looking towards the street with everybody else. He nodded gravely to Marco without speaking.

Marco soon heard a distant rattle of chains and rhythmic chanting that grew louder and more distinct as a formation of men made its way down the street. He stood beside other onlookers as the Ashura procession passed directly in front of him. Men of various ages dressed in white tunics and trousers marched by, lashing themselves in unison with glass-studded chains. Their breasts and backs were cut and bleeding through the white shirts. Some were shirtless, and the blood rolled down their naked bodies. They lashed themselves, first in the front, then in the back, to the rhythm of the chanted Ashura prayers, causing the chains to ring out cruelly in unison. Their voices were deep, gruff, and monotone, giving not the least sign of pain as they marched on looking straight ahead in a masochistic display of devotion to Mohammad's martyred grandson Hossein. "*Yā Hossein! ... Hossein-jān! ... Yā Hossein! ... Hossein-jān!*" The bystanders stood and watched, no one saying a word. When the long phalanx of bloody men had finally passed by, the onlookers slowly began to move on, blank expressions on their faces. A few looked at Marco, probably wondering what he thought of this, whether he understood it.

"It's a religious display," Adarvan told him. "Shia Muslim."

Marco skipped the beer and sandwich that night.

Noruz blues

He had to teach a few more days before the university closed for the Noruz New Year holiday so students could go home to visit their families. Everybody was asking him what his plans were. Would he travel? Ebrahim asked, "Will you go West or East?" In fact, Marco didn't want to go anywhere. All he wanted to do was get Mastaneh to talk to him again.

In the hallway outside the teachers' room, Hassan just looked at Marco and lifted his shoulders a little.

"I know," Marco said.

"I'm sorry, sir."

Azadeh stared down at her desk the whole class. She seemed to be absorbed in writing something. As soon as class was over, she rushed out of the building without a glance at Marco, her eyes averted. She had been insulted before leaving the ice-cream shop when he asked her not to mention marriage to him any more.

Several students gave him New Year's gifts—*gaz* tamarisk sweets from Esfahan, key rings with the seal of Iran, a bookmark with quotes from Hafez. He wondered if he'd be able to give a present to Mastaneh. Parvin gave him a Persian miniature in a *khātam* frame—"marquetry," as his dictionary said the English word was. It was obviously quite expensive. Everybody wanted to see it up close. "Is from Azadeh," Parvin said. "Not me." She added, "She buy *before*."

Lots of male students invited him to come to their hometowns for Noruz—everywhere from Ramsar on the Caspian Sea to Bandar Abbas on the Persian Gulf. He refused, wondering what it would be like to travel to places like that with Mastaneh. She had told him she'd like to travel to small towns all over the country and make sketches.

The Armenian receptionist at the Iran-America Society had news from Farhad, but Marco was having a hard time figuring out what it was.

"He called from Hichja with a message," Yusef shouted. "But it's only for a Mr. Magoo."

"Marco. That's me."

"Glad to meet you. Would you like a membership card?"

"No thanks. What was Farhad's message?"

"Who? He went home for Noruz."

Marco raised his voice. "Did you write the message down?"

Jusef rummaged in a desk drawer. "Message? Here. I wrote it down."

It looked to Marco like a series of lower case *m*s, *n*s, and *u*s. "This is in Armenian!"

"Yes."

"What. Does. It. Say? Please."

"It says, She isn't here."

"Oh. Anything else?"

"What's that?"

"Does it say anything else?"

"All right."

The next day, Farhad burst into the apartment, raced to his room, and threw back the red curtain. "*Pedar sokhteh!* Not here, either? Sorry. Did you get my message?"

"Fatimeh wasn't in Hichja?"

"Right. I jumped out of my uncle's truck and ran to her house. Nobody answers. The door is unlocked. I go in. The whole house is empty."

"Nobody knew what happened to her?"

"They say her husband got there the day before I did. They heard him yelling at Fatimeh in the house. They say he took her to the mullah, got a second witness, and divorced her."

"Nobody saw Fatimeh leave?"

"No. But the bus leaves at 4:30 in the morning, you know. I guess she could have taken it."

"And her husband wasn't there?"

Farhad clicked his tongue and raised his eyebrows *no*. "They say there was more yelling in the house after the divorce, and then he went around asking people where Ziba was, and somebody must have told him something because he suddenly got in his car and drove off."

Farhad started pacing back and forth. "So then I didn't wait to come back to Tehran with my uncle. I took a bus here and went straight to her cousin's house. But they haven't seen her." He stared at his cot. "I was sure she'd come here."

"Yeah."

He dropped his bundle on the floor. "She doesn't even know my plan. Maybe she won't want to get married. I never had a chance to ask her."

He was standing by the table, and Marco poured him a glass of tea. Marco asked, "Do you think she'd try to contact her uncle in London?"

"Maybe. I don't know. The letter from him was over a year old."

"All right, let's say she's in Tehran. Any way to check at the passport office? See if she's applied?"

"You have to bribe people just to get in there. No way they're going to give out any information. Anyway, I hope she hasn't applied for a passport yet. I wanted us to be on the same one. You know, as a family." He finally sat down at the table and lit a cigarette. "Looks like you got a letter."

"From an American friend, Huff. In Esfahan. He wants to come visit us for Noruz."

"Noruz. Right. I'm not really in the mood for it. Reza wants to come visit us for the holiday, too. Of course, I said he could stay. It's not a good time, though. He's coming to the big city for *safā*. R and R, I guess you guys call it. Trips to the House of Heaven, bringing women here, drinking—I'm done with that. I need to find Fatimeh."

"I was just at Mastaneh's—I mean, your aunt's house. They hadn't heard anything from Hichja."

"Naw. They get all their news from my uncle, and he won't be back for a few more days." He dropped his ashes into an empty green beer bottle. "You mean you went to my aunt's to see Mastaneh?"

"Yes. Because Mastaneh's upset. She thinks Azadeh and I are going to get married. Can you—"

"How do you know she thinks that? When did she tell you?"

"When you were gone."

"Oh?"

"She said that's what you told her." Marco didn't add that Mastaneh had seen him with Azadeh in the ice-cream shop.

212

"Yul, maybe I said that." He frowned. "So you met Mastaneh somewhere?"

"Yes. At the Global Publishing Company. And . . . ."

"What?"

"I've met her here a few times."

"And you never said anything? *Father-dog*! I don't get it. It doesn't seem like you."

"I was afraid you wouldn't like it. You know, because men aren't supposed to meet women."

"So you just didn't tell me? She's my cousin. She's like a sister to me. More. What are you saying?"

"Farhad, I love Mastaneh. I can't help it."

"What! I don't believe I'm hearing this. Can't help what? *Kesāfat*! Filth. I have to think." He rushed out of the apartment slamming the door behind him.

Different laws

Farhad hadn't come back to the apartment since he had stormed out, but Marco knew he would have to come back sometime. His friend Reza might arrive any day. Marco walked to the Iran-America Society.

"Who?" Jusef said.

"Never mind." Marco could see for himself that Farhad wasn't in the classroom.

Was he at Mastaneh's house? He wasn't sure he was welcome there any longer. But he got on the bus. What did he have to lose?

Little Mina stood on a stool to let him in. No one else was in the courtyard. He picked her up and hugged her. "How are you, sweetheart? Does your tooth still hurt? I miss you."

Mina hugged him back.

Inside, the house seemed to be in complete confusion. They hardly noticed Marco had come in. Mastaneh's father was back.

They were talking about Shiraz, about Fatimeh, about her mother and Ziba. Marco didn't see Mastaneh.

Her mother said, "I'm sorry. Things are confused right now, Mr. Marco."

Farhad was there, too. He was talking to Mastaneh's father. "So how did you find out they were in Shiraz?"

"Since the bus stops first in Shiraz, I made a phone call to the station there. At first, they wouldn't tell me anything, but I told them I was *Mr. Worthless* and it was information that SAVAK needed. I found out an older woman and a little girl came to meet a young woman who got off the bus with a green bundle and they took a taxi together to the Zand Guest House. So I drove right to the Zand Guest House. There they were."

"You didn't bring them here?"

"Farhad-*jun*, I can't tell you where they are now. Just in case anybody comes asking questions. They're safe. She'll contact you."

Mrs. Sufizadeh said, "Maryam, dear, pour Mr. Marco some tea. He'll think we don't know how to receive guests."

"He probably came to see his *friend*, Mastaneh," Farhad said.

His aunt didn't get the sarcasm. "Oh, I'm sorry. She's sick. She's staying in her room."

Farhad didn't get up to go to work the next day. The red curtain to his room was drawn, and mournful strains of poetry about love and longing and fate streamed out from the radio. He'd only said a few words to Marco since he came back.

The door buzzer rang. It was Fatimeh, in a chador. "Mr. Marco!" She grabbed his hand. "Farhad. Is he here?"

Farhad came out. "Where have you been? Let me see you. Come here."

"Farhad! I don't know what to do."

Marco left them alone and went into his room, but they stood where they were by the doorway. There was no talking for a few minutes, but then he heard Farhad say, "Ziba. Is she all right? Your mother?"

"They're safe."

"Where are they?"

"In Tehran. It's better if you don't know where."

"Don't worry. I'll take care of you."

"What do you mean? How can you?"

"You're divorced, right?"

"Yes. The mullah gave me the paper."

"We could get married."

"What? You'd marry me? How could you? I'm . . . ."

There was another silence for a few moments. Then Marco heard Fatimeh say, "But even if we were married. He would still take Ziba from me."

"Not if we went to London. They have different laws there."

"You mean go live with my uncle? My mother wrote to him, but now he doesn't know where we are."

"Let's get married first, then worry about the rest."

After another silence, he her heard Fatimeh say, "I promise I'll make you happy."

"Tomorrow."

"Silly! You can't just go get married in a day."

"No? How about this? Meet me tomorrow at the *Ham-bur-ger* shop on Takht-e-Jamshid Street. There's a telephone outside. Eight o'clock. We'll call your uncle."

"*Ham-bur-ger?*"

"Right. Then we'll go register or whatever so we can get married."

"Hm-huh! Marry me now."

Marco heard them go into Farhad's room. He went out for a walk, giving them plenty of time.

When he got back, after dark, he heard loud music and laughter before he got to the top of the stairs. Fatimeh was gone, but Reza and Huff were there with Farhad.

R and R

Farhad was glassy-eyed. He had been drinking. "There he is, gentlemen. The American Majnun, my 'friend,' Mr. Marco."

Reza was in the army uniform worn by the *Sepah-e-Danesh*, the Literacy Corps, an alternative military service that sent men to remote villages to teach reading and writing. He was short, with a receding hairline, and spoke slowly and clearly—so the foreigners could understand his Farsi. "Glad to meet you, Mr. Marco. Uh, I didn't catch your last name." He winked at Farhad.

"Just call me Marco, if you don't mind."

Huff spoke only English. If anybody didn't understand, that was their problem. "Hope you don't mind me just dropping in, Mister, uh, *Marco*. The University of Esfahan's been closed for a month. A bunch of students were arrested for something—not much more than a food-fight in the cafeteria. They haven't been heard from since. My bar bill at the Qajar Palace is so high I can't go back there for a while."

Speaking loud and slow, Reza offered Marco some liquor in a clear bottle they'd all been drinking from. "I made it myself on the roof in Kuchak, where I'm stationed. It's the best alcohol in town. He-he. The only alcohol in town."

Marco sipped a little of the cherry araq. "It's good."

"*Bezan bālā!*" Reza told him. Drink it down. "Now that we're all here," he said, "I wonder if our hosts can introduce us to some ladies."

Farhad said, "Yes, Marco, would you take them to the House of Heaven. I'm not feeling up to it myself." He put his hand on his forehead.

"Drink some more of this," Reza suggested. "It'll clear your head."

"I'll have some more," Huff said. "I don't suppose there's any Johnnie Walker?"

Reza pulled out a *vāfur* opium pipe from his sack. "In Tehran it's alcohol. In the desert villages, it's *taryāk*." Opium.

"Goddam!" Huff said.

Marco didn't want to go to the House of Heaven and encouraged the opium distraction. So did Farhad. They sat on his carpet and Reza showed them how to put a ball of opium on the pipe bowl and hold a piece of charcoal next to it to heat it. *"Fut ... fut ... fut ... bezan!"* he said as they blew, blew, blew, then inhaled. After a few rounds, there wasn't much talking.

"Can you turn down that damn radio?" Huff said. "Goddam mournful yodeling."

Reza leaned back against the wall and seemed to be nodding off. Marco said, "You guys must be tired from your trip. How about we postpone the House of Heaven?"

"What?" Reza said. "What did you say?" He roused himself a bit. "I want to change out of this uniform. Mind if I use your shower?"

"I'll go after him," Huff said. "Damn nice not to have to go out to a public bath. You're leading a life of luxury here."

Marco lit the kerosene water heater. "Don't forget to turn it off when you're finished," he said.

Farhad lay back on the carpet. "One of you guys can take my cot. I'm going to sleep right . . . ." He was gone.

Reza came out of the shower in his pajamas, apparently ready for bed. He seemed to have forgotten about the House of Heaven. "Nice hot water!" he said. "I'm a little sleepy."

While Huff went to take a shower, Marco pulled the mattress off his bed onto the floor for him to use, and he dropped down on the box spring himself, still wearing his clothes. He fell asleep instantly, dreaming of snow and mountains and glowing sunsets.

Thermostat problem

Marco woke up to the smell of steam, then a tremendous ear-piercing shriek and boom. He felt himself lifted from the floor—and then all went blank.

He came to consciousness with a gasp under a white dusting of plaster. It was dark, and his head hurt. He heard people's voices. "Here's one!" somebody yelled. Two men wiped off his face and checked for a pulse. "Alive!" He felt hands and arms under him as they carried him outside and put him down in the garden. The men ran back inside the apartment building. Marco managed to turn his head and watch.

The water heater had exploded, he found out later. One whole wall of the four-apartment building had crumbled and fallen away, leaving the building open on that side like a doll house. The neighbors carried Farhad out of the ruins in a blanket, then Huff, then Reza—all of them covered in white dust. Marco saw a group of neighbors looking up at the flat roof of the adjacent building. There was a body from one of the other apartments up there with one leg dangling over the edge of the roof.

"Ali's going to get him," someone yelled. A neighbor put a plank from the roof of one building across the space between the buildings and crawled over to get the dangling body. He dragged him back across the plank to the safety of the flat roof next door. Marco saw the rescued man sit up, holding his leg.

Everybody they found was carried to the same spot. Marco's head was ringing. Huff had some blood on his forehead. Farhad and Reza didn't look wounded but acted too stunned to talk.

A siren blared out and lights flashed as an army paddy wagon followed by an army ambulance squeezed slowly down the narrow *kucheh*. The paddy wagon doors opened and four gendarmes rushed out. "Who was in there? Where are they?"

"These are alive," the neighbors said. "They're bringing another down from the roof with a hurt leg. He was in the top apartment."

"We don't know how many were in there."

"We heard the bottom two apartments were empty."

"There were foreigners in one of them."

The gendarme who seemed to be in charge said, "Arrest them all."

"What have we done?" Reza said. "What have we done?" There was no answer.

His ears still ringing, Marco was loaded into the paddy wagon with all the others. He was happy to hear Farhad start cursing as the vehicle jolted through the streets. Huff was starting to look more alert, too. It was amazing, but none of them seemed seriously hurt. The wall that had fallen away was the farthest from where they were sleeping.

The Tehran jail was not much more than a holding pen. Without being questioned, without any paperwork, they were put into a large dark room with a metal door. There was one small window with bars across it facing outside, but it was still dark out there. There weren't any chairs or benches or anything else in the room. Gradually their eyes became accustomed to the dark, and they realized there were other people in there with them. Some were sitting or lying on the concrete floor.

As daylight began to come through the little window, the prisoners on the floor started to stretch and sit up. They looked at each other, blinking. Soon everybody could see everybody else. A couple of them realized they knew each other.

"What're you in for, Hossein?"

"Driving a taxi without a license. You too?"

"Yeah."

One woman asked another, "What are you in for?"

"Walking unescorted." This meant prostitution. She indicated some other women in chadors crouching against the wall. "Same for all of us."

Marco blinked, trying to focus on one of the women sitting against the wall. He couldn't believe it. She was wearing his college jacket from the missing baggage. He recognized the Jesuit college name and logo.

Huff rubbed grit out of his eyes and mumbled to Marco, "What're you looking at?" Then he saw the jacket. "Is that . . . ? Goddam!"

"Shh! Don't say anything."

"You're not going to go to the police to claim it, huh?"

Then, among the women Marco noticed a face that seemed familiar. It was Fereshteye-Do-Hezari, the Two-bit Angel. She recognized him, too, and secretly gave a barely perceptible nod.

Suddenly the metal door opened and another person was shoved into the room. This man was dressed neatly in a suit and was fingering a string of amber *tasbih*.

"What are *you* in for?" somebody asked the man right away.

The man squinted, his eyes not accustomed to the low light in the room yet. "I'll tell you what I'm in for. I owned an apartment building, and I rented an apartment to an American, and they blew the whole place up. That's what I'm here for. That's all I know." He fingered his *tasbih* in rage.

It was Haji, Marco's landlord. Marco and Farhad were covered with so much dust he didn't recognize them.

"Blew it up?" a taxi driver said. Some of the women said, "Tsk-tsk."

"Honest to God?" another driver said. Marco and his friends kept quiet. Haji said the police suspected people in the apartment building were making a bomb to use against the Shah, and it accidentally exploded. He said the police had asked him lots of questions about bombs and who he had rented the building to.

Haji finally recognized Farhad. "You! You're the one who blew up my apartment."

Marco couldn't keep quiet. He said, "Haji, we warned you it was dangerous not to fix the thermostat."

"*Father-dog*! You're the American, aren't you? You come over here and blow up people's houses. I'll make sure they put you in jail for this."

A few of the prisoners tittered nervously at this threat, but then one of them said, "Why are we in here with these criminals?" Others joined in. "Let me out of here." "Stay away from us with your bombs."

There was a loud banging on the metal door, and four gendarmes stormed in with batons, swinging randomly. Everybody fell to the floor putting their hands over their heads. Marco got hit lightly on the shoulder by a glancing blow. "All right. All right," one gendarme said. "The rule in this prison is absolute silence. The next person who says one word will be punished severely."

When the gendarmes all left, the prisoners gradually pushed themselves up, kneeling in place like people getting ready to pray in a mosque where nobody knows which direction Mecca is. Absolute silence definitely prevailed.

Suddenly a loud "Psst!" came through the barred window. Everybody looked up, startled. "Psst!" they heard again.

Haji went to the window. It was somebody he knew. Haji took a huge wad of money out of his pocket, then turned to Marco and his friends. "Now we're all civilized Muslims, here, aren't we? Nobody here would slander anyone, would they? Nobody would file a false lawsuit—for example, for negligence, would they?"

Farhad said, "No, sir. No lawsuit."

Reza said, "We are your sacrifice, sir."

There was a general murmur from the other prisoners. "No" "We know nothing about negligence." "I swear to God!"

Haji passed the wad of money out the window.

In only a few moments, the metal door opened once again. Instantly, everybody was down on the floor covering up their heads. "All right. All right. One by one, up on your feet. Put your hands behind your head and walk single file through the door." The gendarme clanged against the door with his baton. Some of the prisoners looked towards Haji as if suggesting that he go first. "*Mother-whores!* This is no time for *ta'ārof*," the gendarme yelled. "One by one. Get out. The nearest to the door goes first."

And that was it. They were all "bailed out," including the taxi drivers and prostitutes.

As they passed through the police office, Marco heard a sergeant say they had already determined it wasn't a bomb but an explosion caused by excessive steam pressure in the pipes.

It was well past noon when they were back out on the street.

III

On the street

"**W**ell, well, well."

Marco and Huff stood—covered in plaster—in front of Boggs's desk at the International Teachers Association office on Takht-e-Jamshid Street.

"You guys aren't looking too dapper, I have to say."

Huff gave him a shit-eating grin. "And you thought teaching at a university was a cushy assignment."

"My, my. What are we going to do with you guys? Conspiracy to bomb the Shah is a serious charge." Boggs chuckled. He seemed pleased with the turn of events.

Marco pointed out that the charge had already been dropped. "They say our water heater exploded, and the surge of steam made the other three water heaters in the building explode."

"Yes, yes. Oh, I heard. I heard details from some of the neighbors, too. Apparently, there have been people, including women, going in and out of your apartment."

Huff said, "I see. All right, then. I'll be getting back to Esfahan. Demands of the job, you know."

"Really? The university's been closed for over a month. What have you been doing with yourself?"

"Oh, talking to the local people, you know. Spreading American ideas. They didn't manage to save any of our stuff, did they?" Huff was still in a T-shirt and pajamas.

Boggs told them there was a pile they could look through in the storage room downstairs. "And what about you, Mr. 'Marco,' as you're apparently called. You still look a little stunned."

"I—"

"To the Hotel Caspian. For the time being."

"But maybe I could go—"

"What? Take a blanket and go live on the streets in south Tehran? You look like you'd fit right in."

"No. I mean. Never mind. I'll go to the hotel. Until I can find somewhere else to stay."

Huff found his suit in the pile of remnants the neighbors had gathered up—stained but wearable. They found Reza's uniform.

"I'll give it to him," Marco said.

Huff kept rummaging. "What the hell are these?"

"My pajamas!"

Marco looked for the tie Mastaneh had given him. He found it, but it was stained by water. He found only one of her drawings, the snow scene. But his vinyl briefcase had been salvaged, and zippered inside it were his school papers, *The Golden Road to English Literature*, and his other class books.

Huff pulled a picture frame from a drenched blanket. "Too bad. This is all smashed up." It was the miniature Azadeh had given Marco.

It had been a strained parting with Farhad when they left the jail. Farhad said he was going to his aunt's house and Reza could stay there until he went back to Kuchak. "Guess you guys'll go to a hotel, right?"

Reza shook Marco's hand and said, "Thank you for your hospitality. It will never be forgotten."

Marco took Farhad aside. "I heard you tell Fatimeh you'd meet her early this morning. You don't think she's still waiting for you?"

"How did you know that?" Farhad held his head as if he might still be feeling the effect of the explosion.

"You know. You were standing right by my door talking to her."

"Ah."

"Maybe you don't want Reza to know anything about Fatimeh yet. I'm going to the Association office. We'll go by the *Ham-bur-ger*. If she's still waiting there—probably not, but if she is—I'll try to arrange another place for you to meet."

"You will? OK. But what about Huff? OK. I guess he won't

understand a word you're saying."

"He won't."

"All right. Thanks. Thanks. I'm still thinking about you and Mastaneh."

"I love her. I hope you can accept that."

"I don't know."

"Could you do me a favor?"

Farhad squeezed his head with his hands. "What?"

"Tell Mastaneh I'm not hurt."

He nodded.

"And would you tell her you're sure there's nothing between me and that university girl, Azadeh."

"I don't know. I don't know. I have to get some sleep. If you see Fatimeh, tell her I'm at my aunt's house."

But, as expected, it had been too late, and Fatimeh wasn't at the *Ham-bur-ger* when Marco and Huff passed by.

Over the wall

Huff and Marco carried what they could to the Caspian Hotel and dumped it all on the floor of Marco's room. Huff took a shower and put on his slightly discolored suit. "Great visit," he said. "Hate to leave. But there's a bus this afternoon. I really should catch it."

When Huff was gone, Marco lay down on the bed and stared at the white fan whirring in the middle of the ceiling. He fell into a deep sleep. When he woke up, it was dark and his head ached. It took a while before he realized where he was. The room was bare, with a small heap of clothes and books on the floor. He sat up, and the walls seemed to be spinning.

He felt a little stronger after he took a cold shower. He picked up his trousers from the pile on the floor. Amazingly his wallet, with the money still in it, was in the pocket. His suit was rumpled and covered with white dust. He shook it out. His head pounded when he bent over to put his shoes on. It was only nine o'clock. Lots of families were just starting their dinners this late.

Shah Reza Avenue was bustling with *gardeshers* when he left the hotel. He wasn't hungry, but he thought he should eat something and turned in to the Meikadeh Hafez.

Adarvan said, "We've been talking about an accident they announced on the radio. Have you heard about it? They said there was a foreigner involved. It was somewhere near here."

"Yes. I heard. On the radio."

"They say it was caused by steam in the pipes, but some people think it might have been a bomb."

"I guess the police checked pretty carefully."

"Yes. But they might be hiding the truth for some reason. They didn't say what nationality the foreigner was."

"Not American, I'm sure."

Adarvan laughed.

"Probably one of Saddam Hossein's supporters," a customer said. A few others agreed. "He wants to keep the Shah from taking control of our half of the Shatt ol-Arab river."

Marco nodded, eager to deflect attention away from himself. He ordered a cognac and drank it down in one gulp, Iranian style. Then he had another. He was tipsy when walked out onto the street.

He took a taxi to the end of Mastaneh's *kucheh*, where he got out and walked down the dark alley towards her gate. Two dogs appeared in front of him, their eyes glowing in the single street light at the end of the alley. He kept moving, talking calmly as he passed between them. He stood in front of Mastaneh's gate with his hand on the warm wrought iron, without any plan at all, wondering what he was doing there.

Could he possibly ring the buzzer for someone in Mastaneh's apartment to open the gate? Of course not. Farhad was there, and Reza. Arriving alone at night and asking to talk to Mastaneh would make him a madman or worse in the whole family's eyes. A

Majnun, as Farhad called him.

Peering through the gate, he tried to see across the garden and into the first-floor windows of Mastaneh's apartment. There were some shadows made by people moving, but that was all.

The gate wasn't much higher than Marco's head. He stepped on the hinge, stood up, and scrambled up onto the top of the wall. A dog barked, and Marco lay flat on his stomach on the top edge of the wall for a moment, then pivoted and dropped down into the garden. He sneaked towards the lighted window and stood in the dark, looking in. He could see people only when they stood up. He saw Mastaneh's mother get up, cross the room, and disappear. Then he saw Mastaneh. She was standing, holding a white cloth on someone's forehead—possibly Farhad's. Marco took another step towards the window with the vague idea of signaling to her—a pitiful Porphyro shut out from the life of his beloved Madeline.

But as he stood looking at her in profile, he was struck by the innocence of the domestic scene inside. He shuddered with guilt at his violation of this family's trust, and he sank to a squatting position, now in a panic that anybody would see him. Creeping back towards the gate like a thief, he quietly opened the latch and raced down the alley to the street, the dogs barking after him. He raced all the way back to the hotel, his head aching with each step. When he lay down on the bed, the pounding of his heart was so loud in his ears it drowned out the whir of the ceiling fan.

The pink purse

Marco went to look for Farhad at the Iran-America Society, bypassing Jusef and going straight to Farhad's classroom before any students came in.

"You look like shit," Farhad said. "I guess Fatimeh wasn't still waiting there by the *Ham-bur-ger*?"

"No. So how are you going to find her? Does she know where

your uncle's house is?"

"No. And my uncle still won't tell me where she is. He says he'll contact her."

"You think she heard about the explosion?"

"Maybe. It's on the radio. Maybe she thinks I'm dead or something."

"I guess you told Mastaneh I'm all right?"

"Yul. I told them all."

"I'm at the Hotel Caspian. Want to come to the Association storage room and look through the stuff they saved from the explosion? Reza's uniform's there."

They looked at the pile on the floor. Their short-wave radio was cracked open. Farhad picked out some of his books that weren't torn or soaked. He kicked the pile with his foot, then kneeled and picked up a dirty lump of cloth stuck on a sheet. "Oh, this is depressing."

"What's that?"

"It's Fatimeh's little purse. It used to be pink. She must have left it behind the last time we . . . . You can hardly tell what it is any more." For the first time ever, Marco noticed Farhad's eyes tearing up.

"Look inside it," Marco said.

There were a few coins, a lipstick, and a couple of folded pieces of paper. "Oh my God," Farhad said. "These are guest house receipts. Zand Guest House, Shiraz, and, look! Mosafer Guest House, Tehran. She's probably there waiting. Maybe she thinks I changed my mind. I'm going." He ran out and flagged down a taxi.

Marco walked down towards where his apartment used to be. It was almost the beginning of Noruz, the Iranian New Year, and the streets were packed with people shopping for Noruz presents. He stopped near some women admiring silk scarves. He picked out one with a traditional Iranian *boteh* or paisley design and bought it for Mastaneh.

230

When he reached Kucheh-e-Hamin'oddoleh, it was blocked off, and workers were carting away shattered hunks of cement. Neighbors had to walk on boards in some places to get to their own houses. One whole side of the building he had lived in had crumbled away.

A room without a view

He knocked at the door of the Global Publishing Company.

"Mr. Marco! Thanks to God." Mr. Ketabi hugged him. "But are you hurt? I shouldn't touch you. Merciful God! I have heard the story on the radio. And I have also heard it from Mastaneh. She said nobody was seriously hurt."

"Mastaneh was here?"

"To ask about you." He set a cushion for Marco by the table but didn't sit down himself. He said he needed to send someone a message, wrote something on a slip of paper, then quickly ducked out of the shop. Marco saw him give the paper and some money to a man sitting on the sidewalk next to a cloth spread with limes. The man covered up his limes and started up the street.

"But I'm afraid Mastaneh told me she's quitting this job," Mr. Ketabi told Marco when he came back.

"Quitting?"

"I have a feeling she did not tell me everything." Mr. Ketabi took off his glasses, wiped them on his necktie, put them back on, and blinked. "But, please, you must have some tea. Where are you living, Mr. Marco?"

"In a hotel, for now."

"No. This is not good. Mr. Marco, you must come to live with me. There is a room upstairs in the back. Please, come with me to look at it. It is not worthy of you, but perhaps until you find a better place. There are no windows. And I'm afraid the small shower has no hot water—but perhaps this will be acceptable to you. Khakh-khakh-khakh."

"You can't imagine how much I appreciate this," Mr. Ketabi. I hope it's not going to be a problem. I don't know if you're aware, but there's been some trouble between me and Mastaneh."

"Mr. Marco, no matter. It will please me to have you here with me."

This was just what Marco had been hoping. After some effort, he finally got Mr. Ketabi to agree to accept rent for the room. Mr. Ketabi gave him a key to the Global Publishing Company, and Marco looked at it in the palm of his hand—the key to the place where Mastaneh worked, where she had helped him with his handwriting, where—

From below, the cry of "*Yā'allāh*," rang out. The lime-seller called up to Mr. Ketabi, "She says she can't come," and Marco realized the message must be from Mastaneh.

"Come downstairs," Mr. Ketabi said. "Perhaps another cup of tea, and we can talk."

A warm sunset glow found its way into the production room. They sipped tea in silence. As Marco stretched his legs out under the table, he was hit by the memory of his first days sitting here with Mastaneh.

Finally, Mr. Ketabi said, "So. She can't come now. You heard that. I'm sorry, Mr. Marco. I can see that you are *nārāhat*."

Marco was definitely *uneasy*. He kept silent for a minute. Then he told Mr. Ketabi, "It's not just Mastaneh. Farhad's my best friend, but I never could tell him anything about me and Mastaneh. Finally, I told him I love her. It was just before the explosion. He called me *kesāfat*." Filth.

Mr. Ketabi sat back, shocked. "Your best friend called you this?"

The Red and the Black

در حقیقت چو جمله یک بودست

پس همه بودها نبود بود

—Attar

Dar haghighat chu jomleh yek budast
Pas hameh budhā nabud bud.

Marco moved into the second-floor room of the Global Publishing Company before classes resumed at the university. He dumped the little pile of clothes and books on the carpet. Some of his books were water damaged, but they were all there. He hung Mastaneh's snow scene sketch on the wall. *Like what we did was just a dream,* she had said when she finished it.

When the university re-opened after Noruz, the students were excited, telling each other where they had gone, what they had done. Azadeh still acted as if he had insulted her. Maybe it was for the best, he thought. He wondered if she had heard the report of the explosion on the news—some people were still talking about it. He liked Azadeh but was pleased that she no longer knew where he lived.

He could go *home* now to the Global Publishing Company although Mastaneh wouldn't be there. After class, Marco walked out of the university gate without any idea where he was going. When Ebrahim asked him to go to the tea house with him, he quickly agreed.

They walked south from the university into the poorer section of town where the privileged class of students would seldom venture, where no one knew him. He felt relieved. It was lunch time. Men were sitting on the sidewalk with their legs crossed and backs up against the buildings eating *āb gusht* or green *āsh*, spinach stew, from metal bowls. Delivery men carried glasses of tea or stacks of flat bread to nearby shops on trays held in one arm or balanced on white cloths coiled on top of their heads.

Ebrahim took him to the same tea shop they had gone to before. Two old men at the table next to them were engrossed in a game of backgammon, clacking down wooden pieces on the board. Men sat smoking, with little cups of Turkish coffee on their tables, some in pairs, some alone. The waiter brought Ebrahim and Marco tea in a pot that had been cracked into countless pieces and repaired with strips of metal that Marco hoped wasn't lead.

"I don't know if this is a place where you feel comfortable," Ebrahim said.

"I feel quite relaxed here."

"You can take off your shoes if you want."

Marco did.

"We have *kuku sabzi*," the waiter told them. It was a kind of herb frittata often served for Noruz.

Ebrahim gave him a New Year's present—a book of sufi poems by Attar.

"*Dast-e-shomā dard nakoneh*," Marco said, surprising him. May your hand not hurt.

"It's not much, but I thought you might like it. I know you got some nice presents from the other students. By the way, Azadeh said you went to the Planning Organization with her. That must have been interesting."

"Yes."

"I've never been inside."

"It's very modern. I guess you'd call it a den of Western ideas."

Ebrahim chuckled. "I certainly would never say that."

"So, how was that lecture you went to? Was it religious?"

"Mr. Shariati's a lay speaker, not a mullah. He's a powerful speaker. Every time he speaks, more people come."

"What does he talk about?"

"He says Islam in its original, purest form is simply belief in one God. *Tohid*. He says this idea was revolutionary when Mohammad first transformed his people from worshippers of tribal gods to believers in one single God. That was the essence of Islam. But he says that since that beginning, Islam has degenerated into empty rituals and pointless rules."

"So he wants to reform Islam?"

"Yes, in order to reform society." Ebrahim noticed that Marco had his dictionary out trying to follow this. He slowed down.

Marco said, "You mean make society less Westernized?"

"That's part of it. He has a vision of a monotheistic order, a *Nezam-e-Tohid*, becoming the basis of a revolutionary movement once again. When this happens, there will be a new kind of society. All people will become one."

"Become one?"

"Here." Ebrahim opened the book of Attar's poetry:

> *Truly, since all existence is One,*
> *Then no separate beings can exist.*

"You see?" Ebrahim said. "There will be no different classes. No conflict. Corruption and injustice will be eliminated. There will be a perfect society of people who believe in one God, a perfect Islamic society."

Marco was glad he had his dictionary. "It sounds pretty . . . theoretical. Utopian. Do you think this could really happen?"

"It's something to work for."

Marco thought about Sassan, who had been accused of—or merely suspected of—sympathizing with a Marxist-socialist group, the Fedayan-e-Khalq. He asked Ebrahim, "Would the socialist groups follow Shariati?"

"The Mojahedin-e-Khalq do follow him, it seems. I don't know much about the Fedayan, but they might, too. Mr. Shariati says he stands for *red* Islam, not *black* Islam."

"Red means socialist?"

"Yes. He wants a socialist Islam."

"So black means the clergy, the mullahs?"

"Yes. He wants a classless society, a socialist society, like Marx, but based on the idea of *Tohid*, the oneness of God and the oneness of people. He doesn't want a society based on a religious hierarchy."

"I suppose it's safe for you to go hear him talk?"

"So far it is. It's theoretical, as you say."

Ebrahim asked how Marco's "mullah" friend was doing.

"He went back to his village."

"That's . . . ." Ebrahim was too polite to say "good." He said, "He can talk with passion, but it looked like he was going to get himself in trouble."

"Yes. I was worried. You know, I can't seem to get a feel for what gets you arrested here. I mean, Sassan, for example. Let's assume Sassan was arrested. What did he do? I can't imagine what he could've done."

"*Hesāb ketāb nadāre*." There's no rhyme or reason. "Mr. Marco, sometimes people are arrested even by mistake. They get the wrong person, but the person stays in detention."

"Is there any way to get them out? Any way you know of?"

"I've been thinking about that. I've been thinking about Sassan."

"If you come up with anything, I'd like to help if I can."

Ebrahim said, "I'll let you know." Then he said, "Mr. Marco, do you think you could live here? Live in Iran forever?"

"Lately I've been wondering that myself. I don't know. It would be hard."

In deep doo doo

"**I** went to the Mosafer guest house. Fatimeh wasn't there." Farhad had come to meet Marco at the university gate right after class. He said, "Let's walk," and they headed in the direction of

Shah Reza Avenue. "The guy at the guest house said a woman, her daughter, and granddaughter had been there, but they left. They didn't say where they were going."

"Did your uncle know anything?"

"He would only say it's probably best if she keeps on the move."

"Maybe so."

"So, where the hell are *you* staying? Not at the Hotel Caspian any more, I find out."

"I'm staying with Mr. Ketabi at Global Publishing."

"What? You know him that well?"

"I've been there . . . quite a few times."

"You mean to see Mastaneh."

"Yeah."

"All that time. You didn't tell me. I thought you and I were friends."

"We were. We are. I'm sorry I kept it a secret."

"What did you think I would do if you told me?"

"I knew you would feel wronged. You called me *kesáfat*, remember?"

"Sure. Think about my cousin. What's going to happen to her? I can't believe I didn't see this."

"I couldn't help it, Farhad. The first time I saw her, I—"

"OK, maybe I did notice something." Farhad stopped at a little stand on the street, bought two Zar cigarettes, and asked the man for a light. He blew a smoke ring high into the air. "I could have handled it, I guess. If you had told me."

"I'm sorry, Farhad."

"Yul. You should be."

"But please tell me one thing. I have to know. Did Mastaneh want to marry you?"

"Try to understand. Here's how it is. Even though the *father-dogs* were joking, they put the thought in our minds by saying it so often. Neither of us would've come up with the idea on our own. But maybe we could have accepted it."

"Accepted it?"

"I don't want to think about that any more. I need to find Fatimeh. Let's walk."

They turned into the Meikadeh Hafez. Marco was hoping some araq would reduce Farhad's annoyance with him.

Farhad said he couldn't eat. He finished off his araq in one swallow, and Marco did the same. He felt his eyes watering, then got the hiccups. The tavern keeper Adarvan raised his bushy eyebrows.

"Don't tell him we were the ones that got blown up," Marco said under his breath. "I'll explain later."

Farhad downed another glassful. Then another. "So you're staying at the publishing company? Does this mean we're not going to room together any more?"

"I guess not. If you're going to London."

"Yul. But even if I do. You could go there, too." He had another drink. "Do you think Fatimeh changed her mind and went without me?"

"No."

"You and I had a great time, didn't we? How about that *father-dog* Haji!" He downed another araq. "Fatimeh's bra hanging there! Wouldn't fix the heater and *paid for his sins*. Farhad had "just one more araq" and got serious. "I'm probably never going to see Fatimeh again."

"Listen," Marco said, "You're going to find her. I'll help you."

"If you can do that, I'll forgive you for everything."

They walked back in the direction of his aunt's house. "How about you come stay with us?" Farhad said. "Reza's gone, and there's room."

"That's what I really want, but I can't. Mastaneh doesn't want me there."

"Because of that university girl marriage thing? What's-her-name? I was just joking. Anybody knows you can't be serious about her."

"Did you talk to Mastaneh? You know, tell her you were just

joking?"

"I started to. She wouldn't listen. She's busy sewing something, she says. She just stays in her room."

Marco said, "I think I know why."

Farhad's eyebrows raised until they touched.

"Mastaneh saw me with her. In the European Ice-cream Shop."

"What the hell? You met her there? That Planning Organization bitch?"

"It's a long story. I thought she was going to help me find Sassan, the student who disappeared. But no."

"You're *in deep doo doo.* Is that how you use that?"

"It's not funny to me."

"Marco, how can I explain that to Mastaneh? You'll have to do that yourself."

Fate

Upstairs in his room over the Global Publishing Company, Marco sat on a mat at a low table puzzling over Rumi's ghazals. A bare light bulb hung over the table by a wire. He wondered if he had copied the best verses to send to Mastaneh. Maybe this would have been better. Or maybe this. A day passed, then another, and Mastaneh didn't come to the shop. Finally, he went to her house. Only her mother was there. Mrs. Sufizadeh took his hand. "My boy. What a horrible accident. Are you all right? You've finally come to see us. Farhad said you might not come. Are you all right?"

"I'm fine. Thanks."

"What's wrong, my boy? There's something wrong between you and Mastaneh, isn't there? Sit down. I'll get you some tea."

He said, "Mastaneh's not working at Global Publishing any more, it seems."

"Yes, that's what she tells us."

"And now I'm living over top of the shop."

"That's what Farhad said."

"I brought these Noruz presents. Sorry they're late. This one's for Mastaneh."

Mastaneh's mother seemed to think about this. "She's not here now," she said.

Marco said, "I think I should tell you, since I've met Mastaneh, we've become . . . very close."

"Aiee."

"I know the customs are different here."

"Mastaneh is an Iranian girl."

"I know."

"Maryam, Mina—maybe they could start talking another language and go drive a Mustang. Not Mastaneh."

"I know."

She pushed the sugar bowl closer to Marco. "Your heart."

"Yes." Marco took a tiny lump of sugar and sucked some tea through it.

"I need to speak clearly, Mr. Marco. I don't like to disappoint you, but—"

The gate clanged open, and they looked up to see Mastaneh walking through the yard. She started talking to her mother before she noticed Marco.

"Oh." Mastaneh stood stiff without finishing.

"Aren't you going to say hello to Mr. Marco?"

"Hello, Mr. Marco. Are you all right?"

"He brought you this present." Her mother put her arm around her. "What's troubling you, dear? You haven't been yourself for days."

"Nothing. I'm fine."

Her mother looked at the two of them and said, "I see." Then she grabbed her purse from a table and said, "I'm out of rice. I'm just going to run to the store for a few minutes."

"I'll get it," Mastaneh said.

"No, dear. Wait here. I have a few other things to get, too." And she rushed out of the house.

Mastaneh dropped to the floor in front of Marco, but she didn't touch him. "Are you really all right? Show me. Let me see your hands. No cuts? No burns? Anything? You don't know how much I—"

"I put a note in the book you lent me. Lines from Rumi. I was trying to explain—" Marco reached out to her, but she drew back. He said, "That girl means nothing to me."

"Maybe not. I guess I can believe you."

"It's true."

"But when I saw you there with her, I understood something. That university girl is better suited to you, a girl who probably wants to go to America. I know you love me, but it seems our love has to be a secret, a secret in our past. Marco, I looked into that ice-cream shop and saw our fate."

She wiped her teary hands on her skirt. "I'm afraid neither of us is destined to be happy."

Look out, Texas

There was some kind of commotion in the classroom when Marco walked in. Most of the students were crowding around Ebrahim, and he was wrapping something in a cloth. They seemed to be shielding him from Marco's view as he stuffed whatever it was into his pocket. As they took their seats, they gave Marco guilty glances. He didn't know what it was about and didn't ask.

After class, Azadeh cornered him in the hallway. "Mr. Marco, I ask you to go with me to the Planning Organization cafeteria one more time. Please."

"I'd rather not."

She said in Farsi, "I beg you." Marco softened.

Parvin didn't go with them. At the lunch table, Azadeh said, "I told my father and my uncle everything."

"Oh?"

"Here is what my uncle said." She looked in her notebook. "He said I am espoiled girl."

Marco smiled.

"I see you think this also. Maybe is true. But I want to thank you for good teaching, and for your help." She took a letter from her notebook. "Look! My accept from University of Texas. It is from your help with essay and your letter."

"And your academic record—your numbers. Congratulations."

"I go to Texas when classes are finish."

"Student visa?"

"Yes." She pursed her lips. "I know what you think. I wanted permanent resident. Is true, but—"

"You don't have to explain."

"Is true, but not real reason I write you that letter. Real reason is I like you."

A *ta'ārof* phrase came to Marco's lips, but he was afraid it might be taken the wrong way. Azadeh went on. "My uncle said American girls don't get marry until after university."

"Right."

"I am disappoint. So you see, I don't always get what I want." She smiled. "Do I tell you what my uncle said? He said there are many sons of oilmen in Texas to marry. Is joke, of course."

"I wish you all the best, Azadeh. And thank you for that beautiful miniature. Parvin gave it to me."

"Please keep it forever."

Routine

The next day Ebrahim followed Marco off the campus where they could speak in Farsi. "Mr. Marco, we think Sassan was suspected of being a member of the Fedayan-e-Khalq. And, maybe you know, there's only one way to get somebody out of detention."

Marco recalled his own release from the Tehran city jail.

"I've been taking up a collection in class," Ebrahim said. "I told them this is our classmate. We should help him. Every student gave something."

"But wouldn't it take a whole lot of money?"

"Everybody gave a little, even Azadeh. She fears all these organizations, but Sassan was her classmate. Still, we wouldn't have had enough, but Mr. Davud helped a lot. He gave it to me privately. Actually, about 99 percent of what we have is from him. It's enough."

"Isn't everybody afraid of getting in trouble?"

"For bribery? No. It's kind of routine. The hard part was finding out where he is. I have some connections. They found out for me."

"What's your plan?"

"*One hand makes no sound.* They say it will help if I have an American with me asking for his release."

The Zendan detention center was in the north of the city, not far from an exclusive residential section for wealthy merchants, diplomats, and foreigners. It was in the Shah's territory. Marco and Ebrahim had to take a taxi there from the end of the bus line.

They talked their way past the guard at the door, the clerk at the desk inside, and finally the waiting room attendant before they were allowed to sit on metal folding chairs to wait nervously for their turn to speak to the warden. A huge picture of the Shah in his white uniform hung on the wall.

All the women in the room and some of the men were crying. A few had left the chairs and sat cross-legged on the tile floor leaning back against the wall. They had obviously been there a long time. Some of them were asleep.

The door to the warden's office was open, but his desk was out of view. That room had a picture of the Shah on the wall, too. Now and then a gendarme in a khaki lieutenant's uniform walked out of the office and through the waiting room to another office. Each time he did this, the people waiting looked up at him, but he never made eye contact with any of them.

Marco glanced at Ebrahim. Ebrahim took out his *tasbih* and fingered them. This was the sign they had planned to indicate "That's the man."

"Excuse me, sir," Marco said, standing up the next time the lieutenant passed by. He felt the eyes of everybody in the room on him. "Since it looks like we're going to have to wait quite a while, could you show me the right place to park my car?"

To everyone's amazement, the lieutenant stopped and told Marco and Ebrahim to follow him outside. They went around the back of the building through a dirt lot where a few cars were parked, then into a corrugated metal shed.

Marco crossed his arms in front of his chest to cover his shaking hands. He had rehearsed this again and again under Ebrahim's direction. "Sir," he said, "an innocent man, my colleague at the Iran-America Society has been arrested through some horrible mistake." He took an envelope stuffed with banknotes from his coat pocket. "His name and other information is written here, if you will please read it."

"You understand that the warden will also need the information you've given me."

"Of course. We have the information for his honor, too."

They were led back into the detention center through a door in the rear of the building. "Wait here," the lieutenant told them.

When the warden came in, Marco repeated everything they had said outside. "Oh," he told the warden. "I also brought this. His membership card to the Iran-America Society."

The ordeal of filling out forms and affidavits in the discharge room to the satisfaction of surly government clerks was as humiliating as the bribery itself. Marco and Ebrahim supplied every possible piece of information about themselves, including the names of their parents and all siblings, their religion and sect, and the address of every place they ever lived, on small, flimsy pieces of paper crowded with small print. Like the forms used by the U. S.

Post Office, Marco thought.

Sassan squinted at the light as he was brought into the discharge room by two guards and placed on a metal chair in front of the lieutenant's desk. He didn't notice Marco and Ebrahim at first.

"You're free," the lieutenant said. "Sign this form and go."

Sassan blinked. "Mr. Marco! Ebrahim! *Alhamdulellāh!*"

The lieutenant slapped his hand down on the form that Marco had filled out. It stated that Sassan was a colleague of Marco at the Iran America Society.

"Sign it!" the lieutenant barked.

As soon as he did, a guard brought him a small cloth-wrapped bundle. Sassan picked it up.

"Leave the cloth," the guard said. "Just take what's in it."

Getting the number

Marco tried to think of some kind of final exam question that Ebrahim could get more than zero on. He couldn't. There were voices down in the book shop. It sounded like Farhad, talking to Mr. Ketabi. Then Farhad came up to his room. "I still can't find Fatimeh anywhere. My uncle told me to be patient. I don't know what to do."

"We'll find her somehow."

Farhad frowned.

"So," Marco said. "Mastaneh's still just staying in her room?"

"Yul. I never see her." Farhad took a cigarette from his pocket but noticed something on Marco's little table and put it back. "What's that?"

"My final exam."

"Oh, shit. When is it?"

"Tomorrow."

"Great. I forgot all about it. That means mine will be tomorrow, too."

Sassan was back in class for the final examination. He shook every student's hand before he sat down. Ebrahim must have told him about Davud's generous donation because Sassan went to him, hugged him, and kissed him on both cheeks. Then the class fell absolutely quiet. The "invigilator" had entered the room.

For final examinations, the university placed outside proctors in every classroom. Their job was to walk up and down the aisles watching the students, making sure they weren't cheating. The room was deadly silent, the only sound being the invigilator's steady, scraping footsteps. There was a smell of nervous perspiration in the room. Some students' hands were so sweaty they had trouble writing on the dampened spots on their papers.

The examination was two hours long. No one could ask any questions or say a word. No one could leave the room until the time was up. Davud and Azadeh finished theirs in an hour but knew they couldn't leave. They checked their papers again and again. Azadeh looked at her little gold wristwatch, turned her paper over, and extended her essay on the back. Eventually Davud extended his, too. Ebrahim sat in the back of the room on the highest level. He seemed to be as busy as the others. Marco had put an optional essay topic choice on the exam that he thought Ebrahim might like—if he could read it: "Describe a Sufi poem."

When they handed their exams in, they didn't talk to Marco as they usually did—the invigilator was still in the room. Ebrahim handed in his paper folded in half, watching to see if Marco would open it. Of course, he had to take a look. Everything was blank except one area. Ebrahim had *written* a Sufi poem, in Farsi.

Farhad came up to Marco's room over the bookshop. "Oouee. I went to the Faculty of Translation, walked into the hallway. But they had some list on the wall. You had to be on the list to take the exam, and I wasn't. The teacher had taken my name off because I

246

never came to class."

"Oh, no."

"So, of course, I went to the office and said this is some mistake. I've been to every class. They said all right, you can take the exam if you get the teacher's permission. Just go get his permission. But there were three or four teachers. I didn't know which one was mine. I had to ask some students in the hallway. They pointed him out and I went up to him. I said I swear to God I've been in every class. It must be some mistake."

"Did it work?"

"It did. He let me in. The exam was a *piece of cake*, by the way. Is that how you use that?"

"Yeah."

"Not that I give a shit about the exam."

"Still no word from Fatimeh?"

"No. I found out my uncle doesn't even know where she is any more. Let's go for a walk."

"I can't now. I have to grade these exams before tomorrow morning."

Farhad left to go check again at Fatimeh's cousin's to see if they had heard from her.

Marco sat at the table and leafed through the final exams. He read Ebrahim's poem, translated it the best he could. It seemed good, but he didn't really know. Mastaneh would have known.

He looked at Azadeh's essay. "My Best Summer Vacation." Not one of the topics listed for the exam. This was probably something she had memorized and used since high school. He looked at Davud's. "The Shah's White Revolution." Not one of the topics listed, either, but he subtitled it with one of them: "Learning a Foreign Language." He wondered how many other courses Davud had submitted "The Shah's White Revolution" in.

It was the last week of class, and Marco handed each student a report of his final grade. They were nervous, concerned, and knew that a lot depended on their "getting the number," but, unlike American students, they never thought of questioning their grade. No one expected the highest "number." As long as they got 10 or better out of 20, they were satisfied. That was passing. If they didn't—like Ebrahim—they were resigned and didn't take it personally.

"What will you do in the summer?" Parvin asked.

"I might write something."

"About Iran?"

"Maybe."

"Please don't make it funny."

He took the grade report for the whole class to Dr. Zaban in the teachers' room.

"This is a good. I see Mr. Sassan Gharari took the exam and passed the course."

"Yes. He got back just in time."

"*Alhamdulellāh.* Did he talk about what happened to him?"

"A family emergency, he said."

"Ah. I see." He looked back at the report. "And this is also a surprise. You have given Colonel Ghorbaghi a grade of zero."

"I had no choice. He didn't attend the class or take the exam."

"No choice. Mm. I see."

Marco went into the tea room and gave Hassan ten tomans, thanking him for all of his help. "I'll always remember," he told Hassan.

Sassan was waiting for Marco at the gate.

"Mr. Marco, I've heard from Ebrahim you know Farsi. Here is a letter from my parents thanking you. I hope you can read it. And also my landlord, the dry cleaner, thanks you. He said you came to find me and he wasn't polite to you. He's sorry."

"Good luck from now on, Sassan. I'm sure you're going to become a great engineer. Keep moving down that Golden Road."

Not worth paying for

The main branch of the University of Tehran was on Shah Reza Avenue. Gendarmes holding machine guns were permanently stationed at each side of the entrance gate. Marco walked through and headed for the Faculty of Arts and Sciences building. He was looking for a job. His International Teachers Association assignment—and pay—was going to end two months after the university closed for the summer, and he wanted to stay in the country at least another year. He hoped the university would hire him directly to continue in the same position. Carrying letters of recommendation from Dr. Zaban and three of the students, he entered the office of Dr. Khodpour, head of the English Department.

"I am afraid this is impossible," Dr. Khodpour told Marco. "Government regulations require that only native Iranians be hired in university positions."

And yet, Marco thought, there hadn't been a problem letting him teach for free, on a volunteer's stipend paid for completely by the U. S. government. His services were acceptable as long as they cost nothing, but they weren't worth paying for.

Dr. Khodpour continued, "I admit I'm confused about this American organization you work for. They send people here to work for free. But isn't there this English expression that there is *no free lunch*? We assume America is getting something out of it, if you see what I mean?"

"Yes."

Dr. Khodpour stood up. "Very well, unless there is anything else. Thank you for your work at the university, Mr. Marco."

Doubts

On the last day of class, Marco said a final good-bye to the students. As he headed for his bus stop, a woman coming the other way with a chador held across her face stopped in front of him. She let go of the chador. It was Fatimeh.

"Mr. Marco. I found you. Are you all right? Is Farhad all right? I know they said on the radio nobody was seriously hurt. And Farhad's uncle said so, too."

The sidewalk was busy, and they stepped aside by the university wall. Fatimeh said, "This is the third day I've come here. I've been walking up and down the street in front of the gate hoping I'll see you leave. Can we go somewhere?"

He hailed a taxi. "Park-e-Shahr."

They sat on a bench beside a spring garden filled with narcissus in bloom. A little bubbling fountain murmured softly, covering their almost whispered talk.

"Farhad's going crazy looking for you."

"That's what I need to talk to you about. Farhad didn't come that day to meet me at the *Ham-bur-ger*. So I called my uncle in London anyway. Then, the next day, I heard about the accident. I can't believe you're not hurt. Farhad's not hurt, either, for sure?"

"We're all fine. What did your uncle say?"

"He said not to stay in the same place and not to tell anybody where I am. He said we need to get out of Iran quick. It's too dangerous to wait to get married first. They'd check up on me. We could do that in London. There's no time to apply for a passport. It could take half a year or more. We have to buy a forged one. He told me where I can go."

"Did you go there?"

"Not yet. It costs a lot of money. He's going to send it to me." She took his arm in both of her hands. "Hm-huh! I'm sorry, Mr. Marco, but I told him to send it to you. At your post office box. I remembered the number, 9989, on a letter I saw on your table."

"Oh."

"I couldn't think of anywhere else to send it."

"I hardly ever check my mail. You think it's there now? Should we go get it?"

Fatimeh sighed. "I don't know. I've had time to think about everything. I wanted to talk to you first."

"To me?"

"Do you think I should really marry Farhad?"

"What? Yes. Definitely."

"But what about Mastaneh?"

"Mastaneh? What do you mean?"

"You've met her, you said. What do you think? Everybody in Hichja always talked like she and Farhad were going to get married some day."

"But Farhad loves *you*."

"Yes, but what about Mastaneh? She probably expects to marry him. I've been thinking. I don't want to ruin her life. I don't know what to do." She was kneading the edge of her chador in her hands. "I've always been a little jealous of her. Now I feel sorry for her."

"Maybe you shouldn't. I don't know."

"Why? You mean you've talked to her?"

"Yes. I know her better than you think."

"What?"

"Here's what she said when Farhad left to go find you in Hichja: *Boro bekheir, pesar. Mard beshi.*" On your way, kid. Become a man.

"Okh!"

A woman walking by turned to look at them.

Marco continued, "I think Mastaneh is proud of Farhad for trying to help you."

"Probably smiling through her tears. That's been me all these years. No, I don't know if I can do this. Maybe I'll just go to London with Ziba and my mother."

Marco felt a jolt of panic. "But what if Mastaneh loves somebody else? Would you still—"

"That's not likely." Fatimeh paused, then looked into Marco's eyes. "Wait a minute. You say you know her better than I think? Devil! What are you saying? Tell me everything."

"We fell in love. But then Farhad found out. And then, remember that student Azadeh who brought me that letter when you were staying with us? Farhad told Mastaneh she was my fiancée."

"*Father-dog!*"

"Now she knows that's not true, but she still thinks being with me was a mistake."

Fatimeh put her hand on his chest. "*Bichāreh*," she said. Poor thing.

Marco stood up. "Anyway, let's go to the post office."

The money was there, along with a letter from Dooley.

"Is it from your mother?"

"No. From a friend. He wants me to visit him in Dashtabad. I feel like this isn't a good time. I'll write that I'll come as soon as things are settled here."

"You don't have to worry about us." She put the envelope into her purse. "Thank you, Mr. Marco. Would you just tell Farhad I'll contact him."

"Where?"

"Um, Park-e-Shahr. Same place. You bring him."

"When?"

"I'll come to the university and tell you."

"The Faculty of Letters is closing for the summer."

"I'm scared to go to his uncle's house."

"You might be watched?"

"But mainly I'm afraid they hate me."

"They don't hate you. All right, contact me at the Global Publishing Company on Jaleh Street. If I'm not there, just pretend you're a customer."

Small pale green leaves were springing from the poplar trees along Takht-e-Jamshid Street. Vendors were selling flowers on the sidewalk of Vesal-e-Shirazi Street near the Iran-America Society. Marco met Farhad as he was getting off work.

"*Pedar sokhteh!*" That rascal. "She contacted *you*? I want to see her. Did she tell you where she's getting the passport? Was it enough money? And what about getting married?"

"Her uncle said all of you should get out of the country fast and you can get married in London."

"Sure. Maybe." He thought for a minute. "I don't like it, though. Once she's in London, she won't need me."

"You're not making sense. What's that you're carrying?"

"Something to give to your Mr. Ketabi." Farhad showed him a large brown envelope, and they headed towards the Global Publishing Company.

"Good to see you once again, Mr. Farhad." Mr. Ketabi poured them tea. "Your cousin Mastaneh's place is empty these days."

"She sent you this." Farhad gave him the envelope.

"Let's have a look, shall we? Oh, yes. A sketch for Mr. Byron's *Don Juan*. She chose this scene herself." It was Julia in the convent writing her farewell letter to Juan.

Farhad ignored the sketch. "I have a problem, Mr. Ketabi. I don't know if anybody told you about it."

"No."

"I'm in love."

"Ah. Is that right?" He gave Marco a glance. "I see. Mr. Marco and I didn't think this engagement to Mastaneh—"

"In love with a girl named Fatimeh."

"Oh, this is . . . ." He bobbed his head towards Marco.

Farhad told him about Fatimeh and her mother hiding Ziba from her ex-husband. "I need a place to contact her."

"Contact her? Here?"

"I'll make sure you don't get in trouble. What I'm thinking is, she comes here, just a few minutes, I'm upstairs, we talk, she buys a book and leaves."

"I see. You just talk?"

"Briefly. She gives me a message."

"But what if you're not here?"

"She gives the message to Mr. Marco."

"Of course, a customer can come to my shop and buy a book."

Farhad told Mr. Ketabi his kindness was without end, he was his servant, he was his sacrifice—

"Khak-khak. No need for *ta'ārof*, Mr. Farhad. "I admit I worry about getting in trouble with the law. But I want you to know I also think in this case the mother should keep the child."

Marco walked Farhad to the bus stop. Farhad said, "Nice man."

"Yeah."

"I can see why Mastaneh likes him."

"Yeah. You think she's ever coming back to work?"

"Nobody knows. She's *up to something*. Is that how you use that?"

Book business

Marco and Mr. Ketabi looked at Mastaneh's sketch.

"This will be very good for sales," Mr. Ketabi told him. "It's just a picture of a girl writing a letter, but it makes you feel very sad. What do you think? Does it fit Byron's story?"

"Yes."

"Maybe there are other scenes she could do. I don't suppose you have any ideas? —What's wrong, Mr. Marco?"

"Just thinking about Mastaneh."

"Mr. Marco, do you want me to talk to her?"

"What would you say?"

"I could say we'll lose business without her sketches. I want her

254

to come back."

Marco wasn't encouraged.

Mr. Ketabi tried to hide a smile. "Or, for example, I could say Mr. Marco can't go on living without you."

"What?"

"Khak-khak-khak."

Marco had his first chance ever to say *Bitarbiat*! Impolite! But he didn't.

Mr. Ketabi took off his glasses. "Sorry to tease you, Mr. Marco. But, in fact, I *will* tell her exactly that if you want."

When Marco didn't respond, Mr. Ketabi said, "Yes. Well. We will discuss this matter later."

Marco sipped some tea. "About your business, I've been looking at some of the books you've published. It's true. Mastaneh's illustrations are better than the previous ones. There's more feeling."

Mr. Ketabi bobbed his head. "We don't sell many books, to tell the truth. But I think you can see why we have sold more in the past year or so."

"Yes. How do you choose which scenes to illustrate?"

"You see, I read the books and put a little pencil mark in the margins here and there. Later I discuss these scenes with the illustrator. She reads the book and we choose the best ones."

"Mastaneh, you mean."

"Yes. Then I retype the whole text, inserting the illustrations, and take it over to Goethe Street for printing."

Mr. Ketabi showed Marco the books he was currently working on. "Perhaps you have read these in English?" he asked. Marco had. Marco asked him if he might be of some help in identifying key scenes. "Yes," Mr. Ketabi said. "I have the English originals. But, of course, it would be too much to ask you for such a favor."

And so Marco started work at the Global Publishing Company. Mr. Ketabi gave him a list of English-language classics for which he had identified Farsi translations in libraries, special collections, and bookstores—copyright restrictions didn't seem to be a problem—and

Marco read the English originals putting pencil marks in the margins at dramatic points. The number of scenes to illustrate mounted now that both Mr. Ketabi and Marco were doing the reading.

"I know there are troubles between you and Mastaneh," Mr. Ketabi said. "But it's clear that we need her more than ever."

"Yes."

"I'm still sending her books with scenes marked. I hope she does the sketches at home and sends them here."

"Yes."

Marco woke up early and came down the staircase into the back room of the shop. Mr. Ketabi was at the printer's and wouldn't be in for several hours. Marco was now an employee at the same place Mastaneh worked. He looked around. The back room with the low table where he had sat with her and Mr. Ketabi also served as a workroom. There were long tables against the walls covered with typescripts, slick photocopies, drawings, and piles of published books with page markers in them. And there was Mastaneh's easel. The front room, the sales room, had shelves of books bound in colorful, glossy covers that opened stiffly.

Marco was in the back room reading *A Scarlet Letter*, looking for likely scenes to illustrate and locating these passages in the Farsi translation. He was in charge of the shop for the first time. He was nervous but didn't really expect any customers.

"*Ya'allāh!*" Somebody was coming in the door. He rushed to the front. It was a woman in a chador. "Welcome, ma'am. Come in, please."

"Hm-huh! *Māshā'allāh!*" I'm impressed!

"Fatimeh!"

"I'd like to buy a book, please."

"Fatimeh, where have you been? Farhad asks every day if you came here yet. We were starting to think something went wrong."

A customer came in. He wore glasses, carried a briefcase, and looked to Marco like he might be a high school teacher. Marco quickly said to Fatimeh, "Ma'am, the children's section is over there."

The teacher asked about a new illustrated translation of *Treasure Island* he'd heard of.

"Yes, sir. Here it is."

The customer leafed through the book. "Yes. Yes. You know, when I was at the university, we had this book called *The Golden Road to English Literature*. We read a few pages about Mr. Long John Silver, and that was it. Ever since then, I've wanted to know the whole story."

"This is it, sir."

"I like these illustrations. Yes. I can introduce this book to my class." He bought it and said he would tell his students where they could buy one for themselves. Marco had made a sale.

"*Bārak'allāh*," Fatimeh said when the customer left. Nice job. "You make a good salesman."

"Thanks. And you, ma'am? Are you interested in any of these for your daughter, Ziba? Here's a good one. *Alice in Wonderland*. Just look at the pictures. Done by a local artist. Highly recommended."

"I'll take it. And this one, too." It was *Heidi*. She took some money from a fat envelope and gave it to Marco.

"So it's set? Everybody's going to London?"

"I guess so."

"You're not sure?"

Someone else rushed into the shop saying, "I'm just going to leave these and go, Mr. Ketabi." It was Mastaneh with a large sketch pad. She stopped short. "Oh. I didn't mean to interrupt."

"*Salaam*," Marco said. "Um, you know—"

"*Salaam*," Fatimeh said.

"*Salaam*." Mastaneh reached out to shake her hand.

Marco said, "Excuse me. I need to make some tea." He slipped into the workroom.

They were talking low, but he heard Mastaneh say, "We've all been worried about you. Mina cries if anybody mentions Ziba."

"You're too kind," Fatimeh said. "I don't know what to do."

"What do you mean? The plan is set, isn't it? The three of you are going to London with Farhad. That's what Farhad is planning."

"But should I, Mastaneh? I want to be sure."

"It's not decided?"

"It is for me and Ziba and my mother. I'm taking them to the passport man. Before long I'll get tickets for London."

"I don't understand. Aren't you going with Farhad? Aren't you going to marry him?"

"I want to. But I don't want to hurt anybody."

"Fatimeh, you're going to hurt Farhad if you don't get married. He's already gone back to Hichja to say good-bye to his parents."

"But what about you?"

"Me?"

"All I ever heard was you and Farhad were engaged."

"Akh."

"I know you hated Farhad and me being together."

"Because of the scandal, maybe."

"You must hate me a little."

"No, I don't. The truth is I admire you. Remember that movie everybody in our village went to see in Shiraz? *The Sound of Music*? In my mind, you're like Maria leading the children out of danger into a safer place."

"You don't really think that?"

"Yes, I do. Here. Look at these sketches I just brought in. Look at this one. For the book that movie came from."

"Nice. Maria and the Captain escaping with the children."

"Look closely."

"*Māshā'allāh*. O, my God. Is that me? Maria looks like me. And the Captain—it's Farhad."

"Look at the children."

"There's Ziba! Mastaneh, is this really how you feel?"

"Of course. Farhad does, too. You should hear how he talks about you. But don't tell Farhad about this picture. He would think it's silly."

Fatimeh said, "That could be you in the picture. Escaping, I mean."

"No. I don't have your strength. Look back there, at the easel. That's me. The girl in the convent writing a farewell letter to her departing lover."

"Departing? You mean Mr. Marco!"

"Yes, ladies? Sorry it took so long. Here you are." As if on cue, Marco came out of the workroom with the tea.

Fatimeh said, "You've been in there listening."

Mastaneh said, "Impolite!"

Fatimeh handed Mastaneh an envelope of money. "This is for Farhad's passport and ticket," she said. "The London address and phone number are inside. And the location of the passport man. Mastaneh, you can decide whether to give it to him or not. I'll leave it up to you." As she left, she said, "Look at that picture on the easel, Mastaneh, Mr. Marco. I think both of you need more steam."

Mr. Ketabi stood with pursed lips looking at the *Sound of Music* sketch Mastaneh had left, oblivious of the water boiling wildly in the samovar. He raised his shoulders and inhaled audibly, then turned, sank down cross-legged at the table, and looked up at the sketch of Julia writing her farewell letter to Juan. He didn't notice the samovar until Marco went and turned it off. "Sorry," Mr. Ketabi said. "I was thinking."

Marco filled the teapot.

"I see what you mean about the face of Captain von Trapp," Mr. Ketabi said. "It's a beautiful sketch and a beautiful story. All of Iran knows this story. The book will sell."

"Yes."

Mr. Ketabi said, "And the other one, of Julia. It's beautiful, too. It will sell the book. But it makes me sad."

"Yes."

"I hope everything will turn out well for Mastaneh's cousin. *Enshā'allāh* there will be no more need for meetings here."

"*Enshā'allāh.*"

Mr. Ketabi looked at the sketch of Julia. "Mr. Marco, we need to get in touch with Mastaneh."

"When I go to her house, she stays in her room. She never comes out."

"I don't like that. Are you willing to try again? Perhaps take her another sketch assignment. Perhaps from that book you've been working on most recently."

"*The Scarlet Letter*?"

"Khak-khak-khak! Just kidding, Mr. Marco. But this is a serious matter, of course. Maybe you could take her the fee for her most recent sketches?"

Walking through the gate

Several days later, Fatimeh came back to Global Publishing. She gave Marco a note to take to Farhad. "It's all set for me," she told him. "Me, Ziba, and my mother."

"And Farhad?"

There were tears in her eyes. "I hope Mastaneh gave him the money. I hope he still wants to come."

Farhad opened Mastaneh's gate. "Marco! I wanted to talk to you. I got the money and information from Mastaneh. She and Fatimeh are like good friends now. Did you have anything to do with that?"

"Not really."

"Anyway, I already got my passport. That was scary. I hope it looks real enough. Now I'm ready to buy a ticket as soon as I find out which flight Fatimeh's taking."

"That's what I need to tell you. She's not leaving by plane."

"What the hell? She gave you that message at the bookshop?"

"The passport guy told her she might be on a list of people to watch out for at the airport. He sent her to a travel agent at Aeroflot. Here's the information."

Farhad read Fatimeh's note and said, "Bus to Noshahr. Boat to Baku. Russian plane to London. *Father-dog!* I'm supposed to do this, too?"

"You could just fly to London, she said. But if you want to go with them, there's the agent's address."

"*Pedar sokhteh!*" Scoundrel. "What does she mean *if*? Am I going to let them do this by themselves? Anyway, it sounds like fun when you think about it." He looked at the note again. "Oouee. The boat leaves in ten days. Before long I'll be in London."

"Oh, man."

"You'll come to Noshahr to see us off, of course."

Marco nodded. "How did it go in Hichja? I guess your parents were sad you're leaving."

"Yul, but I said it's only a few hours away by plane. I'll come back now and then. And they said they like Fatimeh. –Would you believe it? They said she was perfect for me." He lit a cigarette and blew a smoke ring into the air. "Here's another weird thing. You know what Reza told me? He said he was going to try to marry Fatimeh if I didn't. Looks like you were right about all that."

"I can imagine Hichja's buzzing with gossip."

"That's one thing I won't miss. But I made my mother and father swear to tell everybody I was going to America alone to study. Reza promised to tell people the same thing. Then, just to be sure, I told that to *Mr. Worthless*. I said I didn't know where Fatimeh is. Where is she, by the way?"

"I don't know either, but she'll be there when you get on the bus for Noshahr."

"Great. I'm off to the travel agent's."

"Hold on a minute. I really want to talk to Mastaneh."

"Good luck. She's not talking to anybody much these days. But come inside."

Marco told Mrs. Sufizadeh he had brought something for Mastaneh from Mr. Ketabi. "May I talk to her, please?"

"She's at the bazaar picking up something for that mysterious project of hers," her mother said. "She just stays in her room working on it."

Little Mina ran up to Marco. "I'll give it to her."

"It's her pay. And Mr. Ketabi says he hopes she'll come back to work soon. I do, too."

As they were leaving, Farhad said, "Coming with me?"

"No. I guess I'll get back to the bookshop. Just in case Mastaneh comes by."

Farhad paused inside the wrought iron gate, holding the bars in both hands, looking out. "My mind is spinning. I'm happy and you're not."

"I am happy—for you."

Farhad pushed open the gate slowly and stepped out as if he were entering an unfamiliar world. "All right, then. I guess I'll be off." He turned and put his hand on Marco's shoulder. "I'll talk to Mastaneh if I can. I think I can convince her that the Planning Organization girl isn't your type."

"And would you tell her you know it's *not my fate* to be with that kind of girl. She'll know what you mean."

Wild goose chase

When he hadn't heard anything from Farhad for a couple of days, Marco went to find him at the Iran-America Society. There was some confusion by the doorway. Then Marco saw Mohammad from Hichja being ushered out, a man holding each arm. They let him go and gave him a little kick in the behind. Marco turned away, but it was too late.

"Mr. Marco!" Mohammad cried out. "You're not dead?"

Marco took him by the arm. "Come on, Mohammad. Let's walk away from here. What are you doing back in Tehran?"

"I came by Merci Days."

"What?"

"With Mr. Ziadpul."

"Who?"

"Fatimeh's husband. He drove me here in his black Merci Days. I showed him where you live. It wasn't there. So I showed him where Farhad works. They said he wasn't there. They didn't know where he is. Mr. Ziadpul needs to find him."

"Where is Mr. Ziadpul right now?"

"He went back to our hotel when they said Farhad wasn't at work. But I didn't. I went into a classroom. Some people remembered me. They weren't very polite."

"Tsk-tsk," Marco said, Iranian style. "So you and Fatimeh's ex-husband are friends?"

"He came back to Hichja again looking for his daughter. Everybody told him I know where Farhad lives. He's very kind. He drove me here and got us each our own room at the Ibn Sina Hotel. With toilet and hot water."

Marco immediately crossed the street and started walking in the direction away from the Ibn Sina. Mohammad was in his brown robe, but he had abandoned the turban. His pale, close-shaved head was covered with short black whiskers. They must have made a curious sight. People glanced back when they passed.

"What happened to your apartment?" Mohammad asked.

"It kind of collapsed."

"God's glory! Crushed by decadence?"

"I guess you could say that."

"Was Farhad martyred when it was crushed?"

Marco considered letting Mohammad assume Farhad was dead. It might be a great way to get Fatimeh's ex-husband off his track. But he didn't want that message to get back to Farhad's parents. He said, "Nobody knows what happened to Farhad."

"I'm sure Mr. Ziadpul can find him."

"Where is he looking?"

"He's going to talk to some people at the airport first. Then he'll try to find where Farhad's aunt and uncle live."

"Oh."

"People in Hichja think Mr. Sufizadeh found Fatimeh and drove her to Tehran. So she might be at the Sufizadehs' house."

"Oh, I doubt it. Anyway, I think they moved. I don't know where."

"He needs to find her. She stole his daughter."

"I see."

"Are we going to your new place?"

Marco swallowed. The last thing he wanted was for Fatimeh's ex-husband to know where he lived. It was time to get rid of Mohammad. "No, not to my place. Somewhere else. Let's take a taxi. —Hosseiniye Ershad," he told the driver.

"What's there?"

"It's a kind of meeting."

"Ah. You want me to preach?"

"No. Promise not to talk at all. This is a meeting where you only listen."

They fell in behind a crowd entering the blue-domed building. The light was dim inside, and more people were standing than sitting.

"Is this a mosque?" Mohammad said.

"No. Shhh. This is a place where you have to be quiet and listen. By the way, do you have money to take a taxi back to your hotel? I mean—"

Mohammad raised his chin and clicked his tongue to say *no*.

"So, here. Just in case."

Mohammad took the money. "In case what?"

"I mean, it's kind of crowded here. Who knows, we might—"

The people all stood and applauded as Mr. Shariati walked onto the platform. Mohammad shoved his way to the front of the crowd, and in a moment Marco was gone.

Marco ran down Mastaneh's *kucheh*, startling the two dogs into barking. He held his hand on the gate buzzer until he heard a male voice shouting, "All right. All right." Farhad opened the gate.

Marco's voice was quavering. "Fatimeh's ex-husband is in Tehran looking for her. And for you. He brought Mohammad with him."

"*Son of a whore!*" Farhad started pacing back and forth in the garden.

"Mohammad showed him where you work."

"I can't believe it. I quit just yesterday."

"I guess nobody at the USELESS told him that. Or where you live, either."

"Yusef. He probably talked to Yusef. Lucky."

"But if he goes back, he might talk to somebody else and find out where you're living."

"This is bad. Let me think. You don't know where the *father-dogs* are staying, do you?"

"At the Ibn Sina Hotel. Mohammad told me."

Farhad stopped pacing. "All right. Here's what we have to do. We can't let that snake know where my uncle lives or where you live, right? There's only one thing. We have to get him out of town right away."

"How can we do that?"

"I don't know if I can ask you to do this. But it's all I can think of."

"Tell me."

"What if you go to the Ibn Sina and tell Mohammad we already left for Tabriz. By train. Say we're flying from Tabriz to Ankara, then to America."

When Marco got to the hotel, a lot of people were taking their siesta. At the end of a long, empty lobby, a man in a white uniform sat nodding behind a mahogany counter.

"Excuse me," Marco said.

The attendant woke up and rubbed his eyes. "Yes, sir?" He looked around. "Just a minute. I'll get someone who speaks English."

"That's all right. I'm looking for somebody who's staying at this hotel. I wonder if you can page him for me. Mr. Mohammad Ahmagh."

The attendant leafed through a registration book. "Of course. Let me see. Ahmagh, you say?"

"Mohammad Ahmagh."

"There's no one here by that name."

"He's with someone else. Maybe the room is in his name. Mr. Ziadpul."

"Ah, yes. Mr. Ziadpul. And, yes, he came with a young man. But, sir, this young man can't be the person you're looking for."

"Yes, he is."

"Sir, you can't be serious. This is a man dressed like a mullah—or something. He arrived back here this afternoon. It looked like he had been in some kind of a scuffle."

"He's the one I want to see."

"I understand. Just a minute, please." The attendant went upstairs. After a few minutes, a fat, gray-haired man in a dark suit came down the stairs followed by the attendant. He stood in front of Marco and said, "I am Ziadpul. Is it true you're looking for me?"

"My name is Marco. I'm an acquaintance of Mr. Mohammad."

"Marco. Yes, I know of you from that jackass Mohammad. Please come with me." He took Marco's coat sleeve and pulled him into an empty waiting room off of the lobby. The attendant didn't follow. Ziadpul held Marco by the wrist. "You must be the American Farhad is living with in Tehran. Don't try to get loose. I need some information from you. Maybe you don't know the laws of this country. Child theft is a crime here. Stand still." Ziadpul called to the attendant. "Summon the police."

"Wait!" Marco said. "I'm on your side. I came here to help you. I lived with Farhad for a while, but now he's gone too far. We had an argument, and now he's left the city. They all left the city today."

Ziadpul signaled the attendant to hold up calling the police. He shook Marco. "What are you saying? Who left?"

"Farhad and the child and the mother and grandmother. I told

266

him it was wrong to steal a child. He wouldn't listen."

"Where did they go?"

"To Tabriz. By train."

Ziadpul told the attendant to have his car brought around and his bags brought down. He took both of Marco's wrists. "What time did they leave?"

"I don't know," Marco said. "Is there more than one train to Tabriz?"

The attendant said, "There's only one train, Mr. Ziadpul. It leaves at 8:00 in the morning."

Ziadpul held Marco's face in his hands. "Where are they staying? Did they say?"

"The Park Hotel." Marco had heard this name from Huff, who had taken a "vacation" there. "That's where they're staying while they try to get tickets on a flight to Ankara, then to America. If it gets too expensive at the Park, they plan to move to a cheaper guest house until their flight leaves."

Ziadpul let go of Marco to look at his watch. He took out some money and gave it to the attendant. "This should cover everything. Put my bags in the car."

Marco watched Ziadpul take off in his shiny black Mercedes.

The attendant and Marco looked at each other. The attendant raised his eyes towards the second floor and shrugged. Mohammad had been left behind.

Veiled sadness

ترسم که اشک در غم ما پرده در شود

وین راز سر به مهر به علم سمر شود

—Hafez

Tarsam ke ashk dar qam-e-mā pardeh dar shavad
Vin rāz-e-sar be mohr be 'ālam samar shavad.

Marco was the first to arrive at the east Tehran bus terminal. Fatimeh had bought ten tickets to Noshahr, which meant Mastaneh was going, too. A *taxi-bar* pulled up, piled high with bundles, and Farhad got out from beside the driver. Marco rushed over to help him unload, but the driver was in a hurry, so they piled the bundles onto the road, blocking traffic. Horns blared, brakes squealed—the *sholugh* had started. Mastaneh's father, mother, and sisters got out of a taxi. Another *taxi-bar* arrived, beeping, with Fatimeh on one side of the driver and her mother on the other. There was a little girl sitting on top of the bundles in the back—Ziba.

Bus number 105 now boarding for Chalus and Noshahr. They managed to get all their baggage to the bus, where the attendants threw some bundles into the lower compartment and some onto the top of the bus.

Farhad said, "Marco, this is Fatimeh's mother. And this is Ziba."

Fatimeh's mother shook his hand but seemed too nervous to talk. Ziba said, "We're going on a bus ride!"

"So, all right," Farhad said. "Come on. Let's all get seats. I'm sitting next to Fatimeh."

Mina sniffled. "I want to sit next to Farhad." Then Ziba started crying. Marco looked around. Mastaneh's eyes were wet, too, and so were her mother's.

Her father said, "Let's get in, everybody. Sit wherever you want." He and Marco let them all go first and ended up sitting next to each other behind the others. Marco noticed there were chickens on the bus, and a baby goat, too.

The bus beeped and jerked its way through the Tehran traffic heading for Karaj and the Chalus road to the Kandevan pass through the Alborz Mountains. Mina was teasing the baby goat with her foot.

The yellow and green sagebrush in the southern foothills of the range gradually thinned as the bus slowly made its way up the dry south face of the mountains. Mina succeeded in making the goat bleat, and everybody laughed.

"Mina!" her mother said. "Impolite!"

The bus driver turned on the radio to *Golhaye Rangarang*, and Mastaneh's father moved his lips along with the recitations of classical poetry. "These lines are beautiful, Mr. Marco. I hope you can understand them."

I fear that tears will break through the veil of our sadness
And the secret we have sealed up will be spread about by all.

Her father continued, "You know, I've heard Mastaneh reciting those lines in her room recently. I asked her if it was because Farhad was leaving. She didn't answer. I got the idea that wasn't the only thing making her sad."

"Maybe the whole idea of going abroad?"

"You might be right. I hear your job in Iran is ending soon, Mr. Marco."

"In a couple of months."

"Have you ever thought of getting a more permanent job here?"

"Yes. I asked at the university, but they can only hire Iranians."

"I see. So you've actually considered staying here longer. I'm glad to hear that. We all wish you would stay."

Just as the road was starting to get steeper, the bus stopped for a tea break. When everybody got back into the bus, Mastaneh's father wanted to sit next to his wife, where Mastaneh had been sitting. Mastaneh had to move back and sit next to Marco.

"*Salaam*," she said. "With your permission."

"I beg you." He let her sit next to the window. "But please talk to me."

"It's all so scary."

"I know. I wish the driver wouldn't go so fast."

"I mean them going to London." She clasped her hands together. "I couldn't sleep much last night thinking about everything."

"Farhad will adjust to the new place right away."

"I'm sure."

"Did he talk to you? About me?"

She whispered, "Yes—a serious talk, for a change. He said good things. I'll tell you about it later."

The road got narrower as it circled and climbed one precipitous cliff after another. The driver seemed to have only one speed—as fast as the bus could go. It leaned in the curves, slid on gravel, and a couple of times jerked to a sudden stop as another bus or a truck appeared from around the bend. Deep down in the valleys, the tops of trees pointed up like sticks, and in a few places you could see a bus, truck, or car that had tumbled down into a ravine. Marco saw one caught by trees halfway down, and a couple that had made it all the way down to the bottom of the valley, one of them still shiny and new.

"*Allāh homā saleh Allāh Mohammad va āleh Mohammad!*" The scare prayer.

"You all right?" Marco said.

Mastaneh put her arm through his and leaned her head on his shoulder. "No, but I'm not looking down."

"Want to switch seats?"

"This is good like this." Her eyes were closed. He felt her hair on his cheek.

The bus leaned from side to side in the turns. Most of the passengers in front of him were holding onto each other. As the bus continued to climb, Marco closed his eyes, removing everything from his consciousness except the feeling of Mastaneh leaning against him. After a while, he felt her body relax. She was asleep. He kept his eyes closed, imagining they were alone together.

Marco felt his ears pop as they reached the highest point of the mountains. The vegetation had disappeared, and the road ran between sheer rock on one side and bottomless cliffs on the other. Mastaneh woke up, confused at first. Then she sighed and snuggled back against him.

"You were asleep," Marco whispered.

"I dreamed I was lost in London. I was with you. I don't know what we were looking for, but we couldn't find it."

The bus started to descend on the northern side of the mountains, heading towards the Caspian Sea. They snaked wildly down the mountainside and emerged into a completely different climate—clouds and cool, moist air, then, as the bus wound its way down, oak forests, at first, then beech, then lush green fields. The spring rains had filled the streams, which rushed high in their banks. Marco heard several passengers saying "Beautiful." This was the part of the country that Sassan was from, he thought. "Have you ever been here before?" he asked Mastaneh.

"No. It feels like we're in a different country."

Everybody on the bus woke up as they drove through Chalus, where most of the passengers got off. The chickens and goat went on to Noshahr with their owners and the Farhad entourage.

The humid, salty smell of the Caspian filled the air at the Noshahr guest house. There were only two rooms. "We'll take them," Mr. Sufizadeh said. One for the women, and one for the men. The women went to the upstairs room that had a door and, the proprietor said, beds. The men walked through a walled garden towards their room. It wasn't clear where the outside left off and the inside began. There was a *mosterāh* or outhouse in the far corner of the garden for all of the guests to use, and against another wall was a sink with a small mirror over it. Next to the sink was an open L-shaped hall that led in to a small dark room with mats on the floor.

"Oouee, this is great." Farhad was more pleased with the accommodations than Marco was. "Can you feel that air? The Caspian Sea. And can you believe those mountains we crossed over?"

"Let's walk down to the water." Farhad stood in the garden looking up at the women's door. "We're going for a walk. Come on. Anybody coming?"

Mastaneh's mother called out that they were too tired, but Mina and Ziba ran down to join them.

Farhad picked Ziba up and took Mina by the hand as they walked to the beach. Mastaneh's father took off the girls' shoes so they could walk in the water. Then the men did the same. The sunset gave the water a fiery glow. Marco looked along the shore and could see the Noshahr port where a Soviet passenger ship was being loaded with bulging burlap bags. He looked back at Farhad playing with the girls and felt a lump in his throat.

The women had already eaten when they got back. Mastaneh's mother said, "There's some rice left—and fish. Nobody liked it."

"I don't like fish, either, but let me try some," Farhad said. The fish and rice were cold, but he finished his before the other two men even started.

"I can see you don't like it," Mastaneh teased him, possibly for the last time.

"It's not bad."

Mastaneh brought out a package wrapped in tissue paper. "Fatimeh, I made something for you."

It was a silk embroidered wedding shawl. Fatimeh held it up in the palms of her hands. "Mastaneh-*jun*, did you make this? I've never seen anything so beautiful."

"I hope you like it."

Farhad said, "Is this what you've been working on? Let me see. God, look at this!"

"I don't know if you could wear this in a London wedding, but

I hope so," Mastaneh said.

"You can," Mr. Sufizadeh asserted.

"You've been there?" his wife said. "I guess you've driven your oil tanker there?"

"No," he said. "But you can wear it there. I'm sure of it."

They all looked at Marco for verification. "You know," he said, "I've never been to London, either, but you could wear that to a wedding anywhere in the world. Trust me."

Fatimeh was holding both of Mastaneh's hands. "But silk is so expensive. And the gold thread!"

"Put it on," Farhad said to Fatimeh.

"No way. You shouldn't even be seeing this before the wedding."

The men went back to their room and stretched out on the cool, clammy mats. Mastaneh's father turned on his portable radio. The poetry hour. They were all in their pajamas, no one talking. "With your permission," Farhad said to Mastaneh's father as he lit a cigarette. He blew a smoke ring into the dark above them. "I don't want to go to London," he said. He was speaking Farsi so his uncle could understand.

"They say you'll be freer in London," his uncle said.

"How about right here? This feels pretty far away. Could anybody find us here?"

"Yes, definitely."

"But there wasn't any *Mr. Worthless* when we checked in."

"Because there's more than one guest house. But you can be sure there's a *Mr. Worthless* in the town somewhere."

"I like it here. I could get used to eating fish."

"You probably couldn't make a living here unless you knew how to *catch* fish."

In the morning, as they entered the boarding terminal, Farhad whispered to Marco, "I'm a little scared."

"Don't be. Everything's going to be just fine."

273

A low wooden rail separated the waiting area from the passengers' entrance. Farhad and the others paused before going through the gate. Everybody hugged everybody, and everybody was crying, at least a little.

"Time to board," someone behind the rail called out, and Farhad led his group through the gate.

There weren't many passengers boarding the Soviet ship. Farhad, Fatimeh, and her mother put their bags and bundles on a counter in front of two customs officials, one Iranian and one Russian, who rummaged through it all, then gestured for the passengers to close everything back up. They moved on to another counter where uniformed Iranian and Russian immigration officers stood at opposite sides of a narrow table. Marco held his breath as the Iranian took Farhad's forged passport. Opened it. Held it up. Leafed through the pages. Looked up and down from the picture on it to Farhad's face. Snapped out questions to corroborate the information on the passport. And finally, with a tight-lipped, dismissive look, stamped it and slid it across the table to the Russian without saying a word. Marco exhaled, glancing sideways at Mastaneh's father, who remained staring ahead motionless as a stone until Fatimeh, her mother, and Ziba had all passed through.

They watched Farhad and the others board the ship, then went out to stand on the pier as it slowly backed out of the port and turned towards Baku. Farhad and the others were waving from the deck. The ship gave out a long and mournful wail of its horn. "I'll come to see you," Marco shouted out.

"Good-bye!"

"Good-bye!"

They stood on the pier watching silently as the ship got smaller and smaller in the distance.

Mastaneh and Mina walked hand-in-hand in front of Marco back to the guesthouse. "I want to go on a boat like that," Mina said. Mastaneh just said, "Hmm."

"Where is London? I want to go there. Ziba's going there. Is it far?"

"You ask a lot of questions."

Mina looked up at her. "Why are you crying, Mastaneh? Farhad's coming back. And Mr. Marco's staying here, right?" Mina turned around and took Marco's hand, too. "Can I sit with Mr. Marco on the way back?"

"I'm going to sit next to him. But you can sit on my lap."

Marco said, "I'm sorry, Mastaneh. Didn't Farhad tell you? He said he would."

"What?"

"I got a letter from a friend in Dashtabad who needs my help. I'm going to take the bus directly from here."

Mastaneh stopped. "No. He didn't tell me."

Their mother turned back and said, "Hurry up, everybody. We're going to miss the bus."

Mastaneh stood looking confused.

"Come on." This time it was their father. "We have fifteen minutes to get our things and get to the terminal."

"Just a minute. We're coming." She held the hair back from her face. "You're joking, right? How can you have a friend in a place called Dashtabad?" It meant something like Desert Habitation.

"He's an American friend. He teaches in the boys' high school there. He just wants me to visit him for about a week. I told Farhad, but—"

"He should have told me."

"I guess I could write to Dooley and say I'll come later."

"No, he's your friend. You have to go. Dashtabad! I almost think I'd rather go to London."

"You would?"

"No, not really."

Walking the line

Marco's bus crossed back over the precarious road through the mountains and into the edge of the Dasht-e-Kavir. He stared out the window at the dusty plains, tan ranges of mountains, and occasional mud-walled villages of the desert. The scene seemed less alien than when he first came to the country. The bent and faded shapes of laboring people didn't seem as remote and pitiful as they previously had. The sense of their differentness from him was fading. He was about to enter a village where no one, probably, had ever seen a foreigner other than Dooley, but Marco knew what to expect. He knew he could count on the ancient civilization of elaborate politeness and sincere hospitality that he or any visitor to the smallest and remotest village in Iran would be welcomed with.

In front of everybody, Mastaneh had held his hand at the bus terminal. Her face was flushed, but she didn't say anything. When her father called for her to get on the bus, she squeezed Marco's hand, then let go, still without saying anything. Marco had ached to ride back to Tehran with her, but he had promised Dooley he would come.

Dooley's letter was intriguing: *I have big news. You have to come. I could use your help. There's a bus that runs once a week or so.*

Everybody in Dashtabad seemed to know that Marco would be on the bus. He had to push through a crowd to get to Dooley, who was standing with the only man there wearing trousers rather than pajamas.

"Mr. Matrukgozasht," Dooley said. "Principal of the girls' high school."

"Please call me Matt. I am too please meeting the friend Mr. Dooley. Please to come my house for tea."

"Tomorrow," Dooley said. He led Marco to his own house. Of course, the principal and lots of others tagged along as they walked through the dusty street. The women watched from doorways wrapped in black chadors, their brown eyes peeping out. "Here we are," Dooley said in front of a door built into the side of a high mud wall.

The principal shook hands at Dooley's door. "Tomorrow," he said, and told the villagers, "Let's go. Mr. Dooley wants to be with his friend."

They sat on mats beside a narrow sluice that ran down the middle of Dooley's room from one end to the other. Dooley had quite a story to tell. "I get really horny here in the desert, you can imagine. I hardly ever get to even see a woman. You know what some of the teachers do? They get a boy. You know, a special boy."

"I've heard something about that."

"Then I met Matt. He's the principal of the girls' high school."

"Yeah, you said."

"We got to be good friends."

Marco wondered where this was going.

"I haven't picked up much Farsi, but he can speak a little English, you noticed. Not much."

"He seems nice."

"Anyway, he saw my problem."

"Uh—"

"He said I should get married. He would line up all the high school girls in the schoolyard. I could walk by and pick one out. He would arrange it."

"No! Are you serious? He said that?"

"And I did it."

"What!"

"There were maybe forty of them, all in their uniforms. He had them lined up by grade inside the wall. I rang the bell, he opened the gate, and he led me down the line. They were embarrassed without their chadors, but curiosity won out, and they stared at me, the foreigner they'd only had glimpses of until then. I took my time going down the line."

"Oh, man."

"Matt slowed me down when we got to the senior class. I told him any one of them would do, but he wanted me to choose. So, OK, I stopped by the most beautiful one and asked Matt how about her. Good choice, he said. And so that's it."

"Damn, Dooley."

"Her name's Hediyeh."

A low gurgling sound started at the slightly elevated end of the dirt floor. "Oh, good," Dooley said. "Did I tell you? My room has running water." A stream of water started flowing through the sluice, across the room, and out under the other wall. "Grab a pot, if you don't mind. We need to scoop up as much as we can before they turn the water off. Keep dumping pots into that plastic container over there."

Soon the flow of water stopped. Dooley seemed pleased at how much the two of them had been able to capture. "It's from a *ghanāt* about ten miles long. That's an underground aqueduct they dig by hand from the mountains. You see all those holes in the ground when you fly over the country? That's where they go down to dig out the *ghanāts* from hole to hole."

"Yeah. But you were saying—Hediyeh?"

"Oh, right. She's beautiful. Too beautiful for me, I admit. I heard somebody say we're *an elephant and a teacup*. But anyway."

"What's she like?"

"Matt says she does her homework."

"What else?"

"And pays attention in class."

"Those are good things."

"She gets pretty good numbers, except in English and Arabic. They have a grading system here where you get—"

"Yeah. What else do you know about her?"

"She gets along with the other girls in the class."

"That sounds good. All according to Matt?"

"Right."

"Have you actually talked to her yourself?"

"Oh, yes. We had a meeting in Matt's house with her parents and her."

"You said she's beautiful. What else do you like about her?"

"She looks right at me when I talk to her."

"That's good."

"She doesn't laugh when I try to speak Farsi."

"Good."

"She's not always giggling. I hate that."

"And she agrees to this marriage?"

"She said she'd do it. She has some questions, though. So do her parents. That's where you come in. When I answer their questions, I tend to ramble onto different subjects—"

"Yeah."

"And then Matt can't understand or translate. Maybe you can help."

"All right. Let me think. So, you're willing to become a Muslim?"

"Sure. No problem. I'm already circumcised."

The principal's room was like Dooley's but a little bigger. Hediyeh's parents got up to give Marco and Dooley their choice of a seat on the cushions. Marco made sure to sit back a little from the sluice. Hediyeh's mother was covered in a black chador and sat behind her husband. The father was in suit coat and pajamas. They looked a bit ragged, definitely poor.

"The thick mud and straw walls keep these village houses cool in the summer," Dooley began explaining to Marco. "That opening in the wall you see over there that looks like an empty fireplace is a *bādgir*, a vent with a chimney to draw in a breeze. They've been in use since—"

"You're rambling, Dooley. See how confused everybody is. Just eat your grapes and drink your tea."

"*Bādgir*, yes," Hediyeh's father nodded. It was the one word he had understood.

Nobody said anything else. It was clear that the discussion couldn't begin until everyone had drunk a glass of tea. They waited for the principal to drink first. Then Dooley and Marco. Then Hediyeh's father. Meanwhile, the principal spoke in Farsi, praising Dooley's intelligence and noting that he'd learned how to cook a number of Iranian meals.

Hediyeh's mother nodded in the background. Finally, the principal asked what questions the girl's parents had.

Her father did all the talking:

Was Dooley married? They'd asked this question before but weren't clear about the answer.

"No," Dooley said in English. "In the United States it's illegal according to civil law to have—"

"No," Marco answered in Farsi, cutting Dooley off.

Was Mr. Dooley proposing a temporary marriage?

"Of course, not," Dooley said in English. "The Iranian custom of *sigheh* is not—"

"*Sigheh?*" both parents said at once, alarmed.

"NOT a *sigheh*," Marco clarified, and they settled down.

Would Dooley beat her? Dooley's previous answer to this had also been too complicated for the principal to translate.

"Just say yes or no," Marco told him.

"No. This is also something that the civil law—"

"Dooley!"

"No. Of course, I won't."

Would she have to become a Christian or Jew?

"No," Marco answered for Dooley.

Would Dooley be able to find a job in America?

"Yes," Marco answered. "High school teacher."

The parents seemed impressed. That seemed to be all their questions. Then Hediyeh's mother poked her husband from behind.

"Yes," he said. "And one more question. Why did Mr. Dooley choose our daughter?"

For once, Dooley seemed lost for words.

The principal intervened. "I recommended her to Mr. Dooley."

This seemed a satisfactory answer to both parents. "We'll do what Mr. Matrukgozasht thinks best," her father said. "We have three daughters and no son. We're glad to have a son in the family and have a way to provide for our oldest daughter." His wife poked him in the back. "Yes, but of course we need to see if Hediyeh has any questions."

Hediyeh apparently had been waiting in the kitchen, and her mother brought her in. She sat next to her mother in an identical black chador. She didn't hold it across her face, however, and Marco could see that she was indeed beautiful, probably about seventeen years old. Her first question for Dooley was, "Why did you choose me?"

Dooley said, "I . . . I . . .You seem nice." Thankfully, he stopped there, and when Marco translated the answer, Hediyeh's mother said, "Yes, she's very even-tempered. You are right. She's a good girl."

Hediyeh's next question: "Is Mr. Matrukgozasht making you do this?"

"I would never allow myself to be forced into—"

"Yes or no, Dooley."

"No."

Did Dooley realize her family was poor?

"Yes."

Was he going to take her with him to America?

"Yes."

And that was all. Everybody stood up, and Dooley shook hands with her parents. Hediyeh took a step forward.

"I guess Hediyeh could shake hands with Mr. Dooley," the principal said. "This is the Western custom, as I understand."

"You're basically right," Dooley said. "It's not done as often in the West as it is here since the time of Reza Shah."

"Reza Shah?" her father said. "Yes, yes. Shake hands. Reza Shah gave us this custom."

Hediyeh put out her hand, but Dooley seemed embarrassed.

"Shake her hand," Marco said in English, and he watched as Dooley touched Hediyeh for the first time.

Marco stayed in Dashtabad a few more days. Dooley cooked him meals mostly of lentils, rice, and cucumbers, all that was for sale in the bazaar this season except melons and grapes. They had melon and grapes for dessert. Dooley scraped out a honeydew melon so thin the skin looked like paper. "You know what they say here? *Marriage is an uncut watermelon.*"

"It'll be just fine."

"That's what Matt says. What food do you miss the most?"

"I don't know. You can get almost anything in Tehran."

"Yeah, even Johnnie Walker, according to Huff. He wrote to me about the explosion."

"Water heater problem. Yeah, we have water coming in through pipes in Tehran and some people even have hot water."

"So why don't you get married, too? You see how easy it is."

"I don't know. Won't Hediyeh miss living here?"

"Actually, Matt asked her that. She said, 'What do I have here?'"

"Her family, of course."

"She meant, what kind of future did she have? Marry a shepherd or at best an older teacher who needs a housemaid? This is how Matt put it. Besides, I said she can bring her family to the States if she wants."

"You think they'd want to go?"

"I'll just say this. You see what food there is to eat here. If they ever get a lamb, they have to make it last them a month, and they eat every single part. You can't even drink the water unless it's boiled first. Anywhere would be a step up."

"If I wanted to marry a Tehran girl, I couldn't say that. I guess it's easier here. But maybe even in Dashtabad not everybody would want to pick up and go to the States."

"Your odds would be better here."

Marco served as a witness when Dooley converted to Islam and then got married. The wedding took place in the principal's house because Hediyeh's house was "too poor." There were mirrors, candles, special sweets, and a white marriage shawl worn by Hediyeh.

"You look kind of down," Dooley whispered to Marco.

"No. This is great. A beautiful ceremony. I'm happy for you two."

"I'm a little nervous. Hediyeh sent me a note. Here's how I translated it: *Please ask your friend to kill the cat at the bridal chamber.*"

"I think I get it," Marco said. "I'll keep them away even if I have to cause a *sholugh.*"

After the wedding, a kind of procession followed Hediyeh and Dooley to his house and waited at the door after they went in. Marco raised his voice. "We have to go now and leave them alone. In America it's considered bad luck to stay near the bride and groom's house. Very bad luck. For everybody." He held out his arms as if he were herding sheep and was pleased to see them disperse. He heard some women murmuring "bad luck."

He stayed with the principal for a few days until the next bus for Tehran.

"Your friend is happy." Matt smiled. "Come back when school is in session again, and I will line them up and do the same for you."

Like a child

When Marco got back to Global Publishing, Mr. Ketabi was sitting on the floor asleep with his head on the table. He sat up, taking off his glasses and rubbing his eyes. "Mr. Marco, I'm so glad you're back. Please, sit here and have some tea. Then I have some big news." There was a pile of books on the table and a notebook that he had been doing some calculations in. "No, I'm sorry, I can't wait for you to have tea. Remember that teacher you sold a book to? He came back. He has a business proposition. It's very exciting."

"You mean the teacher who bought a copy of *Treasure Island*?"

"Yes. He's starting a private after-school program to prepare students for taking entrance exams to foreign universities. The language part of the exam. For schools in Germany, France, England, and America. And he needs books."

"For all those languages?"

Mr. Ketabi bobbed his head. "We thought we'd start with English."

"Textbooks?"

"No. There are plenty of textbooks. Are you familiar with the *rāhnamā* that high school students use?" These were simplified guides to most subjects, sort of like *Cliff's Notes* in the States. "His idea is to publish something like that," Mr. Ketabi said, "but for students preparing to take foreign entrance exams."

Marco thought of *The Golden Road to English Literature*. The largely nineteenth-century language of these "samples" was as alien to English and American university students as to Iranian students. He mentioned this to Mr. Ketabi.

"That's right, Mr. Bahoosh told me he didn't want a book like *The Golden Road*. He said he wanted to have complete poems and stories. Short ones. Modern works like the students in American universities read. With vocabulary aids and illustrations."

"So, not translations?"

"No. And since it's always been a challenge to find translations, this would simplify things."

"I guess you'd have to get copyrights."

"Maybe. But the father of one of Mr. Bahoush's students has a lot of money. He wants to start this business. Do you hear what I'm saying, Mr. Marco? An investor." He grabbed Marco's hand. "They think the illustrations would help the students understand the original text. He imagines lots of illustrations."

Marco recalled trying to draw pictures on the blackboard again and again to explain passages from *The Golden Road*. "That's probably right. But wouldn't the . . . illustrator have to know English or French or whatever?"

"Not if she worked hand in hand with an editor who reads that language. An editor, for example, who knows what literature is used in the first year at American universities."

"Short stories would be best. In contemporary language."

"I thought you would find the idea interesting. The student's father says he thinks high school students throughout the country applying to American universities would buy them. As you know, most students applying to foreign universities have money. We would produce any number of small books. Paperback. What do you think? Shall we give it a try, Mr. Marco?"

"Did you ask Mastaneh?"

"Not yet. I haven't had a chance."

"Maybe I should go and ask her now."

"Khak-khak. There's no hurry, Mr. Marco. Sorry. I've been talking about business before even asking how your trip was." He poured two glasses of tea.

"It was sad saying good-bye to Farhad. You could tell they all wished they could stay in Iran."

"I suppose they left because they were in love."

"Yes, Farhad and Fatimeh have been in love since he was in high school."

Mr. Ketabi bobbed his head. "Like me."

"Beg your pardon?"

Mr. Ketabi looked away, sighed, and took off his glasses. "I knew my wife when we were only children. We played *bāzi lei-lei*. I don't know if you know that game. You draw on the ground, throw stones, and—"

"Hopscotch."

"We grew up and went to separate schools, but I was best friends with her brother, so I would go to her house. Both of her parents worked. The three of us liked reading books. I was lucky her brother didn't mind his sister joining in on our discussions. She came to Tehran to the university. So did I."

"And then married?"

"Yes. We had a wonderful life. No children, though. And then she died young. We were only married eight years."

"I guess it was unusual for you to choose your own wife?"

"Oh, it's more typical than you think. I wouldn't have married anybody I didn't know. Shirin and I knew each other very well before we got married. Very well."

"You know, after seeing Farhad off, I went to see my American friend in Dashtabad. He got married while I was there." Marco told Mr. Ketabi the whole story.

"Believe me, Mr. Marco. This method of choosing a wife is very strange even in Iran."

"What I keep thinking about is how his wife will do moving to America."

"She's only seventeen? Practically a child. She will adapt easily. In my case, it was different."

"I don't understand. What do you mean?"

Mr. Ketabi sipped some tea. "It was after my wife died. Years later, I worked at the Alliance Française."

"I know you said you studied French."

"I got to know a French woman, a colleague. She was very beautiful, light brown hair and gray eyes. I still mourned for my wife, but I started to love Marie-Thérèse, too. I don't know if you remember that translation of the Keats poem Mastaneh was thinking of illustrating? It was Marie-Thérèse who translated it into French. When she went back to France, she wanted me to go with her. I wanted to, but I couldn't." He closed a book on the table as if closing a chapter of his life. "I wanted to go with her, but I knew living in a foreign country would be like becoming a child again. I spoke French like a child. I would be struggling like a child to understand what people were saying, struggling to read, to learn how to act. I would be relying on Marie-Thérèse for everything. I told her I couldn't go, and she left without me." He put the book on top of the pile. "Every day I wonder if I should have gone with her."

Earthquake

Marco took a cold shower and sat on his mat in the room above Global Publishing. The light bulb hanging from the ceiling cast just enough light on the book he was reading. Mr. Ketabi wanted him to pick out a few more passages from Byron's *Don Juan* for Mastaneh to illustrate. "Perhaps the scene of Juan and Haidée walking on the beach," Mr. Ketabi had said. He also wanted Marco to get Mastaneh to agree to the new business plan.

"Mastaneh's gone to Shiraz," Maryam told him. They were standing in the courtyard. "Papa drove her." She pushed her glasses up over her hair and seemed to be fighting back tears. "She didn't tell you, it seems."

"No."

"She volunteers at a hospital there sometimes. In the summer."

Marco couldn't hide his disappointment.

Maryam stepped closer. "Please, I want you to understand, Mr. Marco. It's not because of me. The trouble between you and Mastaneh, I mean."

"I never thought that. But can I talk to you?"

They sat on the edge of the *hoz*. Marco remembered picking up a ball from the water the first time he had come to the house. He said, "It seems like she confides in you."

"Yes."

"I mean, does she tell you everything?"

Maryam picked a red flower petal out of the water and her face turned as red as the flower. "Yes."

"I don't know what to do."

"You could go there and see her."

"I could? Maybe she wouldn't want me to."

"I think she would."

"What do you think I should do?"

"I don't know what you should do, or what Mastaneh should do."

"I understand."

"I know what I wish you would do. I wish you would go to her and—"

"What?"

"And just be with her. I know I shouldn't say that. I didn't used to think that. But I want her to be happy again. I don't care."

Marco needed to stop by the Association office. His visa was still valid, and so was his work permit, and he didn't plan to leave the country right away. But his International Teachers assignment was coming to an end, and he had to sign some separation papers. He walked down the cool side of Takht-e-Jamshid Street thinking of something else Maryam had said to him before he left: "Sufis believe that earthly love is a reflection of love of God. It lifts you beyond earthly bonds." He asked if she really believed that, and she had simply nodded.

The ground floor of the Association office was where the Iranian employees worked. He could tell they had heard some terrible news. Upstairs, Boggs sat at his huge desk listening to the Voice of America. "Hold on," he told Marco. "Sit there. This sounds bad."—*An earthquake has been reported in the east of Iran in the province of Khorasan. Numerous villages have been leveled.* The broadcast then switched to "American Jazz Greats."

Boggs's phone rang. "Right. Right. Will do. Will do. I'll get right on it." He hung up and turned to Marco. "Well, look who it is. The only one still loitering about the country after the schools have closed. You'll get the last couple months' stipend even if you go home now, you know."

"I'll be staying a while."

"Suit yourself. Good luck finding a job."

"I know."

Boggs flipped through some papers in a file he had taken from his desk—Marco's file, presumably—but immediately put them down. "So you can speak Farsi, the staff downstairs says." He shut off the Jazz Greats. "There's been an earthquake, you just heard. 7.3 on the Richter scale."

"It sounds bad."

"All right, then. Since you're here and don't have anything else to do, how about going out to Mashhad? USAID will fly you out. They want somebody to make sure their tents and blankets get into the right hands."

"Me?"

"They just need somebody who speaks Farsi, that's all." He picked up the file again. "Here. We'll just extend your service, say, to three months from now." He wrote something down. "Fine. I'll tell them I have somebody."

Marco had been planning to get a bus ticket to Shiraz as soon as he signed his papers. Now what? He walked towards the post office. Everywhere, people were talking about the earthquake. Whole villages had been leveled to the ground. Tents and blankets were important, Marco figured. He'd have to go.

There were three letters for Marco. One was from his mother. She was excited that his service was almost over and he'd be coming home. Another was from Dooley thanking him for his help. He was leaving with his wife for the States in a week. The third was from Farhad:

We got to London OK. The uncle's apartment is really crowded with all of us. Remember I told you that Muslims believe you can't get into heaven unless you wash up after intercourse before the sun comes up. Fatimeh and I are sure to get in. It's so crowded here we have to do it in the loo standing up in the bathtub. Then it's just splish-splash and we're saved from damnation. We're getting married soon. Come to visit us. And bring Mastaneh.

Red Lion and Sun

From the air, he could see the flashing gold and turquoise of the Imam Reza Shrine and the Goharshad Mosque, which no infidels were allowed to enter. The Mashhad airport was nearly covered with army trucks, preventing the plane from docking at the gate. The passengers, all except Marco in Iranian army uniforms, walked down the portable stairs. A foreigner approached with a clipboard in his hand. "Um, I'm told to call you Marco?"

A car was waiting to take him to the nearby Javad Hotel, where the AID team was headquartered. Marco was the youngest in the room, and the only one not wearing a suit or a U.S. army uniform. A man with a gray crew-cut told him, "We're in a holding pattern, waiting for the DOD to send over its C-141s with the supplies. The locals are on our backs. They can't seem to understand there's nothing we can do until the stuff gets here. Want a drink? Some Johnnie Walker over there."

"I could talk to the locals."

The crew-cut man poured himself a drink. "Jimbo, take young Matt here to that guy who had his panties all in a bunch."

"Marco."

"I don't know what his name is."

"I mean I'm Marco."

"All right. You can settle in when you get back. Traveling with a pretty light kit, it looks like."

The man who had his panties in a bunch was a doctor. They found him outside the airport in a loading area, sitting on a crate. He seemed surprised when Marco introduced himself.

"Daryoush Komak. *Ich bin froh, Sie zu treffen.*"

Marco said, "I don't know much German. Can we speak Farsi?"

Dr. Komak laughed. "Sure. This is weird."

"The AID people asked me to tell you they're waiting for supplies to get here. There's nothing they can do until then."

"I understood that much. I missed the truck that took a group of nurses and orderlies out to Khosh. That's where they're taking a lot of the wounded survivors. He looked at a line of Jeeps parked on the runway. "I was just trying to ask if somebody could drive me to catch up with the truck. Obviously, they didn't understand me. I guess it's too late now."

"Why Khosh?"

"Most buildings are still standing there, including a kind of hospital. Also, there's a small a landing strip they're using to fly some wounded in."

Jimbo was standing to the side, kicking his black military boots on the tarmac, looking bored. Marco explained what Dr. Komak was telling him.

"Can't catch that truck? Hell, yeah, we can! It hasn't been gone that long. Just have to call it in." He radioed somebody and got permission. "Hold on, doctor. I'll get the keys and be right back. The hotel's close enough, Matt boy. I guess you can get back on your own."

"Maybe I'll see you in Khosh," Dr. Komak said.

Marco walked back towards the airport and met Jamshid, a young Shir-o-Khorshid Society truck driver with a pencil-line mustache. The Red Lion and Sun was the Shah's version of the Red Cross. Jamshid's job was to take plasma, disinfectant, blankets, tents, and drinking water to the stricken villages. Like Marco, he was waiting for supplies.

"Game of backgammon?" Jamshid suggested, opening a board on the hood of his truck. But Marco didn't know how to play.

"I could teach you."

Marco was tempted but thought he'd better get back to see if the AID people needed him for anything. In the hotel lobby, he heard continuing reports of the catastrophe on the radio. They were now saying over a hundred villages had been destroyed. In many there were almost no survivors. The Iranian army was flying volunteer doctors and nurses to Mashhad, then trucking or flying them out to the disaster areas. The Voice of America said shipments of American tents and blankets were on the way. Then more American Jazz.

In the crew-cut's hotel room, they went over the plan they had drawn up for the distribution. The AID staff had brought receipts with multiple carbon copies attached. Marco's job was to help get receipts for the tents and blankets signed by the truck drivers, then give a copy to the regional Red Lion and Sun director. The AID man in charge kept the original.

"Sounds like an iron-clad system," Marco muttered.

The AID man said, "Yes, we think so."

Finally, a U.S. transport plane arrived. Tents and blankets were unloaded and counted, and the AID man watched each Red Lion and Sun truck being loaded while Marco explained about the receipt to the drivers. Jamshid shook his head in disbelief as he placed his *emzā* or elaborate signature on the thin little piece of paper. There were far more tents and blankets than would fit in the trucks.

"I guess we'll have to come back for the rest," Jamshid said. "See you then."

Then there was nothing to do but wait again. The next evening, the moon was full, and Marco took a walk out to the airport loading zone to get some air and look around. He talked to an Iranian worker, and as it got late, they lay down under the stars on stacks of blankets. Marco was asleep when Jamshid got back.

"That's right, Mr. Marco. Don't let those things get away from you!"

"Jamshid. You look exhausted. Stretch out here a minute. How bad is it out there?"

"You wouldn't believe it. Some towns are just rubble. No sign there were ever houses or buildings there. Anybody still alive is living in a tent. By the way, about the U.S. tents. They're setting them up, but the zippers won't close."

"You mean none of them?"

"Right. And it's going to be getting chilly at night in a few months."

"Let's go tell the AID guy."

Donald Ledgerman was drinking a Coke in the lobby with his AID assistants. "What is it, Matt? We're trying to relax a bit here. Who's this guy with you?"

"Do the tents come with any set-up instructions?"

"I wouldn't know. Anybody know?"

Nobody knew.

"How about opening one of them up and seeing if there's anything inside?" Marco suggested.

"Bad idea. If we take off the covers, how will people know they're from the USG?"

Marco told Jamshid, "They won't let us look and see if there are any instructions inside."

Jamshid reached into his pocket. "You mean this?" It was a thin booklet about three inches square with about fifteen pages of instructions on onion skin paper. "They're tearing out the pages and using them to roll cigarettes."

Marco looked it over. The print was so small, and the pages were so thin, it was hard to read. There were pages of legal disclaimers and safety warnings followed by two pages of set-up instructions. "Here's something," he said. *Important: Pole orientation is crucial for zipper operation. May be necessary to close zipper with assistant inside tent before final location of side supports.*

"There you go," Donald Ledgerman said. "Tell him that."

Jamshid made another delivery the next day, then another. The drivers slept in the back of their trucks between deliveries. When all the supplies were gone, Marco gave the last of the receipts to Ledgerman.

"We're flying back to Tehran this afternoon," Ledgerman told him. "Made the reservation a couple of days ago. Guess you did, too?"

"No." Marco had a return ticket but hadn't made any reservation.

Was his job really over now that the tent and blanket receipts had been collected?

"Your room's paid up for another day," Ledgerman told him.

Marco watched the AID staff and their military colleagues board the plane. As the plane took off, he noticed Jamshid standing beside his truck. Jamshid looked at the plane taking off, looked back at Marco, and scratched his head.

Marco walked over. "I'm not really with them," he told Jamshid.

"It didn't seem like it."

"I have a room in the hotel," he told Jamshid. "Want to share it with me?"

Jamshid had never been in a hotel before and gaped at the beds, the furniture, and the bathroom. "I can't believe my eyes. This is a different world." He looked askance at the gray wall-to-wall carpet. "I can't say much for the rug, though. Strange." The television in the room was broadcasting a single channel with coverage of the disaster but mostly announcements of what the Shah and the Shahbanu were graciously doing to help. Jamshid stared at the screen. "It's worse than what they keep showing."

In the restaurant, the waiter brought a menu with English translations: *beftek, hmburgr, potat, espinach, chlokab.* They ordered *chelo kabāb,* the only dish Jamshid was familiar with.

"Dessert, sirs?"

Jamshid found something he knew. "Flan, please. I love flan."

Marco sat there watching him eat it. "Where are you off to tomorrow?"

"Taking plasma and medical supplies to the hospital in Khosh. That's where they're putting up lots of tents for the refugees to live in."

"What about the zipper thing? Will you be able to explain to everybody how to set them up?"

"I could use some help."

The tent man

The truck banged over the washboard dirt road into the desert as the gold glow of sunrise spread over the barren landscape. There was so much noise it was hard to talk. Marco read the tent set-up instructions again. "So what have you been telling them? About the tents?"

"Oh. Nothing. I've been busy with other stuff. Now you can tell them."

They pulled off the road for Jamshid to get out and say the midday *zohr* prayers beside the truck. They made tea with canned heat and ate hard boiled eggs and bread Jamshid had brought. "There's a doctor in Khosh who came back from Germany to help out. He showed me how to give people blood, and I did that one day. That was great. Maybe he'll show you, too."

They rattled and bumped southwards towards the disaster area. Marco was sore, thirsty, and covered with dust by the time they reached Torbat-e-Hedarieh, where they stopped for tea. "Almost half way," Jamshid told him. There was nothing but desert for hours after that. Marco's eyes hurt when he closed them, and his hair was as stiff as wire from the dust by the time they reached Khosh.

Khosh was north of the major earthquake damage. Acres of tents were pitched on the outskirts of the village for refugees from the Dasht-e-Bayaz and Ferdows areas to the south. There was a smell of disinfectant in the air. Jamshid had to swerve now and then around bandaged villagers walking or limping towards a water tanker to fill up their plastic buckets.

He pulled the truck up to the hospital. "They bring the worst victims in here. From the hospital, they move them out to the tents after they're treated, or if they die, carry them out behind the building and help the families bury them."

"*Alhamdulellāh*," someone in the hospital called out. "I hope you have plasma." It was Dr. Komak, and he helped Jamshid and

Marco bring in the supplies. "Food out in the hospital courtyard for you two," he said. "I have to hurry." He went into the sick room, drawing a curtain behind him.

It was getting dark. Red Lion and Sun workers, looking exhausted and dazed, squatted in the courtyard by small tents they had set up for themselves. Jamshid led Marco to a kitchen where they again ate hard boiled eggs, bread, and tea. "We can wash off at the *hoz*," Jamshid said. "Don't drink the water, but it's all right to wash with." There was a kind of curtain set up beside the pool, and they stood behind it pouring buckets of water over their heads. "We can sleep in the back of the truck," Jamshid said. "I have a couple of nice blankets, American made."

Before sunrise, Jamshid woke Marco up. "I have to drive to Ferdows. You can get a ride back with one of the other drivers if you need to." He walked with Marco back to the courtyard. "You won't really need a tent yet. The evenings are perfect for sleeping out in the open. Just use the curtain at the *hoz* to change." He shook Marco's hand. "Good luck with those tents."

As Marco walked toward some piles of unopened tents stacked against the hospital wall, a man and woman in torn clothes came up to him. "Doctor, Doctor," they said. "Can you look at our baby?" The woman held up a tiny white-faced infant wrapped up in a paisley chador.

"Sorry, I'm not a doctor, but that's the hospital right there."

"Not a doctor?"

"No. I'm . . . the tent man."

"Ah, the tent man." They took their baby into the hospital.

Some Red Lion and Sun volunteers came to pick up more tents, and Marco introduced himself as they were piling them on a donkey. "They say there's trouble getting the zippers to close right. I might be able to help."

As they were setting up the first tent, it was clear that it was a bad design. Yes, the zipper could be made to close, but in order for that to be possible, the front had to sag a little. The tents Marco and his group set up looked lopsided compared to all the others.

"All right. Thanks," one of the men said. "We'll show the others how to do this. Maybe they'll just want to wait till it gets cold before they go back and set them all up this way."

"Or maybe go back to the hospital courtyard and see about the women's tents," another man laughed. "They have them lined up with the doors facing the wall. You know, because they can't zip them closed."

As Marco walked back towards the hospital, he noticed piles of dried mud and bricks where some walls had fallen down. Most of the buildings were still standing, though. The biggest change in Khosh was the influx of displaced and wounded from the towns that had been directly hit. These were the people being treated in the hospital and sheltered in the fields of tents on the outskirts of town.

He went into the hospital kitchen and picked up the bundle of things he had left there the night before. He nodded to some volunteers in the courtyard. One man started to talk to him, and when Marco had to explain he wasn't a doctor, another said, "Yes, you're the tent man, right? But you don't have a tent. You can put your things in our tent for now if you want."

A man in a white doctor's coat came into the courtyard, tilting his head and rubbing the back of his neck. It was Dr. Komak, and he recognized Marco.

"Mr. Marco, thanks for getting me a ride here from Mashhad. I made it in time to help out with some of the earliest victims. You know, if the severely wounded don't get treatment right away, they usually die."

"I came to help with the tents. But they don't really need me. I wonder if there's some other way I can help out. I mean, the driver Jamshid said you showed him how to do some things."

"Jamshid? Oh, that was you last night all covered in dust?" Dr. Komak smiled. "Let me think. Yes, maybe there's something you can do. Would you come into the supply room."

The room was lit by a humming fluorescent light. There were blue plastic tubs marked *Water* piled high against one wall and boxes with the Red Lion and Sun seal stacked in front of them. On a counter were petri dishes and other kinds of medical lab equipment.

Dr. Komak said, "There are some USAID surveys and questionnaires in that drawer. I don't have time to deal with them, even if I could read them. We keep our own records on this shelf. Here. Maybe you can use them and fill out the forms. If you don't know what to put down, just ask somebody."

"All right."

Dr. Komak went back into the sick room. Marco opened the drawer and looked through the USAID forms. Questions about numbers of victims, number of deaths, and types of injury were followed by other questions about amount of supplies received by the U. S. government, quality of the supplies, and degree of satisfaction with U. S. government aid. Marco wondered: should the quality of the tents be marked *Excellent*, *Good*, or *Satisfactory*—the only choices.

Over the counter there were yellow cabinets. Marco walked closer to see if he could read the Farsi labels on the doors and noticed a pencil drawing taped to one of them with adhesive tape. It was a sketch of Khosh with wounded people being loaded out of a truck in front of the hospital. The picture was done in heart-rending detail. Marco stared at it for some time.

Dr. Komak came in to get a box of syringes. "More wounded are arriving tomorrow. How's it going?"

"All right. Can you also show me how to give a blood transfusion or something?"

Dr. Komak picked up a USAID form and smiled. "Get something put down on all these papers. Then we'll see." He sat down on a box. "This is the calmest day we've had since I've been here. I finally feel like I can relax a little bit."

Marco said, "I'm curious about that sketch on the cabinet. It seems very well done."

"Oh, right. One of the nurses did that. I thought it was good and taped it up there." He looked at the sketch. "She's a good nurse, too."

"A volunteer?"

"I'm not sure. Most of the volunteers aren't actually nurses yet. This one, I don't know. She dresses in white like a nurse—even has a special kind of cap with the Red Lion and Sun stitched on it. I didn't think she knew anything, at first."

"You said she was a good nurse."

"What she's really good at is sutures. It's like, she watched it once, caught on, and now she's the best I've seen. This isn't a situation where you care very much whether somebody has a degree or not."

Marco slept soundly on a USAID blanket next to the tent where he was storing his things. The next morning, the sound of trucks woke him up. They were bringing in more wounded. He helped put the patients on stretchers and carry them into the sick room. An old man was shivering even though he was covered with blankets. A young boy seemed dazed, staring motionless at nothing. One side of his face was wrapped in a bloody shirt. Dr. Komak talked to each one as they brought them in, giving orders to the nurses and other aides. As Marco was going out the door, a nurse was just coming in. She had the Red Lion and Sun logo sewn onto her cap.

"Okh!"

The doctor called out, "Suture! Suture, right away!"

Mastaneh took a deep breath, then turned and ran into the sick room.

Two more trucks pulled up, but the hospital was full, so they had to put the wounded on stretcher-beds in the shade on the west side of the building. One of the drivers said, "God help us. That's the last of the survivors who need hospital care." He wiped the sweat off his forehead. "So now we go to help with the burials."

Marco ran back towards the hospital entrance. He was stopped at the door by a middle-aged nurse. "You're the tent man, aren't you?"

Marco ignored this. "I need to talk to one of the volunteers if I can. I think she came from the Pahlavi University medical center in Shiraz. Her name is Mastaneh."

"I'm sorry. She's in the sick room helping the doctor now. What we need is more tents set up for the patients outside. We're out of room in here." She led him to the stacks of tents beside the new patients on stretchers. "If you and the others could just set up some of these tents right here so we can put these people in them, we'd appreciate it." She went back into the hospital.

"We'll help," a few workers said. "We want to see how the tent man sets these up."

"Just like you've been doing it is fine," Marco said.

"But the zipper?"

Marco said, "We can set them up so the zipper closes, but then they sag down in the front."

"We already knew that," somebody said.

"So which way do they want them?" another asked.

"I'll go find out," a third man said.

He came back shrugging his shoulders. "She says she doesn't care."

One of the wounded was a teenage boy still bleeding through a makeshift bandage on his leg. When the tents were set up, they moved him in. Soon Dr. Komak was making his way through the new tents. "Suture!" he called out. "No room in the hospital. We'll do it here."

Marco stood outside of the tent as Mastaneh rushed in without noticing him. The tent door, of course, was unzipped, and he stood there watching. Her deep brown eyes gleamed out from the gap between the hospital mask and the cap over her head as if she were peering out from a chador. She had never seemed so completely Iranian to Marco. Intent on her task, she put on gloves, cut away the boy's pajamas, and cleaned the wound with iodine solution. "Lidocaine," she said. The word was muffled by her mask, but Marco understood it. He had seen boxes of this anesthetic in the supply room. A nurse injected it while Mastaneh opened the suture package, pulling out a curved needle attached to a black string. She called for another instrument to hold the needle with, held the boy's skin open with forceps, and sewed first one layer, then another. She tied separate stitches with double or triple knots, then moved on along the line of the cut. The boy didn't seem to feel any pain.

"Beautiful," the doctor said.

Mastaneh bandaged the boy's leg. She put her hand on his cheek. "You'll be all right," she told him. "Are you thirsty?"

The nurse beside her gave him some water.

One of the tent crew saw Marco watching. "Pretty, isn't she?"

Marco flinched.

"Knows what she's doing, too, they say." The man patted Marco on the back. *"Movafaq bāshid."* Good luck with that.

While Mastaneh was still talking to the boy, the assisting nurse came out of the tent. "Sir, if you've finished setting up the tents, you can go back to the courtyard and rest. We won't need any more help here."

Marco raised his voice and spoke very slowly. "Thanks. All right, I'm going back to the courtyard now."

Fate, revisited

"Allāh akbar ... Allāh akbar ... Allāh akbar ... Allāh akbar!" The town muezzin was calling the faithful to the evening *maghreb* prayer. Marco stirred, sat up, and rubbed his eyes, then blinked. Mastaneh was standing in front of him, still in her uniform.

"It's me, Marco. We're really here together."

"I must have fallen asleep." When he went to stand up, he suddenly felt faint. Black spots swam in the air in front of his eyes, and he held onto Mastaneh to steady himself.

"Sit down. You're probably overheated." She knelt down and

put her hand on his forehead. "You feel hot." She put her fingers on his wrist to take his pulse. "You need some water." She took a corked bottle from a bag she had with her. "Drink some of this."

He swallowed, then said, "I was going to Shiraz to find you. Then the earthquake hit. They sent me to Mashhad. I ended up here."

Mastaneh seemed confused. Then she said, "It was fate."

He thought about the day she had told him they weren't fated to be together.

"I know what you're thinking."

"And?"

"It looks like maybe I was wrong."

"How did you get here? They think you're a nurse. Maybe even the head nurse."

"I sewed this outfit myself as soon as they reported the earthquake. I knew they wanted licensed nurses, not assistants, but I put on the uniform, and when the bus came, I just got on."

"I saw you sew up that boy."

"I really want to be a nurse."

"You still think you can't?"

"I tried again at Pahlavi. They said they're not taking anybody over eighteen years old." She looked around and noticed somebody watching them. It was the man who had wished Marco luck. "Just let me—" She took a roll of gauze out of her bag and started wrapping Marco's wrist as if he needed it bandaged. The man walked away. "I wanted to ask you to come see me in Shiraz. I was going to tell you that on the bus."

"I couldn't let my friend Dooley down. He needed me to go to a *khāstegāri* with him." A marriage proposal meeting.

Mastaneh's mouth opened slightly.

"He proposed to a girl just graduating from high school. English was her worst subject."

"Did she accept? Wasn't she scared?"

"They're married. He's taking her back to America with him."

"Okh. You went to the wedding?"

"Yes. The bride's shawl was nice, but nothing like the one you made for Fatimeh."

Absently, she made more turns of the gauze around his wrist.

"I got a letter from Farhad," he told her. "He says they're getting married soon."

"We got one, too. He's already married. I have it here." She took a letter from her bag. "There's something here none of us understood. *Komeidi kelub*. See here? What's that?"

Marco translated the Farsi for himself:

*I already got a job. Announcer at a **comedy club** for foreigners. Lots of Iranians. I can't believe I'm being paid to do this. And it's more than I got from the Americans.*

"Oouee," Marco said, Farhad-like. "The perfect job for him." He tried to explain "comedy club" to Mastaneh.

"You're right. It's his destiny."

"In his letter to me, he said to come visit him. He said to bring you, too."

Mastaneh pursed her lips. "He did?" She wrapped more gauze around his wrist. "I don't know. I don't know."

"I guess that's enough bandage."

"Heh-heh."

"That reminds me. Mr. Ketabi has a new business plan." He explained the whole thing to her.

"What do you think, Marco. Would it work?"

"I think it might. Mr. Ketabi says the three of us are a good team. We could actually end up making some money in a few years."

"A few years."

"Right."

"Okh, Marco."

"What's wrong, Mastaneh-*jun*? I thought you'd like the idea."

"I do. It's wonderful. It was my dream that we'd end up working together." She put a strip of adhesive tape over his extremely thick bandage. "But I'll be even older in a few years. Can I ask you something?" She looked away. "I don't know."

"What?"

"Maryam says they aren't as strict about age for new nursing students in America or Europe. Is that true?"

"I think so."

"I mean, I was just wondering. That's all."

Bands of sunset gold streaked through the dark turquoise sky, and the burning glow of the desert sparkled in her eyes. She held out her hands to help him stand up. He stood holding both of her hands.

"What is it, Marco? We can't stand together like this. People will notice."

"Mastaneh, I love you. I never want us to be apart again."

She squeezed his hands. "No. We won't, I promise. We'll find a way."

A man wearing a medical mask brought a search dog into the courtyard to give him a drink from the *hoz*. Mastaneh cringed as the dog walked past her. She whispered, "Marco, I know a place we can go."

"You do?"

"The post office. The post office roof. It's undamaged."

"Are you serious?"

"Put your pajamas on as if you're going to bed. I'll do the same. As soon as you can see the moon over the courtyard wall, get up and start walking down the road. I'll come and show you where it is."

A hundred veils

عشق است بر آسمان پریدن
صد پرده به هر نفس دریدن

—Rumi

Eshq ast bar āsemān paridan
Sad pardeh be har nafas daridan.

He left the courtyard with a USAID blanket over his shoulder, at first heading towards the trucks as if he were going to sleep in one of them, then turning back towards the main road through town. Mastaneh was just ahead in her pajamas, nursing blouse, and cap. He caught up, and they stopped at an undamaged one-story building.

"Around the back," she said. "We picked up somebody from here yesterday, and I noticed there was a ladder." It was made of logs stripped of bark and smaller branches tied crosswise for rungs, and it looked fragile. "We better go up one at a time."

"*Befarmāid*," he said. After you.

"Devil!" she whispered. "Don't make me laugh."

Although the post office was in the center of town, in the silence of the night there was a sense of complete privacy up on the roof. They spread the blanket and lay hand in hand, looking up into the steadily darkening sky. The town was absolutely still since most of the villagers and rescue workers had dropped off to an exhausted sleep at sunset.

Then in the street in front of the building they heard a man's voice. "Psst! Hossein. A man and a woman are up on the roof."

"What? Don't they know it's dangerous? What if it falls in?"

"Crazy, right?"

"Who are they, anyway?"

305

"I think it's the tent man and that Red Lion and Sun nurse."

"What? Are you serious?"

"I'm sure it's them."

"Are they married?"

"Yeah, they must be."

"How do you know?"

"They both have the exact same pajamas. What are the odds of that?"

Mastaneh was shaking with soundless laughter. She whispered, "God bless Farhad's mother for giving you those."

"That's not what you said when you first saw me in them."

She turned over and lay looking down at the town. "A lot of things I used to think were important don't seem so any more." Rows and rows of tents could still be made out in the distance against the last light of the sky. "All these villagers without homes. Grieving for the people they've lost."

A jackal howled at the outskirts of the village, and they heard a baby cry.

"Marco, over there. Those people sleeping on the ground outside their houses. They say a lot of them are afraid to sleep inside ever again. It's not just injury to their bodies. Their spirit is damaged."

"There should be some way to help them, too."

"You wish you could be more than the tent man here, don't you?"

"Yes. It's ridiculous. I was sent to Iran to help people, and I haven't done a damned thing."

"Mr. Ketabi says he was thinking of quitting his business before you came along."

"He was?"

"And Farhad says he wouldn't have had the nerve to marry Fatimeh if it hadn't been for you. She might have ended up a prostitute like lots of other divorced women." She took his hand. "And he told me you helped get a student out of jail."

"What are you getting at?"

"I just mean it seems to me you do your best."

306

"I love you, Mastaneh."

She put her arm around him. "Remember when we went up on the roof in your apartment?"

"I think about it a lot."

"We stood on the wall and weren't afraid."

"Yes."

"I feel like that again."

"We have to be together, Mastaneh."

"We will. I promise."

She snuggled against him, and he thought she was asleep. But then she turned onto her back. He did, too. The Milky Way stretched across the blue-black sky like a clear white road of stars.

She squeezed his hand. "Look, Marco. Now I understand what Rumi meant."

> *What ecstasy to fly through the sky*
> *Tearing a hundred veils with every breath.*

They awoke from a deep sleep as a rooster started crowing. Mastaneh stood up and stretched, looking towards the sun. Marco did the same in his identical pajamas. Just then, a plane taking off from the landing strip banked and flew low over the roof.

All translations of Persian poetry in the story are by the author. The poems in which the lines appear are listed here by chapter.

Pajama party
  Hafez, Ghazal #141

Wayfarers
  Hafez, Ghazal # 47

Not Kansas
  Attar, Ghazal # 15

Dating
  Hafez, Ghazal # 67

Level seven
  Rumi (Molavi), *Divan-e-Shams-e-Tabrizi*, Ghazal #2388

The Coronation of the King of Kings, Light of the Aryans
  Sa'di, *Golestan*, Chap. 1, On the Nature of Shahs, Anecdote 6

A sea without a shore
  Rumi (Molavi), *Robā'i # 11*

The hand of God
  Attar, Ghazal #70

Snow
  Attar, Ghazal # 14

Wind in my ears
  Hafez, Ghazal #35

Lovers' migration
  Rumi (Molavi), *Divan-e-Shams-e-Tabrizi*, Ghazal #1789

Sleepover
  Hafez, Ghazal #42

The green bundle
  Rumi, *Divan-e-Shams-e-Tabrizi*, Ghazal #1855

Returning things
　　Rumi (Molavi), *Divan-e-Shams-e-Tabrizi*, Ghazal #1545

The Red and the Black
　　Attar, Ghazal # 329

Veiled sadness
　　Hafez, Ghazal #226

A hundred veils
　　Rumi (Molavi), *Divan-e-Shams-e-Tabrizi*, Ghazal # 1919

The large collection of Persian poetry at http://ganjoor.net includes the complete version of all the poems quoted from in this story. The numbers given above are those used by ganjoor.net.j

CPSIA information can be obtained
at www.ICGtesting.com
Printed in the USA
LVOW08*0133040417
529505LV00001B/11/P

9 780983 699040